# THE BAYMAN'S DAUGHTER

## THERESA DODARO

Edited by
MELODY HAISLIP

Cover Designed by Lauren Dodaro @ http://laurendodaro.weebly.com

Edited by Melody Haislip

Formatting by AB Book Services

Manufactured in the United States of America

Library of Congress Cataloging-in-Publication Data

Dodaro, Theresa Ann

The Bayman's Daughter

ISBN 13: 9798518412286 (Paperback)

*To my husband, Rob, the greatest love story of my life, and to the people of my hometown, the beautiful hamlet of Sayville.*

*Sayville is the nicest village, that ever can be found,*

*One mile from the bay, sixteen from the sound.*

*It has for its inhabitants, about 2,000 strong,*

*Who can discern the differences between the right and wrong.*

**SAYVILLE RESIDENT, LEWIS NOE (1849-1931)**

# CHAPTER ONE

## 1902

Outside the window, the blazing red and orange leaves on the ancient trees graced the stately grounds of Meadow Croft. Inside the Roosevelts' warm kitchen, Hannah watched as Cook ordered the staff about. As the daughter of a lady's maid and a local bayman, Hannah's prospects in life were not grand. But for all her humble beginnings, this magnificent house on the south shore of Long Island felt like her own, and in her young mind, so did the Roosevelt family.

Hannah was feeling quite content while rubbing her belly which was pleasantly filled with the treats Cook had prepared for the family. When all of a sudden, a loud commotion broke out in the front hall. She slid off the bench and walked toward the sound of voices. Gathering there were John Ellis Roosevelt, his eldest daughter, Pansy, and some men in white coats. Pansy was crying and saying, "No father, don't let them take me!" Hannah stared at the scene before her. She was sure that Mr. Roosevelt would throw those men out of the house and save Pansy; but instead, he turned away from his daughter. The men then grabbed Pansy by her arms, lifted her into the air, and carried her down the mahogany-walled hallway toward the front door. Pansy kicked wildly at them, but they paid her no mind. Hannah felt her own heartbeat hasten in alarm. Frightened, the child quickly hid under Mr. Roosevelt's desk, afraid that the men in white coats would see her and take her away, too. But the longer the screaming went on, the more she thought she should do something. She should stop those men from taking Pansy away. But she was too afraid to try.

So instead, she placed her hands over her ears and started to hum the lullaby her grandmother always sang to her. It soon became apparent, however, that no matter how loud she hummed, she could not shut out Pansy's hysterical cries. Then the men carried Pansy out and Mr. Roosevelt closed the door behind them.

Suddenly, the house was so silent that she could hear the ticking of the big hall clock. Tears spilled silently down her cheeks, her tender heart both aching and fearful. That's when Mr. Roosevelt pulled out his desk chair and sat down, unaware that she was hiding just a foot away from him. Even with her hands over her ears, she heard him release a painful sob, and knew then, that his heart was broken. She tentatively peeked out from under the desk and found herself looking straight into his eyes.

# CHAPTER TWO

## 1902

John Ellis Roosevelt was surprised to find Hannah hiding under his desk. Her long red curls were wet and tangled around her face and caught between her tiny fingers. Through the strands, he could see her button nose and the light sprinkle of freckles on her tear-stained cheeks. And with a heavy heart, he realized that the child had witnessed the devastating scene that had just played out. He had forgotten that Hannah was in the house. The two stared at each other for a moment before they were interrupted by Cook as she came running into the room. When she spied Hannah under the desk, she apologized in a flurry with her thick Irish accent, "I am so sorry, Sir! I was meant to be keeping an eye on the lass until her mother came back. But with all the commotion, I lost track of the child."

"It's all right, Mary, I've got her now." And with that, he reached down for the little girl who then crawled up into his lap. As Cook left the room, he laid his cheek against the child's curls, and overwhelmed with grief, his own tears were finally released. The child unlatched her hands from her ears and reached up to wipe his tears away. And in that instant, they found a special place in each other's hearts.

When he was finally able to get himself under control once again, he wondered how he could explain to her what had happened. How could he, when he didn't understand it himself?

Pansy had never had an easy time of it, and this year had been especially stressful for her. It had all started in January when Pansy was presented to the world as one of its most desirable debutantes. The whirlwind of social engagements that followed proved to be too much for her delicate state of mind. She alternated between bouts of rage and depression, sometimes refusing to leave her bed for weeks at a time. He and Nannie were at their wits' end, not knowing how to help their daughter. When they consulted with their family doctor, he recommended that they send Pansy to a sanitarium where she would get the help she needed.

Wanting to spare their younger daughters from witnessing Pansy's removal from the house, he had told Nannie to take the girls shopping for the day in Patchogue. But even his own resolve weakened when Pansy screamed for him to stop the men from taking her away and he almost intervened. But the doctor had remained firm, continually reassuring him that this was what was best for her, as the orderlies carried Pansy away from Meadow Croft.

Till now, his country home had been his retreat from the world. Built on the land adjacent to his father's summer home, Lotus Lake, and next to his brother, Bert's retreat, The Lilacs. It had been a place for him to enjoy his interest in botany, and to enjoy hunting, fishing, and sailing. But that peace was now replaced by agony, as the halls echoed with his daughter's cries.

He finally spoke, his voice cracking with emotion, "Hannah, you know how sometimes you have to take medicine to get better?"

Hannah nodded her head.

"Well, sometimes that medicine tastes awful, right?"

Hannah pouted, but once again she nodded.

"You know you have to take that medicine to get better, even if you don't want to take it. Well, that's what happened here today. Pansy needs help, and she doesn't want that help right now, but later, she will feel better and be glad."

Hannah sniffed back her tears and gulped for breath before managing to say, "But Gladys and Jean will be sad."

John Ellis Roosevelt replied, "Yes, so you will have to help me make them smile again. Okay?"

The thought of Mr. Roosevelt believing she could help the girls, made her feel more confident. "Yes, Sir. I will."

For all the wealth that he possessed and the power that came with being one of the most well-known families of Dutch aristocracy in America, at that moment, he simply felt helpless. He knew that if the newspapers got wind of what was happening, Pansy's name would be plastered across their front pages. Mental illness was not new to him, both he and Nannie had family members who fought their own struggles with it.

In fact, John Ellis Roosevelt was currently embroiled in a court battle to protect his wife's sister, Blanche, from her husband, Constant Andrews. Constant had committed Blanche to a sanatorium and was attempting to rob her of her inheritance.

In addition, as a child, John had lived in Manhattan, next door to his younger cousin, Teddy. John's father was Robert Barnwell Roosevelt, an older brother to Theodore Roosevelt, Sr., and John's childhood was anything but average. His eccentric mother, Lizzy, had exhibited behaviors considered strange by society, including dressing her pet monkey in human clothes and treating it as if it were her child. His father, Robert, unhappy in the marriage, took on a mistress and lived a double life, producing two separate families.

John had faced adversity before in his life. He thought back to a time when he and his cousin, Teddy, had hunted together in northern Texas, where they crossed wild barren wastelands and experienced terrible thirst, all the pools of water having vanished during a drought. During this hunt, they were nearly trampled to death by buffalo, and fought, side-by-side, against bandits they encountered along the way. And yet, none of that, had been as difficult for him as letting the doctor take Pansy away.

Hannah wiggled in his arms and his attention was brought back to her. He thought that perhaps if he told her a story, it would help them both. So he took his handkerchief out of his pocket and wiped Hannah's tears away and then used it to wipe away his own.

"Did I ever tell you the story about when my cousin's sons walked all the way here from very far away?"

Hannah shook her head.

"You see, the boys live in a town called Oyster Bay and they decided to have an adventure. Well, the boys, Teddy, Jack and John, left Oyster Bay early in the morning. They walked a distance of thirty-five miles in one day. They stopped on the way and walked around Lake Ronkonkoma. Have you ever been there?"

Again, Hannah shook her head.

"I will have to take you with the girls one day and show you the lake. The boys finally arrived here in Sayville around six o'clock that evening. The only telephone in Sayville is at Thornhill's Drug Store. So the first thing they did was to stop at Thornhill's to call home to tell their parents they had arrived safely. They stayed here that night, and the next day, they walked all the way back to Oyster Bay! But this time, they didn't dawdle, and they completed their journey in just twelve hours! What do you think of that?"

Hannah just looked at him with her six-year-old mind trying to imagine walking so far without her parents. Hannah asked, "Did they have to get new shoes after that?"

John chuckled at Hannah's response and almost forgot his own troubles. He nodded and said, "I'm sure they did!"

Just then, Nannie, the girls, and Hannah's mother, Maggie, arrived at Meadow Croft. Upon their return, Maggie walked into the room to find Hannah cradled on her employer's lap. She stammered, "Oh, Sir, I'm sorry if she's been trouble for you."

"No trouble at all, Maggie. Quite the opposite." He winked at Hannah who then smiled in return.

From the hallway, they could hear Gladys say, "Where's Pansy?" Followed by Nannie calling for her husband, "John dear? Please, come here to help me explain."

John gently placed Hannah onto her own two legs and sighed deeply. His smile disappeared as he stood and walked toward his family.

Maggie lifted her little girl into her arms and kissed Hannah's cheek. "Sweetheart, I'm so sorry. If I had known, I would have taken you with me."

"It's all right, Momma. Mr. Roosevelt said Pansy had to go to take her medicine, but she will be back when she's better."

They heard Gladys and Jean stomp up the stairs to their bedrooms, their footsteps heavy on the treads. "Momma," Hannah said, "Mr. Roosevelt told me to help the girls feel better. Can I go to see them now?"

With reservations, Maggie let Hannah run after the older girls. Gladys and Jean, who were now thirteen and eleven, had a special fondness for her daughter. But the affection that they poured on Hannah worried Maggie. After all, they were from two different worlds. Gladys and Jean were the daughters of her wealthy employer, while Hannah was the daughter of a bayman who spent his long days hauling oysters from the waters off of the south shore of Long Island. She worried that when her daughter grew up, Hannah would find herself caught between these two worlds.

# CHAPTER THREE

## 2012

Quaint shops and restaurants lined Sayville's downtown in buildings that had stood for well over a hundred years. Having been settled in the early 1700s, the hamlet had somehow retained its charm through the centuries. In fact, in 1994, California State University at Fresno, designated Sayville "the friendliest town in America."

Philip maneuvered his skateboard down Main Street and was glad to see that Ralph's Italian Ices had reopened for the new season. But at the sight of Officer Joel's police car parked in front of the barber shop, and knowing that bicycles and skateboards were not allowed to be ridden through town, Philip jumped off his skateboard and tucked it under his arm. The tables in front of Starbucks were crowded with locals enjoying the sunny weekday afternoon. He recognized most of them, for after all, he had been born here, and Sayville was a town that families remained in for generations. He also knew that soon the town would come alive with summer visitors from New York City.

Although the village was usually a quiet town, when something happened, it became big news. Like when a couple of months ago, an old but live grenade from World War II was found in the basement of the diner, and the bomb squad had to be called and Main Street shut down. There had been a gas leak and when the plumber went into the crawl space, he found this little souvenir! The diner had first opened during the depression, and someone must have brought home a live grenade after the war and left it in a crawl space next to a box of coupons that expired in 1946. Philip shook his head at the memory, it was crazy to think that people had eaten in that diner for sixty-five years, not knowing that this corroded hand grenade could have exploded accidentally at any time!

Once back on his skateboard, he passed Thornhill's Drug Store. The place was famously known as the location of the first phone in Sayville. He couldn't imagine not having a cell phone, never mind not even having a phone in his house. He followed the road leading toward the Fire Island Ferries until he branched off onto one of the many side streets. The block was filled with older homes, built in the early years of the 20th century. His house was at the termination of the dead end street, just off of Brown's River. Next to his house, was a field of phragmites. In his Environmental Science class, he had learned that, like thieves, this invasive species of perennial reed grasses had encroached upon the marshlands over the past century, robbing the cattails of their domain. A mourning dove sang its sorrowful song on the telephone wire, "Who-who-who-ooo-who." Philip loved where he lived. His little corner of town was tucked away from traffic and remained hidden from most of the summer visitors. With another casual dismount from his skateboard, he opened the front door, calling out, "Hey, mom, I'm home!"

Grace Ferrara responded from the kitchen, "Hi honey, how was History Club today?"

Philip could smell the pasta sauce cooking on the stove. He felt lucky to have a mom who had chosen to stay at home to raise him and his two older brothers. And now that Tommy and Jack were both away at college, he enjoyed having his mom's attention all to himself. He kissed his mother on her cheek, poured himself a glass of milk, and opened the plastic container on the counter to take a homemade chocolate chip muffin before sitting down at the kitchen table.

Philip answered his mother, "It was cool."

"Do they ever teach any local history these days?"

"Not really, except like the Dutch buying Manhattan from the Indians."

Grace corrected her son, "From the Native Americans."

Although her husband's family had lived in the town for many years, Grace was a relative newcomer, having only moved to Sayville as a newlywed. But she knew a bit about the history because she had a particular interest in this quaint old town.

Grace asked, "Did you know that there were once grand hotels, stately homes, and beach resorts in Sayville? Unfortunately, they are all gone now. They either burned down or were demolished before I moved here. It must have been something to see in its heyday. In fact, this is where James Dean and Marlon Brando started out in summer stock theatre."

Philip shrugged, "Who are they?"

Grace shook her head, "We need to have a movie night together soon."

"Sure thing, that would be great, mom."

She asked, "Do you have a lot of homework?"

"I did most of it in school, but I have to go down to the bay later and take some pictures of the sunset for my photography class."

Grace nodded, "All right. Dad will be home early tonight and the days are getting longer now, so you should have plenty of time after dinner."

"Sounds good."

There was a knock at the front door and Philip looked up to see his friend, Gordon, standing there. Philip waved to him, "Come on in."

As Gordon Richter opened the door, the aromas of home cooking assailed his senses, "Oh, Mrs. Ferrara, you're killing me. My stomach is rumbling like a jackhammer."

Grace laughed, "Well Gordon, we're having spaghetti and meatballs tonight and you are welcome to join us if you'd like."

Gordon responded, "I'd love to! But I have to ask my grandmother."

"Well, let me know. There's plenty if she says it's okay."

Gordon called his grandmother from his cell phone and she told him it was fine to stay for dinner, but he needed to come home right after to finish his homework.

Grace placed a muffin and a tall glass of milk on the kitchen table in front of Gordon. With a wide grin on his face he said, "You know, no one would believe this. It's like you can't be a real family. I tell people about you guys all the time. But people don't believe me. Really. They think I'm making this stuff up."

Grace rustled his hair, "Well, no one is perfect, and certainly we are no exception."

"You could have fooled me, Mrs. F." He laughed again, "In fact, I guess you have."

"Go on with you both now. Let me finish this dinner."

An hour later, Tom Ferrara had only just walked in the front door when Grace called up to the boys, "Dad's home. Dinner's ready!"

Tom kissed his wife and pleaded, "Well, just let me get out of these clothes first. It's been a long day."

She looked at him with concern, he worked long hours at a stressful job so his family could have all that they wanted. But she also knew that he thrived on the challenges his job as a biomedical engineer presented and the rewards it offered.

Tom stopped at his son's open bedroom door and said, "Go on down to the kitchen boys and take a seat. I'll be right down."

Philip enjoyed reading, and the shelves in his bedroom were lined with books about the World Wars with some adventure novels scattered between them. Although WWII was his passion, the books from WWI had been his mother's effort to get him to expand his interest in reading, but so far, that effort had failed. Philip's grades had improved when his mother promised him the experience of flying in a WWII plane if he graduated high school with honors. Philip was succeeding in that endeavor, and was excited for his flight that was scheduled for Memorial Day weekend. He would leave from Republic Airport on a C-47. The plane would take him out to Montauk and back. All who participated would be dressed in WWII paratrooper uniforms and would be assigned the identity of a soldier who had actually jumped into Normandy. At the end of the flight, he would find out if the solider who he had represented had lived or died in the war.

Besides his bed and dresser, there was also a large television and a small sofa bed that was often used by Gordon during their many sleepovers. The boys sat together on the sofa bed and played the latest war-themed video game, shooting at each other from the cover of blown-out buildings and grumbling as they lost lives.

Philip gave his father a thumb's up, "Thanks dad."

Gordon chimed in, "Great, Mr. F! I'm so hungry!"

Tom chuckled, "Well my wife loves to feed boys with healthy appetites."

Gordon's smile widened, "And I'm happy to oblige."

Fifteen minutes later, sitting around the dinner table, Tom asked, "So Gordon, do you have any plans for the summer?"

"I hope to get a job in town. If I pass my road test, I'm going to need money to buy a car."

Tom nodded, "How is Driver's Ed going, boys?"

Gordon laughed, "Well, with Phil and me in the same car, let's just say that Mr. Mitchell has his work cut out for him."

Grace warned, "Now don't you boys be giving him trouble. That man's been teaching Driver's Ed for at least forty years. He's old enough to be your grandfather."

Tom added, "And if you want to get a job, you'd better start applying before the college kids come home."

Gordon remarked, "Yeah, I heard they are looking for people to work on the Fire Island ferries. I'm going to check it out this weekend."

Grace placed the dinner on the table and ladled the spaghetti out as the others sat conversing with each other.

Gordon took a mouthful and then closed his eyes and sighed in pleasure, "Mrs. F, your gravy is the best ever!"

Grace corrected Gordon, "Gravy is brown, sauce is red."

"Well, whatever you call it, no one else makes it like you!"

"Thank you, Gordon. The recipe has been handed down in the Ferrara family for generations." Grace had lost her own parents when she was young, and so it was her father-in-law, Angelo Ferrara, who had taught her how to cook. Whenever she made sauce, she felt as if her father-in-law was in the kitchen with her again and she was thankful that she could continue the family traditions that had been passed down through him.

After dinner, Philip said, "Mom, I've got to go down to the park to get that photo of the sunset for my class."

"Go on then. But don't stay out too late, there's school in the morning."

He asked Gordon, "Want to come with?"

"Naw, I've got too much homework. I'll see you tomorrow."

"Okay."

"See ya!" Gordon called out as he left the house, "And thanks again, Mrs. F!"

Philip wrapped the strap to his camera crosswise around his shoulder and hopped onto his skateboard. The street leading to the bay was pretty quiet, but he knew that soon buses and taxis would roar up and down Foster Avenue taking people between the train station and the ferries. He liked when the town was bustling, but he liked it even more when it was quiet. Although it wasn't the most direct route, he branched off on a side street to follow Brown's River to the bay. He enjoyed watching the private boats being unwrapped from their plastic coverings, after which they would be moved from the parking lot and then lowered into the bay. The more boats that were moved, the closer summer was to getting here.

He passed the docked ferries that serviced the beach communities at The Pines, Cherry Grove, and Sailor's Haven. Each beach had its own personality. Sailor's Haven was known as the "family beach" while Cherry Grove was known as a community that was accepting of all family lifestyles and, lastly, The Pines was perhaps seen as the most exotic and counter-cultural of all. But each was truly part of Sayville in its own way. And because of them, Sayville, had become known as a place that was more tolerant of alternate family lifestyles than the average suburban Long Island community.

He flew down the street, faster and faster on his skateboard until he reached the bay and turned west toward Port o' Call and the sailing club, Wet Pants. Like most Sayville kids, he had taken sailing lessons there when he was younger.

Just beyond Wet Pants was Foster Avenue Park. It was nearly deserted as the sun started to sink from the sky. The skeletal remains of wooden piers, probably from one of the beach resorts that his mom was telling him about, reached out from the sandy beach into the bay toward Fire Island. Far away, on the other side of the bay, the lights from houses on Cherry Grove and The Pines were just starting to appear.

Just west of the park was what was one of the last remaining stately homes that had once lined the bay. It belonged to Philip's father's friend, Ben. Ben's grandparents had built the home, and after they moved further east on the island, Ben's parents had taken it over. Now that Ben's parents had moved to Florida, it was Ben's house. Unfortunately, Ben's wife, Alice, had passed away from cancer and so now only Ben and his daughter, Jenny, lived in the grand house. They weren't blood relatives, but Philip's parents and Ben and Alice had been friends from way back, and Philip considered Jenny to be like a cousin.

When he heard someone cough, his attention was brought to the bench on the path in front of him. An old man was sitting in a wheelchair next to the bench that was occupied by a woman; Philip assumed she was the old man's caretaker. He figured they had taken a stroll to the water from the nursing home that was just outside of the park. The old man seemed ancient. His back was bent, his hands were gnarled, and his eyes seemed glassed over with cataracts. Suddenly, Philip had an idea for his photo. He asked the woman, "Do you think he'd mind if I took a picture of him for my photography class?"

The woman's dark face smiled in return and she whispered into the old man's ear. That's when the man's clouded eyes took a better look at his young visitor. With a solemn nod, he gave his consent. Philip stood back, adjusted the lens, and captured the sun as it was setting, all orange and pink, as it sunk into the bay beside the silhouette of the man in the wheelchair. Looking out toward the horizon, Philip could just make out the Robert Moses bridge and the Fire Island lighthouse. Philip glanced at the images that appeared on the screen of his digital camera and thought that the caption, "The Sunset of Life," might be appropriate. Philip sat down beside the woman and they watched together; the old man, the woman, and the boy, as the sun made its final descent into the bay.

Philip stood and then crouched by the old man and said, "Well, thank you, Sir, for letting me take your picture."

The old man's ears perked up, the boy's voice brought back a memory to him. He squinted his eyes and tried to get a better look at Philip and said, "Come here boy."

Philip inched closer to the man. Then, a gnarled bony finger poked Philip's chest and he heard the old man's shaky voice say, "I know you."

Philip didn't think that was an unusual statement, after all, they lived in the same town. Philip asked, "What's your name, Sir?"

The old man responded with a wry laugh, "Louis."

"Well, Louis, I don't remember you, but it's very nice to meet you."

Louis nodded and said, "But I remember you, Philip. I met you a long time ago. We were once good friends."

Philip felt chills run up and down his spine at the old man's words. He said, "Well, uh, I've got to get home now."

The old man poked Philip in the chest again and asked, "What year is this?"

Philip responded, "It's 2012."

The old man nodded as if some old puzzle had finally been solved and said, "One hundred years then. Young man, there's going to be a sand storm. Go to her on the harvest blood-moon. She'll be waiting for you at Meadow Croft."

In his confusion, Philip repeated, "Meadow Croft?"

The woman seated next to Louis pointed to her head and whispered, "He's not always with it, if you know what I mean."

The old man looked at her with disgust and waved a hand in dismissal as he said, "Bah!"

Insulted, the woman stood up and proceeded to unlock Louis' wheelchair. But Louis stopped her by swatting at her hand. Again, he turned his attention to Philip and asked, "Listen to me boy, you know where Meadow Croft is?"

"Sure, it's the old Roosevelt estate."

Louis smiled, "Good, good." He patted Philip's hand, "Go to her. She needs you."

"Who needs me?"

A twinkle seemed to come to Louis' eyes, but all that he said was, "Hannah. Don't forget, Philip. The sand storm is coming."

Then Louis waved to his caretaker, "We can go now. I've done what I was supposed to do."

The caretaker rolled her eyes at Philip and proceeded to push the wheelchair back down the path toward the park entrance.

Philip skated home in the dark. The street lights were on, but they seemed extra dim to him tonight. Luckily, he knew the streets by heart, and avoided the cracks and potholes. This time he took the more direct route, straight up Foster Avenue. When he got home, he set his skateboard alongside the front stoop and felt thankful for the safety of the yellow glow coming from the front door and windows. Inside, he found his parents in the living room. Grace was on her computer, doing what she loved most, researching their family tree, while Tom was inserting old silver coins into books with slots made for such collections. Grace was playing one of her old Italian CD's and Jerry Vale was singing the song, *"Mama"*. She always said it put her in the mood to do her research.

His mother asked, "Did you get some good shots?"

"Yeah."

He paused a moment before deciding to tell her about his encounter, "There was this old guy there. I took a photo of him against the sunset. He said he knew me."

Tom asked, "What was his name?"

"He said it was Louis."

"Can you show me the photo?" Tom asked.

"Yeah." Philip found the photo on his digital camera and showed it to his father.

Tom gave Grace a knowing look before saying, "He's an old-timer. He was one of those orphan kids who used to live in the buildings across from St. Ann's Church."

Philip questioned him further, "Orphan kids?"

Tom explained, "You know Gillette Avenue?"

"Sure."

"Well, it's named after the Gillette family. Ida Gillette donated land across from St. Ann's Church in the early 1920s. They brought orphans out from the city and built two dorms for them. One for boys and one for girls. The town's people chipped in and paid for their schooling and necessities. Louis lived there when he was a boy."

Philip offered, "Well, the guy seems a little out of it. He was talking crazy. He said something about a sand storm." Philip shrugged, "I don't know what he was talking about."

Tom offered, "He's got to be over a hundred by now. In fact, a long time ago, he was a good friend of Ben's grandparents. Don't worry about it. He's harmless."

"Sure, dad. 'Night mom."

"'Night, honey."

But when Philip went upstairs the old man's words still repeated themselves in his head. So he turned on his computer and typed in, "harvest blood moon." What he saw, made him shiver.

*"Also known as the Hunter's Moon, it comes right before Halloween. During this time, the Gaelic festival Samhain (pronounced saah-win or saa-ween) is celebrated to mark the end of the harvest season and the beginning of winter, the darker half of the year. The leaves have fallen and the fields are brown and dead. The nights are longer and there is a chill in the air as winter looms not far behind. It is the time of year when the earth dies. This pagan festival gives us the opportunity to celebrate the cycle of death and rebirth. Séances are popular rituals during this time of year since the veil between this world and the spirit realm is at its thinnest."*

He thought again about what else Louis had said, something about a sand storm. It just didn't make sense. They didn't live in the desert; there weren't any sand storms in Sayville. He shut off his computer and picked up a book on his nightstand as he got into bed. He flipped the pages until he found the ear-marked page where he had left off. Chapter 2 of *The Time Machine* by H. G. Wells, page one. He read until his eyes grew heavy and he fell into a deep sleep. In his dreams he saw the beach sand rise up and sweep through Sayville on the wind. He could hear a dog barking in the distance and a girl crying out as the black of night lowered itself over the land.

# CHAPTER FOUR

### 1903

President Theodore Roosevelt had snuck out of his home, Sagamore Hill, in the wee hours of the morning after a thunderstorm. Without anyone in government knowing where he had gone, he rode from Oyster Bay to Sayville on horseback with his son and two of his nephews. Mrs. Roosevelt had expected to join them, but the bad weather deterred her. However, when he didn't return by the next morning, she informed the Secret Service of the President's departure and two men immediately boarded a train and headed for Sayville.

President Roosevelt had set a rapid pace on their journey, riding on his favorite horse. His son, Theodore Jr., was riding a horse they called Wyoming, a gift presented to the President by the citizens of Douglas, Wyoming. The small group followed a route through Huntington, then through Smithtown, and finally, past Lake Ronkonkoma, and completed their journey in less than four hours. Unfortunately, the journey had been hard on the President's horse, and so they decided that they would not only spend the day, but also stay the night at his uncle's home on Lotus Lake so that his horse would have the time necessary to recover.

While the President enjoyed an automobile ride with his Uncle Robert and cousins, John Ellis and Bert, his son and nephews had spent the day fishing with their cousins in West Lake, a trout preserve on the grounds of the Roosevelt estate. That afternoon, they all came to Meadow Croft for lunch.

Meadow Croft was buzzing with excitement at having the President as a surprise guest! Hannah sat on the floor in Jean's bedroom and watched the older girls get ready for their luncheon with the President. Gladys and Jean were joined by their cousin, Olga, the daughter of John Ellis' brother, Bert. Olga's mother, Grace Woodhouse, had died when Olga was just three years old, and then her father had married her stepmother, Lillie Hamersley, when she was seven. Olga and Jean were both twelve now, and they were very excited to have their male cousins, who were each about fourteen years old, in the house. Gladys dabbed on a little perfume and then handled the bottle to Jean.

Gladys warned her younger sister and cousin, "Be polite, only speak when you are spoken to. Let them take the lead."

Jean shook her head, "Really, Gladys. It's 1903, I will not wait my turn to speak."

"Well," Gladys responded, "They are making matches, so if you want a good match, you will behave."

Olga remarked, "Perhaps after lunch, we can take the boys out in our rowboats on the lake?"

Jean winked, "Which of the boys do you want in your boat, Olga?"

"Why, the son of the President, of course. No reason not to aim high." The cousins exploded into giggles.

When dressed and ready for lunch, Gladys, Jean, and Olga left Hannah sitting in the bedroom by herself. Hannah picked up the perfume bottle and squirted too much of it on her face, which sent her into a coughing fit. Next she ran her fingers over the discarded dresses on the bed, any of which Hannah would have loved to wear. Out loud, she said longingly, "Like princess dresses." Then quickly looked about her to make sure no one had seen her touch the beautiful fabric. She walked over to the window and looked out over the front lawn to where Brown's River crossed the road. She knew her father and brother were shucking oysters at the cull shack where the river met the bay. She left the bedroom and quietly descended the stairs and skirting around the dining room where everyone was seated, she entered the kitchen. "Momma, can I go to the cull shack? I want to see Harry."

"Yes, dear. Tell your father, I won't be home for dinner. With the President's visit, there's too much to do here."

"All right, Momma."

Hannah left through the kitchen door and ran all the way to the cull shack in the July heat. When she pushed open the flimsy door to the shanty, the smell of oysters filled the air. Andrew Trumball was happy to see his daughter, "Hannah! Have you come to help us?"

"Yes, Pa. Momma says she won't be home for dinner. The President is at Meadow Croft and she's very busy there."

Andrew scowled. He hated the fact that Maggie had to slave over the Roosevelts' every wish and fancy. And he hated that he wasn't able to give her the life she deserved. But if the President was there, what could he say to her? He supposed she thought of it as an honor. But that wasn't how he saw it.

Harry called to her, "Hey, Hannah, come and help me sort these oysters."

She sat on a stool beside her brother, Harry, as Andrew watched his children. They looked so much alike; twins from birth. But as much as they looked alike, they were very different from each other. In fact, of the two of them, Harry was the more docile, while Hannah was more spirited. They complemented each other and each supported the other in their own way.

Hannah told Harry about the President's visit and how the girls were all dressed fancy for the luncheon.

Harry said, "Aw, let them have their fancy luncheon, we've got oysters!" And with that, he shucked an oyster and dropped the sweet meat into his mouth. Then shucked another, and offered it to her, which she accepted with enjoyment.

Late that night, Maggie arrived home exhausted. She washed her face and climbed into bed alongside her husband. Andrew asked angrily, "Doesn't that man know you have a family of your own?"

Exasperated, Maggie responded, "Andrew, the President of the United States was their guest."

"I know, I know. But how are we supposed to raise our children with you over there and me out on the bay?"

Maggie thought for a moment, "Maybe I should ask my mother to move in with us?"

That wasn't the response Andrew wanted, but he agreed, it would help to have his mother-in-law there for the children. He took a deep breath and asked, "How was the President's visit?"

"Well, all went fine, although it was quite unexpected to have him for lunch today and that threw everyone in the household into a tizzy. But it all worked out and he is spending the night at Lotus Lake and expects to return to Sagamore Hill in the morning. When I left, the President and the others had walked over to Nohowec's Saloon."

Andrew knew the saloon well. It had been known to be one of John Ellis' favorite places to meet up with his wealthy cohorts. Andrew brushed aside his thoughts of the Roosevelt men and drew his wife close to him. He massaged her tired shoulders with his calloused fingers. He kissed her head and said, "I love you, my Maggie girl." But there was no response for him; she had already fallen fast asleep.

# CHAPTER FIVE

## 1905

Hannah ran to Meadow Croft after her mother told her about the accident. Poor Gladys and Jean had been thrown from a wagon when their horse bolted. Jean had been thrown against a tree and had struck her head and lost consciousness. Gladys suffered painful bruises and cuts, but had retained her senses. After being taken to Dr. Krichbaum's office for treatment, they had just been transported back home to Meadow Croft.

Hannah rushed up to Jean's bedroom to find her lying in bed with a cut lip and her face badly scraped. Drs. Krichbaum and Vandiense were speaking to Nannie and John Ellis. Dr. Vandiense said, "They have excellent constitutions; both will recover. Just some rest and indulgence and they will be fine."

Hannah knew that the sisters were expert horsewomen, and had always attracted much attention as they rode, unattended, on horseback on the Long Island roads. She also knew that they were very popular at the annual horse show held at Bay Shore. So she wondered how this accident could have occurred.

Hannah sat on Jean's bed and asked, "What happened?"

"Gladys was driving. An automobile startled the horse and it dashed down Main Street until we got to Candee Ave. Then the horse turned left and the cart flipped onto its side and struck a tree. We were both thrown from it and that was the last I remember until I woke up sitting against the tree." Jean closed her eyes and reached up to touch her head, "I have such a headache."

Nannie said, "Hannah, perhaps you should leave and let Jean rest."

Jean complained, "No, Momma. Let her stay."

"All right, but be quiet Hannah. Jean and Gladys need to rest."

Hannah agreed, "I'll be quiet. I'll just sit here and keep an eye on them."

Nannie smiled at the little girl who loved her daughters so well. "And you let me know if Jean or Gladys need anything."

Hannah perked up, "Yes, that's good. I can go back and forth to the kitchen to get them something to eat when they're hungry."

Jean shook her head with difficulty, "Oh, I'm not hungry. I don't think I could keep anything down. But perhaps some water would do."

Hannah ran to the kitchen and told Cook what she needed. Cook gave her two glasses, and a pitcher of water for both of the girls. Then she added a bowl and two towels, "You can wet the towels in the bowls and place one each of their foreheads. It will help with their headaches." Hannah carefully balanced the weight of the tray and carried the contents up to the girls' bedrooms. She then poured them each a glass of water and, taking a towel, she dipped it into a bowl of water and placed the cool towel on Jean's head. She asked, "Does this feel better?" Jean responded, "Yes, thank you, Hannah. What would I do without you?"

Hannah felt important. She placed the other towel on Gladys' head and said, "Do you feel okay, Gladys?"

Gladys responded, "It wasn't my fault, the horse got frightened by the automobile."

Hannah nodded, "I know, Jean told me." Hannah tucked the light blanket around Gladys. Then adjusted the face of the metal fan toward Gladys. Gladys said, "Oh, thank you, Hannah. That's much better."

Hannah then walked back into Jean's room and sat down on the divan to watch over the older girls. She felt proud to have been given this important task by Mrs. Roosevelt.

# CHAPTER SIX

### 1910

John Ellis Roosevelt had just returned from a business trip to Scotland and was excited to see his wife and daughters. He lifted the puppy into his arms, a gift for the girls to make up for his absence. He soothed the puppy by petting its fur and whispering gently into its ear. But he hardly set foot outside of his automobile before the girls came rushing out to greet him. Hannah lagged behind, watching the reunion.

"Father, what have you brought us?" Jean squealed in excitement at the sight of the puppy.

"He's a Cairn Terrier, born in the highlands of Scotland."

Gladys affectionately reached for him and her father placed him gently into her arms. She cuddled the puppy close to her, "He's such a wee little thing."

Nannie appeared at the doorway, smiling in relief at the safe return of her husband. John Ellis walked past his daughters and embraced his wife. He kissed her and said, "I've missed you, dear." Nannie hugged him close and said, "I wish we never had to part, but it is always sweet to be reunited again." John Ellis smiled at his wife, "It is, indeed."

Jean called out, "Let me have him!" Gladys handed the puppy over to her younger sister.

John Ellis remarked, "They've grown up so much."

Nannie replied, "Well, dear, they are young ladies now. Nineteen and twenty-one. I'm afraid they aren't your little girls anymore."

"Nonsense. They will always be my little girls." And with a pang in his heart he thought of Pansy. He said, "I visited Pansy before coming here. She's doing well."

"I know, John. It's still hard, but she's happy there."

John Ellis still felt the emptiness at not having his eldest daughter in his home, but each time Pansy visited, she would wait nervously to return to Dr. Harrison's small sanitarium in Whitestone, New York. He had to accept that at this point, Pansy was never going to return permanently to be with him. She now considered the residents at Breezehurst Terrace to be her family.

John Ellis whispered to his wife, "I think Pansy is sweet on one of the other residents."

Nannie pressed for more, "Really, John? Did you meet him?"

"Well, no. But she kept looking across the room at him and I caught them smiling at each other."

Nannie sighed, "Thank you for that, John. It's good to know that her life goes on, even if she isn't with us."

"She's all right, Nannie. Don't worry." Then he turned his attention to their other two daughters.

Jean called to Hannah, "Come, meet the new member of our family."

Hannah walked slowly over to the girls, "He's so sweet! I wish my parents would let me have a dog."

Jean said, "Well, we can share him with you. Let's see, what should we name him?"

Nannie answered, "Let's name him Billy. He can be the brother you always wanted."

Jean and Gladys laughed, and Gladys said, "All right, brother Billy. Let's go get you some water after that long journey. You must be thirsty." Gladys took the dog back into her arms and carried him to the kitchen with the other two girls following.

Seeing Maggie in the kitchen, Hannah excitedly introduced Billy to her mother, "Look what Mr. Roosevelt brought home! His name is Billy." Maggie smiled weakly at her daughter trying to hide the burning pain she was feeling in her chest. She told herself it was just indigestion, but she worried that it might be more than that.

Cook bustled past Maggie with a bowl waiting for Billy. Then she set to cutting up some chicken for him and saying, "The little thing is probably famished."

Billy drank and ate heartily and then the girls brought him out to the backyard. They watched as he searched out every chipmunk hole in the ground and chased the squirrels up their trees. At fourteen, Hannah laughed along with Gladys and Jean, but inside, she felt saddened. Lately, the tug she felt between wanting to be part of the Roosevelt family and knowing she never could be, was always playing out within her. She wasn't a little girl anymore and neither were Gladys and Jean. She wondered how much longer they would welcome her into their confidences. After all, it was time for them to find matches, to marry, and start families of their own. She shook away the thoughts that worried her and ran to catch up with the girls as they chased Billy around the yard.

That night, she walked home with her mother. She said persuasively, "Momma, we should get a dog too. I think a dog would help keep the chickens in line. Don't you?"

But Maggie didn't answer. Hannah looked up at her mother and saw sweat beading down the sides of her face. Something was wrong, and Hannah asked in concern, "Momma, are you all right?"

Maggie reached out unsteadily to lean on her daughter. Hannah tried to hold her mother up, but the weight of her mother's body was too much for her. They both crumbled to the ground. Hannah cried out, "Momma!" But Maggie couldn't respond, she felt as if a horse was standing on her chest.

Hannah looked around her, but no one was on the street. She ran to the corner and burst in to Thornhill's Drug Store. "Doc! Ma needs help!"

Sewell Thornhill was the pharmacist who owned Thornhill's, but everyone just called him Doc. He came out from behind the counter and said, "Where is she?" Hannah pointed and begged, "Please, help her." He turned back toward his wife and said, "Call the doctor." Then he followed Hannah to Maggie, but there was nothing he could do for her. Maggie was gone, and so was Hannah's childhood.

# CHAPTER SEVEN

## FEBRUARY 1912

Harry was registered for the ice boat race that was to take place today, but he was sick in bed with a fever. Without fully thinking it through, Hannah seized the opportunity. She tucked her hair under Harry's knit cap and slipped undetected out of the cottage. Their father's oyster sloop was still at its mooring on account of the creek having frozen over. Instead, Andrew had left early to meet up with the other baymen at the cull shack. She faltered momentarily, fearing what his reaction would be when he discovered what she had dared to do. This, she reminded herself, was why she must win the race.

She then pushed the bay scooter undetected through the tall cattails and off the bank. With the expertise of one who had grown up on the water, she quickly sailed down the icy surface of Brown's River to join the other participants at the bay. She could see the shanty that was used to cull the oysters; smoke rose from the chimney in an attempt to warm the baymen inside. The giant wheel apparatus that was used to dry and mend fishing nets loomed over the shack, looking to Hannah like a Ferris-wheel. Hannah prayed that her father would not peek outside and spy her at the starting line. She hid her face behind Harry's scarf. A few of the boys called out, "Hey Harry!" so she raised her gloved hand in silent response.

Her muscles were tense as she waited alongside the other scooters. But she didn't waste a moment to take a breath when the gun shot signaled the beginning of the race. The Stalwart's sail filled quickly, leaving most of the others in her wake. While in the thick of it, only a few boys struggled to keep up, and there was only one scooter in front of her. His long blonde hair whipped freely in the wind as she closed the space between them. She saw the look of surprise and recognition on his face after Harry's scarf fell below her chin. As he faltered, she swiftly moved past him and into first place. Like other bay scooters, the Stalwart had two rails or "sled runners" attached to its bottom making it capable of traversing open water and then jumping onto stretches of ice. With no rudder, the only means of steering the scooter were the main sail and jib sheet. Hannah now adjusted the main sail and it billowed in the wind as the Stalwart continued to race across the ice. She held onto the jib sheet and leaned as far left as she dared, her elbow almost touching the icy surface. She and her brother, Harry, had sailed the Stalwart many times over the years, but she had never imagined she would secretly take his place in a race. And yet here she was, in the lead, and she wanted to keep it that way. The frosty wind stung her face and caused Hannah's tears to crystallize on her cheeks. She was glad to be wearing her brother's woolen pants and oversized jacket, but even with the extra weight of his clothes, she and her scooter were lighter and faster than the others. With a full 75 square feet of sail, she flew over the frozen Great South Bay as if on wings and wielded the Stalwart on to victory. When she finally crossed the finish line, it was to the cheers of all who had gathered along the shore in front of the four-storied Elmore Hotel with its many gabled roof. The first place prize of five dollars was hers!

On shaky legs she stood upon the ice, and with a reticent smile, she faced the members of the Sayville Yacht Club. She knew that the crowd would turn on her once they realized she was a girl, but she approached the judges without showing a hint of the fear that bubbled within her. She suppressed the instinct to run, embracing the adrenaline that ran through her veins. After all, her father had always told her that without fear, there was no true bravery. Hannah watched as the group of well-dressed men approached. Although she hadn't seen him in two years, she recognized the leader of the group immediately. Others were intimidated by him, after all, he was the cousin of President Teddy Roosevelt, but she knew his kindness and her eyes silently pleaded with him to extend it to her now.

As he stood beside the frozen bay, Commodore John Ellis Roosevelt was faced with a dilemma. He suddenly recognized the young winner of the ice boat race who was now standing in front of him. "Hannah Trumball, is that you?" In response, Hannah pulled the knit cap off her head and exposed her abundant red hair as it whipped around her face in the wind. The crowd responded with audible shock and gasps, followed by jeers. One boy in the crowd yelled in disgust, "She can't win! She's disqualified, she's a girl!" A chorus rose in agreement with him. But the Commodore's eyes never left Hannah's face. Flanked by the other wealthy and influential members of the Sayville Yacht Club, he was uncertain of how he should proceed. That was when he felt the presence of his wife, Nannie, as the men parted so that she could join him. He heard her whisper gently in his ear, "Give it to her, John. She won. She deserves the prize." John Ellis Roosevelt loved his wife with every fiber of his being, and for that, he would have done as she bid. But there was another reason he would stand up for Hannah. He would never forget the little girl who had comforted him when he had to send his own daughter away.

Now, nearly ten years later, he thought it was fortunate for Hannah that he had decided to come to Sayville to judge the ice races on this long winter weekend. For he was certain that if it weren't him standing here, her deception would have left her alone as she faced the scorn of the crowd. He looked away from her now and addressed those who were calling for her disqualification and announced, "Hannah has won this race."

He attempted to calm the crowd that roared with disapproval, "Now, now, I know that it has been tradition that this is a race for boys, but there is nothing written in the rules stipulating that girls cannot partake in it. The only qualification is that participants must be 'youths' between the ages of fourteen and twenty." Turning back toward Hannah, he handed her the five-dollar-note prize, "Congratulations, young lady. You sailed a great race and you won fair and square."

Hannah lifted her chin and faced the crowd as a silent sigh of relief escaped her lips. Hannah took the money and tucked it quickly into her pocket. She curtsied, "Thank you, Sir," and then with her head held high and her green eyes blazing, she faced her audience. No one wanted to challenge the Commodore's ruling; the grumbles died down quickly. A few of her competitors even came forward to congratulate her. As the crowd turned their attention to the next race, one of her competitors held his hat in his hands, his eyes averted to the ground. His blonde head sparkled where the sun's rays found ice chips embedded in his hair. He stood alone, he wore wide-legged pants, as was the Dutch tradition. He was kicking a stone at his feet until she finally approached him. I'm sorry, Carl, you would have won if it weren't for me."

Carl Hendricks and his sister, Ilsa, were Harry and Hannah's dear friends. Although they were all the children of baymen, Carl and Ilsa's father was Dutch, while Harry and Hannah's father was English. Andrew Trumball's family had been in the United States for over 200 years; whereas, Horace Hendricks had been born in Zeeland, Holland, and had come to America as a young man with his bride in 1890. For the most part, the English families lived in Sayville, while the Dutch families had formed a community of their own in West Sayville, and the towns were divided by such distinctions.

The Great South Bay was the home of the flavorful Blue Point oyster, named after a town just east of Sayville. The shoreline from Oakdale to Blue Point was once cluttered with Oyster shanties where the men shucked their oysters and clams. But as the affluent city-folk started to build mansions along the shore, the shanties became fewer. Instead the shacks became confined to designated areas, mainly at the end of West Avenue near Green's Creek in West Sayville and at the end of River Road in Sayville alongside Brown's River.

Although independent baymen had made a decent living in the past, that was become increasingly more difficult. In 1851, Jacob Ockers came to America from Holland. He rented the shoreline in Oakdale, just west of Sayville, and founded The Blue Point Oyster Company. Soon he became known as the Oyster King. Before building his home on Main Street in Oakdale, he created a hill on which to build it by stacking oyster shells and filling the mound in with dirt. The Blue Point Oyster Company was housed by the bay in West Sayville and it grew to become one of the largest oyster shipping companies in the world. As Ockers purchased more and more of the bay lots, the independent baymen were forced to harvest from both the shrinking public oystering grounds in the east bay and the disappearing public clamming grounds in the west bay. This change in the economy of those who relied on oysters and clams to feed their families, caused rifts between the Dutch and English communities.

Carl shook his head at her apology, "You were faster, you won."

The cheers rose around them as the next race neared the finish line and not knowing what else to say, she bowed her head and turned in the direction of their beached scooters. Carl walked quietly beside her in a companionable silence. They reached their scooters and prepared to sail them in opposite directions when Ilsa and another friend, Anna Koman, joined them. Ilsa's blonde hair was tucked neatly beneath her woolen cap; her heavy skirt was of a somber dark gray. Of sturdy Dutch lineage, Ilsa was taller than Hannah and had crystal blue eyes. Although she had been born in West Sayville, her Dutch accent was strong, and like the other Dutch children, English was her second language. Anna was also a sturdy girl, but in contrast to Ilsa, she was a quiet, shy girl with brown hair. It was only when speaking to their American classmates, that either spoke in English.

Ilsa said, "Oh, Carl! I'm sorry you didn't win, but Hannah, you astonished us all!" Then looking down at Hannah's clothing, Ilsa exclaimed, "Oh my, you're wearing boy's pants! Does your father know? Does Harry know?"

"No, Harry has a fever and couldn't race today, so I entered instead. I am hoping that the five dollars I won will be enough to distract Pa from my charade." The thought of her father's reaction still worried Hannah.

Ilsa exclaimed, "A fever! Why I hope he will recover."

Hannah assured her, "Gran is watching over him. She will take good care of him."

Ilsa lowered her voice, "Please tell him that I will say a prayer for the return of his health."

Hannah smiled, she knew that Ilsa was sweet on her brother, but she was pretty sure that Harry wasn't interested. However, she didn't have the heart to tell her friend so, "I'll do that, Ilsa. Thank you."

Ilsa asked, "What will you spend the money on? Will you buy yourself new boots? Or perhaps, a new dress? We could take the trolley to Patchogue! I'm sure you will find something divine to purchase there!" Ilsa's wish to accompany Hannah on a shopping spree to Patchogue had to do with her desire to live vicariously through Hannah, since her own strict parents forbade any show of vanity.

Of the two Dutch churches in West Sayville, Ilsa and Carl belonged to the True Holland Church, which was the stricter one on the west side of Atlantic Avenue, while Anna belonged to the Reformed Dutch Church on Cherry Avenue. The children who belonged to the True Holland Church were not allowed to listen to music other than church music, nor were they allowed to dance or even play cards. However, those belonging to the Reformed Dutch Church were not held to such strict rules. It was a severe upbringing, and Ilsa did not easily conform to it.

But Hannah had other plans for the prize money. "I will give it to Pa." Although her family was far from destitute, five dollars was a lot of money and she felt proud to be able to help her father provide for the family. Since her mother's death, her father spent most of his time out on his oyster sloop or at Nohowec's Saloon or at the Kensington Hotel in town. He left the care of his children to his mother-in-law, while he drowned his sorrow in ale.

Feeling a bit disappointed, Ilsa replied, "Well, I'm sure it will help."

Anna added, "You were so brave, Hannah. I wish I could be more like you."

Hannah revealed that her hands were still shaking, "Oh, Anna, I was terrified."

Anna hugged Hannah, "But you did it anyway."

Hannah then turned to Ilsa and said, "Sorry my friends, but I've got to get back and explain where I've been. I'll see you all at school on Monday."

Carl blushed as Hannah put out her hand to him. She said, "Thank you, Carl, for understanding." After an awkward moment, he took her hand and bowed his head to her, "You won, Hannah. But we shall see who wins the next time." A sly smile appeared on his face.

Hannah laughed, "All right, Carl! I will be sure to take you up on that challenge!"

When she got home, Hannah's grandmother was standing by the kitchen stove as the back door swung open and Hannah entered with frost covering her head.

"What on Earth? Where have you been, lass?" Cathleen O'Connell exclaimed.

Hannah held up her prize money in full view, "I've won the scooter race!"

Gran's voice rose an octave as she asked, "You've won what?"

"I raced in Harry's place and I won."

"Oh, my, my, what have you done, child?"

"It was nothing, Gran. Commodore Roosevelt was there and he declared me the winner, fair and square. But tell me, how is Harry doing?"

Gran looked tired as she wiped her brow with a dish rag, "His fever is still high, I hope he will sweat it out and it will break by tomorrow."

Hannah saw the concern on her grandmother's face, "It will, Gran. Don't worry."

Hannah ascended the stairs two steps at a time, knowing full well, that her grandmother was watching in disapproval at how unladylike it was for her to do so. She peeked in at Harry's door and saw that he was sleeping peacefully. She thought that sleep must be a good sign. She opened the next door which led to her own tiny bedroom and discarded the wet clothes and dried her raw skin with a large rough towel before dressing in her own clothes. She collapsed on her bed and held the five dollar note up against the light shining through the solitary window. Then she imagined what five dollars could buy. She thought about her desire to attend college someday, perhaps she should save the money for her own future. She knew that if there was enough money to send one of them to college, it would be for Harry. Her father saw no purpose in sending a girl to further her education. She was lucky, in fact, to be allowed to finish high school. Many girls who had graduated from primary school with her had been sent to work at the lace mill in Patchogue.

Her thoughts moved on from those unfortunate girls to the Roosevelt daughters. She had always loved spending summer days at Meadow Croft with Gladys and Jean. Over the years, she had become like a little sister to them. She longed for the afternoons when they had invited her to lounge in their bedrooms as they told her stories of life in Manhattan. But after her mother's death, those afternoons had stopped. The sisters were, respectively, eight and six years her senior and at the ages of 23 and 21, they were high society ladies now, not just the girls who had once taken her under their wings.

Later that afternoon, Hannah peeled potatoes and dropped them into a boiling pot of water. She had worried all day about how her father would take the news of her entering the race. When she heard his heavy footsteps on the back porch, her stomach took a lurch and she rubbed her belly to quiet her nerves. The door opened, and as her father entered, so did the smell of the sea. His metal lunch pail clanked on the counter as he set it down. He sat on the bench by the door and pulled off his heavy rubber boots and then slipped his feet into his dry shoes while he looked first at Hannah and then at Gran.

He asked, "How is Harry doing?"

Gran replied, "He's resting. I brought him some soup earlier and he had a few spoonful's. I think the worst is over."

The unvarnished floor boards creaked beneath Andrew's weight as he shuffled off toward his bedroom, only stopping to look in on Harry. Satisfied that his son was sleeping, he continued on to clean up before dinner. As he washed his calloused hands in the bowl set for that purpose on his dry sink, he looked at the image in the mirror that hung above it. In it he saw a man with gray hair and whiskers. It was still a surprise to him to see that old man looking back at him. He had been looking out of the same eyes for sixty years, but somehow the face that those eyes were set in had changed. There was a lot on his mind, his salary of $2.50 for working a ten-hour day was just not enough. He wanted his children to get the education he didn't have. He wanted them to have a better life than his had been. Fevers often ended in death and his only son was resting in the next room with only the help of a cool towel across his forehead to ease the heat that rose from his young body. Andrew Trumball felt like a failure. He had worked his whole life and had little to show for it beyond his children. If he were to lose them, he didn't think he could go on. His heart wrenched. With a coarse towel, he rubbed his face dry and returned to the kitchen. As his daughter and mother-in-law flew about the room, he took his seat at the table. He felt blessed to have a daughter who reminded him so much of his wife, but the sight of her also caused the pain of his loss to well up in his heart. She looked so much like Maggie, and she carried both that same flaming red hair and fire within her, as his wife had. Although he admired that fire, it also caused him concern. He worried that someday she would find herself in a precarious situation and that her strong will would end up causing her harm.

He had learned that it was all too easy to lose someone in this life. There had been the babies that Maggie had lost, the loss of his own parents and brother, and then the loss of his wife. This was the saddest part of growing old, losing loved ones along the way. And he knew that the world was not ready for the fire he saw in his daughter. Perhaps, it was partly his own fault for bringing her along with him and Harry so often after Maggie's death to help on the oyster sloop and in the cull shanty. Others warned him that it was no place for a girl, but he liked having her near him. Harry even seemed to look to his sister for strength. She challenged him and often encouraged him to do things he would never have tried on his own. On the other hand, Harry was the only one who could quell Hannah's fire. It seemed that only when they were together, were they truly whole. Andrew sighed, resigning himself to the things he could not change.

Hannah served her father and then sat across from him. She tried to read his face to see if he was in a good mood or not. She remembered the man her father had been before her mother had died and she missed that man. She knew that his heart was broken, but his sadness struck a fear in her. So she had made it her personal responsibility to bring him happiness. And it was because of that responsibility, that she now felt at odds with herself; unsure of how he would take the news she would need to share with him.

Gran interrupted the silence, "Andrew, I think Hannah has something to tell you."

Hannah was almost grateful to her grandmother, because she wasn't sure that she could have found the mettle to bring the subject up on her own.

Andrew Trumball looked at his daughter and said, "Well, let's have it."

Gathering her courage, she spoke in a steady voice, "I took Harry's place in the ice-sailing race today."

Andrew stared at his daughter and could see the energy that emanated from her core. He knew he should reprimand her for being so unorthodox, but something about the way she held her head high and almost dared him to do so, stopped him. He admired her.

So, instead, he asked, "And did you win?"

Hannah let go of her breath and held up the five-dollar-note. "Yes, Papa, I did."

He nodded at his daughter, "Well, then. It was all for the best. I bet they gave you a razzing though."

Hannah rushed on without a second thought to her words, "Oh, they almost disqualified me! But Commodore Roosevelt was there and he told the crowd that I had won fair and square."

Hannah held the five-dollar note out to him, "Here Pa, this is for you. I hope it helps."

But a shadow had passed over Andrew's face when he heard her mention John Ellis Roosevelt. "You keep that money, Hannah. You earned it." Then gruffly he said, "I can take care of my own family."

Immediately, Hannah regretted mentioning the Commodore, "But Papa, I did it for you."

Andrew stood up then and angrily slammed his fist on the table, "I don't want his money." Then he walked over to the wall and took his hat from the hook that hung there. He placed it on his head, grabbed his coat, and as he went through the door, he said to Gran, "Don't wait up for me."

Hannah and Gran looked at each other. They both knew he was heading toward a tavern and that he wouldn't be back home until he was good and drunk.

# CHAPTER EIGHT

1912

The day after the race, Hannah walked down the long dirt driveway to Meadow Croft. It was lined on each side by tall willow trees, their sweeping branches, now bare of leaves, encrusted in ice. A thin layer of snow covered the pockmarked road. To the east, Brown's River was frozen, but the sky was clear and the air was crisp and still. To the west, the bells of St. Ann's Episcopal Church chimed three times to announce the hour. Hannah's parents had been married in this very church, to the displeasure of Maggie's Catholic family.

Hannah's ear caught the sound of an engine running and she noticed that the Commodore's Searchmont automobile was outside of the carriage house and evidently being prepared for his departure. The main house stood before her; its yellow façade and wide wooden porch, accentuated with stately white columns, was supported on a foundation of red brick. The portico of the summer house extended out over the driveway in a porte-cochère, so that guests dismounting from their carriages would find themselves under shelter. As a result, the second floor windows could access the roof over the front entrance, as if it were a terrace. Hannah remembered the many times she had climbed out of those windows during a game of hide-and-seek. Somehow, Gladys had always known where to find her. Hannah knew that there was a great divide in status between herself, the daughter of a humble bayman, and the Roosevelt daughters. But she had spent so much time with them over the years, that she had often imagined she belonged to their family.

Now standing before the two columns on either side of the brick front steps, she observed them closely. The column on the left had a button that was labeled, STABLE, the one on the right had a button labeled, HOUSE. Clutching her winter cape about her, she pressed the button on the right column and waited for a servant to answer the door. To her astonishment, the Commodore was the one to greet her with a look of annoyance on his face. She stammered, "Oh, hello, Sir. So sorry, I just wanted to stop by and thank you once again for standing up for me yesterday."

John Roosevelt's face quickly changed to an expression of pleasure at the sight of Hannah. "No need to apologize, come in, Hannah. As you see, my staff was taken by surprise when we came out this week-end." The sound of footsteps scurrying about echoed from the rear of the house. He continued, "It's all for the better; we're leaving today, anyway. The fact is, in all this time, I haven't been able to find a suit-able replacement for your mother, Hannah. She was an efficient lady's maid, but when she became housekeeper for Meadow Croft, she was magnificent. On a moment's notice, no matter what the time of year it was, she would have the house ready. Mrs. Roosevelt and I have missed her very much these past years." Hannah felt a jab to her heart at the mention of the loss of her mother. But it gave her solace to hear the Commodore speak so highly of her.

"Well, Sir. If there is ever anything I can do for you, please let me know."

John Roosevelt took another look at her. "How old are you now, Hannah?"

"I'm fifteen, Sir. I'll be sixteen this August."

He nodded as he twirled his handlebar moustache between his finger and thumb as he observed to himself, "Young, but you have your mother's character. You know the house and you're trustworthy." He seemed thoughtful for a moment and then he said, "Well, why not?"

"Sir?"

"Hannah, would you be interested in watching things here over the winter months? You know, keeping an eye on the house?"

Hannah was surprised by the offer, "But what of the caretaker? Doesn't he manage it all?"

"He does, but he has a family to think of in West Sayville and he can't always be here during the off-season. With you living so close, I'm sure he would welcome the extra help. Why don't you come by, say, once a day to make sure the house is dusted and aired out. And if we decide to take another visit before spring, we will send word for you to make the house ready."

Hannah was overwhelmed with pride that he would ask this of her, "Well, yes, Sir. I can do that."

"Great! I will give the caretaker instructions to pay you a dollar a week, then."

"Thank you, Sir!"

Nannie entered the room and smiled as she saw who their guest was and in her gentle voice she remarked, "Hannah, that was quite a race you ran yesterday!"

"Thank you, Mrs. Roosevelt."

Nannie continued, "We need more young women with gumption if we are ever to win the right to vote. I was very impressed with you, Hannah." Nannie paused for a moment in thought and then said, "One day this summer, I'd like to have you meet a friend of mine. She is very influential in the Suffragist movement and I think she would enjoy hearing about your little scooter race."

Hannah blushed at the praise, "That would be wonderful, Ma'am."

The Commodore cleared his throat, "Dear, I've asked Hannah to check on the place for us while we are gone. I thought, perhaps, she could come by once a day and just air out the place and make sure all is in order. What do you think?" He threaded his fingers through what was left of his hair. At 59 years of age, he had developed a severe widow's peak. There was only a tuft of hair at the very top of his head, whereas, the hair from his ears to the nape of his neck was neatly trimmed.

Nannie was pleased with the idea and replied enthusiastically, "I think that would work out fine! Can you start immediately, dear? I don't believe we will be back again until April."

"Yes, of course, Ma'am."

Mrs. Roosevelt exclaimed with a bright smile, "Wonderful! Then it's all settled." Although Nannie possessed wiry hair and features that Hannah often thought were more masculine then feminine, when she smiled, her whole face softened and became almost beautiful. Nannie walked purposefully toward the butler's pantry and retrieved a set of keys. "Here you go. Take these. We leave today, so you can start tomorrow."

"Very well, Ma'am."

Hannah was happy with this arrangement. But as she walked home, she wondered how her father would take the news that she was now working at Meadow Croft. Then again she thought, perhaps he didn't need to know. A sound from the marsh beyond the willow trees caught her attention. It was sort of a squeak but at the same time, a cry. Hannah walked off of the driveway and into the marsh expecting to find a mouse, but instead, she saw a ball of white and brown fur among the virgin snow. Earnest brown eyes looked up at her, a little black nose at the center, twitched, as its mouth let go of another cry. Hannah unbuttoned her cape and immediately bent down to pick up the puppy. Even through her gloves she could feel it shiver in her hands. After further inspection she asked, "So little lady, wherever did you come from?" When there was only a whimper in response, Hannah placed the puppy near the warmth of her heart and buttoned her cape around the small body.

She could see from the matted-down dead leaves that lay beneath the fresh coating of snow, that someone, or something, had made a bed for the puppy. The tiny dog squirmed and settled itself comfortably against her warmth. Hannah said, "Where is your mother, little one?" But the puppy remained silent. The tips of Hannah's lips rose into a smile, "Well then, I guess you need to come home with me." So she walked back to the driveway and toward the road. A few feet further, just as she was about to reach St. Ann's Church, she saw a Shetland sheepdog lying on the side of the road. Hannah cried out, "Oh, dear!" The dog must have been run over by an automobile. Hannah shivered and her heart wrenched for the second time that day. She spoke to the puppy that sheltered beneath her cape, "Poor thing. You have lost your mother just as I have. But I've got you now and you'll be safe with me." Hannah felt the tears freeze on her cheeks, it was so very cold out. She was sure the puppy wouldn't have survived another night alone. Hurriedly, she turned onto Foster Avenue and then down the side street to her cottage. All the time, whispering soothing words to her little charge.

When she reached home, she burst into the kitchen exclaiming, "Gran! Look what I found!"

Cathleen O'Connell looked at her granddaughter and sighed, "What have you brought home now, lass?"

"Oh, Gran, look how sweet she is."

"Like that opossum you brought home when you were little? You thought that vermin was sweet too." But as Hannah opened her cloak to reveal the little puppy, Gran's face softened, "Aye, now what have we here?"

Hannah placed the puppy in her grandmother's hands and knew that she now had an ally. "Do you think Papa will let me keep her?"

"He's down at the cull shack, why don't you go there and tell him what you have found. I'll take care of this little one in the meantime."

"Thanks, Gran!" She kissed her grandmother and then headed back out into the cold. She ran until she was out of breath and felt a stitch in her side, and then was forced to walk the rest of the way. When she opened the wooden door of the shanty, the sight that greeted her eyes was a familiar one. The building itself was not much more than a crudely made shelter. Rudimentary wooden tables lined the walls and there were barrels and baskets everywhere. Glass lanterns hung from beams to give the men some light. Shovels, tongs and rakes were left discarded on the floor or leaning against the walls. Wheelbarrows full of oysters were keeping the men busy. They were all at work, washing, sorting and shucking oysters. William Smythe, holding a culling iron, pointed to Hannah and shouted, "Hey, look who's here!" The men all stopped what they were doing to look in Hannah's direction.

Randall Fergerson exclaimed, "Why if it isn't little Hannah Trumball! You're a site for sore eyes, to be sure."

Andrew Trumball smiled at the sight of his daughter. He asked, "Come to lend a hand now; have you, Hannah?"

Hannah hung her cloak on a peg by the door and joined her father at one of the tables. He offered her a pair of sturdy gloves and a stool as she took her place beside him. It had been several months since she had been in the shanty and in that time, her spindly body had grown shapelier. She reached into a barrel and took out an oyster, handing it over to her father she said, "I miss this, Papa."

Andrew nodded, "We've had good times. But a cull shack is no place for a young lady and you're growing up, my dear."

"Oh Papa, times are changing. You'll see, women don't have to spend all their time in the kitchen anymore. Why there are so many modern conveniences these days that a woman is surely left with time to fill in more interesting ways."

Andrew kept his eyes on the oysters as he said, "Hannah, someday, you're going to say something and someone is going to set you straight. There are differences between men and women. That's the way God created us and that is never going to change."

Not wanting to upset him further, she quietly handed him oysters as he continued his work. Finally, he asked, "So what brings you here? I'm sure it wasn't that you missed the smell of this place."

"Actually, I do miss it. I miss the men's laughter. I miss the companionable atmosphere and the old stories you all tell each other."

Andrew knew his daughter better than she realized, "Uh, huh. But that's not why you're here, is it?"

"Well, Pa," she took a breath, "I found a puppy." She rushed on before he could react. "The poor thing is an orphan. Her mother was lying dead at the side of the road. She would have frozen out there. I had to take her home. Please Papa, please can I keep her?"

"What does your Grandmother say about this?"

"She's already preparing for the little thing. But she sent me here to ask you if it 'twas all right."

"Well, I guess if she doesn't mind the extra work, it's all right with me." He wasn't thrilled about the extra expense but it was obvious that Hannah was already attached to the puppy. He thought back at all the other "orphans" she had brought home in the past. There were injured birds, a bat, a squirrel, an opossum, and once, even a rat. It seemed that there was always another animal to be rescued. But at least this one wasn't wild.

She whispered, demurely, "Thank you, Papa."

It was then that she heard Clarence White start in with a story about a time when he was caught in a squall while tonging for oysters. That was followed by another story, just as frightening, being told by Frank Winfield Greene about his nearly being struck by lightning, "It missed me by an inch," he boasted. Hannah silently rejoiced in being part of this special brotherhood for one more time.

At the end of the long day, she accompanied her father home. More snow had fallen during the late afternoon and now the dirt roads were difficult to traverse. Andrew wrapped his arm around his daughter to give her some warmth, but he could see that her fashionable boots were not sufficient for such conditions. In a gruff voice he said disapprovingly, "I hope that this puppy hasn't cost you your health, marching through the streets without proper winter boots on."

She had worn the fashionable boots that Nannie had once given her. They were boots that Jean had outgrown and she felt they were the most appropriate for her visit to Meadow Croft. In her haste, she hadn't taken the time to change into the more practical snow boots that had been stacked by the kitchen door. Then again, she reasoned, she hadn't known that it was going to snow again, either. By the time they made it back to the house, Hannah's legs were frozen through and Gran made a huge fuss about it.

Gran ordered, "Go sit next to the fire and wrap yourself in a blanket!"

Hannah obeyed, she could feel the pins and needles as the blood began to rush to her feet once again.

Gran worried over her, practically in tears, "You're near to frostbite!"

Andrew didn't even take his coat off. He took a quick look at the puppy and shook his head, then said, "I'll be down at Kensington's." And walked back out the door.

Harry came down the stairs then, looking recovered from his fever. He asked, "What's all the commotion about?"

Hannah exclaimed, "Harry! You're better!" She jumped up on her numb legs and felt the pinch of pins and needles as she hugged her brother.

He protested, "Aw, stop that now. I'm all right." But he actually enjoyed his sister's display of affection.

They sat down next to each other by the hearth and he asked her, "So what have I missed?" And with that, the puppy came playfully up to him and nipped at his toes. Harry asked, "Who is this?"

Gran said, "Your sister has brought home another orphan."

He laughed and picked up the puppy who then licked his face. Harry asked, "Does she have a name yet?"

Hannah shook her head, "No, we haven't had time to name her. I was just down at the cull shack asking Pa if we could keep her."

Although Harry already knew that his father rarely said "no" to Hannah, he asked anyway, "And what did he say?"

Hannah replied, "He said that as long as Gran didn't mind the extra work, it's all right with him."

Gran protested, "Oh no, she's not my dog, lass. It's you who will be doing the extra work, Hannah." But Gran couldn't keep from smiling as the puppy barked her approval. Gran said, "That's a smart one you have there. She's a loyal one, too. She followed me 'round the kitchen like she was waitin' for a chore to do. I dropped a kitchen towel and she picked it up for me, sat back on her hind legs, and waited for me to take it from her, the dear."

Harry said, "Like a little sage attending to her lady."

Hannah exclaimed, "That's it Harry! Sage! That will be her name."

Harry leaned in close to his sister, "And did I hear right? Did you win the scooter race for me?"

Hannah's cheeks filled with color, "I won the scooter race, but not for you Harry Trumball. I won it for me. Fair and square, I should say!"

Harry lifted his arms in defeat, "All right, you won." He smiled at his brave sister, "You are a wonder, Hannah Trumball."

She lifted her chin and smiled, "Yes I am, Harry Trumball. And you'd better get used to it."

He put his arm around his sister's shoulders, "I bet you're the talk of the town, now." She shrugged, "As I should be." Sage nipped at the edge of Hannah's stockings, so she bent down to pick up the puppy and snuggled her face into the dog's fur. Hannah looked around the small kitchen at her brother and grandmother. She missed her mother's presence, but that loss had taught Hannah to appreciate what she did have. She had learned that nothing lasts forever. Still, her heart sank at the thought that her mother would have loved Sage. Hannah wondered how long it would take to get over her mother's death. Tears began to spill from her eyes, but Sage licked away the salty tears from her face before anyone else could see them.

# CHAPTER NINE

## 2012

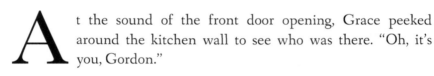t the sound of the front door opening, Grace peeked around the kitchen wall to see who was there. "Oh, it's you, Gordon."

"Hey, Mrs. F, is Phil around?"

"Sure." She called up the stairway, "Philip, Gordon is here."

"Be right down, mom," came the answer from behind Philip's closed bedroom door.

"Gordon, why don't you come into the kitchen with me? I'm just making Philip's birthday cake."

"Sure thing, Mrs. F." Gordon followed Grace into the kitchen and took a seat at the table. She took a good look at him and could see that something was troubling him. "What's going on, Gordon? Is your grandmother all right?"

"Yeah, yeah. She's fine. I'm just a little bummed, that's all."

"And what does a boy your age have to be bummed about?"

Gordon took a deep breath before answering, "I asked Courtney to the prom, but she said I was too late. She's already going with Jack Collins."

"Well, that doesn't mean she wouldn't have preferred to go with you if you had asked sooner."

"Naw, I could tell, she was glad she had an excuse not to go with me."

"Why do you say that?"

"'Cause I'm a nobody and I've got nothin'. I'm just a joke to everyone."

Grace saw how his shoulders slumped and she knew how deep his wounds were. His grandmother was raising him because both of this parents had died in a car accident when he was young. His grandfather had also passed a few years ago and now all that he had was his grandmother. Gordon had found out early that causing others to laugh covered up a lot of pain, and so, he had become the "class clown." Now, as a senior in high school, it was hard to shake that reputation.

Grace put the cake in the oven and set the timer. She took out her tarot cards from the kitchen drawer and then set the box on the table.

Gordon asked, "How did you know I wanted you to read my cards, Mrs. F?"

"I'm psychic."

They both laughed.

When Philip entered the kitchen he took a seat next to Gordon and looked over the cards that were already spread across the surface of the table. He saw the death card and pointed to it, "Uh oh, Gordy, that doesn't look good!"

Philip was used to his mother reading cards to his friends. There were times when he and his friends would come home from a late night at the local Applebee's and he'd knock on her bedroom door to tell her they wanted their cards read. Grace would always get up and come down to spend some time with his friends. She liked that they came to her for guidance. She even suspected that they all knew she wasn't psychic at all, but it was a safe way for them to ask the difficult questions without feeling embarrassed. And Grace always knew what they needed to hear. They needed to hear that it would be all right, that everything happened for a reason, and that they just weren't privy to that reason yet. Time would tell; all would even out in the end. They just needed to trust themselves and learn from their mistakes.

Grace waved her hand over the death card, "This card means a great change is coming. It is the death of an old way of life and the beginning of a new way."

Philip poked Gordon, "What did you ask?"

Blushing, Gordon answered, "I want to know if I'm ever going to find a girl."

Philip eyes widened and he whistled, "Well, okay then."

Grace turned over the next card, it was the fool. "This card shows what has passed. You have often played the fool." Both Gordon and Philip snickered. Grace gave them each a look of warning, then she turned over the next card. It was the sun. "Ah, this card represents the present, it shows growth and liberation from limitation. This indicates your upcoming graduation and entering college in the fall."

Gordon responded, "Some liberation! I'm only going to Suffolk Community College, it's like an extension of high school. Half our class will be there. How's that going to mean liberation."

Philip said, "I'll be there with you, Gordy."

Gordon responded, "My point, exactly."

Grace looked from one boy to the other and said, "It will be what you make of it. That is up to you."

She turned over the final card and said, "This is your future." The card that was revealed was the lovers. Philip pounded Gordon's back, "There you go, Gordy! You can't beat that card!" Grace ignored the outburst and continued, "This card means an end to isolation and the formation of a bond based on love, honor and trust."

"Wow, Mrs. F! I hope this is for real!"

"Trust in yourself, Gordon. You can make it happen if you believe you can. But it's time to put the fool in the past and start to become serious about your future."

"I got this, Mrs. F! You'll see!" Grace was glad to see Gordon's expression transform into one of determination.

Philip said, "It's my turn now, mom."

"All right." Grace collected the cards and handed them to Philip, "Here, shuffle the cards and think of the question you want to ask."

When Philip handed the cards back to his mother he said, "I don't really have a specific question, I just want to know what my future will be. Will I be successful? Will I ever leave Sayville?"

Grace looked at her son who had grown so quickly into the man seated before her. Gone was the little boy who had clung to her with such fierce devotion, promising her he would never leave her side. He was now of medium build and still growing every day. He had thick chestnut brown hair and kind green-speckled hazel eyes, shaded under long dark lashes. His nose was just a tinge too large for his face and he had a bright smile that could light up her heart in an instant. She laid the first card on the table and said, "This card is you."

Upon seeing it, Philip exclaimed, "The wheel of fortune? What kind of card is that to get?"

She smiled at her son, "The wheel is ever turning, unfolding fate. It holds both gain and loss. You are changing, Philip, becoming the man you will one day be. But you need to learn to have more patience."

Philip made a gesture with his hand that told her to move on with the reading, "Okay, okay, keep going." Philip was disappointed with the card that represented him.

Grace announced, "This next card represents the forces that are working against you." She turned over the hermit and said, "In order to receive great wisdom, you must seek the light alone. It is something you will have to do without your father and me, even perhaps, without your friends."

Grace went on without waiting for a response, "And this next card reveals your hopes for the future." Gordon interrupted, "Yeah, mine was death." Grace corrected him, "Yours was *change*, Gordon." Gordon shrugged.

The next card turned over was the magician. Grace looked at her son with pride, "You seek wisdom and skill, you want to harness energy into a force that will benefit others."

She turned over another card, "This is your past, temperance. In the past you have been hesitant and have restrained yourself from acting on your feelings. While caution is a great virtue, if taken to the extreme, it can cost you to experience life."

She continued, "And this next card represents the present. It is the moon. Darkness magnifies your fears. It is difficult when you don't understand the circumstances that surround you, but you must move past the darkness to reach the light." Both Philip and Gordon were silent now. Both caught up in the spell of the moment. Waiting to see what the future would reveal. Grace turned over the final card.

"This is the tower." Both boys drew in their breath. The image of the wooden tower on fire, being struck by lightning as bodies fell from its great height could not be a good thing. Philip wondered how his mother would interpret this.

Grace looked almost pained as she spoke, "The tower means that in a flash, the road one has traveled comes to a sudden halt. Change will prevail. Disruption to all you have known. But you will be up to the challenge, you will conquer the adversity no matter what is presented to you."

Philip complained, "Oh, come on now! How do you get that from this card? That looks like utter destruction."

He was surprised when he looked at his mother again and saw tears welling up in her eyes. "My son, just as I told Gordon, the future is what you will make of it. It is up to each of you to rise to the challenges ahead. To face the struggles and find a way to survive. Your future is your journey, not mine. Wherever it takes each of you, be strong, be wise, watch and learn. Philip, *she is waiting for you.*"

Philip shook his head when he heard those last words. They were so much like the ones he had heard from the old man, Louis, at the park. He asked, "Wait. What did you say?" Grace responded, "I said, 'See what is waiting for you.'"

"Oh." Philip wondered, had he heard it wrong? Had she said what he thought she had said? He wasn't sure anymore. "Okay, but I wish I was going away to college like Tommy and Jack did."

Grace put her hand on his shoulder, "Just give it one year at Suffolk, Philip. If you still want to go away next year, we will work that out."

Grace put the cards away. "Your cake will be ready soon and Dad will be home. He's picking up Jenny and Ben. Gordon, are you staying for dinner and for cake?"

"Sure, Mrs. F!"

Later that afternoon, Jenny came bursting into Philip's room.

"Hey guys! What'cha up to?" Jenny bounced on Philip's bed and then pulled her long legs up under her to sit cross-legged.

Philip's and Gordon's eyes never left the television screen as they continued to press buttons on the PlayStation handsets, "Ah nothing. Just figuring out our entire futures is all."

Jenny laughed. She knew these boys; they had been a threesome for as long as she could remember. Her dad and Philip's dad were best friends. Their families went way back together. That's how extended Italian families were, they were *paisans*.

Philip explained further, "Courtney shot down Gordon."

Jenny dramatically placed her hands over her chest as if she had just taken a bullet to the heart, "What? Why?"

Gordon responded, "She's going with Jack. He asked her first."

Jenny looked at Gordon, "I'll go with you Gordy. We'll show her. She'll be jealous as heck. You wait and see."

Philip was ecstatic, "Wow, Jenny. Would you do that? That would be great!"

"Well, I said so. I don't say something if I don't mean it."

Philip turned to his friend, "What do you think, Gordy?"

Gordon kept his eyes glued to the television screen as he shrugged, "I-I think that's a great idea."

Philip slapped Gordon on the back, "Great, then it's settled. See, we're starting that new life already."

Jenny asked, "What new life?"

Gordon explained, "Mrs. F. was reading our tarot cards again."

Jenny rolled her eyes, "Oh, well, then it must be true. Do you think she'll read mine later?

Philip laughed, "I'm sure she will, Jenny. Just ask her."

After dinner and the birthday cake, the boys and men moved into the living room to watch the baseball game. Jenny was helping to clear away the dishes when she asked, "Aunt Grace, the boys were telling me that you were reading cards today. Do you think you could read mine?"

Grace smiled, "Of course. You know where they are Jenny. Get them out and I'll sit down with you in a minute."

When Grace joined her, Jenny had already shuffled the cards and was ready to hand the deck to her.

Instead of the usual ten, Grace laid only six cards on the table, making a cross within a cross, and asked, "What is your question, Jenny?"

Jenny whispered, "Will Gordy ever see me as more than just a friend?"

An almost imperceptible smile crossed Grace's face before she hid it behind her hand. "Well, let's see."

Grace turned over the first card, "Jenny, this card represents you. It is strength. You are one who is filled with both courage and compassion. You have a determination that enables you to succeed where others fail."

Jenny liked that, "Wow! Awesome!"

The next card that was turned over was, judgment. Grace continued, "This card represents those forces working against you. While others may sit in judgment of the two of you, you will stand up to that judgment. Although you may have your work cut out for you, you will give Gordon purpose. This will be a turning point for him."

Jenny observed her Aunt Grace, it seemed to her that the older woman was almost in a trance. Something had come over her. Some greater awareness.

Grace turned over the next card, "The world, ah, this is your hopes for the future."

Jenny tried to interject some levity into the situation, "Well, that's not too daunting!" she joked. But Grace did not smile this time. "You hope for recognition and understanding of who you are. You desire a change in status. This will come, in time."

Grace continued without a moment to pause, "This next card represents the past, it is, the charioteer. Your past has been divided. Notice that the heads of the two horses are leading the chariot and facing in opposite directions. Your existence is a result of life's victory over opposing forces."

Jenny interjected, "Wait, what does that mean?"

Grace looked at this girl whom she loved as much as if she were her own daughter. Jenny's mother, Alice, had been her childhood friend. In fact, she wouldn't have even met Tom if it weren't for Ben and Alice. "You are very dear to me, Jenny. You are here at my table because the past has deemed it should be so. But the past has held conflicts, as does the future. We must accept that this is the way it was supposed to be."

Jenny still didn't know what her aunt was talking about, but she didn't want to seem obtuse, so she refrained from asking any more questions. Grace continued with her reading, "This is the fifth card, it is the present." Grace turned over the high priestess, "You possess both intuition and foresight, they are aspects of great wisdom. You know what is right. Follow your intuition, it won't mislead you."

"And lastly, this is your sixth and final card." Grace's hand shook as she turned it over, and then sighed with relief when she saw what it was. "It is the star. It represents your inner light. That inner light will guide you to a full and happy life. Gordon is a lucky man, you will marry and raise a family together. These cards are quite clear."

Grace closed her eyes, her face looked pale. "Aunt Grace, are you all right?"

Grace shook her head, "Perhaps I have said too much."

Jenny asked, "What do you mean?"

"Jenny, there have been secrets I have held within me for a long time. It is time for me to let Philip go, so that others can live the lives they were destined to live, including you and Gordon. But letting go is a hard thing for a mother to do."

# CHAPTER TEN

## 1912

With the approach of the new summer, Hannah found herself once again welcomed by the Roosevelt household. She had missed Jean and Gladys terribly. But the girls seemed to not have noticed that there was any interruption in their friendship at all. Quite the contrary, and Hannah's presence among them was simply accepted as the natural course of events.

Hannah was now sitting on Jean's bed, listening intently as Jean and Gladys described the woman who was coming for a visit.

Gladys explained, "Our mother is entertaining Alva Vanderbilt Belmont for lunch today. She was once married to William K. Vanderbilt and it was at her direction that the grand mansion, Idlehour, was built in Oakdale."

Jean added conspiratorially, "Her marriage to William lasted twenty years, but mother told us that, back in the day, her divorce was fuel for the gossip mill. It is said that she received an enormous sum of over two million dollars, and an income of $100,000 a year for life." Jean's eyes widened as she mentioned the large settlement.

"Don't forget that she also received Marble House in Newport and was awarded sole custody of their three children." Gladys added, proud of her knowledge on the subject.

Jean continued, "I should add that she has often been the subject of gossip for the simple reason that she is not afraid to live life on her own terms. Her husband, like so many men, was a womanizer and when she found out that he was having affairs, she divorced him. But unlike so many women, she fought for what she felt was rightfully hers, and she fought for her children, too. A year later, she married Oliver Hazard Perry Belmont, the son of a wealthy banker. Oliver was actually a few years younger than Alva and had been a friend of William's. In fact, he had joined them more than once on their yacht, which, by the way, was named Alva."

Jean laughed, "Well, Oliver was wealthy in his own right, he received a substantial inheritance when his father died, and then later, around the turn of the century, he became a New York Congressman. He and his brother, August, had a particular fondness for horses. It was August who built Belmont Park, the famous racetrack."

Hannah shook her head; racetracks were not part of Hannah's world, "I don't know any racetracks."

In response, Jean shook her own head at Hannah's lack of knowledge, "Well, anyway, after their marriage, Oliver built a new mansion for Alva in East Meadow and called it Brookholt. They had some good years together, but then he died in 1908 leaving Alva as one of the wealthiest women in the world and in a position to do whatever she wants with her money."

Gladys agreed, "Yes, mother says that after Oliver's death, Alva became a motivating force for the Suffrage movement. She joined the National American Woman Suffrage Association and convinced them to move their headquarters from Ohio to Manhattan. She even purchased a building for them to work out of on 5th Avenue. Then she started an organization of her own, Political Equality Association. She feels strongly that the involvement of working women is crucial to winning the right to vote for all women. So PEA, as it is called, was created to spread the word to the working women of New York City. She has opened meeting places throughout Manhattan and has organized lectures and discussion groups that attract women from all walks of life. In our circles, having her here at our lunch table this afternoon is quite a humdinger!"

Hannah's head was spinning, but she tried to keep up as Jean explained further, "Well, NAWSA, is an old organization and they are made up of older women who frown on the ideas of younger women, like us, who are now taking up the torch. You've heard of Alice Paul, haven't you?" Mutely, Hannah shook her head once again. The more that was explained to her, the more uneducated she felt.

Jean continued, "Well, Alva's daughter, Consuelo, is a Duchess in England. While visiting her daughter, Alva became acquainted with the cause in Britain and met Alice Paul. Although Alice is an American, she became a leader of the movement in England, and Alice believes it will take more aggressive action than we have seen so far to change minds. Alice has now taken the fight back to America and believes that it is not good enough for individual states to pass suffrage bills, she wants to strive for an amendment to the U.S. Constitution."

Hannah asked an honest question, "Why would wealthy women care if women get the right to vote? Their husbands and fathers will give them anything they want."

Gladys replied, "Even wealthy women are controlled by their husbands. Our Aunt Blanche had all of her assets destroyed by her husband, Constant Andrews."

Hannah questioned, "What do you mean? How did he destroy them?" This whole conversation was reminding Hannah that the world of the wealthy was still mostly a mystery to her. She lived on its edges, only because of the generosity of the Roosevelts, but she had not been educated to be a part of it. Although an excellent student, her education was limited to literature, science, history and math. Society and its workings were an enigma to the daughter of a bayman.

Gladys said, "Let me explain, our grandmother, Augusta Vance, died here, in this house, in June of 1901. But only months before her death, she pleaded with the court to have her daughter, our Aunt Blanche, committed to an insane asylum in an attempt to save her. Our Uncle Constant had hired a housekeeper who was trained as a nurse. Together they were medicating our Aunt Blanche and causing her to become fearful and distrustful of everyone. But the court fight took years and our parents had to take up the cause after grandmother's death. Aunt Blanche was finally taken from her home in 1907 and institutionalized. But by then, Aunt Blanche had even lost control of her own limbs. She was placed in an asylum in Manhattan near our home. You see, as a woman, our mother could not speak for her own sister, so our father was assigned as co-trustee along with Aunt Blanche's husband. Uncle Constant tried to prevent our mother from visiting Aunt Blanche. But at least the courts protected our mother's right to see her sister and ensured that she could speak to her without the presence of our uncle."

Hannah realized now that all of this had been happening around the same time that Pansy was being sent to the sanitarium. How sad for Mrs. Roosevelt to have lost her mother, been separated from her daughter, and to have nearly lost her sister, all within a few years of each other. "How horrible!" Hannah exclaimed.

Gladys continued, "Occasionally, our uncle would take Aunt Blanche out of the asylum for a period of time, and each time he returned her, she was physically and emotionally in worse shape. The court battles went on for years over control of the trust, and in the meantime, our uncle's extravagant spending decimated our aunt's inheritance to the point where he even lost their home. When the court intervened and threatened to remove both our father and our uncle as trustees, Uncle Constant claimed that our aunt was miraculously cured and could permanently return home. But when the judge visited Aunt Blanche, whatever was said between them, he determined that she should not be released into her husband's custody. However, our uncle was successful in having our aunt transferred to an asylum in White Plains, closer to his new home and further from ours."

Hannah asked with concern, "So, what happened then?"

Gladys shook her head in despair, "She died a few months later, on November 29, 1909. A week after her death, our uncle produced a will he said she had signed shortly after their marriage in 1880. The will proclaimed him the sole-beneficiary."

Hannah questioned, "And what happened to the housekeeper?"

Jean added, "While our aunt was in the asylum, the housekeeper accused her husband of abandoning herself and their children. But her husband said it was only a ruse, because he was about to file for divorce himself." Jean continued in a whisper, "You see, the housekeeper had been working for our uncle for years and had not been intimate with her husband. If you ask me, I believe our uncle and the housekeeper were having an affair. Although much of the trial was plastered all over the papers, the most sordid of the details were hidden from the public's eye."

Hannah asked, "So, your aunt was never insane?"

Gladys answered, "No, but as we said, declaring her so was the only way our grandmother and mother could protect her from him. Women need to be able to speak for themselves, protect themselves, support themselves, and make choices for themselves without the consent of their husbands. This all begins with the right to vote."

Jean explained, "The whole experience has taken a lot out of our mother. She just hasn't been the same since her sister's death. Our father tried to fight our uncle in court after Aunt Blanche passed away, but it was useless. Since our aunt had been declared insane, she couldn't have signed a will protecting her inheritance. In the end, Uncle Constant got whatever was left."

Jean had barely finished her thought when they heard the bell announcing Alva's arrival. Jean jumped off of the bed and examined herself with the hand mirror on her dresser. As they descended the stairs, Hannah noticed for the first time that one of the spindles on the railing was set upside down. She knew it was impolite to ask, but Gladys saw her touch the spindle and hesitate on the steps. Gladys explained, "The builder, Boss Strong, intentionally placed that spindle upside down, it was his trade-mark. He felt that only God made things that were perfect."

When the girls walked into Nannie's parlor, they waited for their mother to introduce them to their guest. Nannie was speaking to Alva and saying, "I read that James Clinch Smith of St. James was on the Titanic. I know you were a friend of his, I'm so sorry for your loss."

Alva replied, "Yes, he and his dear sister, Bessie, were frequent and welcome visitors when William and I lived in Oakdale. The sinking was quite a terrible occurrence. A tragedy on a grand scale for so many."

Looking up and seeing her daughters and Hannah at the doorway, Nannie extended her arm out toward them in a gesture beckoning them to join in. After Alva exchanged greetings with Gladys and Jean, she set her piercing eyes on Hannah's face. "And who do we have here, Nannie?"

Gladys made the introduction, "This is our young friend, Hannah Trumball."

Hannah walked toward Alva and gave a slight curtsy before saying, "How do you do?" Alva rebuffed it, "Now, I'll have none of that. Shake my hand young lady." Alva reached out her hand and grabbed Hannah's forcefully, and said, "It's all in the handshake, remember that. If you take someone's hand as if you were a fish, then they will think you are weak. A firm handshake is the calling card of a forceful woman. Trumball, did you say? Of the Southold Trumballs?"

Hannah blushed and with as much pride as she could manage replied, "No Ma'am, I'm sorry, but I'm not. My father is a bayman from Sayville."

"Well, that's fine with me. That's nothing to be ashamed of. There have been times in my life when I was near penniless. It's not about what is in your bank account, it's about what is in your character. Are you interested in our cause, Hannah? We need all women to join and it's the working women who will be on the front lines of this war."

Hannah replied, "Well, it sounds very interesting and I'd like to know more about it." Alva shook Hannah's hand enthusiastically. "Very well. The reason for my visit is to inform you all that there will be a Suffrage march going through Sayville next month. Dear Edna Buckman Kearns of Rockville Center will be teaming up with other like-minded young women to bring the word of our fight to every town on Long Island. There will be several caravans spreading out all across the island, they will come in automobiles and will then march on foot through each town. Edna is even bringing her young daughter, Serena, with her."

Nannie reacted with surprise, "The child can't be much more than five years old! Isn't that a bit young?"

Alva said, "Pish-posh, never too young to join the cause. After all, it is the next generation that we have all been fighting for since 1848. The men pushed us aside during the Civil War and deemed our cause unsuitable; we will not allow that to happen again. The fight must go on until we have won the right to speak for ourselves. And dear Edna is the perfect woman to represent us, she has quite a way with words. Publicity is the answer! The more we place our demands in front of the world, the harder it is for others to ignore us."

Hearing the bell that announced lunch was ready, Hannah was about to excuse herself when Nannie said, "Hannah, won't you join us?" Taken off guard, Hannah replied, "Oh, of course ma-am, if it would please you." Nannie led the group to the dining room and suggested, "Please, have a seat next to Mrs. Belmont, Hannah." Jean and Gladys took the seats opposite Alva and Hannah, while Nannie sat at the head of the sturdy mahogany table.

Hannah replied, "Thank you, Mrs. Roosevelt, it is very kind of you to include me."

Nannie responded, "Nonsense, Hannah, you are part of our family."

Although Nannie might think so, some of the staff did not. And as the trays of sandwiches and raw oysters were set before the women, there was a maid or two who scowled at Hannah's presence. There was this attitude among them that Hannah was imposing herself on the Roosevelt family. After all, her own mother had been part of the help at one time. But Hannah did the best she could to avoid their scowls and concentrated on the talk at the table. She was very interested in this movement that was spear-headed by women for women, and she thought that she would like to be part of it.

Alva once again turned her attention to Hannah, "How old are you, young lady?"

"Fifteen, Ma'am."

"Humph, you appear older. But we need young women to follow us now and to become the leaders of tomorrow."

Nannie told Alva about Hannah's unconventional entrance into the ice scooter race and how she had won the first prize. "My husband was there and he ensured that Hannah was given the acknowledgment that she deserved. It is brave young women like Hannah that will be the most valuable to your organization."

Alva clapped, "Well done! Glad to hear! And we can count on your donation as well, Nannie, to fortify our girls with the means to achieve our goal?"

Nannie assured Alva, "Of course."

The French doors were opened to the front of the house to allow a breeze to pass through the dining room. Thankfully, screens over the doors prevented mosquitoes from pestering the guests. After their meal, Nannie pressed the annunciator button at the head of the table and the maids appeared, as if by magic, to remove the lunch plates and serve afternoon tea and an array of delectable petit fours. It was at times like this that Hannah forgot that she was the daughter of a bayman and, instead, thought that she could perhaps one-day rise to this level of society. Perhaps Alva guessed what she was thinking because she patted Hannah's hand and said with a chuckle, "Dearie, I always say that your first marriage should be for money, your second marriage should be for love."

Seeing Hannah's expression at having her mind read, Jean laughed, "Don't look so startled, dear, Mrs. Belmont has been telling us the same thing for years!"

# CHAPTER ELEVEN

## 1912

A month later, on July 7th, Hannah and Ilsa were standing in front of the Methodist Church on Main Street when the contingent of Suffragists marched through. As it was a Thursday, both the shopkeepers and their patrons lined the streets. Some of the Suffragists marched on foot, while others followed in automobiles. Together, they navigated the hard-packed road made of dirt and oiled ground oyster shells. The Suffragists marched in white dresses with black stockings and black shoes. Mercifully, their wide-brimmed straw hats shaded their faces from the burning sun. They were accompanied by several men, including Edna Buckman Kearns' husband, Wilmer. Edna's mother, May Begley Buckman, walked alongside her daughter, while Edna's six-year-old daughter, Serena, rode in the back of an automobile with other young girls. Even the children held signs that read "Votes for Women" as they waved bright yellow flags. Some of the marching women held baskets from which they sold buttons, arm bands, and pennants to those who would support them. Others handed out literature explaining their demands for self-representation.

Hannah was swept up in the pageantry and excitement. She purchased a button from one of the women and proudly pinned it to her bodice. Another woman shoved a yellow flag into Hannah's hand. As much as Hannah admired these women, not all the bystanders were supporters of the movement, and there were men who shouted at them, "Go home you ungrateful women! Go home to the protection of your husbands and fathers!"

Ilsa grabbed Hannah's hand, "Let's follow them!"

They crossed Green Avenue and walked east on the south side of Main Street and passed the Jedlicka Brothers Plumbing and Heating store. Hannah peeked in the windows and glanced at the coal stoves that were displayed along with the multitude of plumbing fixtures. Then they passed the Pearl House at 116 Main Street, but in 1907, the hotel had closed and was, subsequently, moved closer to the street and renovated for business purposes. Beyond that, they passed the Hook & Ladder Fire House, yellow with green trim and red-framed windows, it boasted a tower that matched the Hook & Ladder Fire House, yellow with green trim and red-framed windows, it boasted a tower that matched the height of the Methodist Church's bell tower and had been designed by the revered architect, Isaac H. Green, Jr. At Candee Avenue they met Gladys and Jean. Together, they followed the parade down Candee to where the road met the bay at the South Bay House.

The hotel was one of the finest in Sayville. Every summer, the wealthy families would come to Sayville for the seaside breezes. While the families stayed all summer, the wealthy bankers and businessmen would take the railroad back to the city during the week and return for the weekends. The South Bay House was especially desirable because of its convenient location. The trolley ran down Candee Avenue from the railroad to the bay and this hotel was located right next to the dock where ferry boats crossed to Fire Island and

Patchogue. At three stories high, the South Bay House was also the tallest building in the area. It's handsome covered front porch extended the entire length of the building and the American Flag waved from the towering flagpole beside the hotel.

After the owners of the hotel, Charles and Delia Brown, treated the Suffragists to a meal, sixty-year-old Ida Gillette, beloved citizen of Sayville and the daughter of Captain Charles Zebulon Gillette, a distinguished sea captain who had led his ship into the Civil War Battle of New Orleans, introduced Edna Buckman Kearns to the crowd who had gathered around the porch. With her hair neatly curled on top of her head, Edna addressed the crowd.

"We as women have been silent too long. We have let our brethren move us aside for matters that they deemed more worthy. We will not let this happen again. We call on each and every one of you to join our cause. We know that the road will not always be easy. We will have to make decisions that our families and friends may not approve of, but we cannot change anything by hiding in the shadows. We must stand in the sunlight, we must stand on the city streets and the farm fields, we must stand on the mountains and by the bays, we must make our presence known. For far too long we have been shielded by our husbands and our fathers, it is time to take up the torch for ourselves and our daughters. We demand the right to be heard, the same right that every American male has by birth. We stand together, shoulder to shoulder, and we will not give up until the right to vote is granted to every woman in this country, be they the daughter of a railroad baron or the daughter of a bayman."

Hannah heard the crowd break out in a mixture of both cheers and jeers. She was reminded of the jeering crowd after she had won the iceboat race. She now raised her hand high and waved the yellow flag with Ilsa, Gladys, and Jean. And in a strong and clear voice, she shouted from the midst of the crowd, "Votes for Women! Votes for

Women!" The fears that her father had for her, forgotten in the moment.

Hannah was startled by Jean, yanking on her arm. Jean shouted above the crowd, "Hannah, come back with us to the house, we have some friends joining us there. We're going to take a dip in the pool to cool off. It's hotter than Satan's pepper patch out here!"

Hannah looked toward Ilsa, but Jean did not extend the invitation to the girl. Torn between her desire to go and her loyalty to Ilsa, Hannah hesitated. Ilsa, seeing that her friend wanted to go, said, "You know I couldn't go anyway. Father would never allow it. Go, and have a good time."

Hannah nodded and turned toward Jean, "All right. I've just got to stop home to get my swimsuit."

Jean responded, "No need. I have some that will fit you."

An hour later, dressed in Jean's fashionable swimsuit, Hannah admired herself in the mirror. The bloomers style one-piece woolen swimsuit, was far more revealing than any Hannah had ever worn. Jean called to her, "Catch!" and tossed Hannah a kerchief to wrap around her head.

Hannah had been in the Roosevelt pool often over the years. It was quite the talk of the town since it was the first in-ground pool on Long Island. The pool was 20 feet wide by 50 feet long and enclosed by screens and a roof with sky lights. At the beginning of the summer it was filled with the water from Brown's River and at the end, it was emptied into the marsh. Gas powered pumps were used occasionally to empty the pool. Then the grounds keeper would wash the moss, mold, and grime from its walls and fill the pool again. Having just been filled prior to Independence Day, the pool was still crystal clear. But Hannah knew that by September, despite the grounds keeper's fastidious attempts, it would become dank and cloudy.

The maids gave Hannah a sideways glance as they brought out an array of snacks and drinks in preparation for Jean's and Gladys' guests. Gladys sat on the swing that hung over the pool, "Come and join me, Hannah!" Feeling self-conscious, Hannah sat at the edge, her long legs dangling into the cool water. The Roosevelt's dog, Billy, sat beside her and accepted her generous petting. The presence of Billy, helped to calm Hannah's nerves. Gladys noticed the exchange between the maids and Hannah, so she slipped off of the swing and waded through the water to reach her.

"Hannah, don't let others define who you are. We live in America, anything is possible here. After all, it's the 20th century."

Hannah lowered her eyelashes and replied, "I'll try."

A flurry of voices announced the arrival of the guests and Gladys left the pool to greet them.

Hannah watched her reflection become distorted in the watery surface as she quietly moved her legs. Circles appeared in the water as the vibration generated ripples of tiny waves. She was surprised when she heard a deep voice address her.

"Hello, there!"

When Hannah looked up, the sun streamed through one of the skylights in the wooden roof directly into her face. She shaded her eyes to get a better look at the figure standing over her. The man looked familiar. It took a moment, but she remembered seeing him several years ago at one of Jean's parties. At that time though, she had been a gangly twelve-year-old. Both he and the young lady who he had been talking to, had been unaware of Hannah's presence until someone bumped into Hannah from behind, and the tray of drinks she had been carrying was thrust into the air and all over him and the young lady.

She had been mortified, but he had laughed it off, while the young lady had scurried out of the room in a huff. He had then turned to Hannah and said, "Don't worry, little one, she was boring me anyway."

But now, this same man, was smiling down at Hannah. He said, "I don't believe I have had the pleasure of your acquaintance, I'm Walter Grayson III." He smiled, then added, "But that is too ostentatious a name, so if you please, Walt will do. May I ask your name?"

Suddenly, her mouth felt very dry, "I'm Hannah, um, Hannah Trumball."

Walter asked, "Of the Southhold Trumballs?"

For a moment, Hannah thought about lying, but instead she said, "No, Sir, of the Sayville Trumballs."

"Oh, I don't believe I know them, how interesting."

Walt tossed a towel on a chair and lowered himself into the pool in front of Hannah. His physique was well defined and his grey eyes were watching her intently. He said, "You live in Sayville and I haven't met you before now?"

"Well, we have met, sort of. But I'm sure you don't remember."

His smile widened and her heart melted when he begged, "Please, remind me. I can't imagine that I would have forgotten such a pretty face." No one had ever spoken to her like this before. She could feel her heart beating wildly and wondered if he could see the movement of her heart through her swimsuit. Quickly, she placed her hands over her bodice to hide her heart's betrayal.

Walter was completely intrigued by her. He closed the space between them as he waited to hear her reply.

Hannah was unnerved by his closeness but she managed to say, "Well, unfortunately, the last time we met, I spilled a tray full of beverages all over you."

Walter looked confused for a moment and then, as the recollection of the event hit him, asked, "The little maid? That was you?"

"Yes, Sir."

"Well, it seems you have moved up in the world. No longer a maid, instead a guest of the Roosevelts." Hannah blushed again, searching for a response to a conversation that was way beyond her experience. Walt continued without waiting for her to reply, "So lucky for me."

At that moment, Jean appeared, rescuing her. "Walt, have you met my little friend, Hannah?"

"Yes, I have, and she just reminded me that we have actually met once before." Jean looked at him with amusement and then sat beside Hannah and sunk her own legs into the cool recesses of the pool. Then she said, "Hannah is more of a little sister to me. When I was younger, she was always in the house under the foot of her mother, our housekeeper, so naturally, she became my little playmate. We have a long history together and I love her dearly. So be forewarned, I will not have you playing with her affections, Walt."

He replied, "I would never dream of doing such a thing!"

But to Hannah, Jean warned, "He's a wolf that needs some taming. But I believe the right woman could make a perfect pet out of him."

Walt's expression turned to one of shock as he protested, "A wolf? Jean, darling, never have I been called such a thing. You know me better than that."

Jean stared intensely at Hannah and then tilted her head, motioning with it toward the house. Hannah quickly understood that Jean was silently instructing her to leave them. Dutifully, Hannah said, "It was very nice to meet you, Sir, but I think I should be leaving now." And with that, she drew her shapely legs out of the water and walked away from him.

Walt then jumped out of the pool and grabbing his towel, he quickly caught up to Hannah and followed her toward the garden behind the house. Walt bent down and picked a rose off of a bush and handed it to her, "Can we start over again, Hannah?"

Hannah looked at the rose and then turned away from him. "No, Sir, I am not a toy to be played with. I would thank you to leave me be."

But Walter did not give up, "Perhaps I could take you for a drive someday in my automobile? Would you like that?"

Hannah had never ridden in an automobile and she was sorely tempted to say yes. But it was clear that Jean had been warning her that this was not a man she could trust. Still, she wondered if just a ride in an automobile would be so terrible of a thing to accept.

"And where would you take me?"

"We could drive to Lake Ronkonkoma if you'd like."

She remembered Mr. Roosevelt promising to take her to see the lake once, long ago. The lake wasn't so far away; still she had never been to it. She felt a tingle down her spine as she threw caution to the wind and answered, "Well, yes, I think I would like that very much."

Surprised by his luck, Walt said, "Well then, would next Saturday work for you?"

Lifting her chin, she replied, "I believe I am free."

"Around noon then, where shall I pick you up?"

As Jean approached them, she hurriedly offered, "You can meet me here. But I must go now."

Walt nodded, "I will pick you up at noon, then. This Saturday."

As Hannah walked to the back porch, she felt her nerves unravel. What had she just agreed to? Jean caught up with her at the door, "What happened?" Hannah explained that Walter had invited her to take a ride to the lake with him on Saturday. Jean looked concerned, "Well then, I think I will join you both."

"Would you?" Hannah exclaimed, "I would feel so much better if you were with us."

"Of course! You are much too young to go unaccompanied." Hannah replied, "Thank you, Jean."

# CHAPTER TWELVE

## 1912

Hannah sat behind Jean in the back seat of Walt's 1912 Buick Model 29 with a self-satisfied smile on her face. Walt had not expected Jean to join them, but had quickly recovered his composure when faced with the two women, arm-in-arm, in front of Meadow Croft. Jean simply put out her hand for his assistance as she climbed up into the left-side passenger seat of the sleek brown automobile with its polished brass fixtures and wooden-spoked wheels. Walt was forced to make some quick adjustments to his plans for the afternoon.

The drive was a pleasant one, passing by farms and meadows along the way to the lake. Lake Street, which led from Sayville to Ronkonkoma, was lined with oak trees, and the sound of birds chirping could be heard above the automobile's pistons. The combination sounded like a symphony to Hannah. Occasionally, they passed another car going in the opposite direction, but the road was pretty much left to them. On their arrival at the lake, Hannah marveled at the size of it, "My, it's so much larger than I expected it to be!"

There were picnic tables beckoning from the welcome shade of trees, as well as a bathhouse for changing into their bathing suits, and a selection of rowboats tied to a dock nearby. Walt carried a wicker picnic basket with him as he chose a table for them. It was already a warm July day and the sun was not yet directly above them. Jean opened the basket and exclaimed, "Walt dear, what a nice assortment of goodies you have brought for us!"

There were fresh succulent strawberries, a variety of cheeses and soft bread rolls. A bottle of wine and two glasses accompanied the treats. As Jean pulled the glasses out of the basket, Walt shrugged, "I'm sorry, Jean, I hadn't realized that you would be joining us."

"Not to worry," she replied, and from her beach bag, she produced another glass. "I came prepared."

The afternoon was wonderful! Hannah and Jean enjoyed a boat ride on the lake while Walt rowed for them. The children bathing by the shore screamed and laughed with delight as their parents watched from the shaded picnic benches. Hannah mused, "It's so wonderful here! Safer than the bay, I would imagine. There's no chance of a changing tide or an aggressive undertow on a lake."

Walt stopped rowing then and allowed the boat to drift, "Perhaps," he responded, "But there is a curse on this lake."

Hannah's eyes widened, "A curse?"

Jean nodded, "It's true, dear. There is a saying that this lake takes the life of one young male each year."

Hannah felt a shiver run down her back, "Jiminy Christmas!"

Walt's baritone voice quietly told the story, "It was in the 1600s when this land was first being settled by Europeans. There was a Setauket Indian Princess named Tuskawanta who fell in love with a young Englishman named Hugh Birdsall. The two had first seen each other on the opposite shores of the lake, and they would send messages to each other on floating pieces of wood. But Tuskawanta's father forbade them from ever meeting. For seven years the young lovers sent messages, till one day, Tuskawanta became distraught. She could not live any longer without her love, but also knew she couldn't disobey her father. So she got into a row boat and rowed out to the center of the lake. Hugh Birdsall was watching her; he imagined she was finally rowing to him. But instead, she stopped halfway across and then stabbed herself in the heart and fell into the lake. Lake Ronkonkoma is said to be bottomless, so they were never able to recover her body."

Hannah took in a deep breath, the laughter of the children on the shore seemed far away from the quiet center of the lake where they now floated.

Walt continued, "Now, without any hope of ever meeting the lovely young princess, Hugh Birdsall returned to England and married. But it is said that 'The Lady of the Lake' claims the life of a young man every year to share her watery grave with her in place of her lover."

As the rowboat rocked unexpectedly, Hannah grabbed onto the side and said, "Please, let's return to the shore."

Later, at their picnic table, Walt asked, "Jean, would you mind if I took Hannah for a walk . . . alone."

Jean smiled and said, "As long as you remain in view, that would be fine."

Walt took Hannah's hand in his and her mind focused on the feel of his touch. She had never held hands with a suitor before. Her insecurities started to mount, he was so much older than she; more sophisticated and polished than any boy she had ever spoken to. She was at a complete loss as to what to say, so she walked in silence.

The picnic tables were filled with families and a chorus of voices reached her ears. She could hear them talking in many different languages. Thanks to her education, she could differentiate some of them. They spoke in Dutch, of course, as well as, French, Italian, German, and Russian.

Walt cleared his throat before speaking, "Are you having a nice time?"

Hannah nodded.

He smiled, "My family is very wealthy, Hannah. They expect a lot of me. But I like you and would like to spend more time with you."

Hannah mulled his words over in her mind, fearing she was unworthy of him. She replied, "My family is not wealthy, Walt. But I also like you and would like to spend more time with you."

Again he cleared his throat, as if the words were getting caught inside and he was having to force them out, "I know you are very young but if you'd like to live in Manhattan, perhaps, I could buy an apartment for you."

She narrowed her eyes, and then looked at him with some confusion, "I can't leave home, my family needs me. Besides, I am not sure of what you are suggesting."

"I could give you fine clothes and jewelry. A life you could easily become adjusted to, I'm sure. I would even be willing to pay your father if that makes you feel better."

Someone shouted to their children in Italian, "Venite qui bambini, mangia!"

Walt shook his head, "This country is turning into a cesspool with all these immigrants. It's getting to the point that there's no place for a decent fellow to spend a day anymore. Well, anyway, you think about it and let me know."

Hannah pulled her hand from his grasp. "I think we should go get Jean. It's time to return home."

He said, "I couldn't agree with you more." But Hannah knew now that they didn't agree at all. Still, she thought, it would be so nice to have all the pretty things that Jean and Gladys took for granted. She blushed, feeling ashamed of herself.

# CHAPTER THIRTEEN

### 1912

Hannah and Harry sped across the bay in their old sailboat as they headed for Fire Island. It was their sixteenth birthday, and they and their friends had decided to celebrate with a clambake on the barrier island that separated the Great South Bay from the Atlantic Ocean. Carl and Ilsa, and another friend of theirs, Edmund Schaefer, were meeting them there. There were fishing and clamming boats dotted across the bay as far as they could see. Above them, a flock of black birds changed direction in perfect rhythm with each other. Hannah wondered how the birds communicated their precise coordinates to each other. It was beautiful to watch them do their dance in the sky. A seagull squawked at them as they neared the barrier island, while other gulls stood in silent watch on wooden pilings jutting out of the surface of the clear water. After securing the sailboat to one of the pilings, the twins waded to the shore. They sat down in the sand and waited for their friends to arrive.

"Harry, can I tell you something?"

Harry looked at his sister and wondered at her serious tone, "What have you done now, Hannah?"

She picked up a handful of sand and threw it at him. "I haven't done anything, but I've met someone."

Harry's interest perked up, "Is he a summer visitor?"

"Yes, I suppose he is. His name is Walter Grayson III. His father is a banker who works on Delancey Street in Manhattan. They live near the Roosevelts on Madison Avenue, and he's very rich. He took me in his automobile to Lake Ronkonkoma."

Harry looked concerned, "Father would kill him if he knew."

She nodded, "I know, but Jean Roosevelt was with us."

"How old is he, Hannah?"

"He's twenty-three."

"And does he know how old you are?"

"Yes, of course, I told him." Then defensively she added, "There are plenty of girls my age that marry men older than he is."

Harry's voice rose, "Marry? You sure jumped to that quickly."

She thought about Walt's offer to buy her an apartment. She wondered if she had initially mistaken the meaning of his words. She fantasized that perhaps it really was a proposal. And as far as his insensitivity to others, perhaps she could change his thinking? Perhaps he just hadn't had enough exposure to people who were different? She had been wrestling with these thoughts since she had seen him. She worried that she was letting go of her chance to improve herself and her standing in the world.

"I'm not saying we *are* getting married, I'm just saying he's not too old for me."

Harry put his arm around his sister, "Be careful, Hannah. There is more than age between the two of you."

Hannah felt her anger rise. She had only seen him once since their trip to Lake Ronkonkoma. It seemed that every time he tried to get close to her, Jean inserted herself between them. She knew that Jean was trying to protect her, but she felt that she was old enough to take care of herself. Resentment started to mount and she wondered if Jean was just jealous.

She decided that the next time that she saw him, she would make sure they had a chance to really be alone.

Harry's friend, Edmund, arrived first, and then Carl and Ilsa anchored their sailboat offshore and waded through the shallow waters of the bay.

Hannah asked, "How did you get away, Ilsa?"

"Carl told father we would come over here to collect clams. We need to be back before nightfall, and hopefully, we will go home with a few bucketfuls."

The group picked some blueberries and munched on them as they followed the path to the ocean side of the island. At the beach, Hannah and Ilsa started to gather pretty shells to add to their collections. There were old stories of shells being collected from the island to be made into wampum long before any white man saw this strip of land. The waves roared across the sunken sandbars in front of Hannah. She knew that in the 1600s, Indians killed right whales from the beach and had taught the white settlers how to do the same. She tried to imagine them in dugout canoes hunting whales with their bone harpoons and lances. It was said that sometimes, they even drove the whales into shallow water, where the women and children were waiting to bludgeon the whales to death. The island had a rich history, one full of pirates, Indians, the illegal slave trade, and even ghosts. But more recently, it was becoming a refuge for those who wanted to be free of responsibility and to spend a few hours of leisure. And it was a place where these friends of different nationalities, British, Dutch, and German, could be free to enjoy time together without the restrictions and prejudices imposed by their parents.

The boys dug a rectangular pit far enough from the advancing tide and lined the bottom of it with grapefruit-size rocks that the girls had collected. Then making a teepee with pieces of wood, Edmund lit the fire with matches. They spent an hour or so feeding the fire with more wood and then let the fire burn for another couple of hours. Finally, they returned to the bay side of the island and began to stomp around the beach, waiting for the tell-tale breathing holes to appear, indicating that a clam was buried beneath that spot. With their shovels, the boys dug down to retrieve their prizes. The bigger the hole that appeared when they stomped, the bigger the clam that was buried there. The girls collected the clams in nets and carried them back to the ocean side. When the rocks had cooled, the boys covered them with damp seaweed and watched as the smoke rose through the leafy covering. They scattered their clams over the surface of the seaweed and covered them with a canvas tarp moistened with seawater. Lastly, they shoveled sand on top of the tarp and allowed the clams to bake for an hour.

As they enjoyed their clambake, Harry asked, "Hannah, how about you tell us one of your ghost stories?" Hannah was the storyteller of the group. She had even started to write some of them down in a little book that she intended to give to Harry this Christmas. As the others gathered around, Hannah related one of the Fire Island ghost stories that had been passed down for generations.

"Long ago, three farmers came to Fire Island in order to cut down the grass that grew on the beach. They used it as hay on their farms. It grew late and in spite of their fears of an Indian attack, they decided to stay on the island overnight and to continue gathering hay the next day. The next morning, one of the men awoke before the others. He took a quiet walk toward the ocean and on his way, saw a woman lying in a ditch. At first, he thought she was asleep, but on closer inspection, he realized that she was dead. She was dressed in a black velvet dress and had ornate jewelry on her fingers, wrists, and around her neck. He pulled off her ring and went back to tell the others about the body he had found. But when they went in search of it, they couldn't find it. It is believed that she was the paramour of a pirate who had lost his favor. She had been thrown overboard and she had managed to swim to the shore and crawl over the island to the place where she had died of exposure. They say that the Indians had been watching the farmer and that after he left, they stole the woman's body and swept away any evidence that they or the body had ever been there. Then at their leisure, they had taken the rest of the jewels from the woman's body. And now, many who stay on the island overnight have seen a woman dressed in black walking across the sand and beach grass, looking intently for her jewels and the thieves who stole them."

Ilsa cried, "Pirates!"

Hannah replied, "Yes, indeed. Captain Kidd hid some of his treasure on Fire Island over two hundred years ago. Some of that treasure has been found, but not all of it. In 1790, two pots of gold were dug up on the east end, but he may have buried treasure all along the island with the intention of coming back to dig it up again."

Ilsa asked, "Why don't people look for the pirate treasure?"

"Well, it is told that the pirates would bury a corpse on top of their treasure to scare off plunderers. I suppose superstition and the fact that no one knows where the treasure is buried has delayed its discovery."

Harry responded, "And if you found the pirate treasure, Ilsa, would you tell anyone?"

She blushed, "Probably, not."

Finally, Harry asked Ilsa, "So, has my sister told you about her newest beau?"

Hannah protested, "He's not my beau, Harry?"

Harry laughed, "Well, maybe not yet. But we all know what happens when you set your mind to something. You don't let it go until you have what you want."

Harry and Ilsa both laughed, but Carl did not join in the laughter, instead his face beneath his hat became paler than usual.

"What have you been keeping from me?" Asked Ilsa.

But it was Harry that explained, "She met a man who has an automobile and he took her to Lake Ronkonkoma for the day."

Ilsa was scandalized. She couldn't imagine doing such a thing. "By yourself?"

Annoyed with Harry, Hannah replied, "No, I wasn't by myself. Jean Roosevelt came with us."

"Is he a friend of the Roosevelts?"

"Well, yes, he is. I met him at Meadow Croft."

"Oh, well what does your father think?"

Harry responded, "He doesn't know."

Carl spoke up then, "It doesn't sound like a good idea to me."

Hannah felt like her friends were judging her and tears welled up in her eyes. Carl immediately regretted saying anything. He should have kept his mouth shut. He said, "I'm sorry, Hannah. I didn't mean to make you cry."

Ilsa hugged her friend, "Don't cry, Hannah. What do boys know? Perhaps yours will be a love story like the ones we read in newspapers. Stranger things have happened." Hannah appreciated her friend's words, but she also knew they weren't true. She was a bayman's daughter, she wasn't good enough for him. Ilsa added, "Besides, look at me, I'm going to be stuck with Will Amundsen. Our parents have already decided. They didn't care to ask me what I thought."

Will was a sullen boy who went to school with them. His father, Oliver, was also a bayman from West Sayville and both families were longstanding members of the True Holland Church on Atlantic Avenue, where traditional Dutch values and a moral life were held in the utmost regard. She worried that he would be a difficult match for Ilsa. But knowing that Ilsa had no choice in the matter, she tried to be positive. She said, "Give him time, Ilsa. You may grow to care for him if you give him a chance." Ilsa turned her head away from Hannah, but not before her own eyes had filled with tears.

They loaded bushels of clams into Carl and Ilsa's sail boat and the group departed from Fire Island as they made their way, separately, to their homes on the south shore of Long Island.

# CHAPTER FOURTEEN

1912

Hannah ran home from Meadow Croft as fast as she could with tears streaming down her cheeks. But she quickly wiped them away when she opened the door. She was stopped in her tracks at the sight of her father's pale face. Looking over his shoulder, she saw the front page of the Suffolk County News. The bottom had fallen out of the oyster market.

"What does it say, Pa?"

He spoke slowly and steadily, but there was an underlying fear that crept into the tone of his voice, "It seems word has spread across the country that oysters, especially those from the bay waters surrounding Long Island, have become contaminated. The ensuing panic has resulted in Blue Point Oysters being stricken from all menus." Then he read from the newspaper, *"Dr. George W. Stiles, Jr., Chief of the Bacteriological Laboratory of the Bureau of Chemistry of the U.S. Department of Agriculture announced that after intensive investigation, he has reported to Secretary Woodrow Wilson, that oysters "floated" in the polluted Jamaica Bay were contaminated with the bacillus typhosus and were responsible for the outbreak of typhoid in the weeks that followed a banquet last October, in Orange County, NY."*

Hannah could see the strain on her father's face and wished that there was something she could do to alleviate it. But instead, the news she had to tell him was only going to make it worse.

Hannah knelt beside her father and took his hand in hers, "Pa, Mrs. Roosevelt is dead. The typhoid took her."

Andrew swiped his free hand over his face in disbelief, "But they said only a week ago that she was getting better and that they expected her to make a full recovery."

"I know. But I just saw Dr. Ross at Meadow Croft, he said that the typhoid had turned to pneumonia and that she hadn't been able to fight it any longer. He said that both Mr. and Mrs. Roosevelt had been infected with typhoid and that it was most likely caused by the unfiltered water in their pool."

But now, she wondered silently if oysters had been the cause. Hannah knew that raw oysters had been a favorite of Nannie's. There was no way to know. She sat down heavily on a chair at the table.

Andrew instantly put aside his own worries upon hearing this news and seeing the distress that Hannah was in. He knew that for Hannah, losing Nannie, was like losing her mother again. "I'm sorry, Hannah." He put his hand over hers on the table. "How is the Commodore doing?"

"He has regained his health, but I'm afraid that losing his wife may be more than he can bear. Pa, would you come with me to the funeral?"

"Of course, dear."

Four days later, Meadow Croft was packed with those who had come to mourn the loss of one of the most famous women who summered in Sayville. All of the Roosevelt cousins were present at the funeral except for the former president. Colonel Theodore Roosevelt was currently traversing the country by railroad to solicit support for his bid for the presidency with the newly-formed Bull Moose (Progressive) party. His opponents were the Republican incumbent, President William Howard Taft, and the Democratic party candidate, Woodrow Wilson.

Hannah recognized Jean's and Gladys's cousin, Olga, sitting next to her husband, Joseph Breckinridge Bayne. Olga held her infant daughter, also named Olga, in her arms. She thought back to the time they had congregated in Jean's bedroom, anticipating the afternoon they would spend with their male cousins. It seemed a lifetime ago to Hannah.

It was 9:30 in the morning on Monday, September 30th, and Hannah still could not believe that Nannie was gone. She and her father stood just inside the entranceway to Nannie's parlor.

Walt stood against the wall, opposite Hannah. She hadn't seen him since she had told her brother and friends about him. When he noticed her, he lowered his gaze away from her. Her heart skipped a beat. She wasn't sure if she wanted him to approach her or not. After all, how would she explain him to her father? And yet, if he didn't approach her, what did that mean? Why had he left for New York so early this summer and not given himself a chance to get to know her better? Evidently, he had chosen not to see her again.

Reverend John H. Prescott started speaking and everyone fell silent. Commodore Roosevelt sat before his wife's coffin, his head bent, his shoulders slumped, a devastated man. The dog, Billy, sat beside him dutifully and quietly licked his master's hand. John Ellis' father, Robert, had passed away in June of 1906 in Sayville at Lotus Lake. With both parents gone, and now his wife, a feeling of loneliness overtook him. Seeming to understand without the need for words between them, his younger brother, Bert, patted his back. Their half-siblings, the Fortescues, sat stone-faced. If it weren't for their father, none of them would have come to own land in this place. They had followed his lead and created this compound for their family. For many years, the good times had outweighed the bad, but now there didn't seem to be much reason to feel joy any longer. The Commodore tried to put on a brave face for his daughters. During the days that Nannie's body lay in wake at Meadow Croft, Jean and Gladys, had tried to console him. But the depth of his grief was beyond their reach. When the service concluded, the Commodore followed the casket, accompanied by his daughter, Gladys, and her fiancé, Fairman Rogers Dick. He saw Hannah and Andrew standing just inside the front door, and as he passed them, Andrew's eyes met his. The Commodore nodded to Andrew and Andrew returned the nod. Comrades at last in their common loss, now both had lost their beloved wives.

Walt passed by her with Jean at his side, he did not even glance in Hannah's direction. Hannah's face turned red with shame. Nannie's casket was loaded onto a train and her immediate family and close friends boarded the passenger car to accompany her body to its final resting place. Hannah was not invited to join them.

Back at home, Hannah walked out to the chicken coop in the backyard with Sage at her heels. She let herself in, as the chickens ran and clucked. Ever calm and patient, Sage did her best to ignore the flutter of wings around her. Hannah spread a blanket on the floor and sat down as the chickens surrounded her. She lifted a baby chick into her hands and caressed its soft body against her cheek. Sage laid down and rested her muzzle on Hannah's thigh. Hannah's heart was broken, but the animals helped to alleviate the pain.

# CHAPTER FIFTEEN

## 1912

Although the Roosevelt family often stayed at Meadow Croft until early November, they decided to return to the city in mid-October. The Commodore sent word to Hannah through the caretaker that they would not be returning until late spring and asked that she resume her duties of checking on the house over the winter.

Hannah sat alone in her bedroom and lifted the heart shaped pink velvet box that had once belonged to her mother. At the center, was a white heart made of satin thread with the word, *Memories*, embroidered in gold, interspersed with threads of delicate green stems and white daisies. With her finger, she traced the faded pink velvet that surrounded the white heart at the center. The outer edges of the box were trimmed in lavender brocade. Opening it, she found her mother's pearl rosary beads, her mother's yellow gold wedding ring set with three small diamonds, a sterling silver and mother-of-pearl teething ring from when Hannah was a baby, a cameo made from some sort of shell that had once belonged to Hannah's great-grandmother, the five-dollar note Hannah had won in the ice-boat race, and the silver dollar coins that the caretaker had given her each week from mid-February through mid-April. She counted the money, fourteen dollars was a fortune to her. There was also one final item, a postcard from Washington D.C. from when her mother had accompanied Nannie on a trip. She lifted the postcard out of the box. It was frayed around the edges from the many times she had held it in her hands. On the front, was a picture of The White House and on the back, in her mother's handwriting, were the words,

*"Dearest Daughter,*

*There is so much to see in this city on the Potomac! Perhaps, one day, I may be able to show it to you. I hope you are keeping up with your studies while I am away. Your mother misses you very much.*

*Always in my heart,*

*Mother."*

The postcard was dated 1908.

The loss of Nannie was like losing another piece of her mother; the two women were forever entwined in Hannah's memory. She missed her mother so much and wondered if now her mother and Nannie were together in heaven. She could not help but feel abandoned by them both. Placing the items back in the box, she decided it was time to tell her father about her job at Meadow Croft, especially since it would be starting up again and would last for months.

Andrew was reading a book in the living room by the fire, "Pa, I wanted to talk to you about something."

Andrew patted the seat of the sofa he was sitting on and said, "Come sit next to your old man and tell me what's on your mind."

Hannah sat down and leaned the side of her head on his shoulder for a moment. She soaked in the comfort that he offered and took in a deep breath. He smelled like strong soap and sawdust. "Pa, remember when I won that scooter race in February?"

He took a deep breath and nodded, "I do."

"Well, I went to see the Commodore the next day to thank him. He and Mrs. Roosevelt asked me then to keep an eye on the house and to come over to check on it each day. For a few months in the spring, they paid me a dollar a week and now that Mr. Roosevelt has returned to the city, he has asked me to resume these duties." She held her own breath, worried about what his response would be.

Andrew looked at his daughter and nodded, "I know. The Commodore told me. I was waiting for you to tell me."

"I'm sorry, Pa. I should have told you right away. But since you didn't want to take the money I won for the race, I was afraid to tell you."

"It's all right. You save that money for yourself. I don't have much to give you, but I can take care of us for now. Someday, you might need that money, so you keep it."

"So it's all right for me to watch the house again this winter?"

"That's fine. As long as you get your school work done. Your schooling was important to your mother. I want you to finish. We will see what happens after that."

Hannah kissed her father's cheek. "Thank you, Pa."

Never one to show much emotion, Andrew's only response was a nod and a pat on Hannah's leg.

A week later, on Friday, the caretaker met her at Meadow Croft with her pay. He was a simple Dutchman who was used to hard labor. He explained, "I've given me' notice to the Commodore. I be movin' my family to Michigan before the snow comes. Mr. Roosevelt said to tell you, Hannah, that you can see the Clerk at The Oysterman's Bank each Friday from now on to receive your pay. He asked that you continue on as you have been doin', and in the spring, he will hire a new caretaker to take my place. If'n you see anythin' that needs a-fixin, in the meantime, you let the clerk know and he'll hire a handyman."

"Thank you. But what will you do in Michigan?"

"My brother has a farm there, and it's expanding. He be needin' my help. So we'll be off in a few days. Good luck, here, Hannah. And again, if you be needin' anythin', you just let the clerk know. You hear?"

"Yes, and good luck to you and your brother. Godspeed and be safe on your journey."

"Thank'ya. I be goin' now."

As the days continued to get shorter and colder, Hannah spent more and more time at Meadow Croft. She enjoyed having the big house to herself and took great care of the family's cherished belongings. On the Tuesday before Halloween, Hannah sat in the empty house. A draft whipped by her and brought goosebumps to her arms. Outside, she could hear the wind howl and the trees protesting as they swayed. Dusk was falling and a storm was coming. She knew she should head back home, but she couldn't quite bring herself to leave Meadow Croft just yet. As the floors creaked, Hannah hoped that Nannie's ghost still walked the halls of this house that she had loved so much.

Sage nipped at Hannah's toes and cocked her head, waiting a moment for Hannah to understand her meaning. Then she ran toward the kitchen door and scratched her paw on the wood. "Down, Sage!" She demanded. "You'll scratch the door and then what will the Commodore think when he returns in the spring? You will get me fired." She stood up from the wooden table and crossed the room intending to lift the dog into her arms. But Sage ran in circles and came back to the door, scratching once again. "Do you want to go out? Well then, why didn't you say so?" Hannah laughed.

Sage ran out into the yard as soon as the door was opened. Hannah could hear the bells ringing from Saint Ann's announcing the hour as six o'clock. She walked away from the door and took one last walk through the house. After assuring herself that all was in order, she wrapped her cape securely around herself and locked the kitchen door behind her. She called out to Sage, but the dog did not return.

The wind was howling more than ever and the moon was rising. Clouds shrouded the sky with an ominous glow as the last of the sunset sunk into the horizon. Hannah called out again, "Sage? Where are you? We need to go now." She heard Sage bark somewhere among the woods that bordered the marsh and river. "What is it girl?" her words carried on the wind. Hannah walked past the empty in-ground pool and entered one of the winding wooded paths in search of Sage. She pulled her cloak tighter against her body, it was late October and the nights were becoming increasingly colder. She looked up at the moon, it was larger than usual, a blood red moon. Becoming ever more concerned for her pet, she called out again and again, but Sage's bark seemed farther and farther away. Hannah started to pick up her pace and followed the path to the edge where the woods met the marsh grass, just before the river. She tripped on a fallen branch and cried out as her ankle was wrenched to a difficult angle. Collapsing onto the ground, she grasped her ankle in an attempt to alleviate the pain. She held onto to it and cried out desperately for Sage. Then she heard a sharp piercing yelp. She tried to stand but the pain that shot up through her leg made it difficult. She cried, "Sage!"

With only the dark red moon to guide her, she searched for the branch she had tripped over. Then using it to leverage the weight of her body, she hobbled through the woods toward the crying dog. When she found Sage, she dropped to the ground beside her. A raccoon trap had closed around Sage's front left paw. The dog whimpered as Hannah cried out "Sage!", all the while, trying to pull open the jaws of the trap in an attempt to release Sage from her agony. All of a sudden a boy came out of the woods. He looked even more surprised to see her than she was to see him.

# CHAPTER SIXTEEN

## 2012

Although she had always known that this day would come, Grace wished with all her heart that it didn't have to. At forty-nine years old, she was not ready to let go of her youngest son. Tears ran down her face as she filled Philip's old backpack with the items she thought he might need. He was eighteen years old. She wondered where the years had gone. How had they passed so quickly?

As she had done a thousand times before, she tried to find a way around it, but any other path still led to the loss of ones she loved. Had her husband realized what today was when he left for work that morning? If he had, he hadn't let on. She looked through the backpack one last time wondering if she had forgotten anything.

She said out loud, "Photos, of course!" Frantic that she had almost forgotten them, she retrieved her photo albums and looked through the many pictures. She pulled back the clear plastic sheets as she turned the pages and took out a select few. One by one, she placed them in an envelope. There was the one of Philip, just days old, cradled against Tom's chest on their bed, both father and son deep in sleep. Another of Philip at three years old, a conductor's hat on his head and a little blue train held lovingly in his chubby hand. A third was taken on Christmas morning when he was ten. Flanked by his brothers, they sat cross-legged on the floor in front of their Christmas tree surrounded by presents and wrapping paper. She looked long at a picture of their family, taken while on vacation in Yellowstone, when he was fifteen. A family of five, her husband, herself, and their three sons. Her heart ached.

She folded the letter she had written so that he would have it to comfort him when he was feeling lonely. How many times had she rewritten the words, trying to get it right? She had lost count long ago.

She heard Jim Cantore's voice coming from the television in the living room, "This storm is going to be a big one. It's slow-moving, with dangerous winds, and tonight's autumn blood moon will create higher tides than usual. Extensive flooding is expected."

Grace sealed the envelope that held the photos and her letter, tucked it in Philip's old backpack and closed the zipper before placing the backpack in the closet near the front door. There was nothing more to do except count down the last hours that she would have with her son.

# CHAPTER SEVENTEEN

## 2012

There was a girl sitting across from Philip in the Student Union Building of Suffolk Community College. Every time Philip would look up, he'd catch her looking at him, but then she would quickly shift her gaze away. His notebook was opened before him and he tried to concentrate on the words he was trying to study. It was late October and he was in the midst of midterms. But he kept getting distracted by the girl sitting at the next table. Finally, he collected enough courage to pick up his notebook and walk over to her, "Mind if I sit here?"

She responded, "Um, no. Sure."

He pointed to his notebook, "Midterms."

She smiled, "Yeah, me too." She lifted up her own notebook that was opened on the table.

He reached out his hand, "My name's Phil, what's yours?"

"Michele." She took his hand and shook it. Her hand felt so small in his.

He asked, "Where are you from?"

"Commack. And you?"

"Sayville."

Michele asked, "What's your major?"

Philip shrugged, "I'm not sure yet. I'm just taking the general ed courses right now. I'm not sure if I'm even staying here at Suffolk next year."

Michele nodded, "I'm doing the same. Hoping to get into a nursing program. Maybe at Stony Brook, but I'm not sure yet, either."

"Well, that's good."

"Yeah," she agreed with a shy smile.

There was an uncomfortable silence that followed. Finally, Michele said, "I've got to get to class. It was nice to meet you Phil. Maybe I'll see you around?"

Always feeling awkward around girls, he responded, "Yeah, that would be nice."

She walked away from him and he looked back down at his notebook. He thought he should have asked her out. But it was too late now.

Three hours later, he was waiting in the parking lot for Tommy. He noticed that the wind was picking up and the sky was looking threatening. He hoped that his brother would get there soon.

As he waited, a girl in a car honked at him and pulled up next to him. It was Michele. "Hey, you need a ride?"

He responded haltingly, "Oh, thanks, but my brother's on his way. Uh, besides, Sayville's the opposite direction for you."

"Well, it wouldn't be a bother."

Philip considered calling Tommy on his cell phone and telling him that he got a ride, but he hesitated for a moment too long. Michele nodded, "Okay, well, I'll see you soon. Try to stay dry. The hurricane is on its way."

"Yeah, I know. Thanks."

Just then Tommy pulled up in the car that the two brothers shared, and Philip watched Michele as she drove away. Tommy smiled at Philip, "Got your game on, huh?"

"Not really. I think I already messed that one up. Twice!"

As they drove home, they listened to the radio. The announcer was warning that the local utilities were expecting wide-spread outages from wind damage. So Tommy said, "We'd better stop to fill up the gas tank. If the electricity goes out, we won't be able to get any gas."

They passed several gas stations, all with long lines. Finally, they decided to wait in line at a Hess gas station. People were not only filling up their gas tanks, they were filling up gas cans as well. They heard one guy mention that he wanted to be prepared in case he needed gas for his generator. Philip said, "Maybe Dad should have gotten a generator?" Tommy said, "It's probably too late for that, I doubt there are any left in the store."

After filling up the gas tank, Tommy dropped Philip off at home, "I'm going to hang out over at Val's house, so tell Mom and Dad I'll be back tomorrow." Val was Tommy's girlfriend and since she lived alone with her mother, Tommy probably figured it would be best if he was with them in case they needed him.

At home, the newscaster on the television in the living room was announcing that the hurricane had just been reduced to a tropical storm. Philip found Jenny and her father, Ben, in the kitchen with his dad. Jenny told Philip, "Our house is in the mandatory evacuation zone, so you're stuck with us tonight." Ben was a Pediatrician and he and his daughter, Jenny, lived in the large house by Foster Avenue Park, just feet from the bay.

Philip perked up, "Great! We can hang out together." He put his backpack down on the couch and said, "Let me just change my clothes, I'll be right down."

Philip went to his room and pulled on gray sweatpants and a blue hooded sweatshirt. He was glad that Jenny would be staying with them for the night. It reminded him of when they were kids and used to have sleepovers. Having her around helped to fill the house with activity. As he passed his parents' bedroom, he heard his mother call out to him, "Philip?"

"Yeah, mom?"

"Hi honey, could you come here for a moment?"

His mother didn't look right, her eyes were red and swollen. Right away he asked, "What's wrong?"

"Oh, nothing. I'm just feeling sentimental is all. Here, come give your mother a big hug."

Philip smiled, he put his arms around her, squeezed, and kissed the top of her head. Grace held on to him just a moment longer and said, "You're a good boy. Always remember, I love you, to the moon and back."

The words were the same ones she had said to him each night when he was little while tucking him into bed. He repeated them, "To the moon and back," and he gave her another hug.

"You coming down to for dinner?" he asked.

"Yes, I'll be there in a minute. Jenny and Ben are making some home-made pizzas."

Concerned for the sadness he saw in his mother, he said, "Come downstairs, mom. Everything's going to be okay."

Grace nodded, "Yes, I know it will be."

Philip raced down the stairs and into the kitchen, "Can I help?" he asked.

"Sure, take a stone." There was a selection of stone baking pans that his mother had collected over the years. She always had insisted that cooking on them prevented burning and made everything cook more evenly.

Philip stood in front of one of the stones as Jenny directed him. "First spray the stone so the crust doesn't stick. Then roll out the dough with this rolling-pin. We need to put it in the oven for a while so that it cooks a bit before we put the sauce and cheese on it."

Once the dough browned a little, they took the pans out of the oven and spread sauce, mozzarella cheese, and slices of meatballs and sausages on top. They drizzled some olive oil and grated pecorino romano cheese over the pizza, and then placed the stones back in the oven and let them cook longer.

Grace finally joined them, and when the pizzas were ready, they sat down to eat together. They could hear thunder erupt in the distance. Philip tasted the sweet sauce on the salty cheese and closed his eyes, "M-m-m-m, mom's sauce."

Jenny replied, "Actually, I made it, Aunt Grace showed me how. Right Aunt Grace?"

"And you did a great job. Tastes just like my mother-in-law's."

After dinner, they all sat around the television set, glued to the minute-by-minute reports of the storm on the Weather Channel. Suddenly, Philip heard the words, "Although the clouds may soon block it, if you take a look now, on this 29th day of October 2012, you may still get a chance to see this year's harvest blood moon. But as Super Storm Sandy is quickly bearing down on the metropolitan area, the opportunity to see this rare sight is dwindling quickly."

Philip felt the blood leave his face. He suddenly remembered the words that the old man, Louis, had said at the park months ago. He had mentioned the harvest blood moon and a sand storm. It dawned on him that Super Storm Sandy was the sand storm. Without a second to lose, Philip jumped up and grabbed his jacket. Since Tommy had taken the car to his girlfriend's house, Philip was without a car. So he picked up his skateboard and said, "Mom, Dad, I have to go out for a minute. I'll be right back. Promise!"

Tom and Grace didn't argue; they didn't tell their son to stay home. Jenny looked at them both like they were crazy and then spoke up, "Buddy, you can't go out now. Look at that sky, the storm is going to be here any minute!"

Philip ignored her, he didn't have a minute to lose. He took a flashlight that was on the kitchen table and went to put it into his backpack, but his backpack wasn't on the couch. "Mom, where's my backpack?"

Grace said, "I noticed there was a rip in it. I took it upstairs to sew it. Use your old one. It's in the closet."

Philip opened the closet, shoved the flashlight into his old backpack and with his skateboard under his arm, he headed for the front door. Tom grabbed him before he could leave and placed him in a giant bear hug. "Be careful, son. And remember that I love you."

Grace looked at her son and said, "Wherever you go, you take my heart with you." There was nothing unusual about that, those were the words his mother said to him every time he left the house.

"Sure, love you guys too. Like I said, I'll be right back. So don't worry."

As Philip left the house, he could hear the bells from St. Ann's announce that it was 6 o'clock. Philip skated as the wind roared in his ears. There were only a few blocks between his house and Meadow Croft. His house bordered Brown's River just south of the old Roosevelt estate, but he had to skate around the blocks since there was no road along the river. When he came to the end of his block, he turned north on Foster Avenue and then back east on Middle Road. He passed St. Ann's Church on his left and the old St. Ann's Orphanage on his right. He stopped at the sign that read "Meadow Croft, John E. Roosevelt Estate" and a second sign that read "Loughlin Vineyards." The Loughlin family had been the caretakers of Meadow Croft from the 1920s until the property had been bought by Suffolk County in 1974. The Loughlin family now ran a vineyard on the property behind the old mansion.

He dropped his skateboard at the entrance and walked cautiously down the driveway to the old Roosevelt house. Over the sound of the roaring wind he could hear a dog yelping. He looked up at the sky and saw the moon just before the clouds fully engulfed it. It was the largest he had ever seen the moon and instead of being white, it was a deep red. He listened intently to determine which direction the sound was coming from. It was hard to tell with the wind picking up and the rain starting to pour from the sky. Super Storm Sandy was here and he knew he should really be getting back home, but the dog sounded like it was in trouble. The dirt driveway was much as he expected it would have been in the days that the Roosevelts lived here at Meadow Croft. It was really just a narrow dirt path bordered by the phragmites on both sides. Just to the east, the tall marsh grass fell away as Brown's River reached high tide and crested its marshy banks.

Coming up to the house, the barking became louder. It was coming from the woods. There were paths through the trees that had been reclaimed when a Boy Scout had cleared them for his Eagle Scout project in the 1980s. Barney Loughlin had helped the boy find the routes that he had used when he was just a child. Philip passed the Roosevelts' old built-in pool. While on a tour of the main house, he had learned that it was the first built-in pool on Long Island. He remembered seeing a photo of what it had once looked like in its heyday. In the photo, the pool was shaded under a wooden structure and a woman sat in a swing hanging from its rafters. But now the wooden structure was long gone. The pool sat empty with cracks running throughout its bottom and walls. He had taken this path many times. Eventually, it wound its way between the Roosevelt property and the river and on to the Loughlin Vineyards. Just beyond the vineyard were the railroad tracks, and then, Union Cemetery.

Even though he knew the paths well, following them became much more difficult as the light of the moon disappeared and the heavens opened up with torrential rain. The rain was so heavy and the winds were becoming so strong, that the rain started to fall sideways. He was about to turn around and head back to his skateboard when he heard the dog yelp in pain again, followed a second later by the voice of a girl calling out in terror, "Sage!"

The sound was coming from further up the path. Philip ran toward it, his sneakers slipping on the wet ground covered in leaves. Off the path, he saw a girl desperately trying to pry something apart as the dog continued to squeal. Assessing the situation quickly, Philip bent down and using all his strength, he was able to part the mouth of a long spring raccoon trap and release the dog. The girl picked up the puppy and cradled it against her body. Blood was dripping down and staining the dog's white fur. Hail started to pound the ground around them and the roar of what sounded like a train grew louder. The storm increased in force and the girl cried above the winds, "Please, help me back to the house. I've twisted my ankle."

Philip wrapped his arm around her and helped her back to the house. She unlocked the kitchen door and just as they entered the house they saw a tree in the yard being ripped off of its trunk and sailing through the air. Philip closed the heavy wooden door behind them. The girl turned a knob on a gas lantern and light filled the room. This was the first time Philip had a chance to get a look at her. She was wearing a turn-of-the-century costume. She pointed over Philip's shoulder, "There are bandages in that cupboard." Philip grabbed the bandages and watched as she expertly cleaned and wrapped the dog's paw. Outside the winds howled, the skies darkened, and Philip felt the cold inside the house seep into his bones.

# CHAPTER EIGHTEEN

## 1912

Hail pounded against the windows as Hannah, hobbling on her sore ankle, lit another gas lantern in the servants' dining room. A warm reassuring glow was reflected against the dark wooden beadboard that lined the walls of the small room. Warily, she watched through the open doorway as the boy put the bloody rags into the kitchen sink. Sage rested on a blanket next to the table and licked at the bandages covering her wound. Now that the panic of the moment was over, Hannah felt the first trickle of fear. She took a seat beside Sage and wondered, "Who is this boy? Where had he come from?" She was alone with him in the house while a violent storm raged outside. She knew that no one would come looking for her until tomorrow. The storm had surprised them all by how quickly and fiercely it had come, her father would have assumed she was staying at Meadow Croft for the night.

The boy now took a seat across the table from her, "Hi, I'm Philip." With the table between them, he smiled. Hannah relaxed a little. Philip continued, "I heard on the news that they had down-graded the hurricane to a tropical storm, so it shouldn't be as bad as they first thought."

Hannah was confused by his words. Even the way he spoke, the cadence of it was different from anything she had ever heard before.

She spoke softly, "My name is Hannah. Where are you from, Philip?"

Philip felt disconcerted, something wasn't right. The tiny hairs on the back of his neck stood up on end. "Did you say your name was Hannah?"

"Yes"

Louis had mentioned her by name, the moon was a blood moon, the storm was called Sandy. Philip continued in spite of the uneasy feeling that came over him, "Um, wow. I'm, um, from Sayville. I live right around the corner. I told my parents I'd be right back, but the storm hit quicker than I thought it would and now I think it's best if I stay here until it's over." He hesitated, "Do you mind?"

Hannah knew she didn't have a choice in the matter. She couldn't very well turn him out into the storm. "No, of course not. And thank you for rescuing both Sage and me. I couldn't get the teeth of that trap to open. I'm afraid to even think of what would have happened to her if you hadn't found us when you did."

Trying to keep his tone within a normal range, Philip asked, "Hannah, do you work here at Meadow Croft?"

"Yes."

Well, considering the costume she was wearing, that made some sense to him. "Maybe I should call home. Is there a phone here?"

Hannah pointed to the wooden phone on the kitchen wall. Philip walked over to it and started to laugh, "Very funny!" The wall phone was an antique, the kind that even predated rotary phones. There was a mouthpiece built into it that kind of looked like the nose on a face. There were two bells above it that looked like eyes and a shelf below that could have been a mouth. Then there was something attached to a wire hanging onto the side of the phone, he guessed it was a listening device. He said sarcastically, "I mean a phone that works."

Hannah responded, "That is the only telephone. It was installed just a few years ago."

Philip shrugged thinking she was making fun of him, "Well, the lines are probably down anyway." He rationalized that a real phone probably wasn't needed because with cell phones, it wasn't necessary to have a stationary phone. He rubbed his arms, "It's getting cold in here. Can I turn the heat up?"

Hannah pointed to the fireplace in the front hall. She thought he was becoming odder by the minute.

Pointing to the gas lantern on the table he said, "Oh right, I guess the electricity is out. My cousin, Jenny, used to play on the old Roosevelt piano whenever the Historical Society had their Christmas Open House here. My mom loves coming to it, she won some pretty cool Christmas decorations like wreaths and even a fake Christmas tree once. It was decorated with little birds. Barney Loughlin, the old caretaker, donated it. My mom was really proud of that one. But it had this string of lights built into it and when the lights stopped working, she tried to replace them with another string of lights. They didn't look as good, but she still put that tree out every year. Until it just got too messed up and she had to throw it out."

Hannah questioned, "Barney Loughlin? I don't know that name."

Philip replied with a nervous laugh, "Barney? You have to know Barney. Everyone knows Barney! He was the caretaker here, and before him, his father was caretaker. In fact, he runs the little vineyard behind this house."

But Hannah just looked at him like he was crazy. He decided to busy himself by starting a fire in the hearth.

Philip saw that there was a nice pile of wood set aside and some matches beside the fireplace. He piled the kindling and then larger pieces of wood. When the fire was finally going, he watched as Hannah limped into the hall, carrying the dog in her arms. Her face was lit by the flames and her beauty made him catch his breath for a moment. He was glad that she didn't seem to notice. Unlike most of the girls he knew, she didn't wear any makeup. She had a natural beauty and her hair flowed wildly around her face.

Hannah sat down on one of the cushioned benches that lined each side of the hearth. She had also been trying to make sense of their conversation. She asked, "What is a Christmas Open House? The family is never here for Christmas; they always spend it in the city."

Philip felt the sweat bead up on his back. Slowly, he turned to face her. "What family?"

"The Roosevelts, of course."

In the silence that followed, all Philip could hear was the crackling of the burning logs and the pounding of his heartbeat. "Hannah, I know this is going to sound crazy, but what year is it?"

Hannah looked at him suspiciously, "It's 1912."

Although he already knew, instinctually, that what she said was true, his rational brain refused to accept it.

Philip went to the kitchen and grabbed his backpack and brought it to the fire. He sat down on the bench across from Hannah and unzipped it. When he looked inside, he was astonished by what he saw. He pulled out the flashlight he had taken from his house and turned it on. A beam of light shot out from it and Hannah screamed, "What is that?" Without bothering to answer her, he directed the light into the bag. One by one, he took out the items. There were

THE BAYMAN'S DAUGHTER 121

several gallon sized plastic bags filled with a variety of medicines and personal hygiene products. Next he pulled out his dad's coin books filled with old silver dollars along with rolls of paper bills, and batteries for the flashlight. Astonishingly, he found a copy of the family tree that his mother worked so long on. There was also a journal book, a bag of ball-point pens, a newspaper from October 28, 2012, and a scanned photocopy of the front page of another newspaper. He read the date, *November 6, 1912.*

Philip handed the photocopy to Hannah who read it out loud,

*"Woodrow Wilson was elected President, yesterday, and Thomas R. Marshall, Vice President, by an Electoral majority which challenged comparison with the year in which Horace Greeley was defeated by Grant. Until now, that year has always been the standard of comparison for disastrous defeats. But the downfall of the Republican Party this year, runs it a close second. The Republican Party is wiped off the map."* Hannah looked up at Philip for a moment and then continued to read, *"Nearly everywhere Taft ran third, with Roosevelt capturing a large majority of the old Republican vote, and in many states, Taft's vote was almost negligible."*

Once again, Hannah looked up from the newspaper and eyed him with suspicion, "How can this be true? What kind of paper is this? This isn't the type of paper that newspapers are printed on."

Philip tried to explain, "It's a copy. But here, take a look at this." He handed her the front page of the newspaper from 2012, and she read,

*"Sunday, October 28, 2012,"* she stopped for a moment to regain her composure after reading the date, *"Broadway Shuts Down as Hurricane Sandy Approaches. Theaters have closed for the Sunday evening and Monday performances as New York prepares for the mammoth storm heading our way."*

The newspaper dropped from her hands as she took another look at the boy who sat across from her. "What does this mean, Philip?"

He didn't want to frighten her, but he couldn't think of any other explanation, "Hannah, I know this sounds crazy, but I left my house a couple of hours ago, just before the storm hit. It was October 29, 2012, and when I came here I heard Sage cry out and you calling for her. I-I don't know how, or why, but somehow, I think I've been transported back in time one hundred years."

Hannah stood on her sore ankle and backed away from Philip.

"Hannah, please, you have to believe me. I didn't know this was going to happen, but it has. And I-I don't know if I can go back." Philip's voice cracked toward the end of that sentence as what he was saying sunk into his own brain. But he could see that his anxiety was causing Hannah to become even more fearful of him, and he needed her. He needed her to believe him. He needed her to help him.

Hannah saw the fear and terror on his face and she stopped backing away. None of this made any sense. But it was clear that he was not a threat to her, he was even more frightened than she was. Slowly, she returned to her seat by the fire and asked, "Is there anything else in your bag?"

Seeing that the main compartment was empty, Philip opened the zipper to the front pocket and took out an envelope. It was addressed, "To Philip, Love Mom."

Philip explained with disbelief, "It's a letter from my mom." Philip was visibly shaking as he opened the envelope, first taking out the photos, and then, by the light of the fire, he read out loud the words his mother had written to him.

*"My son,*

*Please don't be frightened. Your father and I know where, or perhaps I should say, when, you are. When you came home after taking a photo at the park of an old man and the sunset, we knew this day was close at hand. Louis is an old friend of yours, you met him many years ago when he was just a boy. As difficult as it has been for me, I have come to accept that you were meant to live your life in the past. Ben became a doctor so that he would be able to send broad-spectrum antibiotics and antiviral medications back in time with you. History cannot be changed because it has already happened. You must understand that your history has already been written. All of those hours I spent researching through old census records, I was looking for you. When I found you, I knew that the story that had been handed down through generations of your father's family was true. I hesitate to tell you too much, because your life must unfold the way it was meant to without interference.*

*Today, I must let you go so that you can have the life that you were born to live. I will miss you so! I do not know how I will get through this; but somehow, I have to find the courage. I must let you go, my son. And although tears come to my eyes at the thought of you leaving, I am comforted by the knowledge that you will find the people you need in your life and that they will help to keep you safe. Someday, you will have a daughter of your own and she will have a son. That grandson of yours is Ben. Jenny is your great-granddaughter. If I try to stop you from leaving, they will never be born.*

*Your father and I have placed items in your backpack that we think will help you in the past. While we may not be together, you will always be my son. Please never forget that I love you and that wherever you go, you take my heart with you.*

*To the moon and back.*

*All of my love, forever,*

*Mom"*

Philip drew in a deep breath and said one painful word, "Jenny." If he were able to get back home, Jenny wouldn't be there.

Hannah stood up and crossed the space between them. Sitting beside him, she placed her hand on the crook of his arm. "Tell me about your parents." But when he couldn't answer, she let the moments of silence pass between them. Philip was still grappling with all that had transpired in the last few moments. His first emotion was disbelief, that had quickly changed over to fear and now anger was starting to bubble up inside of him. His parents had known all along and they hadn't told him. They hadn't given him the choice. It was his life after all, damn it! Frustration at a situation he had no control over washed over him. And with that frustration, a feeling of profound loneliness also crept in.

Tears were welling in his eyes with the realization that all that he had ever known in his life was now gone. He fingered the items he had taken out of the backpack, they were his only connection to the life he knew.

Philip's large hazel eyes were framed by dark lashes that were now wet and heavy. As Hannah had once wiped away the Commodore's tears, she now reached up and wiped tears away as they landed on Philip's cheeks. "Philip, please, tell me all about yourself. Tell me about your family and your life."

Philip was so grateful that she was here with him and that they had this time alone to sort it all out. As the storm continued to rage outside, he showed the photos to Hannah and told her about his family.

"My parents are Tom and Grace Ferrara and we live just south of here along Brown's River. I have two brothers, Tommy and Jack. Tommy just graduated college and Jack is a sophomore, I'm a freshman; well, I guess I should say I *was* a freshman. A few months ago, I met this old guy down by the bay by Foster Avenue Park and he told me I had to come here."

"There's a park by the bay? What kind of park?"

"Just a little beach and a playground for the kids, some tennis courts. That sort of thing. Why?"

Hannah explained, "That's where The Willow Grove Pavilion is now. The summer visitors love it there. They can spend the day swimming, having clam bakes and dances, and renting row boats. You can get a ferry from there to go to Patchogue or Ocean Beach. And then there's the Shoreham Café at the end of Candee Avenue near the Sayville Golf Course." She laughed, "Sometimes they call the Shoreham the tenth hole because all the golfers end up going there after they finish their game." As Hannah spoke, Philip regained his composure. Her questions pulled him out of the depths of his sorrow.

Philip wiped his eyes with the back of his hands and nodded, "There used to be a place called The Shoreham at the end of Foster Avenue, but it's been gone since before I was born. I guess it moved from the end of Candee Avenue to the end of Foster Avenue at some point. Anyway, I met this old guy there, his name was Louis, and he told me that I was supposed to come here to Meadow Croft on the harvest blood moon during the sand storm because you needed me. I guess he meant Hurricane Sandy. We were all watching the TV when I heard the weather man say it was the harvest blood moon. That's when I knew I had to get over here fast."

Hannah asked, "What were you watching? I don't understand. What is a TV?"

"Oh, right, you don't know about TV yet. It's a box you can have in your house and it has a screen on it. You can see people on the screen and hear them even though they are far away," Philip explained.

Hannah looked puzzled, "Sort of like a telephone?"

Philip nodded, "Yeah, right, like a telephone. Only you can see the person who is on the other side while they're talking to you."

Hannah exclaimed, "Can you talk back to them, too?"

"Well, no. It only works one way."

"Oh, my goodness!" Hannah was fascinated, but wanted to get back to Philip's story, "So, who was this old man who told you to come here?"

"My parents told me that he's lived here in Sayville all his life. He had to be about 100 years old. Come to think of it, he's probably only an infant right now if it really is 1912."

Hannah said emphatically, "It is 1912."

Philip shook his head, still not fully comprehending the truth but searching for some normalcy, asked, "Now it's your turn, Hannah, tell me about your family."

"Well, I have one brother, Harry, he's my twin. Our mother worked for the Commodore, that's John Ellis Roosevelt who owns this house. Momma was a lady's maid for his wife, Nannie, and then later, she became the housekeeper. But my mother passed away a couple of years ago and, sadly, Nannie Roosevelt recently passed away from Typhoid."

Philip's eyes widened, "Typhoid!"

Hannah didn't understand his surprise. Typhoid was notorious for being a deadly fever. "Why are you so surprised?"

"Because, Hannah, in 2012, people don't get Typhoid in the United States. There's a vaccine for it."

Hannah smiled, "Oh, that's wonderful! It's such a dreadful disease. So many are lost to it and it is still not fully understood how one contracts it. Some even say it's contracted by eating tainted oysters."

"Well," Philip assured her, "That will all change one day."

Hannah wondered out loud, "I bet there are many things that are different about life in your time."

Philip nodded, "There are, but please, tell me more about your family. I'm sorry I interrupted you."

She continued, "My father, Andrew Trumball, is an independent bayman. He harvests Blue Point oysters for the shipping companies. And then there's Gran. She's my mother's mother. She cared for us when my mother had to work and, well, now I'm just really grateful that we have her."

Philip saw the shadow pass over Hannah's eyes and responded with a distraction, "A bayman? Ahhh."

Hannah replied, "Yes, but the livelihood of an independent bayman isn't what it used to be."

Philip knew something of the lives of the baymen of Sayville and the devastation of the supply of oysters in the bays around Long Island. Some thought it was caused at first by the waste from the duck farms, and later, in general, because of pollution. But he thought it best to keep what he knew to himself. So, he said no more about it.

He asked, "Do you go to school, Hannah?"

"Yes."

Philip smiled, "Old '88?"

Hannah looked at him in shock, "We just call it the Sayville School, but it was built in 1888 and has that date inscribed on the front of the building."

"Yeah, we call it Old '88, but it's not there anymore. It burnt down or something. That's where our new library is now."

Hannah was incredulous, she couldn't believe how in spite of the hundred years, there were commonalities that had touched each of their lives. It was uncanny that the places she knew so well had become part of Sayville's history. It gave her what felt like an eerie connection to Philip.

After talking late into the night, and long after the storm had left, they fell asleep on the floor in front of the warm fire. When Hannah awoke the next morning, his arm was wrapped around her and the fire had grown cold. Sage was curled up on the floor besides them. At first, feeling alarmed by Philip's close proximity, she felt the blood rush to her face. When she was finally able to steady her breathing, she gently lifted Philip's arm off of her and slowly sat up. The storm had passed and the sun was already shining. She stood carefully, not wanting to wake him. She gingerly placed her weight on her injured ankle to test it out. It wasn't too bad. She carried Sage with her into the kitchen. Hannah took two glasses from the shelf and a glass bottle of unopened milk from the ice box and set them on the table. Then she looked in the pantry and found some crackers and preserves.

When Philip opened his eyes he was confused at first. But then, one look at the contents of his backpack sprawled over the bench brought back all that had transpired the night before. He could hear Hannah singing in the kitchen. When he stood, he felt light-headed and had to sit for a moment to regain his equilibrium. He was trying desperately to understand what had happened and went into the next room where he saw the polished Roosevelt piano standing grandly in the corner. One peek out the window and he could see that several trees had been broken off in a twisted fashion as if they were splintered toothpicks. He realized that the hail and thunderous roar of the wind last night had probably been caused by a small tornado. But it seemed that, thankfully, the house had been left unscathed.

When Philip returned to the fireplace, he noticed a pile of discarded newspapers and was caught by surprise when he read the headline of the one on top of the pile. It was dated October 15, 1912 and the headline, *"Theodore Roosevelt Shot in Milwaukee by a New York Saloon Keeper."* He picked up the paper and approached Hannah in the kitchen. She said, "Take a seat at the table, I'll be right in."

Hannah carried the tray of crackers and preserves into the servants' dining room and noticed that Philip was reading the paper. He asked Hannah, "What's this? Teddy Roosevelt was shot?" Hannah was suspicious, "You mean, you come from the future and you didn't know that he was shot on the campaign trail?"

"I-I never heard of such a thing."

Hannah sat down opposite from him and pointed to a photo on the newspaper, "This man, John Flammang Schrank; he shot the President." Then she took the newspaper from him and read, *"The bullet lodged in his chest muscle after penetrating both his steel eyeglass case and a 50-page single-folded copy of a speech that was in his jacket pocket. If he hadn't shouted out to the crowd to leave Schrank unharmed, his assailant would most likely have been lynched on the spot. Instead, he was taken into custody by the police. The President knew the bullet hadn't entered his lungs, because if it had, he would have been spitting up blood. So he went on to give a 90-minute speech before accepting any medical attention. His speech started with, 'Ladies and Gentlemen, I don't know whether you fully understand that I have just been shot, but it takes more than that to kill a Bull Moose.' Since then, the doctors have decided that it is less dangerous to leave the bullet where it is rather than to try to remove it. He only took off two weeks from the campaign trail before getting right back to it. Even Taft and Wilson took those two weeks off, they agreed that it wouldn't be fair to keep campaigning while Theodore was recuperating."*

Philip exclaimed, "Wow, he lived through all that, he took a bullet and everything, but still lost the election."

Hannah glared at him, "Well, not yet. The election isn't until next week."

"Yeah, but Hannah, you saw the article from the paper I showed you."

Hannah nodded and lifted her chin, "I know, but I will still wait to see what happens for myself." Then she instructed, "Now have something to eat, I've been making some plans for you. The fire alarm sounded this morning, so there's no school today. I'm going to go home and find some suitable clothes and shoes for you to wear from my brother's closet. In the meantime, you can make yourself at home in one of the rooms on the third floor. The Commodore will not be back until spring and the caretaker has moved away, so no one will bother you. I realize that you may not know how a house in this time functions, so when I come back, I will teach you all you need to know."

Philip was overwhelmed with appreciation, "Thank you, Hannah." He smiled and Hannah's heart did a little flip flop at the sight of his dimples and the darling cleft in his chin. When they had finished their meager breakfast, she led him up the stairs to the servants' quarters. The room was small and simple with white beadboard walls. Looking out the window, he was surprised by the unobstructed view of the bay and Fire Island. The storm had indeed passed, and in its wake, the sky was a clear blue dotted by a few white puffs of cloud. He knew that his own house should be visible from this vantage point and so he tried to find it. He did see a house where his should have been. It had a small second floor but it was shaped different from his house. Then, he remembered his house had been expanded and dormered over the past hundred years. That's when he realized that he was seeing the original building as it had looked when it was first built in 1898.

Hannah was watching him from the doorway and saw his shoulders slump in surrender. She realized he was slowly coming to terms with his new reality and suggested, "Why don't you just lie down and take a rest until I come back. I know that everything always seems worse when you're tired."

He turned to look at her. She could tell that he didn't want her to leave, but she needed to go. She said, "I won't be long."

As Hannah left Meadow Croft, she looked up to the third floor and saw him watching her with a frown. Then and there she resolved to find a way to bring that smile back to his face.

# CHAPTER NINETEEN

## 1912

Hannah carried Sage home in her arms. The poor thing continued to lick at her paw and unraveling the bandages. As soon as Gran saw that the puppy was injured, she went into action. She cleaned the wound and rewrapped her paw, then cut down and tied one of Hannah's old bone-lined petticoats around the dog's neck to prevent her from licking the injured area again.

Hannah asked, "Where's Harry?"

"He's working at the Kensington."

If there was any one place in Sayville where people gathered, it was the Kensington Hotel and Harry was a busboy there.

"Okay, I've got to grab a few things and then I'm meeting Ilsa in town."

Gran mumbled an acknowledgement but was too distracted taking care of Sage to do much more. Hannah found some of Harry's clothing and a pair of old shoes and stuffed them in a potato sack. She realized Harry might notice his clothes and shoes were missing. She was going to have to tell Harry about Philip.

Gran was sitting in her rocking chair, cradling Sage, and singing an old Irish lullaby to soothe the puppy. The song brought back memories of Hannah's own childhood. She kissed Gran gently on the cheek and whispered, "I've got to go Gran. I'll be back in time for dinner," and then Hannah was out the door.

At Meadow Croft, she handed Philip her brother's clothes. She instructed, "Quickly, change into these and then we can walk into town. You can't go to town in what you're wearing. And take the coins and bills your father left for you in your bag so that we can purchase necessities."

Once he had changed, Hannah appraised his new look. Although the shirt sleeves and pant legs were a bit too short for him, he already looked like he belonged. She liked the way his shaggy hair framed his high cheek bones and the stubble that covered his square jaw. She made a mental note to pick up some grooming supplies for him.

As they walked down South Main Street, Philip noticed a sign above a store that read, Thornhill's Drug Store. This surprised him, because the Thornhill's he knew was around the corner from this store. He checked the address on the door, 56 South Main Street. He tried to remember what was in this spot in his time, but couldn't figure it out. He said, "I've heard that Thornhill's had the first telephone in Sayville. Is that true?"

Hannah was surprised that this little piece of information had become important enough for Philip to know. "Yes. Their telephone number is 001. Not all the houses have telephones, so if someone needs to receive a call, they can call Thornhill's. Then Mr. Thornhill will take a message for them."

"Hey, can we just step in there for a minute? I want to see what it was like, way back then."

The two walked into Thornhill's and Philip marveled at the newly installed marble and onyx soda fountain. Sewell Thornhill stood behind the counter and asked, "Can I help you with something, Hannah?"

"Well, this is my friend, Philip and he just got to town. He needs to pick up a few things. To start, I think he needs a razor and some shaving cream."

"All righty, let's see what we have here."

Mr. Thornhill showed him a few straight razors, finally Philip just pointed to one. "Cat got your tongue, son?"

Philip cleared his throat, "No, Sir. It's just that this is all new to me."

Mr. Thornhill chuckled, "I understand, time to start cleaning it up for the ladies. This one is best for a beginner."

Hannah gave Mr. Thornhill some of Philip's silver coins, and then he placed the items in a paper bag. He handed each of them a free piece of candy.

Hannah thanked him and they started to walk out of the store when something caught Philip's eye. Behind a counter was a display of cameras. He hesitated for a moment and glanced at the various models. He seemed fascinated by what he saw, so Hannah asked, "Do you like photography?"

Philip nodded, "Yeah, I took a photography class in school." Philip thought back to his encounter with the old man by the bay again. "But I don't have any idea on how to use a camera like this." There was a sign above the cameras that read, "Film Developing Available on Premises."

Philip asked, "How much are the cameras?"

Mr. Thornhill replied, "They start at $10." Philip nodded, he didn't want to buy the camera just yet since he was unsure of how far the money he had would stretch and what else he might need. So he simply responded, "Thank you."

Standing in front of the drug store, Hannah popped the candy into her mouth and sucked on it. Philip looked at the piece he held in his hand, "What kind of candy is this?"

"It's horehound candy. Not only does it taste good, but it clears congestion and makes it easier to breathe."

Philip repeated uncertainly, "Horehound candy? Never heard of it."

Hannah encouraged him, "Just try it."

He touched the candy with the tip of his tongue. It wasn't bad. Hannah was watching him and rolling her eyes. Embarrassed, he placed it in his mouth. Hannah asked, "How is it?" He thought for a moment, "It tastes somewhere between root beer and licorice, with a touch of mint thrown in." He could feel the effect she had mentioned; it was like a cough drop.

Hannah nudged him, "Well, we better be going. We've got a lot to do over the next couple of hours."

The rain from the night before had left the streets a muddy mess. When they approached the main intersection in town, Philip let out an exclamation, "Holy Crap!"

The scene before him seemed to be out of a movie set. The horse-drawn wagons, the costumes of the people milling about on the sidewalks, Model T Fords and the like parked along the curbs, and antique bicycles left beside the shops. Every detail in living color before him. Hannah touched his arm, "Really, Philip. That language will not do."

"Oh, yeah, all right. I'm sorry."

Hannah redirected him toward Gerber's General Store. "Come this way." Since Harry's feet were a bit smaller than Philip's, the first thing they looked for was shoes. The sizes were all different from the ones he knew, but after trying on several, he finally found a pair that fit his feet well. Next, they looked through the clothes racks. When he found a rack of suspenders he blurted out, "Cool!" Hannah nudged his arm to remind him to be quiet. When they were done, he had a couple of new outfits, a tweed cap, and a winter coat, along with other necessities.

Francis Gerber, the owner of the store, took the silver coins that Hannah held out for him.

Mr. Gerber's eyes narrowed, he could see that Hannah was nervous about something and seeing her with this unfamiliar young man set off an alarm bell in his mind, "Is everything all right, Hannah?"

"Yes, Sir. This is my friend Philip, he's new in town and I'm helping him out today."

Something didn't set right with him, so he said. "Well, all right then. But you be careful. You hear?"

"Yes, Sir. I certainly will. Thank you, Sir."

Mr. Gerber followed Hannah and Philip as they left his store and watched them cross the road toward Joseph Arata's produce store. Chickens ran past them and under Philip's feet. They walked between two wagons and harnessed horses, each tied to a hitching post in front of the store. Crates of potatoes and apples and a variety of produce were stacked on the wooden porch. Hannah took an empty basket and filled it with a selection of fruits and vegetables and then entered the store to conduct her business while Philip stood outside mesmerized by the town that looked so much like Sayville, but was not the Sayville that he knew.

They made one more stop at Otto's Meat Market where Hannah purchased a freshly slaughtered chicken and some ground beef before heading back to Meadow Croft together.

Hannah asked, "Do you know how to cook?"

"No, my mom always did that for us." The word "mom" caught in his throat.

Hannah knew from what he had told her last night, that for all intents and purposes, he had not only just lost his mother, but had, in fact, lost everyone he knew in his life. She knew how lost she had felt after losing her own mother, and understood that it could only be a fraction of the loss that Philip was experiencing at this moment. "I can help you. I'll show you how do to things. Just be patient with yourself. It's going to take time." The word "patient" reminded him of the card reading his mother had given him and now he wondered if, even then, she was trying to prepare him for this experience. He tried to remember what else she had told him.

At Meadow Croft, they descended the stairs to the basement, Philip saw the considerable pile of coal in the corner of the brick-walled basement under a window. Expecting to have to shovel coal into a stove, he was surprised when Hannah touched his arm and turned him in the opposite directions. She said, "The coal is leftover from when the house was heated by a coal stove. Most homes are heated by coal in Sayville, but Meadow Croft has a gas machine. The Roosevelts don't keep it on while they're away, so when I'm here I just use the fireplace and kerosene lanterns. But if you are going to be living here for a while, we will start the gas machine.

Philip was amazed by the cables and pulleys that were set beside a large tank. On closer inspection, he read the label on the tank, *Tirrill "Equalizing" Gas Machine*. Fascinated, he asked, "How does it work and what does it do?"

Hannah explained, "The caretaker explained it to me in case I ever need to turn it on. You see, there's a generator tank buried in the ground outside along with the mixer. You store gasoline in the generator tank and the mixer turns the gasoline into gas that can be used to

light the house, heat water, and operate the gas stove in the kitchen."
Then pointing to the tank in the basement she said, "This here is the
air pump, it works when that cast iron tub, full of rocks, is lifted and
suspended by the cables. You turn this crank and that lifts the
weights and then the machine produces gas." There were huge stones
in a large cast iron tub below a contraption of pulleys and cables in
the corner of the basement. Hannah asked, "Help me turn the
crank." A soft hiss reverberated through the basement.

Ascending the stairs to the main level, Hannah showed Philip that
the stove and the lights could be turned on or off by turning individual keys, allowing only as much gas to be used as was necessary.
Further, she explained, "The heat works its way up these pipes and
into the upstairs of the house. Each room has heat registers on the
floor or walls, and you can adjust them to allow in more heat or you
can even close certain ones if you only want to heat a part of the
house."

Philip asked, "What about water? Is there a well or something?"

"Of course. There's an electric water pump that pumps the well
water up to a cold water tank on the roof. There are pipes leading to
the necessary areas like the kitchen, bathrooms, and a hot water tank
that is heated by the gas machine. I will turn on the electric water
pump and then the water will be accessible when you need it."

She showed Philip how to pluck the chicken, remove the bones and
cut it into small pieces. Then she filled a pot with water and added
some chicken, potatoes, carrots, and onions to make a stew. She
showed him how to knead dough and left it to rise, "Tomorrow we
will make a meatloaf and bake bread. But I have to go home now. I'll
be back tomorrow after school." Try not to get into any trouble while
I'm gone and maybe you can come up with a story to tell people that
won't sound as crazy as the one you told me."

Philip watched Hannah leave from the front Dutch doors. The trees had been shaken by the storm and there was now a carpet of colorful autumn leaves on the ground. He heard the bells of St. Ann's ring four times and felt the fear rise within him once again. He had almost forgotten about his predicament while Hannah was with him, but now that she was gone, he felt very much alone and out of place. In spite of the heat slowly filling the house, he felt a chill. He put his sweatshirt over Harry's old clothes and taking off Harry's shoes, he slipped his feet back into his sneakers. With an audible sigh of comfort, his feet filled the cushioned interiors and he wondered how he was ever going to get used to the shoes of the time. Then he decided to take a walk around the property.

The first thing he did was to go back to the spot where he had met Hannah. The trap that Sage had been caught in was there. He noticed at once that it was in the center of where one of the tornados must have touched ground. All around him were splintered trees and the grass was flattened down like something heavy had been laid down on it. He wondered if the tornado, or whatever strange weather phenomena had occurred here, plus the hurricane that occurred one hundred years in the future, also, combined with the harvest blood moon, had caused some sort of time portal to open which he had unwittingly walked through. If that was the case, how would he ever hope to get back? When would those exact conditions replicate themselves? He sat down on the flattened grass and looked up at the piece of sky visible between the broken trees. It was the same sky, he was in the same place, his home was just a few blocks away, but he knew that he would never see his family again. The silence that surrounded him was deeper than any he had ever experienced before. But as he concentrated, he could hear the water birds squawk over Brown's River. A moment later, a rooster crowed in the distance. This was a pastoral world, one that had a slower feel to it. He took in a deep breath and felt a calm wash over him. He closed his eyes and let go of the anxiety that was plaguing him.

But then the silence was interrupted, and Philip was surprised to hear Hannah's voice calling him. Returning to the house he saw her standing there with a boy. The newcomer was looking at him with skepticism.

"Philip, this is my brother, Harry. I told him about you and how we met, he wanted me to bring him back here to meet you."

Harry looked at this boy who was wearing his old clothes under a strange looking jacket. As much as he had the desire to protect his sister, he had long ago learned that she was too headstrong ever to listen to him. Harry extended a hand to Philip and Philip took it in response. Philip said, "I can't thank your sister enough for helping me out."

Harry was struggling to believe the outlandish story that his sister had just told him about this stranger. But he decided it was best to play along with it until he could decide for himself if this was some sort of a ruse.

"My sister tells me you are from the future," Harry smirked. Philip nodded and shrugged his shoulders. He couldn't blame Harry, he doubted that it would be something he would believe if someone told him the story.

Philip tried to explain, "Yes. Just yesterday, I was in 2012 and living my life in Sayville, but somehow, I have walked through some sort of time portal and am now in 1912."

Harry replied, "Your family must be worried about you."

Clearing his throat, Philip continued, "Well, that's maybe the strangest thing. They seem to have known this was going to happen. They sent me back with a letter explaining that they know where I am."

Harry's eyes widened in disbelief, "But they never told you?"

"No. Not a word. The letter says they didn't want to chance my changing what had already happened. I-I don't really understand it myself, yet."

Harry shook his head, "Well, I can't say I completely believe your story, but you are here now no matter where or when you came from. So what is the plan. You can't stay here at Meadow Croft."

Philip nodded, "Yes, I know. I was just thinking that."

Hannah cut in, "Harry, I told Philip he can stay here. At least, for a while. No one will know. He needs some time to assimilate. From what he has told me, he has a lot to learn about life in 1912. Once he's more accustomed to our culture, he can get a job and we'll help him find a place to live."

Harry knew his sister's desire to help injured animals and people in need, but this seemed dangerous to him.

Philip kicked a stone and Harry looked down to Philip's feet and saw his sneakers. The material that the shoes were made of was unlike anything he had ever seen. Perhaps, Harry thought, Philip really was telling the truth.

The group walked over to the ice house and Harry showed Philip how to chop ice off of the block and helped him to carry it back to the house. Then Hannah and Harry, introduced Philip to all the odd-looking appliances in the kitchen and laundry rooms. Philip exclaimed, "No washing machine or dryer?" Hannah thought it was almost as if they were speaking a different language than Philip.

She explained, "We wash the clothes in that tub and then hang them on the line out back."

Philip smiled, "Like in the old movies?"

Harry asked, "Old movies? You mean moving picture shows?"

Philip scratched his head, "Well, yeah. But I watch them on TV. They're old reruns. They used to be in movie theaters, but now everyone has a box in their house." Hannah smiled and continued Philip's explanation, since he had already shared this information with her, "It's like the telephone, Harry, only you can see and hear the person on a screen on this box even when they are far away."

Philip shrugged his shoulders, "Yeah, well, something like that, Hannah." Her smile turned into a frown and Philip realized he had hurt her feelings. "Sorry Hannah, it's just a lot more complicated than that. But you've got the general idea." Harry tried to hide his laughter at their exchange of words, but then Hannah laughed, too, and said, "Well, Philip, I guess we both have a lot to learn."

Harry asked, "Would you mind showing me the letter from your parents?"

Philip led them to the bedroom he had taken for himself. The three of them sat on the floor with the contents of his backpack spread between them. Each item was a source of wonder to Harry. After reading the newspaper stating that Theodore Roosevelt had lost the election, he let out a low whistle. He could feel goosebumps pop on his arms as he read the letter from Philip's mother. Finally, he swallowed hard and put his hand out to Philip, "I'm sorry I doubted you, but I can't explain all of this any other way. So whatever you need from us, we'll be here for you."

Philip nodded in response, grateful for the support Harry was offering him. By the time Harry and Hannah left him that day, Philip thought things had gone as well as could be expected. As crazy as it seemed, they appeared to have the beginning of a genuine friendship. He thought about Gordon and Jenny and how they had been the only friends he had ever felt he could be comfortable around. Now there were Hannah and Harry. Amazingly, he realized he didn't feel awkward around them. He almost felt like he belonged.

A week later, on the morning of Wednesday, November 6<sup>th</sup>, 1912, the students of Sayville were gathered together as Principal Noll addressed them in the assembly room. He held up a copy of the New York Times and announced, "As you can see, the results are in on the election of our new President. The Democrat, Woodrow Wilson, has prevailed. He has defeated the Republican incumbent, William H. Taft, as well as our beloved Past President, Theodore Roosevelt, of the Progressive Party."

As the murmurs among the students rose like the sound of the ocean, Hannah and Harry grabbed each other's hands. Harry squeezed Hannah's hand and whispered, "Philip was right."

# CHAPTER TWENTY

## 1912

The Kensington Hotel stood at the northeast corner of Main Street and Railroad Avenue. It was the main crossroads of the town and had been the location of the first tavern in Sayville. Hannah had explained to Philip that the building was originally owned by the Howell family and housed the hamlet's first tavern, store, and post office. It was in this tavern that residents met in 1836 to name the town. They had decided on naming it Seaville, but a misspelling of the name that was sent to Washington ended in the town being called Sayville. Andrew Kennedy and his wife, Emma, purchased the hotel and property in 1900 and had part of the original building moved across the street to Joseph Arata's farm in 1907. The famous local architect, Isaac H. Green, Jr., then designed a new three-story addition to the hotel, which now boasted steam heat, electricity, and telephones in each of its fourteen guestrooms. In addition, the hotel had two parlors, a wide welcoming porch to gather on, a handsome curved staircase from the entrance to the second floor, and a spacious dining room, complete with a generous mahogany bar for guests and visitors. It was in this very dining room that Philip now stood nervously on his first day of work. Harry was able to arrange for

Philip to be hired as a waiter. It was early December and there was a flurry of activity going on as employees decorated the hotel with evergreen boughs and red ribbons. Feeling self-conscious, Philip tried his best to fit in, but felt like a fish out of water.

Hannah and Harry had done their best to prepare him for mingling with the townsfolk and had come up with a story he could tell people. The story went like this: He had been born in Philadelphia and was new to Long Island. His family had died in a fire, and he was now alone in the world trying to make a way for himself.

"Young man?" he heard Andrew Kennedy's voice and quickly spun around to face his employer. "While we are waiting for our guests, please take a rag and polish the tables."

Philip replied, "Yes, Sir." The bartender was already extending a rag to him, so Philip quickly crossed the room to take it from him and then went about wiping each of the gleaming wooden tables.

A female voice whispered to him, "Don't worry, his bark is worse than his bite. Mr. Kennedy is actually a very fine person to work for as long as you perform your job to his standards."

Philip looked up from his work to see where the voice had come from. A pretty young woman in a maid's outfit was standing in front of him. She extended her hand to him, "Hi, my name is Bernice. I work here as well, taking care of the guest rooms."

Philip nodded, keeping his head low. Bernice continued, "Well, I know you are new to town. If you need anyone to show you around, I'm your gal."

Philip mumbled, "Thank you, but I think I'm okay."

Bernice produced a saucy smile and said, "Well, if you change your mind, you know where I am."

Later that day, the dining room was crowded with guests and Philip didn't have a moment to think about anything. Harry was there and from time to time, if Philip felt at a loss as to what he was supposed to do, Harry helped him. Some of the foods on the menu were foreign to Philip, such as *Grilled Mutton Chops* and *Grilled Ox Kidneys with Bacon*. But for the most part the choices were familiar, *Roast Duckling, Sirloin of Beef, Salmon*, and the like.

Over the coming weeks, Philip became more confident and more at ease. He was able to make suggestions to diners, talk to them about the weather and the latest news in town and, in general, began making friends with locals and staff members. He was actually starting to feel like he belonged here.

On the Friday before Christmas, Philip saw Harry talking to a group of men who had gathered at the bar and were drinking drafts of ale. Harry called over to Philip and asked him to join him, "Phil, I want to introduce you to my father, Andrew Trumball."

Andrew's gaze bored into Philip's eyes and Philip wondered how much Harry's father was privy to. Philip offered his hand, "It's a pleasure to meet you, Mr. Trumball." Andrew shook his hand and then said, "So you are the young man I've been told was with my daughter a couple of months ago."

Philip took in a deep breath, not sure of what was coming next. Andrew said, "Francis Gerber told me that he had seen Hannah with a young man whom he didn't recognize. When I asked Hannah about it, she told me that you lost your family in a fire. I'm very sorry to hear that."

Philip felt like a hamster running on an exercise wheel, spinning but going nowhere. He would have preferred to be better prepared for meeting Hannah's father, and he was terribly nervous. "Yes, sir." Philip replied.

Andrew continued, "Well now, my son told me he was able to get you a job here at The Kensington. Hearing that, I thought it was about time that I met this mysterious young man who had befriended my children." Andrew watched Philip closely, he knew there was more to the story then any of them were telling him. Andrew continued, "Anyway, they've asked me to invite you to spend Christmas dinner with us next week. What do you think?"

Philip relaxed just a bit, "Well, Sir, that is very kind of you and I'd like that very much."

"Very well," Andrew said while clapping Philip on the back. "Harry will give you the details."

Philip heard Mr. Kennedy clear his throat from behind him. "Young man, I believe there is a table of guests waiting for their meals, and Harry, there are tables to clear." Philip and Harry quickly went back to their jobs.

The following day at Thornhill's, Hannah, Ilsa, and Anna Koman, sat in a row at the counter and sipped on hot chocolate to melt away the chill. Icy rain started to fall from the sky as Hannah glanced out the window and wondered how much she should tell her friends about Philip. Hannah began, "A very strange thing happened to me a couple of months ago. Remember the night of the storm when Sage got caught in the raccoon trap?"

Ilsa nodded.

"I wasn't able to open the trap on my own. But at that moment, a boy came into the woods and found us. He was the one who parted the teeth of the trap so that Sage could be freed."

Ilsa's head tilted in confusion, "A boy?"

"Yes. I-I, well, *we* brought Sage into the house at Meadow Croft and we were trapped there for the night by the storm."

Anna's eyes widened in terror. "You were alone with a stranger?"

"Yes." Hannah's cheeks took on a warm color. And making a decision not to tell the girls the whole truth, said, "He's not from here. He didn't have a place to live, so I let him stay at Meadow Croft."

Ilsa exclaimed, "No! Hannah, what are you doing?"

"I know, Ilsa. But Harry and I are his only friends right now and he needs us."

Ilsa shook her head, "This doesn't make sense, Hannah. Who is he? What are you not telling us?"

Hannah struggled within herself. If the story got around that Philip said he was from another time, the authorities might lock him up in an asylum. So instead, she continued with the story that she and Harry had come up with, "He's from Pennsylvania. He had just gotten off of the train in Sayville and was walking down the road when he heard me call out and Sage crying in pain. So he left the road to find us. If he hadn't been there, Sage could have lost her leg!"

Anna asked, "And you said Harry knows about Philip?"

"Yes. I needed his . . ." she almost said clothes, "help."

Ilsa sat back on her stool and took another sip of the hot chocolate and considered what she should say next. She couldn't help but feel hurt that her friend hadn't trusted her enough to tell her this secret. "Why didn't you tell me this before?"

"Well, I was afraid to tell people because I didn't want anyone to know I was letting him stay at Meadow Croft. I could lose my job and he could be arrested for trespassing."

Ilsa looked away from Hannah, "I would have kept your secret, Hannah. We have always kept each other's secrets."

It was then that the door to Thornhill's opened and Harry and Carl entered. Finding their sisters and Anna together at the counter, they joined them.

Carl asked, "What are you girls up to?"

Ilsa shrugged, "We're just talking."

Hannah looked over Ilsa's head and caught Harry's eye. "I was just telling them about Philip." Harry looked warily at his sister, "Oh?"

Carl's brow furrowed, "Who's Philip?"

Hannah then explained what she had just told Ilsa and Anna. Carl responded with a whistle.

Harry added, "He's been working with me at The Kensington. He's a good guy, really."

"So can we meet him?" Carl asked.

Hannah offered, "Sure. He's off today so we will probably find him at Meadow Croft. We could go there now if you'd like."

When Philip heard Hannah's voice call to him up the stairway, he put down the book he was reading. The Roosevelt library had been the one thing that saved him during the lonely hours he spent in the house in-between work hours and visits from Harry and Hannah. As he descended the stairs, he was surprised to see Anna, Ilsa, and Carl standing there.

Philip reached out his hand to Carl as Hannah introduced them. "I've explained to them how you recently arrived in Sayville from Philadelphia. They have been sworn to secrecy regarding your staying here at the house."

Following Hannah's lead, Philip acknowledged, "Hi, it's nice to meet friends of Hannah and Harry."

Ilsa immediately put aside her reservations when Philip smiled at her and took her hand in his. She said, "It's nice to meet you, too." She lowered her long lashes over her blue eyes and blushed. He then shook Anna's hand and, like a man comfortable in his own home, Philip offered, "Would you all like some coffee, it's still warm on the stove."

By the time Anna, Ilsa, and Carl parted ways with Harry and Hannah, Ilsa said, "He's very sweet, Hannah. Thank you for telling us your secret." The three girls hugged each other in unison. Ilsa left feeling relieved that all was well between them. But Hannah was worried that Ilsa would be hurt again if she ever learned the full truth of the story.

On Christmas Eve, the family sat around the warm hearth at the center of their cottage. Gran held Sage in her rocking chair. The dog had grown too large for Gran's lap, but neither she, nor Sage, was quite ready to give up the comfort that rocking the dog gave to them both. Sage's leg had healed, but the fur hadn't yet grown over the scar. Andrew sipped at his mug of spiked hot apple cider as he spoke, "So where is young Philip living?"

Hannah looked up in alarm.

Harry said, "I asked Hannah to put him up at Meadow Croft. Like I said, when we met him he had just arrived here, he was all alone, and had nowhere to stay."

Andrew placed his mug on a table that sat beside his chair and asked quizzically, "So, you did now? And who gave either of you the right to offer him Meadow Croft for a temporary home?"

Harry's hand partially covered his mouth as he said, "We thought no one would know, Pa."

Andrew responded, "I see. Well, we will have to find him a new place to stay."

The next morning, Philip woke to silence in the big house. He couldn't help but feel a sense of loss, remembering Christmas mornings with his family. He looked longingly at the photo he had of himself and his brothers in front of their Christmas tree. He remembered the joy of tearing open their presents and the big meal his mother would prepare. He wondered if at that very moment, his mother was playing her old Christmas albums on the record player that his father had bought her the year before. He knew the holiday would include a visit from Jenny and her father, playing Po-ke-no, and pulling apart holiday crackers with a pop. The aroma of smoke from the small firecrackers would linger in the air as they found the treasures within, a colorful paper crown, a tiny trinket, and a riddle.

He descended the stairs to the main floor. A few days ago, Hannah, Harry, and he had chopped down a small tree and placed it in Nannie's parlor beside the piano. The three had cut paper chains and paper snowflakes and decorated the tree. But as he entered the room, he was surprised to see a second package under the branches waiting for him. He knew that one was a gift he had bought for Hannah, but was unsure of where the other had come from. He sat cross-legged under the tree and lifted the box with a smile. He shook it a little to see if he could tell what was inside, but it made no sound. He wanted to preserve this moment. A little piece of Christmas. It was then that he realized this would be the first Christmas that his parents and brothers would be missing him as well. It felt like an anchor was sitting on his chest. It took a moment for him to be able to breathe normally again. He blinked back the tears that threatened to seep from his eyes.

He heard the front door open. Startled, he turned quickly, ready to run at a moment's notice, when he heard Hannah's voice calling, "Philip?"

Relief flowed through him at the sound of her voice. "In here, Hannah."

Hannah saw him sitting on the floor, holding the present in his hand like a little boy. "You haven't opened it yet?"

"Oh, no, I haven't."

"Well then, open it."

Hannah took a seat on the floor next to him and watched as he carefully unwrapped the brown paper. When he saw what was beneath it, he let out a low whistle. It was a Kodak 2a Brownie folding bellows camera. The description on the box said it produced 2 ½ by 4 ½ inch photos. He had seen a picture of one once in a book he had about WWI. The soldiers took them to the front line since they conveniently fit into the pocket of their jackets. Some of the most dramatic photographs of the war were taken with these little cameras.

"Hannah, you really shouldn't have. How much did this cost?"

"It's a present, you're not supposed to ask questions like that."

"But Hannah, it's too much."

Hannah frowned, "Don't you like it?"

"Sure, I do! I just feel bad, that's all."

Hannah was beaming now.

Philip reached under the Christmas tree and picked up a tiny brown paper bag and handed it to Hannah, "This is for you."

Surprised, Hannah's voice rose as she exclaimed, "For me?"

"Well, yeah."

Hannah opened the bag to see what was inside. It was a hollow rock. Growing inside the rock were beautiful purple crystals. Hannah let out her breath, "I've never seen anything so beautiful in my life."

Philip explained, "It's called a geode. Anyway, it's nothing compared to a camera and now I feel terrible!"

Hannah had tears in her eyes as she shook her head, "No, Philip. Don't feel that way. It's really beautiful! I love it!" Philip sat back and relaxed as he realized she really meant what she said. He promised himself that he if he was still here in the past next year, that he would get her something nicer.

Hannah said, "I've come to bring you to my house for Christmas dinner." Looking at his sweatshirt and sweatpants she said, "Now go change into something respectable."

Together they walked the few blocks between Meadow Croft and Hannah's house. Philip hadn't known exactly where Hannah lived. The streets were familiar to him, the old houses that were there now were also there a hundred years from now. This was an older part of the town, south of Main Street. When they turned down the side street, Philip's heart really began to race. This was also the street he had lived on.

Finally, they approached Hannah's house and Philip stopped in his tracks. From a tree branch far above, a mourning dove sang her song. Philip felt a shiver run up his spine and it was not from the cold, "Hannah, is this your house?"

"Yes."

He shook his head in disbelief.

With concern on her face, she asked, "What is it, Philip?"

Philip was standing in front of his own house. Only, as he had seen from the third floor of Meadow Croft months before, it was a simple cottage now. "Hannah, this is where I live." Chills ran up and down his spine.

Hannah looked confused, "What do you mean?"

"I mean this is my house in 2012. Only the house will be bigger by then. It will be expanded over the years and when I'm living here, both the downstairs and upstairs are enlarged and two bathrooms were added, as well," looking at the outhouse in the back yard he continued, "and all the modern conveniences."

Philip looked toward the dead end where, unlike in 2012, the river could be seen clearly. The edge of the river was closer to his house then it would be one hundred years from now and there were no phragmites to obstruct the view. The mourning dove called out again and it brought back the memory of another day when he was standing in this very spot. He felt disconcerted as he tried to wrap his brain around this coincidence.

Hannah was tugging at his arm, "Come on, they're waiting for us."

Philip's stomach felt uneasy as he entered the cottage from the side door straight into the kitchen. In 2012, this part of the house was a bathroom. He noticed the cabinets on the wall, they were in the same place as they were in his bathroom. But the kitchen sink was where the toilet would be and the ice box was where the shower would be. The ornate grate in the wall was only an ornament in his time, but now, it allowed the coal heat from the basement to enter the kitchen and warm the house. His mind was doing flips, trying to see this space in both time periods at once.

Gran saw Philip's face turn white, "Come, have a seat young man." Philip felt faint, but he tried to rouse himself. Andrew walked into the room at the same time and reached out his hand for Philip's. Philip shook Andrew's hand weakly. Andrew asked, "Are you all right, son? Feeling well? You don't have a fever do you?"

Gran shuffled over and immediately placed the palm of her hand on Philip's sweaty brow. "No fever," she determined, "The boy just needs a good meal. Look at how thin he is."

Philip sat down at the table as Gran and Hannah placed their Christmas dinner of goose, gravy, sausage, mashed potatoes, corn, and green beans in front of him. Philip nodded silently.

Andrew watched the boy as he ate and waited for everyone to have their fill before he began to ask questions. There was something here that just didn't add up and he was determined to find out the truth.

Andrew pushed his dish away as the ladies cleared the table. Looking directly at Philip he asked, "So you're from Philadelphia?"

Philip nervously cleared his throat, "Yes, Sir."

"Where in Philadelphia?"

Philip had been to the city a couple of times, once on a school trip and once with his parents, and knew a little about the old city. He remembered that the oldest part of Philadelphia ran along the Delaware River and that the streets closest to the river had numbers, he took a chance and said, "2$^{nd}$ Street, near the river."

Andrew's eyes narrowed, "And what is it that brought you here to Sayville?"

Remembering the story that Hannah had spun for him he said, "After the fire, I took what I had left and went to Manhattan. I saw signs there saying that there was work for Italians in Patchogue. But when I saw Sayville, I thought it was so beautiful, I got off here to take a look. I met Hannah and Harry then and decided to stay for a spell."

Andrew nodded but still looked warily at Philip, "You're Italian then."

"Yes, Sir." He wondered if he should feel ashamed of that fact.

"Hmm, my children tell me that you are staying at Meadow Croft until you can get yourself set somewhere." Andrew shook his head and spoke disapprovingly, "It's not their place to offer anyone a room at Meadow Croft." Hannah shifted in her seat, aware that her father's eyes had settled on her. Philip noticed the tension between Hannah and her father and sought to alleviate it if possible.

"I understand, Sir. That's why I need to find a place to live soon."

Andrew sat back in his chair and tried to figure Philip out. Something wasn't right, but he couldn't put his finger on it. But then, looking at his daughter and seeing the way she looked at the boy, he knew that something had to be done. Andrew stood up and went over to where the coats hung on the wall. He took a slip of paper out of his coat pocket and placed it on the table, pushing it with two fingers over to Philip. "This here is a friend of mine. He and his wife have a room available in their house, just down the road in Bayport. I've told him about you and he said he's willing to rent it to you."

Philip read the name on the paper, "Giorgio Valenti."

Philip thanked Andrew and the subject was dropped.

Once the dishes were cleared, Gran put out a steaming apple pie, a pumpkin pie, and her famous bread pudding. By now, Philip's suspenders were about to pop, but he had enjoyed every bite.

Hannah said, "Come into the parlor." She led them all into a tiny room that was taken up mostly by a player piano. She chose a music roll, opened the compartment and placed it on the spindle there. Harry handed out the words to the songs to each person gathered there and as Hannah started to pump the pedals, the rich tones of the piano played one Christmas song after another. Gran's voice could be heard above the rest. She had once sung in music halls long ago, and her voice was still beautiful. Hannah's voice was not as strong as her grandmother's, but it was sweet and melodic.

Philip did his best to sing along. Some of the tunes were new to him, while others were ones he had heard sung on his mother's old Christmas records. He missed his own family terribly, but he somehow felt at home with Hannah and her family. He thought perhaps his mother was right. There were people here, good people, who would help him through whatever awaited him in this life he was meant to live.

# CHAPTER TWENTY-ONE

### 1913

Giorgio and Elisabetta Valenti had come to America in 1875 and settled a year later in Bayport, just east of Sayville. They purchased a small cedar shingled cape cod style home and hoped it would one day be filled with the voices of their children. But the only child that God had ever granted them had died of measles when he was just three years old. Now, all these years later, Philip knocked on their front door. He held a leather suitcase in one hand and a piece of paper in the other. The suitcase was filled with everything he owned, including the backpack and its contents, and the few items of clothes that he had purchased over the past months. The piece of paper held the address that Andrew had written down for him.

At his knock, a round woman opened the door and beckoned him to enter before all the heat escaped. "Come'a in, son, and'a take off'a your shoes if'a you don't'a mind'a. My name is 'Lisabetta Valenti and you must'a be the young'a man that our friend, Andrew, has told us about." Philip heard the southern Italian accent and felt instantly at ease. She sounded just like his memories of his Grandma Virginia, his father's mother. Although she had died when he was young, just hearing that accent immediately brought back to him the sound of her voice.

"Yes, Ma'am, my name is Philip." Philip removed his wool cap and coat and then untied his shoes. Elisabetta took the wet items and hung them on a coat rack by the door.

"I really appreciate this Ma'am."

"Non'a'sense, Filippo, this home is'a too big'a for my husband and'a me. Come'a in. Come'a in." She took the suitcase from his hand as if it weighed no more than a few ounces and he realized she was much stronger than he had first thought. She waddled down the hall with the suitcase and placed it down beside the stairs that led to the second floor. "You can'a take it up'a stairs later. First, you sit'a down'a and'a have a decent meal. Look at you, skin and'a bones."

And with that, she piled sausage and cheese on a large seeded roll and placed it on the table before him along with a glass of red wine. The kitchen was small but welcoming with a white starched table cloth, embroidered with flowers, covering the square wooden table. She took a seat opposite him and watched him intently as he took his first bite. He made an okay sign with his thumb and announced, "Delizioso!"

Satisfied, Elisabetta pushed her chair back from the table and busied herself about the kitchen, humming an Italian melody as she worked. The sun had set early, as it did in January, and Elisabetta pushed a button on the wall and the kitchen suddenly flooded with light.

She took the empty plate from him and instructed, "Now'a, you can'a go upstairs and'a take the room on'a the left'a. Get'a yourself'a comfortable and we will'a eat'a when'a my husband gets'a home." She pushed him to the stairway and shooed him upstairs. Philip had thought the sandwich was dinner, but as it turned out, it was meant to be just an appetizer.

At the top of the stairs, he saw two identical bedrooms, one to the left and one to the right. Directly in front of him, he was grateful to see a bathroom. He turned left and closed the bedroom door behind him. The ceiling followed the slanted roofline on one side of the room, and he had to bend in order not to hit his head when he tried to stand near that wall. There was one window, facing east, and a small closet next to the door to the room. It was sparsely furnished with a bed, nightstand, and one dresser. He placed his suitcase on the bed and proceeded to unpack and fill the dresser and closet with his clothes.

He heard the front door open and Elisabetta welcomed her husband home after a long day at work. She said, "Our young'a guest has arrived, Giorgio. A nice'a young man."

Philip made his way to the kitchen to find the old couple sitting together about to enjoy their meal. "Come'a sit down'a," Elisabetta ordered, "mangia."

"No, no, no," Philip waved his hands, "I've had enough. Thank you very much." He rubbed his full belly.

"Then sit'a with us. Maybe you get'a hungry?" she replied.

Giorgio had a long white beard and mustache and his hair swooped to one side across his forehead. He extended a square hand to Philip, "Nice to meet you. My friend, Andrew, said you are a friend of his children." Giorgio's English was much better than his wife's.

Philip noticed that Giorgio's fingernails had old blood bruises beneath the nails, and his hands looked as though they could never truly be cleaned no matter how many times he washed them. His face was lined in a way that told Philip he had had a hard life. His blue eyes were bloodshot, but his smile was warm and friendly.

Philip replied, "Yes. Harry and Hannah. Thank you very much for offering me a room in your home."

"No problem. You have a job?"

"Yes, I'm working at The Kensington as a waiter."

"That's good. But I take you to see my job tomorrow. You see if you like."

Philip smiled nervously, "What do you do?"

Giorgio explained, "In Palermo, my father and his father before him were Bottaio, or as they say in America, Coopers. I continue to do the same as them."

Philip had heard of the job but wasn't entirely sure of what it meant. "What is a Cooper?"

Giorgio looked at Philip suspiciously. How was it, he wondered, that this young man didn't know what a Cooper was? "I make barrels. You will see, tomorrow I show you."

The following day, Philip accompanied Giorgio on the trolley to The Bayport Barrel Company. His first impression of the building in which Giorgio worked was that it was filled with sawdust which made it hard to breath. Philip sat beside Giorgio as the old man, sitting behind a workhorse, showed him the art of barrel making. The precise measurements to cut each piece of wood was critical and the uniform shaving of the individual slats to fit inside the iron rings was necessary to have a barrel that would hold oysters to be shipped by boat and railroad to other parts of the country. Philip was impressed at the ease with which this master cooper could make a perfect barrel with such primitive tools and machines. Giorgio explained, "There are wet barrels made to hold liquid like wine or milk and there are dry barrels to hold, for instance, grains, sausage, or olives. We make them all here. Barrels for whatever you need."

Philip had never guessed at the work that went into making something that was so commonplace. And he thought that he would never again look at another barrel with the same indifference as he had in the past.

Over the following weeks, on the days when he was not at work at the Kensington, Philip found himself spending time learning this craft from Giorgio. It felt good to make something with his hands that he could be proud of. Giorgio grew attached to this boy who now lived in his home, and before long, he thought of Philip more as a son than as a tenant.

One day in May, Philip was looking through the family tree that his mother had made for him and noticed the names of his father's ancestors. He remembered that his mother had told him they had settled in Patchogue. Taking note of this information, he decided to weave another chapter into the story he had been telling of his arrival in Sayville. He said to Giorgio, "My mother once told me that some of my father's relatives from Calabria lived in Patchogue. When I saw the signs in Manhattan that told of work in Patchogue, I thought I might find them, but I never made it that far. I got off in Sayville and stayed there. But I think I'd like to go and see if I can find them."

Giorgio thought or a moment, "Ferrara is'a your name. I think I know your relatives. They have a construction business in Patchogue. Two brothers own the business, Carmine and Pasquale. How are they related to you, exactly?"

Philip's heart skipped a beat, but he said, "I really don't know." That wasn't the truth though, he did know. According to the family tree his mother had given him, Carmine was his Great-Great-Grandfather.

"Well let me see what I can'a do."

A month later, on a Sunday afternoon, Philip found himself with Giorgio and Elisabetta on the trolley to Patchogue to meet his own ancestors.

The town was larger than both Sayville and Bayport put together. Even though it was Sunday, the cobblestone streets were congested with traffic, both from wagons and automobiles. The shops that lined the streets were closed, but they kept their striped awnings rolled out to give pedestrians a respite from the afternoon sun. Residents and visitors, dressed in their Sunday best, strolled along the pathways. They walked past Swezey's Department Store in the center of town. Philip could remember going to Swezey's when he was a boy, but the store had closed in 2004 after operating for over 100 years. What he remembered most about the store was the wooden floors that made a creaking sound when you walked on them, and the narrow pathways between racks of clothing and other items for sale. The store was closed now on account of its being Sunday, but he made a mental note to make sure he found the time to revisit the store when it was open.

They walked up Waverly Avenue to a simple white clapboard house with an adequate front porch. Directly across the street from the house was a cemetery. One he was sure they were buried in, in his time. Philip felt nervous prickles up and down his spine as he approached the front door. This all seemed so unreal.

A short, but robust man, with a handlebar moustache answered the door, "Hey'a, Giorgio, paesano, it's a good to see you, my friend."

The men embraced and Giorgio stood back, "Carmine, this here is'a the young man I told you about, Philip Ferrara, your cugino." Philip looked at the man standing before him. He was looking at his own great-great-grandfather.

"Eh! Come'a in'a!"

Philip could hear the commotion in the kitchen as the women finished preparing the Sunday meal. A large wooden table was set up in the dining room, with several smaller tables set up in the small living room. Children ran by chasing each other in a game of tag. One almost knocked Carmine over, "Eh! Outside'a with you!" He yelled at them and opened the front door as the children giggled and ran out.

"Come'a take a seat. Dinner is almost'a ready."

Another man entered the dining room and Carmine introduced him, "This is'a my fratello, my brother, Pasquale. Pasquale, this is'a our cousin, Filippo, here." Philip shook the other man's hand, Pasquale looked just like his younger brother, only a little shorter and with less hair. Philip knew that they were in their mid to late thirties, but they each looked at least ten years older than they were.

Pasquale asked Philip, "How are we related?"

Philip explained, "I don't know exactly, my parents died in a fire in Philadelphia. But I remember my mother telling me that my father's family were in Patchogue and so I wanted to come here to meet you. My own family is all gone now."

Pasquale's face was very expressive and the sorrow that emanated from it was honest and real. "I'm'a so sorry. What was your'a papa's name?"

"Tom Ferrara."

Pasquale's face lit up, "Ah, Gaetano? I didn't know he come'a to America. Ah. Well, now'a you found us." Pasquale was short but powerful and he lifted Philip out of his chair and gave him a big bear hug. "Mia famiglia! Cugino benvenuto!" Everyone was smiling now and Carmine said, "From now on, you call me Zio Carmine and my brother, Zio Pasquale. Si?"

Philip swiped at the real tears that were welling up in his eyes and replied, "Grazie, Zio." It was crazy, but Philip had found his family again. His mother had made sure of it, even though she was one hundred years away.

Philip could hear one of the women calling to the children who were playing outside and soon the rooms were full of people as everyone took a seat. The women entered with trays of pasta and meat cooked in sauce.

Carmine introduced them, "This'a is my wife, Rosa, and that is Pasquale's wife, Francesca." A teenage girl followed them and Pasquale said, "This'a is my daughter, Adelaide." Even though there was no real physical resemblance, something in her expression reminded him of Jenny. "Addie, this is your cousin, Filippo."

One of the children called out from the living room, "Eh, he's got my name!" Carmine smiled and then he spoke, "Filippo, meet Filippo, my oldest son." Philip looked at the boy who was about thirteen and realized that this boy was his own great-grandfather. He took a deep breath to steady his breathing. This was a lot to take in all at once.

From the first spoonful of spaghetti, Philip knew he was home. It was his mother's sauce, the sauce that had been taught to her by her father-in-law, the sauce recipe that had been evidently handed by through the generations. Rosa noticed the tears that welled up in his eyes, "What's a'wrong, ragazzo?" Philip shook his head, "It's the sauce, Ma'am, it's just like my mother made. I miss her."

And with that the woman's plump arms were around him and his face was being crushed against her apron. "Ah, tears of happiness then. No tears for sadness, you found'a your family again."

Philip nodded, but could not make a sound. He was so overwhelmed by all of this.

After dinner, Carmine ushered everyone outside onto the porch. Young Filippo ran to the next door neighbor's house and a moment later, the neighbor arrived and took the camera that Carmine held out to him. The children gathered together, some on the porch, others on the steps, while still others stood on the grass in front of the house. Philip willed his eyes to stay open as the shutter closed on the camera and a photo of this family gathering was eternally captured on film. Philip couldn't help but wonder if his mother had somehow found this photograph in her research and had seen him standing here next to his own great-great-grandfather, Carmine.

# CHAPTER TWENTY-TWO

## JULY 1914

John Ellis Roosevelt stood along an inside wall of the Sayville Opera House. Drink in hand, he watched Gladys dance with her new husband, Fairman. He was thankful that Gladys had recovered from her recent tumble from her horse. After all, this was the second time that she had been thrown. This time she had been riding a green hunter. When she was putting it to a jump, the horse threw her, knocking her unconscious. Jean had been there and had taken her sister home by draping Gladys across the pommel of her saddle. Now he only hoped that Gladys wouldn't experience any anxiety that might affect her ability to compete in future horse shows.

Suddenly, he caught sight of Hannah and Walter on the dance floor. He was not at all happy to see them together. Jean stood by his side, while Edith Hammersly Biscoe, his new bride of six months, stood a few feet away. Edith was speaking amiably with her sister, Lillie, who also happened to be the wife of his brother, Bert. Lillie was Bert's second wife, and his junior by sixteen years. But Edith was thirty-one years younger than John Ellis. Edith's beauty and youth had bewitched him at a time when he had felt hollow after the loss of Nannie. But now, just a few months later, he struggled not to openly show how much he had come to dislike his new bride. He knew now that marrying her had been one of his greatest mistakes. Unfortunately, there was no easy remedy for it.

The string quartet played as Hannah danced with Walt across the floor. It was the annual Grand Ball to benefit the Resolute Hose Company. One of his hands was holding onto her waist, while his other hand was clasped in hers. Walt held her waist possessively, almost hungrily, as he swept her off her feet. His eyes were glued to hers, searching to see if the passion he held in his own eyes was reflected in hers.

John Ellis turned to his daughter and asked, "What is going on with Hannah and young Grayson?"

Jean explained, "He's been traveling abroad and has only just returned to the states. He had shown interest in her a couple of years ago, but then Hannah had got it in her head that he and I were an item. Of course, there was nothing to that. I've cautioned Hannah, and told her that he's not the settling down type. But the girl has her head turned about. It hasn't helped that Alva Vanderbilt Belmont had shared with her that a girl should first marry for money, and then secondly, for love."

The Commodore grumbled, Walt's father had earned the family fortune through railroad investments; however, Walt did not share his father's desire to work. Instead, his fortunes ebbed and flowed with his incessant gambling on horse races and card games, his doting father always there to replenish his bank accounts when necessary.

John Ellis simply said, "I don't like it."

"Father, I've given her the whole story, but I think it only makes him seem even more dashing and dangerous. All this seems to have aroused a sense of excitement in our Hannah."

"How old is young Grayson?"

"Twenty-five, eight years her senior."

The dance ended and Hannah and Walt walked to the side of the room to get a glass of punch.

The Commodore said, "Do me a favor, Jean, and keep an eye on them for me."

"Of course, Father."

Just then, the Commodore's thirty-nine-year-old half-brother, Granville "Rolly" Fortescue, limped toward him and immediately noticed the scowl on his face. Rolly then glanced toward Edith and Lillie, and knowingly observed, "Not bad, a five-month honeymoon to the Holy Land with a woman half your age! How are you doing, Jack?"

Rolly's limp was a result of being wounded at San Juan Hill when he rode with his cousin, Theodore Roosevelt, as a corporal in the Rough Riders. Although his foot had pained him ever since, his injury did not stop him from leading a very full life and he had just recently returned from exploring the interior of Venezuela, while the Ex-President had, himself, been busy exploring the Amazon in Brazil.

Rolly and the Commodore had the same father, Robert Barnwell Roosevelt, Sr., but Rolly's mother, Marion "Minnie" O'Shea, had been Robert's mistress. For propriety's sake, Minnie was said to be "The Widow Fortescue", however, there had never been a Mr. Fortescue. And although Robert didn't publically acknowledged Minnie's children as his biological children, after the death of his wife, Lizzy, Robert married Minnie and legally adopted her children. At his death in 1906, Robert left his property on Lotus Lake to his Fortescue children and the name of the estate was changed to Wildholme.

The Commodore replied, "Ah, well, I could be better."

"Cheer up, old man. At least the stocks are doing well. That wireless they built in West Sayville is really helpful when one has been out of the country for a while. It gives us a chance to catch up on the news before returning."

The Commodore nodded in agreement.

The German company, The Atlantic Communication Company, had erected a wireless tower in West Sayville called the Telefunken to communicate with trans-Atlantic liners keeping their passengers informed of the world's latest news and stock market reports.

Rolly continued, "I dare say, you can travel anywhere and be on top of your business at all times. It's amazing how times are changing."

Thankful for the distraction from his wife, the Commodore agreed, "Yes, indeed, I hear that the tower is in communication 24-hours a day. Just the other day they were able to transmit a lengthy press message all the way to Nauen, just outside of Berlin. That's more than 4,000 miles. And even more remarkable, I hear that replies were promptly received."

Rolly asked, "Did you have a chance to meet Frederick Vander Woude? He's the expert wireless engineer who built the Telefunken plant."

"Yes, I did, on several occasions. He was a friendly chap."

Rolly replied, "I would have liked to have met him as well, but I heard that he's already returned to the fatherland."

John Ellis Roosevelt mused at the achievement, "It boggles the mind; I can only imagine what will come of it next." He downed the rest of his drink. "Excuse me, Rolly. Time for another, can I get you anything?"

"Not for me, Jack." But noticing his brother's dejected demeanor, he followed him to the bar.

While the Commodore ordered another scotch, Rolly asked, "Do you want to talk about it, Jack? Something's got you."

After the Commodore downed another, he said, "I've made a mistake, Rolly. I never should have married her. I was lonely, she was beautiful, but we are very different people and it has become exceedingly obvious that we should not be married to each other."

"Well, man, what's to be done about it now? You've made the commitment. She's Bert's sister-in-law for heaven's sake."

"I know, I know." He shook his head in despair and ordered another drink.

# CHAPTER TWENTY-THREE

1914

Ilsa had just finished washing the family's clothes when Hannah arrived for a visit. A washboard was left leaning against a tub of soapy water that gave off a perfume of its own. She wrung out each garment and then placed them in a wicker basket.

Hannah asked, "Can I help you hang them?"

"I would never turn down an offer for help with the housework." Ilsa replied.

The girls each grabbed a rope handle on the heavy wicker basket and carried the load out to the yard. The clothesline that stretched across the grass was held up on each end by a broken oyster rake. As they fastened the clothes to the line with pins, they chatted about their new lives. Having each just graduated from high school, the girls had taken up jobs as weavers at Bailey's Lace Mill in Patchogue. The mill was the largest employer of young women in the area and was famous for the lace curtains it generated. Although Hannah still yearned to go to college, this was not a good time to leave her father.

Ilsa asked, "What do you think of the rules at the mill?"

The superintendent of the lace mill, Frank E. Guttridge, had just that week, sent two girls home from work to wash their faces and warned the rest of them not to come to work with painted cheeks and whitened noses. Hannah imitated the superintendent as she held up Ilsa's father's suit jacket in front of her.

"Young Ladies!" She cleared her throat and spoke in a deep stern voice, "I will have none of this frivolous nonsense on my factory floor. If you value your jobs here, you will throw away your powder puffs and rouge boxes."

Ilsa laughed at Hannah's impression. "Well, my father would never allow me to paint my cheeks so I suppose I have nothing to worry about."

Hannah nodded, "Yes, but I don't feel that an employer has the right to tell employees that we aren't allowed to wear a little make-up if that is what we desire." She raised her chin in defiance of such injustices.

Ilsa had noticed a sadness in her friend lately, and asked, "Have you seen Philip recently?"

"No. I don't think that Walt would approve."

Ilsa sighed, "Walter Grayson is going to hurt you, Hannah. He makes promises and then doesn't keep them. I know he showers you with gifts and compliments but his character is questionable. Why are you wasting your time with him?" It was Ilsa's fervent belief that Hannah was in love with Philip, not Walt.

Hannah sighed, she had asked that question of herself quite often. She knew she wasn't in love with Walter, but then, she wasn't sure that she knew what love was. And as far as Philip was concerned, he had all but disappeared from her life. It was hard to believe that it had been almost two years since she had first met Philip at Meadow

Croft. She and Philip had been such close friends and had spent so many hours in each other's company in the beginning. But once he moved out of Meadow Croft and started a life of his own, a distance had grown between them that accounted for more than the miles between their homes. She hardly saw him anymore except around The Kensington when she stopped in to see her brother at work. On the other hand, Walt made an effort to seek her out whenever he was in town, and she appreciated that. He still asked her to move to the city with him, but so far, she had refused. She thought that if she was stubborn enough, perhaps he would ask her to marry him. She promised Jean that the only way she would live with Walt, was if it was as his wife.

"Have you told Walt that you are working at the lace mill yet?" Ilsa asked.

Hannah frowned, thinking about how Walt had not even attempted to hide his disgust. The look on his face was still etched on her mind and made her feel . . . less. Less worthy, less valuable, less desired, less respected. Yes, just less. She nodded, "I told him."

"And what did he say?"

Hannah shrugged, "What could he say?"

Ilsa glanced at Hannah with a knowing look. Hannah decided to change the subject, "Harry will be leaving for college in Manhattan soon. We've never been apart before."

Ilsa saw Hannah's frown and attempted to ease the impending loss for her friend, "He will be with my brother, they will keep each other from being homesick and you and I will keep each other from missing them too much. Besides, we have work to keep us busy."

Hannah thought of her father, he needed the extra income since the oyster industry had fallen into a slump since the typhoid scare. Her poor father was spending more time clamming these days to make up for the loss of the oyster business. But his health was not what it used to be, and she worried about him.

When the laundry was hung, the girls took a stroll into town. It was a warm August Saturday afternoon and the streets were filled with shoppers. The girls stopped in at Thornhill's for some ice cream.

When the bell jingled to announce customers, they looked up to see Carl, Harry, and Philip entering. Hannah didn't need any rouge on her cheeks. When she saw Philip, a rosy tint filled her cheeks.

"What are you girls doing here?" Carl asked.

Ilsa replied, "We finished with the laundry and decided to cool off with some ice cream. Would you like to join us?"

"Sure, but we came in to check out the new Nickelodeon we've been hearing about."

The girls slid off their stools and joined the boys around the machine that stood in the corner. Carl put a nickel into the slot and started to crank the handle. He bent over the viewer and watched the moving images within. Ilsa cried, "Let me have a look!" and Carl lifted his head to give his sister a chance.

As each took their turn watching the silent moving images of life on a street in New York City, the scene in front of them played over and over again. Hannah watched the images of horse-drawn wagons competing with trolleys for space on the road. People walked by on the sidewalk in front of a barber shop and grocery store. Finally, a couple walked by, and as the woman stepped over the subway grate, her skirt bellowed up into the air and she quickly pushed it back down.

Hannah stepped away from the Nickelodeon and let Philip have his turn. She wondered what this young man from the future thought of their entertainment. She imagined that it must seem simple to him. From what he had told her about his life during their time at Meadow

Croft, she knew that the future held so many inventions that she could not even fathom. When he lifted his head from the machine, his brown hair fell in front of his eyes, but she saw a look pass across his face in that instant before his eyes were covered. It made her catch her breath.

She hadn't seen him in quite a while and was truly hurt that he had seemed to adjust to his new life so quickly and had left her behind. She felt almost jealous that he didn't need her to help him anymore. His finding a new place to live, new friends, and new interests that had nothing to do with her, left her feeling hurt. But then she felt guilty for wanting him to need her. Wasn't it a testament to his inner strength that he had been able to survive the devastating experience that had brought him into her life? What was wrong with her?

Philip approached her, "How are you, Hannah?"

"I'm fine," was her curt answer. She immediately regretted the way it sounded and softened her next words. "How are you, Philip? I haven't seen you in a while." She lowered her eyes, afraid that he would see how much he had hurt her.

Philip replied, "I've been working a lot, trying to get enough money to start a business."

Hannah found this piece of news exceedingly interesting, "What kind of business?"

"A photography shop."

Hannah impulsively reached out to Philip and grabbed both his arms with her hands, "That's wonderful! I'm so happy for you! I know that is something you would really love to do."

Philip nodded and glanced down at his shoes, "Yeah, and I have you to thank for that. If you hadn't bought me a camera, I wouldn't even have considered the idea. But I think there's a future in it." He smirked as he said those last words. "In the meantime, I've picked up extra hours at the Kensington and I help out Giorgio sometimes at the barrel shop. How about you, Hannah? I've heard that you are working at the lace mill. Do you like it?"

She frowned, "I sew hems on lace curtains. It's not the most exciting job. The foreman makes sure that we girls don't talk to each other; heaven forbid we slow down on a stitch. I honestly can't see myself doing this for long, but it does pay ten dollars a week and that is a big help to father. He hasn't been feeling well lately, and between his own health and the oyster industry being under attack by accusations of typhoid contamination, it's been difficult for him. To top it all off, Harry is leaving for college soon."

"Hannah, do you know Addie Ferrara? She works at the mill."

Hannah knew Addie, she was a pretty petite Italian girl with large dark eyes and delicate hands fit for intricate lace work. Trying to cover her jealousy she responded, "Yes, I do."

Philip's face became animated, "She's my cousin."

Hannah looked at Philip like he was crazy, "What do you mean, she's your cousin?"

"Well, more precisely, she's the daughter of my great-great-granduncle."

Hannah had to close her eyes and try to picture what that genealogical connection would look like on paper. Then she opened them in alarm, "Are you saying you found your own great-great-grandfather?"

Philip's smile broadened, "Yup. I did. Remember that family tree my mother put in my backpack? Well, it showed my connection to my father's family in Patchogue. When I asked Giorgio if he knew them, he said they were old friends. So he brought me over to meet him and I met the whole family. I made up a story that my father was a distant cousin of theirs and they seem to actually have had a cousin named Gaetano, which is Thomas in Italian, and so they assumed I was his son. They've kind of taken me under their wing. Honestly, it's been great."

"Wow, Philip, I'm so happy for you." Her heart genuinely lifted for him. He had found his own family. She didn't feel as betrayed anymore if he was spending time with them.

When Hannah left the group at Thornhill's, she walked home thinking about her future. She saw a sign posted to the wall of 14 South Main Street and read it, "Soon to be home of the first Sayville Library and Sayville Suffrage Club. To be established in November 1914. Joan Hoag, Sayville Chapter of the Equal Suffrage Association." Hannah decided it was time for her to get involved with this organization.

# CHAPTER TWENTY-FOUR

As Philip placed the dishes in front of the men seated in the dining room of The Kensington Hotel, he heard a bit of the conversation that caused him concern. A couple of years ago, he had been amused as the town excitedly awaited the first transmission from the West Sayville tower of the Telefunken. Now, it was becoming clear to him that there was something more sinister afoot.

The company had erected a wireless transmitter tower in 1912 to broadcast primarily to ships that were crossing the Atlantic. It served several purposes: to communicate with the Nauen Wireless Tower in Germany, to keep the wealthy businessmen abreast of the news and stock market, to receive S.O.S. messages, and for ships to report their positions and estimated times of arrival at port. The ability to transmit wirelessly was applauded and seen as a feat of astronomical proportion. Communication industries were in their infancy and Philip understood that this new technology would one day lead to radios, televisions, and computers in the homes of ordinary American citizens.

But for now, in 1915, there was a war in Europe; and Germany was at the center of that war. Britain had been able to cut the underwater cable that connected communication between Germany and the United States, and now the only way to send messages across the ocean was through the wireless towers. Philip knew that no matter how much President Woodrow Wilson might want to keep America out of that war, it was only a matter of time before the United States would be shipping soldiers out to fight and Germany would become their enemy.

Justice Daniel D. White lived at The Kensington Hotel and Philip had often engaged in conversation with this man who he had come to admire. Justice White was sitting with Francis Hoag, the editor of The Suffolk County News, when Philip heard Justice White say, "Francis, you know the two U.S. Navy radio operators who have been assigned to monitor messages sent from the station, Cogswell and Cuzzens? Well, you will remember that Cuzzens was electrocuted in April while trying to photograph the additional towers that were just erected?"

Hoag replied, "Sure, I do. Luckily, he still had one foot on the ground when electricity shot into the tower he was about to climb. Although he was thrown twenty feet away, it could have been even worse. He was unconscious for six hours and was burned quite severely."

Justice White nodded, "For some reason, Cogswell has been unable to remain at the plant, and now, even though Cuzzens has recovered, he's not physically able to monitor the messages going in and out of the tower around the clock. I have a feeling that the electrocution was not an accident. I see the Germans, here at the Kensington, filling Cuzzens with alcohol till he is unfit to man his post at all."

Hoag responded, "Marconi's patent infringement trial has just started in the city. He's trying to get the Sayville wireless shut down. He says that the technology it uses is an infringement on his own patent. Now, I've heard that Germany is sending over some heavy hitters to testify in that trial."

Justice White concluded, "Soon they will have three 500 foot towers, and it is already one of the most powerful wireless plants in the world. Something is going on at that plant that doesn't smell right."

Philip felt ill at ease; the wireless plant was guarded by burly German men with rifles and surrounded by an electrified fence. No one got inside without permission. Cogswell and Cuzzens were the only deterrent to whatever the Germans were doing, and it seemed that they were not deterring anything at the moment. Try as he may, he could not recall ever learning about the wireless tower in school or even in History Club.

That night he tossed and turned, his mind leaping to conspiracy theories that kept interrupting his sleep. The following morning, Philip came down the stairs and heard Elisabetta humming in the kitchen.

"Philip, is that'a you? Come in'a, I made you a nice'a breakfast."

She smiled as he entered the kitchen and directed, "Mangia."

The sun was shining, and that, along with a good meal of eggs and sausage improved his mood considerably. "Where's Giorgio?"

"He's gone to work'a early; he has a busy day today."

Philip noticed the newspaper that Giorgio had discarded after eating his own breakfast earlier that morning. Across the table, Philip saw the headline on the South Side Signal, *"Steamer Lusitania Hit by Submarine."* Philip felt a chill run down his spine as he pulled the weekly Babylon newspaper closer to read the full article.

*"Wireless dispatches sent out by the English steamer, Lusitania, about 2:23 o'clock this afternoon, told of her having been struck by a torpedo fired by a German submarine off the Irish coast. There were 1,253*

*passengers on board, including many Americans. Steamships responded to the Lusitania's wireless calls, and it is believed all on board were saved. The vessel sunk shortly afterward."*

Aloud, Philip said, "No, that's not right."

"What's not right, caro mio?" Elisabetta asked.

"Uh, it says here that the Lusitania was hit by a German submarine earlier today." He looked confused.

"Ah, well, is it the timing that has'a you confused? It is hours earlier there in England, you'a know. When we hear'a something here, it has already'a happened there. You'a understand? Capiche?"

"No, uh, yes, but uh, it says, 'all were saved'."

"Yes, isn't that good'a news?"

"Uh, yeah, sure." But Philip knew better. And soon the newspapers did too.

Two days later, the Sunday edition of The Brooklyn Daily Eagle put the number of survivors at 645, and the number lost at sea at 1,200, including 128 U.S. citizens. A month later word was going around that a message sent to Germany from West Sayville was intercepted and decoded and then sent to Washington D.C. The message was reported to have said, "Get the Lucy," and then gave the coordinates of where the Lusitania was in the Atlantic Ocean.

Another month later, Philip sat in his bedroom reading an article in The Suffolk County News. A reporter from the New York Tribune, who spoke fluent German, had rented a room at The Kensington Hotel and pretended to be interested in renting a summer cottage. He spoke at great length with Dr. Jonathan Zenneck, the German Wireless expert, who denied that any coded messages were being sent or received through the West Sayville Wireless Station.

The reporter wrote, *"Dr. Zenneck is an instructor at the Institute of Technology in Munich. As a captain of the marines, Dr. Zenneck served through the German campaign in Belgium and was at the front when he was recalled and sent here to testify for the Atlantic Communications Company in defense of the patent suit brought by the Marconi Company. Along with Zenneck, the Germans sent Mr. Behrendt to West Sayville. Behrendt is an engineer of the German army who has been aiding in the installation of the new towers."*

The reporter went on to say, *"When I asked the residents of Sayville about Dr. Zenneck's claims of innocence and insistence that he and Mr. Behrendt work for an American company, the residents responded with a laugh, 'Maybe it is; but they are all Germans or German-Americans out there.' The residents point out also that if the company is American owned, it is odd that the German government should have recalled two men from the battle line in Belgium and allowed them to come to America for the sole benefit of the company."*

Philip folded the newspaper and grabbed his camera. He softly closed his bedroom door behind him, knowing that Elisabetta wasn't feeling well and that she was resting in her living room chair. He quietly descended the stairs and as he passed by her, he looked at her kind face, and realized how attached he had become to her. She had taken some of his loneliness away by stepping into the role of substitute mother, with her arms wide open.

When he arrived at the wireless plant, he saw the crowd that had already gathered. Standing with his back to the railroad tracks, he could imagine the Cherry Avenue field in front of him where he had often played soccer as a boy. Instead of the soccer field, there was a collection of several small buildings in the shadow of three giant towers. The base of each metal tower came to a point or fulcrum, held up by what looked to him to be concrete supports. Philip held his camera up to his eyes and took a photo. The United States Navy had just sent soldiers to guard the towers and new radiomen to oversee the messages going in and out of the station so that messages could be observed 24-hours a day. As he took another photo, he thought, "History, in my own town. I can't let this be forgotten."

# CHAPTER TWENTY-FIVE

1915

Alva Vanderbilt Belmont took Hannah's hand and said, "Dear, everyone wants to be liked, but in an attempt to be liked by everyone, don't forfeit your true self. If you want to stand up for something, then there are going to be people who will disagree with you and even dislike you. To be disliked for who you are, is better than to be liked for who you aren't."

The recently formed Sayville Suffrage Club, consisting of Margaret Stone, Belle De Graaf Otto, Ida Gillette, Dorothy Blayney, Hannah, Lena Hoag and her daughter, Jane, met in the Village Improvement Society room of the Library. Hannah admired all of these women who surrounded her now and she wondered how she had gotten to this place. She reminded herself that it all started when she began writing articles about the girls who worked in the lace mill for the Suffolk County News. She wrote articles to bring awareness to the community of the dangers that the girls faced on the factory floor. She wrote about the desperation of young girls who were forced to work long hours to support their families. One article was about two girls who tried to escape their dismal life and ran away together to

Pennsylvania only to be brought back against their will. Another, about a girl who found her situation so dire that she had attempted to take her own life by swallowing bicarbonate of mercury. In these articles, Hannah wrote about the struggles young working women faced in a society that wouldn't recognize them as intelligent human beings who should be able to make their own decisions. Instead, fathers, husbands, and the men in their lives, including the foreman on the job, dictated what they could and could not do, causing them to take drastic measures. These articles eventually led to articles about women's rights, especially the right to vote, in order for women to have a say in determining the future of their own country. At the moment, the war in Europe was inching closer to involving the United States, and she believed, above all, that women should have a voice in whether America should enter this war.

When Alva saw these articles, she remembered the girl she had met at Meadow Croft and made a trip to Sayville to meet with her once again. Alva recognized talent when she saw it, and this girl had a way with words that attracted attention. The one thing that the suffrage movement needed more than anything else, was attention. Somehow, over the past year, Hannah had become the "voice" of the local working girl in Suffolk County. And so now, Alva had traveled to Sayville to join the women at their monthly meeting of the Sayville Suffrage Club and to help elevate Hannah's participation in their cause.

Hannah replied, "I know this, but Mrs. Belmont, this is such a difficult path. I've lost friends and family; I've lost the respect of people in my town. When I walk down the street, I wonder what people are saying about me. They whisper. The other day, a man I have known my whole life approached me and he spit at me!" Tears filled her eyes.

Alva softened her voice, "I have seen women walk hundreds of miles with blistered feet for this cause. I have seen women pelted with stones and cursed as they march in parades. I have seen women who have been arrested and bravely entered into hunger strikes in order to make their voices heard. I've seen those same women force fed with tubes shoved down their noses when they refused to bend on their principles. And you are afraid of spit?

Whenever you stand and point a finger, there will be three fingers pointed back at you. But if you don't stand to point that finger, things will never change. Will you accept a world where not only you, but someday, your daughters, will continue to be ruled by the men in their lives, both personally and publicly? If not, then you must stand with your sisters here," she gestured to the women gathered on the porch, "for you have the ear of the young women, you have the skill to persuade with your writing, you have the support of working women who do not see themselves in me. To them I represent the unattainable, they see me as privileged, they see me as bored old woman in search of a cause, but they see you as they see themselves. That makes you invaluable to this movement."

Hannah listened to this woman who she admired so greatly and felt her resolve strengthen. Where before she had felt weak, now she felt strong. Where she had felt undecided, now she felt defined. Where she had felt frightened, now she felt brave.

Alva continued, "We want you to keep writing. To cover the local events, to put a human face on the sacrifices that are being made and to shine a light on the travesties that are being played out in local work places and on local streets. Will you do that for us?"

Hannah saw the faith that Alva had in her. Alva was unshakeable, she was a woman who in spite of the opposition against her, had continued to push forward for the rights of women. There were many who would describe her as a brash and difficult woman. But in reality, they feared her because she was a woman of means who could speak for herself and because, as such, she was unstoppable.

"Yes, I will do it."

The women around her applauded.

Ida Gillette spoke next, "Next Monday we will be hosting the largest gathering of supporters for our cause at the Opera House and will be honored to have the distinguished, Dr. Katherine B. Davis, as our guest speaker." The women all sat straighter and proudly nodded their heads. For Hannah's benefit, Ida explained further, "Dr. Davis is a member of New York's Mayor Mitchel's administration and the Commissioner of Corrections of the City of New York. She draws a respectable annual salary of $8,500 for a position in which she administers the affairs of fourteen institutions with thousands of inmates." She paused as the women clapped their hands. "Now, Margaret, you are in charge of the procession that will meet Dr. Davis at the train station. Please let us know what you have planned."

Margaret stood and faced the group, "I have enlisted the fife and drum corps of the Uniform Rank to lead us as we march down Main Street and up to the station. We will gather people along the way. Everyone should gather in front of the Methodist Episcopal Church at 6 p.m. and we will march from there. After we have collected her from the train station, we will then escort her to the Opera House."

Ida took over once again, "Thank you, Margaret. The panel seated on the stage will include a number of local clergymen, politicians, and other prominent ladies and gentlemen from the area. And Belle, will open the meeting with a song, followed by a blessing offered by Reverend H. H. Mower, pastor of the M.E. Church, and then Judge Arrington H. Carman, of Patchogue, will present opening remarks to the assembly. Lena will then introduce our honored guest. Finally, the evening will be concluded with another song sung by Belle. Dorothy, do we have any idea of how many we can expect to attend the assembly?"

Dorothy rose, "All I can say is we are expecting to fill the Opera House with the largest crowd it has seen in some time. We have sold well over three hundred tickets so far and have raised quite a bit of money for the cause."

Ida smiled, "Thank you, Dorothy. We have arranged for Dr. Davis to have a room reserved for her at the Hotel Kensington for the night. She must board a train bound for the city early the next morning to attend a Budget Committee of the New York City Board of Alderman. We are only a month away from state elections and the New York Suffrage Amendment #2 will be on the ballot. The right of women to vote in New York hangs in the balance."

A week later, the Opera House was packed with people. Hannah sat in the audience and watched as Dr. Davis addressed the assembly. Dr. Davis spoke about her own experiences and about her remarkable career. In conclusion, she said, "I have been vilified by my opponents because I am a woman and because I believe women to be equal to men. I have had to work harder and longer then my male counterparts to rise to my current position. But I do not regret a moment of my struggle. The challenges I have had to meet and exceed, have made me stronger and smarter and more determined than ever to succeed. As women, we have been held back for far too long. We were told to wait while the right to vote was given to freed men after the Civil War, we will not wait any longer. This battle cannot be won by women alone, it is our men who will go to the voting booths in November and decide our destiny. I implore you, the open-minded men in this assembly, to vote to give us the right to stand beside you and vote for ourselves."

Hannah was overwhelmed by this speech. Dr. Davis was an unassuming woman with kind eyes, about the age of Hannah's own parents. When Hannah reached her hand out to shake Dr. Davis' hand as she passed down the center aisle of the Opera House, the woman held on to Hannah's hand for a moment longer than was usual. Hannah looked down at the woman who only came up to her chin. Dr. Davis patted Hannah's hand and said, "I've heard great things about you, young lady." Then she winked at Hannah and added, "Make me proud." Before letting go of Hannah's hand, Dr. Davis squeezed it tightly and Hannah squared her own shoulders, straightened her back, and stood taller than ever.

On November 2, 1915, the New York Suffrage, Amendment #2, was defeated with 748,332 votes against and 553,348 votes for.

A week later, Hannah received a letter from Walt.

*Dearest Hannah,*

*I am writing to you to let you know that I have become engaged to the daughter of my father's business partner. She is a woman of propriety, who respects the natural roles of men and women.*

*Your stubborn campaign to recruit the working women of America to follow your cause has soured me on any future I may have considered with you. I warn you, you are playing a dangerous game and are completely destroying any prospects you may have once had for a better life. I pray that someday you will see the error of your ways.*

*Walt*

# CHAPTER TWENTY-SIX

## 1916

Hannah expertly guided the sail boat across the bay as Philip watched. In his previous life, he had been to Fire Island many times by ferry, and had even manned a sailboat when he was a young student at the Wet Pants Sailing Club which was located at the foot of Foster Avenue. But he was by no means the sailor that Hannah was, and so he contented himself with observing her ability to command the sail.

If anyone had been there to paint the scene, he figured they would have scratched their head to see a girl dressed in white with a straw hat on her head, guiding the boat, as the young man relaxed in his seat. It was 1916, and he realized that Hannah was not your normal girl for her time. It felt good to get away from the hamlet for a little while. A virus epidemic had hit Sayville hard and as a result, people had stopped congregating together. Even the Suffrage movement that Hannah had become so passionate about was stalled.

They took this opportunity to spend some time together, something that they hadn't done enough of lately. When they reached the island, Philip jumped out into the water to tie the boat to a stake in the sand that had been put there for that purpose. He lifted Hannah into his arms and carried her to the shore.

Hannah opened her umbrella to protect herself from the worst of the late afternoon sun and walked to the ocean to look out at the great expanse of blue. The island was deserted, only the two of them stood together on the beach. Philip thought about asking her if he could kiss her, but as always, his fear that it would not be welcomed, stopped him from doing so. Instead Philip asked, "I've always wondered, why was it named Fire Island?"

Hannah explained, "Fire Island isn't just one island. Long ago, there were more islands, but the surf has since filled in the inlets with sand and now there are only two islands that make up Fire Island. There are old maps calling it Fire Islands, some think it was supposed to be 'Five Islands', but perhaps, the original name was written incorrectly by the cartographers as 'Fire'. It is also possible that it was known to the natives as 'Fire' Island long before the name was ever written down on any map. There is a legend that at one time, the island was consumed in smoldering fires that lasted for years in duration so that the Indians could safely guide themselves across the bay at night. And thus, the name 'Fire Island' was given to it. But the truth is, no one knows for sure how it got the name."

Hannah showed Philip how to collect clams and, following her instructions, he built a fire to bake them. She had spread a blanket on the sand and they sat together talking about how their lives had changed since first they met.

Philip asked her, "How are things going at the lace mill?"

She replied, "I am worried that I will lose my job. I know my father needs the money. But it has been brought to the attention of Mr. Bailey, the owner of the mill, that I've been writing articles about the girls who work there and their situation. I'm sure he doesn't like what I'm saying in those articles."

"So why don't you stop writing them?" Philip asked.

She looked at him with disappointment, "Philip, I thought of all men, *you* would understand. The conditions under which these girls work need to improve. Women need to be able to speak up about the lack of safety in the workplace and the lack of say in how things are run. If I don't speak up, who will?"

Philip was embarrassed, "I'm sorry, Hannah. You're right. I just don't want to see you hurt by any of this."

His eyes were kind and Hannah felt the strength of a special bond that they shared so easily. She wished they could spend more time together, but her long working hours made free time hard to find. Still, theirs was the type of friendship that didn't require them to be together daily. Each time they saw each other, they were able to pick up where they had left off. That feeling of mutual understanding was comforting. There were times when she wished for more than just friendship, but somehow she sensed that he wasn't quite ready, and so she waited.

After spending the afternoon and evening together on the beach, the campfire had burned low and Philip poured a bucket of seawater over the remaining embers. He shoveled some sand on top, to be sure, and Hannah picked up their belongings ready to head home. But then, without the light from the fire, Philip looked at the dark sky filled with stars and exclaimed, "Those are more stars then I've ever seen. In my time, there are too many electric lights brightening the sky at night. Before we go Hannah, tell me about the stars." She hesitated and instead said, "Don't you think we should be going. It's getting late."

But Philip reasoned with her, "It's already dark, waiting a little longer won't matter at this point."

They lay back on the sand and stared up at the brilliant sky. Hannah pointed in the moonlight. "There is Orion, it is the easiest constellation to find, it is supposed to be the image of a hunter. You see the three stars in a line, they make up Orion's belt. And the stars hanging off of his belt make up his sword. Look up and you will see a red star on the right shoulder of the hunter. That is the star, Betelgeuse, a red super-giant. The brightest star appears where the hunter's right knee would be, that star is a blue-white star named Rigel. Now follow Orion's belt toward the horizon. Orion's belt points to the star Sirius, which is the brightest star in the sky. Sirius is part of the constellation, Canis Major, or the Great Dog. The only objects in the night sky that are brighter than Sirius, are the moon and the planets Venus, Jupiter, and Mars."

Philip pointed, "I can see the Big Dipper over there."

Hannah explained, "The Big Dipper is part of the Ursa Major constellation, known as the Great Bear. The handle of the dipper is the bear's tale. The cup of the Big Dipper points to Polaris, but we know it as the North Star. Polaris is the last star in the handle of the Little Dipper. The Little Dipper is part of the constellation Ursa Minor, or the Little Bear."

Philip asked, "What is your favorite constellation, Hannah?"

"Cassiopeia. It's easy to find because the stars make a giant W shape. It is named for a famous queen in Greek mythology, who boasted that both she and her daughter, Andromeda, were more beautiful than the daughters of the sea god, Nereus. As a result, Poseidon, sent floods to her lands. Cassiopeia chained Andromeda to a rock by the sea as a sacrifice to Cetus, the sea monster, in order to appease the gods. But Perseus managed to free her and kill the sea monster. Perseus, the half-god, half-human son of Zeus, then married Andromeda. But Poseidon was still angry, so he tied Cassiopeia to a chair and placed her in the heavens to revolve upside down in the sky for eternity."

Philip was impressed with her knowledge of the stars. He also understood that, although his modern education included things she could not imagine, in Hannah's time, education was more focused on the arts, civics, literature, history, languages and stories that had been passed down through generations.

As the night sky deepened, they boarded the sailboat once again, and Hannah guided them back to Brown's River. After helping her to dock the sailboat, Philip felt the strangeness of the situation creep over him once again. He was standing outside of his own house, but it wasn't his house. He missed his family. He missed home. His heart ached. He said goodnight to Hannah and began the twenty-minute walk to his little room in Giorgio and Elisabetta's house. The only light to guide him, came from the stars.

# CHAPTER TWENTY-SEVEN

### 1916

Hannah heard the scream above the roar of the sewing machines. It was a sound unlike any she had ever heard. She dropped the lace she was working on and stood to see where the scream had come from. Philip's cousin, Addie, was standing beside the thread cutting machine. The purpose of the machine was to wind thread onto giant bobbins, and once the bobbins were filled, a sharp flat blade was released to cut the thread. A girl named Gladys had fainted and was lying on the floor beside Addie. Men soon surrounded Addie, and Hannah could no longer see what was happening. Hannah walked toward them as if in a dream, the other women around her falling silent.

As the men parted for her, she saw that Addie had crumbled to the floor. Her bloodied hand, or rather, what was left of it, had been cut and mangled by the blade. Addie's face was pale and her body was trembling. By the time the ambulance arrived, Addie was barely conscious.

That night, Hannah sat at her writing desk with Sage resting against her leg. The dog sensed that something was wrong and she nuzzled

Hannah's ankle, trying to get a reaction. Hannah reached down to pet Sage's silky fur. The contact helped calm both her and her canine companion. Armed with her fountain pen, she wrote about the accident at the mill and the lack of safety measures that were in place. She wrote about the girls who were put at risk and the callous attitude of their employer. If before she had held back a portion of her anger, this time, she gave it free rein. When the article appeared in the Suffolk County News the following week, Hannah achieved a recognition for her reporting unlike any she had received before. Alva Belmont sent her a note congratulating her on her eloquent and persuasive writing. This was followed by invitations to appear and speak at local clubs and organizations. At nineteen years of age, Hannah was a force to be reckoned with.

Philip read her article as he sat at the kitchen table.

*"The changes that have taken place in the past five years since the tragedy at the Triangle Shirtwaist Factory, have not gone far enough. How can we expect justice, when the factory owners of that said factory, Isaac Harris and Max Blanck, were found not guilty of manslaughter in the deaths of 145 workers? It is now the responsibility of The Factory Investigating Commission to ensure that each and every employee in factories across our nation is both protected and valued.*

*However, today a young woman by the name of, Addie Ferrara, lost her hand in an accident at our local lace mill. I ask you, why are there not more measures put in place and safety mechanisms installed on the machines that we work on daily? Whose responsibility is it to keep these young women safe? The government's? The employer's? The foreman's? Or is it yours and mine? We need better laws, more enforcement, and more humanity all around!"*

When Philip read the news article that Hannah had written, he was immediately alarmed for Addie's sake. He knew that an injury like Addie had sustained could lead to an infection and death without antibiotics. He lowered the paper to the kitchen table asked, "Elisabetta, did you hear what happened to Addie at the lace mill?"

Elisabetta nodded, "The poor'a girl is suffering terribly. They say'a she will not live'a long. The poison is in'a her now."

He wondered why no one had told him about this accident. Why did he have to read about it in the newspaper? Immediately, he returned to his bedroom and rummaging through his old backpack, he found what he was looking for, a bottle of Penicillin. A moment later, he was out the door and caught the trolley to Patchogue. When he was finally face-to-face with Addie's father, Pasquale, he held the bottle out to him. "Please, Pasquale, don't ask me about where I got this. But these pills will help Addie. Give her two now and then one tonight, tomorrow give her one in the morning and one at night. You see, there are directions on the label. Keep giving them to her until the bottle runs out."

Pasquale looked at the unusual brown plastic bottle. He had never seen a bottle like it before in his life. His eyes met Philip's once again and he nodded. There was something odd about this cousin of his, but if this bottle could help his daughter, he would ask no questions. Philip followed Pasquale up the stairs to Addie's bedroom. The girl was pale and a terrible aroma emanated from her wounded hand. The telltale signs of blood poisoning were evident as blue and red lines were visible traveling up her arm. Barely conscious, the girl swallowed the first two pills and Philip took a deep sigh of relief. Pasquale looked from his daughter to his cousin and said, "If this does not work, I will lose my daughter."

Philip replied, "It will give her a chance."

A week later, Pasquale arrived at Giorgio's house and knocked on the door. When Philip answered, Pasquale fell to his knees. He kissed Philip's shoes and wept with gratitude. "She lives. The fever has passed, the wound is healing, I am forever grateful to you. You saved my daughter's life."

Philip knelt beside Pasquale, "I am so glad. Thank you, cousin, for trusting me."

Pasquale embraced Philip and the two held each other until Pasquale patted Philip's back and said, "I don't know where you are really from, my cousin. But I know you are my flesh and blood. No matter what your true story is, we are family."

Philip assured him, "We *are* family. That *is* the truth, I swear it."

In December, Jean Roosevelt invited Hannah to dinner at their New York City mansion. This was her first visit to the beautiful brownstone, and she admired the paintings on the walls. Some were of the Roosevelt family, while others were surely paintings by famous artists about whom Hannah knew nothing. Hannah had never before been invited to their Manhattan residence.

As Hannah had continued to write articles about the plight of the working woman, Jean and Gladys had found a new respect for their young friend. Gladys said, "You have become a brave voice for the women's movement and are helping to shed light on the hardships of the working class. In doing so, you are gaining a following of influential women in the Suffrage movement. You have come a long way from the little girl we once knew. We are so proud of you, Hannah!"

John Ellis Roosevelt listened as the young women spoke of Hannah's accomplishments, but remained silent. Hannah noticed this and began to worry that he was unhappy with her actions.

Jean placed a hand on his arm and said, "Father, what do you think of our little Hannah?"

He reflected for a moment, trying to sort out his feelings. The truth was he was ashamed. Not of Hannah, but of himself. He cleared his throat and announced, "Hannah, you have become someone I admire very much. You bravely stand up to those who would discredit you. This world will be a better place when women like you have the right to vote. After all, you have proven to be a far better example of integrity than I have been of late."

Then turning his attention to Jean and Gladys, he continued, "My dear daughters, I am afraid I owe you an apology. I have put you through an ordeal over the past few years. I want you to know how sorry I am. I admit, I allowed my loneliness to bring me into a poisonous relationship with Edith. Unfortunately, that reckless decision to marry her has caused us all a great deal of embarrassment. The courts have made their decision and the divorce is now final. Edith has been awarded a handsome sum, plus a continued monthly alimony of $400. But the discord between us has also led to a division between my brother, Bert, and myself. He has even erected a fence between our properties in Sayville and this has divided our family to a point which appears to be irreconcilable. To put it bluntly, I have been a perfect ass. But what has been done, has been done. We must look forward and I must try to be a better example for you in the future."

Jean stood and wrapped her arms around her father, "It's all right, Father. None of us is perfect. But admitting your mistakes takes a bigger man than one who chooses not to acknowledge them."

Gladys wiped away a tear and said, "Perhaps less Scotch would be a good beginning."

The Commodore nodded, "Well said, my dear. Too much alcohol does tend to lead to undesired consequences."

Jean remarked, "And this is why the Women's Suffrage movement wishes to make alcohol illegal."

But on this, her father disagreed, "Well now, restraint is one thing, prohibition is quite another."

# CHAPTER TWENTY-EIGHT

## 1917

Andrew held onto the door when he entered, preventing the winds from blowing it off its hinges. The end of February was like that, one day could be bright and sunny, while the next was dark and blustery. Gran and Hannah sat at the kitchen table warming their bellies on Gran's Irish stew. Andrew took off his coat and hung his hat before joining them. His face was set in a frown and his eyes were shaded with worry. Before he even lifted his spoon he looked around the table and said, "Something has happened. I think we will have to enter the war now."

The women gave him their full attention as he continued, "I know President Wilson was reelected last year on the premise that he had previously kept us out of the war. But he's going to have to change his tune now. You all know Harry's friend, Charles Richter? Well he works at the Telefunken and he told me something today that is about to be all over the papers. It seems that the German Foreign Secretary, Arthur Zimmermann, sent a telegram to the German Minister in Mexico in January. This telegram was intercepted by three wireless stations, one of those locations was our own in West Sayville. It was sent in code and it took a while for it to be deciphered, but earlier this month, some British cryptographers were able to discover the true message. It was then sent to Washington and the contents of the telegram are expected to hit the newspapers tomorrow."

Hannah asked, "What did it say?"

"The Germans are promising Mexico that if they side with Germany against the United States when we enter the war, then they will return Texas, New Mexico, and Arizona to them. It's a direct threat against us. Wilson can't just look the other way now."

Gran nodded, "That, along with the increased submarine attacks, it can't be ignored."

Andrew continued, "There's more. Charles said that Batterman, Stoye, Schleenvolgth, and Krebbs have all been moved to Telefunken's New York City office. The station is now being fully run by the U. S. Navy crew. And there is word that, as we speak, a Telefunken wireless station is being built in Mexico and that all the German engineers from West Sayville are going to be sent south of the border to man that station as soon as it's ready."

Gran lifted Sage onto her lap and let the dog lick her fingers. "War." Gran shook her head. "Thank goodness Harry is at college. They can't take him as long as he's enrolled."

Over the next few weeks, Sayville and the rest of America prepared for what was surely to come. Finally, on April 6, 1917, President Wilson declared war on Germany.

The Sayville Suffrage club met in late April. Ida Gillette said, "As we were forced to do during the Civil War, we will once again have to set aside our fight for now. We have been successful in obtaining the right to vote for New York women, but the fight to get Congress to approve the 19th Amendment will have to wait until after this war is won."

# CHAPTER TWENTY-NINE

## 1918

Philip read Andrew Kennedy's obituary. The owner of the Kensington Hotel, a hotel known as "one of the best in the country," had died of pleurisy and pneumonia on April 1, 1918, just three days after falling ill. He was 58 years old and had been predeceased by his wife, Emma, three years earlier.

Philip looked long and hard at the cause of death and wondered if, just maybe, it was a harbinger of things to come. After all, it was 1918, and Philip knew that it was the year of The Great Influenza Epidemic. Philip sat in his bedroom and counted the money he had saved over the years. It was time for a change in his life.

He remembered his mother's tarot card reading. She had said that although there were forces working against him, there would also be an unfolding sense of his part and purpose in the world. Everything was somehow interrelated to each other. She had said that until he had figured it out, he would feel like he was walking in the dark. He looked out his window and saw a poster in the store across the street from Giorgio's house. The poster said, "IF THE CAP FITS YOU, JOIN THE ARMY TO-DAY." He had always loved to learn about

WW2, but his knowledge of WW1 was limited. This was his chance to learn it, firsthand.

Philip arrived at Camp Upton in the late spring of 1918. He was amused by the memory of having been there before. When he was a child, it had been the location of Brookhaven National Laboratory. His fourth-grade science fair experiment on sound decibels had won at Sunrise Drive Elementary School. He had been proud to have it move on to the island-wide competition at Brookhaven. During that competition, he learned that the lab had been built on the grounds of the old U.S. Army Camp Upton in Yaphank.

All that he had knew about this war was that the sinking of the Lusitania had something to do with bringing the U.S. into the war, and that once the U.S. had entered the fray, the war was near its end. Of course, now he was better informed. But that didn't change the fact that the Yankees, or the Doughboys, as they were called, had saved the world, and he wanted to be a part of that. Besides, he had his trusty little Kodak 2a Brownie folding bellows camera, and he intended to take some of those photos that had made their mark on history.

Now, in the July heat, Philip stood at attention in a line of young men and listened as Commanding Officer, Major General Franklin Bell, introduced Private Irving Berlin to the men. "This young man has agreed to put together a show for all of you here at Camp Upton. This show will raise money for a community building to be built on the camp grounds." Philip kept his head facing forward but looked sideways to see the private whom the Major was addressing. Philip knew that name, Irving Berlin. After all, Philip had played the trumpet in the school band and they had played the songs that this man had written. He was the man who wrote *White Christmas* and *God Bless America*. He felt a chill run up and down his spine. This was surreal.

Harold Kowalski was his bunk mate, Harold had the upper bunk and Philip had the lower one. They were both training to become medics in the 308th Medical Detachment. Philip thought that his knowledge of injuries and illnesses, although not extensive, was probably an advantage to him in this time before the discovery of antibiotics.

Harold asked Philip, "Hey, Flash, what's up with these guys dressing like women for the show? I mean, why can't we have some real dames to look at?"

Everyone in camp had a nickname, and the men had taken to calling Philip, *Flash*, because he always had a camera in his hands.

Philip replied, "It's called humor, Stilts." Harold had long skinny legs and so, of course, he had been christened Stilts.

The guys who had come from the city had been in enemy gangs from the lower east side of Manhattan and from the docks of Brooklyn, but now they were sharing the same barracks. They were Irish, Polish, Italian, and Jews all living together. These city boys were immigrants and the sons of immigrants. They were raised in a world that was violent, desperate, and yet it was one that prized a fraternal order. And with the enemy established in Europe, these ragtag boys had somehow become united.

# CHAPTER THIRTY

JULY 1918

Ilsa pleaded with her mother, "Please, don't let father make me marry Will Amundsen. I don't love him."

Cornelia looked at her daughter, and although she worried that Ilsa might be right, she knew her duty as a mother, "You will come to love him in time. Your father thinks he is a good match. Will is doing well as a bayman and he comes from a good Dutch family."

Ilsa hung her head as she fought back the tears and whispered once again, "But I don't love him now."

Just then, Horace Hendricks walked into the house. He saw that his wife and daughter were consumed in a serious conversation, but there were more important matters at hand, "We just got word that the U. S. Armored Cruiser San Diego is sinking off of Point o'Woods. Word is that it was hit by a U-boat. I'm heading over to Fire Island now. Walter Suydam and Bert Roosevelt are asking for all boats to come help ferry the survivors back to the Naval Reserve Base in West Sayville."

At the beginning of the war, Navy Department Lieutenant Robert B. Roosevelt had been given command of the Naval Reserve Base No. 5, along with Lieutenant Walter L. Suydam, Jr. They had converted their yachts into naval ships for the purpose of patrolling the waters off the south shore of Long Island. But now, more help was needed. The cruiser's crew numbered over 1,200 men. Word went out requesting help from everyone in the area who had a boat. Thankfully, the weather was clear and the sea was calm.

Horace and Will set out in Horace's oyster sloop. When they came upon the scene, they saw men being unloaded from lifeboats onto the shore of Fire Island. Other sailors, who had been holding onto debris from the sunken ship, had been rescued by oil tankers and freighters, and they were being taken directly to the New York City Naval Yard.

When all was done, twenty-five sailors and six officers had landed in lifeboats on Point o' Woods. Between the Coast Guard and the local residents, the men were provided clothing and food, and then transported by various boats to the local Naval Base.

Horace and Will were able to take three men from Fire Island to the West Sayville docks. While transporting them, one of the seaman explained, "Captain Christy said it was a torpedo. We returned fire on what looked like a periscope, but I don't think we hit it, and then we ran out of time."

Will asked, "When did this happen? How long did it take for the cruiser to sink?"

"The explosion happened amidships, around eleven hundred hours. Within a half hour, the ship was in the soup. We know that there are German mines in the waters off Long Island, but it's unlikely that a mine was the cause."

Will questioned, "Why?"

The sailor continued, "Well, it wouldn't have hit us amidships for one, and Cap said there was a sub."

Horace asked, "Where were you coming from?"

The seaman responded, "We left Portsmouth, New Hampshire, this morning, after having some repairs. And we were bound for New York to convey more troops to England." He shook his head, "It's a shame. That cruiser was 502 feet long, with 6-inch armored walls, and equipped with thirty-six rapid fire guns."

After dropping the men off and returning to find more, Horace mused out loud, "Amidships is where the boiler is. The Cruiser was armored, the explosion could have originated in the boiler and then exploded the magazines that were loaded on board."

Will noted, "But the Captain said he saw a submarine."

Horace frowned and said doubtfully, "Yes, I know."

The Lieutenants Suydam and Roosevelt, scoured the sea for the missing soldiers and the suspected submarine, but no signs of the U-Boat were found.

In the days that followed, some of the sailors were transported by automobile to the City Naval Yard, while those who were injured, were brought to Camp Upton. Six sailors had lost their lives in the explosion.

# CHAPTER THIRTY-ONE

Louis stared at the light above his bed and wondered how long he had been asleep. His tiny body ached and his head pounded, the light hurt his eyes so he closed them again. Time passed. He heard his mother's voice as she comforted him and placed a cool cloth over his forehead. In the distance, he could hear crying, it sounded like his little sister, Amelia. He may have only been five years old, but he was Amelia's favorite person. He was the one she always came to when she was scared, he's the one who could comfort her the best. He was her big brother and he wanted to go to her now. She needed him, but his body would not comply with his commands. In spite of her sobs, he fell back to sleep once again. The days passed. Finally, he awoke and the sun was shining through the window. He could hear children playing outside. They were singing and he could hear the beat of a jump rope hitting the cobblestone streets, "I had a little bird, her name was Enza. I opened the window, and in flew Enza."

He looked across the room and saw his mother tending to Amelia. She was washing his little sister's face with a wet cloth, tears running down her own face. Louis was finally able to sit up in his bed, alert and aware that something wasn't right. His voice was hoarse as he called for his mother. She turned to look at him, and with the back of her hand, she wiped the tears from her own flushed cheeks.

Relief evident in her voice, she said, "Louis, you are awake."

It bothered him that his little sister was so quiet. "Amelia?" The name came out as a question. Amelia heard Louis and opened her eyes, "Louie, Louie." Her tiny voice called out to him. He pushed away the sheets and stood on shaky legs. The floorboards creaked beneath him as he crossed the room. Amelia looked blue, her skin was blue. His drowsy brain tried to make sense of it all. "Momma, what's wrong with Amelia?"

"Darling, she has *the grippe*. You had it too, but you are awake now." He noticed now that his mother had beads of sweat on her own forehead.

Two-year-old Amelia reached her hand out to Louis and he grasped it in his own. Her hand felt clammy, sweaty, cool. Too cool. Amelia gasped for breath and coughed so hard that her body shook. She gasped once more and then went silent as her hand went limp in his. His mother cried out in pain.

Louis felt his chest constrict and his heart felt fear. He called his sister's name again, "Amelia!" but there was no response this time.

His mother said a prayer over Amelia and then took the cloth she had been wiping Amelia's face with and used it to cover the child's face. Through her tears she said, "No more pain, my baby."

Louis asked, "Where is Papa?" He looked around the small tenement apartment, but there was no sign of his father. There was only his coat and hat on a hook by the door.

"Papa is gone to heaven, Louis. He went to heaven so that Amelia wouldn't be alone. He knew she was going to go soon, too."

Through the window, he could hear the wheels of a wagon pulled by a mule, and a man's voice called, "Bring out the dead."

His mother wrapped Amelia's body in the sheet that she had been lying on, then lifted her daughter into her arms. He watched as his mother shakily walked out of their door, past the common toilet in the hallway, and descended the stairs. He ran back to the bedroom window and watched as the wagon stopped and his mother placed his little sister's body in the back of the full wagon. He cried out, "No!" But his mother did not look up toward his voice and she did not pull Amelia's body back into her arms. Instead, she wiped the constant sweat off of her brow and weakly reentered their brick building. Louis greeted her at the door to their apartment. He could see Mrs. Anderson in the doorway across the hall. Mrs. Anderson watched with tired eyes, but did not say a word.

In the apartment, his mother walked through the kitchen and into the bedroom. Three beds occupied the same room, she sat down on her own bed and said, "Louis, there is some porridge on the table and some milk in the ice box. Go get something to eat."

"Momma?" Louis began to cry. His mother held her head in her hands, her face flushed, "Darling, I just need to lie down for a while." He knelt in front of her, "Momma, what can I do for you?" His mother shook her head, "Take care of yourself. If . . . if I don't wake up, go to Mrs. Anderson and tell her what has happened."

His brown eyes filled with tears, "What's going to happen, Momma?"

But she didn't answer. Deep coughs wracked her body and she fell back onto the bed. Louis went to the kitchen and took a wash rag and stood on a kitchen chair so that he could reach the pump. He was grateful when water came out of the faucet. He let the water run over the rag and then brought the cloth to his mother and laid it across her forehead.

# CHAPTER THIRTY-TWO

SEPTEMBER – NOVEMBER 1918

By September, Camp Upton was bursting with eager soldiers, each barracks held about 2,000 men. It was mid-way through the month when one barracks was put under quarantine. It was filled with soldiers who had recently arrived from Massachusetts, and they were all sick. Philip stared at the yellow flag that hung outside the building warning others not to enter. Word started to spread in whispers, "The Spanish Flu is here."

To distract the soldiers, from the illness that was spreading throughout the camp, a stage was erected for the show they called *Yip, Yip, Yaphank*. Irving Berlin led a group of soldiers onto the stage and announced to the thousands of men who sat packed before him, "The show must go on." And with that, Philip watched as the soldiers on the stage performed song after song. There was a carousing wave of laughter during the performance as these lyrics were sung,

*Oh! how I hate to get up in the morning,*

*Oh! how I'd love to remain in bed;*

*For the hardest blow of all, is to hear the bugler call;*

*You've got to get up, you've got to get up, you've got to get up this morning!*

*Someday I'm going to murder the bugler,*

*Someday they're going to find him dead;*

*I'll amputate his reveille, and step upon it heavily,*

*And spend, the rest of my life in bed.*

By the end of the song, the whole audience was singing the chorus along with the performers. Harold, slapped Philip on the back, "This is like being at a Broadway show! Who'd have thought we'd get to see something like this at boot camp?" Another soldier who Philip knew from Sayville was sitting behind him, Jack Koman. Jack was the older brother of Ilsa and Hannah's friend Anna from West Sayville. Their father was known as one of the best baymen in the area. Jack put a hand on Philip's shoulder, "Great show! We never imagined we'd be treated to a show like this when we signed up!"

Philip asked him, "Did you get your assignment yet?"

Jack's face lit up with excitement, "I ship out next week."

Philip nodded, "I'm sure you'll be fine. We Yanks are going to end this war."

Philip, like the rest of the men, was caught up in the excitement of it all. They were young, invincible, training to go to war and being treated to a first-rate show in their own camp by their fellow soldiers. Their adrenaline was pumping and they all agreed that they couldn't get their orders to cross the Atlantic soon enough. During the final song, the entire company of men stood and saluted as the audience listened to the words of *"God Bless America"* for the first time. Only Philip knew the words. He sang along with the performers.

A few days after the show, Philip was walking to mess hall, when he saw a group of civilians wearing masks over their mouths and noses.

He was surprised to see a familiar face in the crowd, it was Hannah. Philip pulled her aside, "What are you doing here?"

"Oh, Philip! It's so good to see you!" She surprised herself by throwing her arms around his neck and hugging him. Philip held her body against his and felt the yearning stir inside of him. He had missed her. They had somehow kept each other at arm's length throughout the years, and he never regretted that more than he did now.

"Hannah?"

Behind her mask she said, "I'm here to cover the news."

"What news?"

"You see that man and woman over there, talking to Major General Bell? Well they are scientists from New York City. His name is William Park and she is Anna Williams. They work for the New York City Department of Public Health and they are experts on vaccine therapy. They are here to collect samples from the men who are suffering from the influenza at this camp."

Philip at once felt concern for Hannah's wellbeing, "It is influenza then? I've heard the rumors."

"Yes, Philip. I'm working full time as a reporter now. I no longer work at the lace mill, thank God." She made the sign of the cross and then continued, "I'm writing an article about Anna Williams. Did you know that she is the premier female medical scientist in America? The women of the Sayville Suffrage Club, along with many other women across the state, will be very interested in hearing what she has to say."

Philip and Hannah listened as the experts explained to the press that they had swabbed the throats and nasal passages of the sick men in the barracks. Anna Williams announced, "Death occurs so quickly, it leaves little or no marks of disease anywhere except for the lungs. We are hoping that these samples will lead us to discover a vaccine that will help protect the population in the months ahead."

As the group disbanded, and the press began to exit the camp, Philip asked Hannah, "How is everyone at home?"

Hannah responded, "People are dying, Philip. People I have known my whole life. The stores and streets are empty. Everyone is sheltering inside their homes and hoping that this plague will pass them by. Parents are hanging garlic around their children's necks to keep other children away from them. You should wear a mask, Philip; it will help protect you." A soldier told Hannah to keep moving, it was time all the civilians left.

"Be safe, Hannah."

"I will. You too, Philip." And before she left, she asked, "May I write to you?"

Philip fumbled, "Y-yes, of course. I would like that very much."

Her presence warmed his heart and he regretted that he didn't have more time to spend with her now.

A few days later, Philip felt the fever take over his body. He lay on his cot in the barracks. Every bone in his body ached and each cough brought more pain as his lungs tried in vain to fill with oxygen. At times, he lost consciousness and experienced terrifying nightmares. As the days passed, he struggled to take breaths and it felt as if there was a fire in his throat. He remembered his mother talking about secondary infections being bacterial. With difficulty, he reached into his military issued bag and pulled out the pills that had been placed in his old backpack by his mother. He unscrewed the top of the brown plastic pill bottles and took two from each. Twenty-four hours later, his fever broke, and he took another pill from each bottle. The antiviral medications and antibiotics were working. While those around him lost their battles, Philip survived.

When he and Harold crossed the Atlantic Ocean on a crowded ship, Philip made sure to take the remainder of the antibiotics with him. The bottle of antiviral pills was now empty.

Once in France, at the Battalion Aid Post, Philip and Harold were assigned to accompany the 308th on part of what was being called The Meuse-Argonne Offensive. The dense Argonne Forest in north-eastern France was a place where the Germans were heavily entrenched, and it was their job to push through the German front line to reach a critical railway junction near Sedan. This junction was being used by the Germans to bring fresh supplies to almost the entire German army. If they could capture this junction, it would inflict a devastating blow to the enemy. Major Charles Whittlesey of the 77th Division would be their leader. On the early morning of September 26th, 1918, 600,000 American soldiers, stretching for miles between the Meuse River and the Argonne Forest, began their mission. Six hundred of those men followed Major Whittlesey into the forest expecting the French to cover them from their left flank.

Leaving the comparative safety of their base camp, Philip and Harold held on to their medical equipment with the fierceness that comes from finally being able to do what they have trained long and hard for. The men around them had been with them at Camp Upton, the same tough New York City former gang members were street trained and ready to prove themselves in battle. What they lacked in real wartime experience, they made up for in grit. It wasn't long before what had been the distant roar of artillery, engulfed them.

First, they crossed the battlefield. Pits filled with dirty rain water and blood alternated with muddy barren hills. Barbed wire crisscrossed the landscape and prevented them from moving quickly. Philip's knuckles turned white as his hand clasped his bayonetted rifle. Shells whistled far overhead in both directions. Harold looked at him with frightened eyes as the mud slowed him down. The mud was like quick sand; it could swallow a man whole. In fact, dead bodies littered the area known as *no man's land,* half hidden in the thick mud. Philip encouraged, "A few yards, that's all we need to go. And then a few yards more. Just keep moving forward." Harold nodded, but didn't say a word.

Finally, they entered the dense trees of the forest. Their progress was slowed by the fallen leaves, sticks, and branches on the ground. The rain started and quickly increased in intensity. They inched forward. It wasn't long before they came under direct fire. The men around them were hit by bullets and Philip hurried to save them as they called out desperately, "First Aid!"

There were many casualties, and Major Whittelsey radioed to let General Alexander know they were taking on heavy fire. But he was ordered to keep going forward. So the men walked into the barrage of gunfire. As they fired back, Harold called out, "You Dirty Krauts!" After hours of pressing on, finally, they reached their mark, The Charlevaux Mill area. The Germans were entrenched just yards away from them; hidden by the forest. As it turned out, a German sniper quickly had them in his sight, and one-by-one, picked off the Americans over the next grueling couple of days.

With the radio communication lines cut between Whittlesey's men and base camp, the Major ordered the men to send a pigeon home with their coordinates. They were now out of both food and water, but they couldn't get to a stream without the sniper opening fire on them. They finally knew that the pigeon had made it to base camp once the American artillery started to fly through the air. For a moment, they thought they were saved. But soon it became apparent that there had been a mistake made. Instead of hitting the Germans, the shells were raining down on what was left of Major Whittlesey's men.

In desperation, another pigeon was sent, telling base camp of the error and pleading with them to stop the barrage of artillery. A sniper shot the pigeon in the air, but somehow, it continued to fly. Miraculously, it made it back to base camp. Philip wondered how the soldiers behind the heavy guns of artillery took the news that they had been firing on their own soldiers. But after hours upon hours of heavy losses, the shelling finally ceased.

In the quiet that followed, Philip and Harold did what they could to tie off severed limbs, bind up wounds, and triage their brothers-in-arms. The woods began to stink of rotting flesh, and the men's cries, moans, and coughs quickly filled the silence. Philip tied a handkerchief across his mouth and nose and felt the fevered foreheads of the coughing soldiers. It was clear to him that there was also another enemy afoot, influenza. He said out loud, "Stilts, the wounded and sick need water now." Harold responded, "I'll go." Harold collected empty canteens and scurried down the tree-covered hill to the stream below, holding a white flag above his head. He had just made it to the stream when a shot rang out and Harold fell, lifeless, to the ground. The canteens jingled like bells as they hit against rocks and then floated away on the stream. Philip cried out, "Stilts!" But there was nothing he could do.

The men slept when they could. Five days had passed since they left base camp. Suddenly the sound of an aeroplane could be heard above. The men cheered as they saw it was their own. The pilot was trying to find the lost battalion. Upon sighting them, he rolled his plane from side to side, signaling to the men on the ground that they had been found. Hope spread through the camp that reinforcements were finally on their way. However, the rolling of the aeroplane's wings had also grabbed the attention of the Germans. Shots rang out as the pilot was hit. The plane sputtered away, barely under the control of the wounded pilot.

The men waited. Piercing the silence, came a terrible sound. German soldiers approached them, armed with flame throwers. Blood-curdling screams came from the men as they were engulfed in fire. Still, they did not retreat from the onslaught; instead, the gritty city boys ran toward it. The Germans had obviously never encountered men like these before. The streetwise 308$^{th}$ charged their enemy and grabbing hold of the flame-throwers, turned them against the Germans. The German soldiers fled in retreat.

Philip attended to the men whose skin had been seared off by the flames. Their pain was unbearable, and there was little Philip could do to alleviate it. While attending to one young man whose red hair reminded him of Hannah and Harry, gunfire erupted above his head. One of the bullets entered his patient's head and the young man's body fell backwards to the ground. Before Philip had a chance to react, another bullet whizzed through the air and Philip felt the burning sensation as it passed through the muscle in his own thigh. He collapsed into the bloody mud. The pain was excruciating, but he had the presence of mind to take a piece of material from his medic pack and tie it above the injury. Then he opened the last half-empty bottle of antibiotics and swallowed one pill before he passed out.

On the sixth day, a medical unit made its way to the trapped men and began the task of carrying the wounded and dead out through the forest. They had become known at base camp as "the lost battalion." There were so many wounded that the men of the regimental band were pressed into service as litter bearers. It took thirty-six hours for the ambulance companies and volunteer riflemen from the regiment to bring the wounded out. Each trip taking twelve hours. Some of the men pressed into this service were of slender physique, yet upon arriving at the opening to the forest, faint and exhausted, they only took a short respite before returning with empty litters and more medical supplies. Philip was eventually transferred to a field hospital, the last of the antibiotics that his parents had sent with him were now gone.

Out of the 600 men that Major Whittlesey marched into the forest, only 194 men walked out on their own power. 600,000 Americans began the Meuse-Argonne offensive, over the next six weeks a total of more than 1.2 million American soldiers in twenty-two divisions assaulted the German positions in northeastern France. By the time of the Armistice, more than 120,000 American soldiers were wounded and 26,277 had died in The Meuse-Argonne Offensive, which had spanned from September 26th to November 11th. Because of them, on the eleventh hour, of the eleventh day, of the eleventh month of 1918, the war was finally over.

# CHAPTER THIRTY-THREE

## OCTOBER – NOVEMBER 1918

Hannah and Jean arrived at the French railroad station in early October along with a dozen other young women who volunteered with the YMCA. They were quickly initiated into the fray. The women were told to build a shelter under which they would serve coffee, sandwiches, cheese, and bread to the doughboys before they boarded trains that would convey them to the front lines. From the seemingly endless barrels of Loganberry jam and 8o-pound blocks of cheese, they made sandwiches for the soldiers. They took turns in 8-hour shifts, making sandwiches, sleeping, and serving food to the men. They worked through the ink-black nights, hiding beneath the shelter, with only a wood stove to heat the coffee and a single lantern for light. All around them, was darkness. There were no streetlights and all windows were shuttered due to the air raids. The Gothas (German Bombers) dropped their bombs just a short distance away, testing the women's courage. Shrapnel fell on the YMCA shelter, as the surrounding forts engaged in contra bombardment. When it was her turn to sleep, Hannah's dreams often turned to nightmares in which Philip was injured or worse. He had written to her and told her he was being sent to France as a medic along with the 308<sup>th</sup> Infantry. She had wasted so much time. She had been afraid to give him her heart, fearing that one day he might just disappear. His existence had always seemed so tentative. But now, she worried that he might die on a battlefield in France, and she would regret for the rest of her life not telling him her true feelings.

Each day, the women met a fresh group of soldiers. Each day, they filled their canteens with coffee and provided them with cheese, bread, and as many sandwiches as they could, before each battery of men was loaded onto the next train. As the cars pulled away, the men reached their hands out of open side doors and broken windows to shake the hands of the women. They were desperate for their last glimpse of the women who, for them, represented home. Hannah searched the faces that came and went, hoping that among them, she would see the one she had come to find in this hellish place. But there was no sign of Philip. She knew that there were many points for the troops to embark from and that there were hundreds of girls like her sending them off on railroad platforms. She hoped that somewhere, Philip was being well fed by one of her comrades. She hoped that his hands were grasping those of another woman from the open door of a train. As long as he was offered the same comfort that she tried so desperately to impart to these young soldiers, she didn't mind. There were still times when Alva's words would nag at the back of her mind, "Marry first for money, then for love." She had tried to convince herself that she loved Walt, but was relieved when she received his final letter. And once she had seen Philip again at Camp Upton, she knew that her feelings for him could no longer be denied. The truth was, that from the moment she had met Philip, she had been irreversibly in love with him. It mattered not to her that he had nothing to offer her, she knew that she could not breathe without him.

After a month at this post, Hannah and Jean were transferred to an Army hospital. What they saw there, changed who they were.

They were not nurses. They were there to serve the wounded soldiers their meals, to help them write letters home, and to be there to hold their hands. But as the cots filled with bodies bloated with mustard gas, with burns and tattered limbs, they threw themselves into whatever role was demanded of them. Pushing themselves beyond anything they had thought possible, Hannah and Jean grew closer. War had a way of leveling things out. The difference between being fortunate or not, had nothing to do with money here, it had only to do with life.

As Hannah sat beside the bed of a young soldier who was burned beyond recognition, she read to him a letter he had received from his wife. She could not even hold his hand while she read, for fear of causing him more pain with her touch. Instead, she sat as near to him as she could so that he could feel her presence, for his eyes were hidden behind his bandages.

*"My Dearest,*

*While you have been away, our daughter, Eunice, has finally been born. She is perfect. Ten little fingers and ten little toes. She looks just like you; her sweet brown eyes are as large as saucers with long dark lashes that flutter when she smiles. I can't wait for you to see her and for you to hold us both in your arms! Please do not worry about us, all is well at home. Take care of yourself, you need not be a hero. Please, just return home to us.*

*With all my Love,*

*Miriam"*

A sound came from his mouth, a sound that went beyond physical pain. She could see his body tensing beneath the bandages, knowing that every movement he made caused excruciating agony. She did the first thing that came to her mind. In her sweet voice, she started to sing the lullaby that her own mother used to sing to her, the same one that Gran had sung to Sage.

"*Too-Ra-Loo-Ra-Loo-Ral,   Too-Ra-Loo-Ra-Lie.   Too-Ra-Loo-Ra-Loo-Ral, Hush now don't you cry.*

*Too-Ra-Loo-Ra-Loo-Ral,   Too-Ra-Loo-Ra-Lie.   Too-Ra-Loo-Ra-Loo-Ral, That's an Irish Lullaby.*

*Over in Killarney, many years ago, my mother sang a song for me, in tones so sweet and low.*

*Just a simple little ditty, in her good old Irish way, And I'd give the world if I could hear that song of hers today.*

*Too-Ra-Loo-Ra-Loo-Ral,   Too-Ra-Loo-Ra-Lie.   Too-Ra-Loo-Ra-Loo-Ral, Hush now don't you cry.*

*Too-Ra-Loo-Ra-Loo-Ral,   Too-Ra-Loo-Ra-Lie.   Too-Ra-Loo-Ra-Loo-Ral, That's an Irish Lullaby.*"

The soldier calmed down as he listened to Hannah sing. Then she noticed that the whole ward had suddenly become silent. Every ear was turned her way, every man, in every cot, was transported back home and into the arms of a loved one as they listened to her voice.

Suddenly she heard someone clapping and looked up to the doorway. A doughboy stood there with a crutch under one arm. His face as familiar to her as if it had been etched into every dream she had had for a year. Philip flashed his brilliant smile and she rushed into his arms.

# CHAPTER THIRTY-FOUR

### 1919

On May 6th, 1919, Corporal Philip Ferrara returned to the states and on May 15th, he was discharged from the service.

While still in France, Philip had sold photographs he had taken during the war to Life Magazine, and in doing so, made a name for himself and a bit of money, too. As he disembarked from the train at the Sayville station and walked down the street toward his beloved hamlet, he felt all the weight he had been carrying lift off of his heart. He was home. Sayville would be his home no matter *when* it was. His loved ones, both now and in the future, resided here. This place was woven into every fiber of his being and he had somehow survived to return to it. The buildings along the road were all decorated with flags for the upcoming Decoration Day Parade. He felt a personal connection to the holiday now. So often as a child, he had marched in the parade, with the Boy Scouts, with the baseball team, or with the school band. He had never seen the holiday as anything but a long weekend off from school, a day for barbecues, or a day trip to Fire Island with friends. But now, the true meaning was etched into the lines on his face and the scar on his thigh where a bullet had once been lodged. He still had a slight limp, he favored his right leg, but was thankful he no longer needed a crutch or cane.

As he reached Main Street, he saw Thornhill's Drug Store in front of him. While he was gone, the store had been relocated. Now it stood where it would in 2012, at the corner of Gillette Avenue and Main Street. Directly across the street from Thornhills, a sign on a building caught his eye. He walked over to get a better look. He read, "Building for Sale" and a broad smile spread across his face. He lowered his army pack and took out a pad of paper and a pencil and wrote down the details. He thought the building would make the perfect location for a photography studio and, in addition, above the store, there was an apartment that he could live in.

He continued walking until he reached Hannah's house. It was so natural for him to walk this way. He remembered riding his skateboard to this exact location. Hannah's house was his house, just one hundred years apart. He knocked on the kitchen door and Gran answered. Her face lit up at the sight of him, "Philip, you sure are a fine sight to see, my lad!" She grabbed hold of him in a warm hug and with a strength surprising for her age, pulled him into the kitchen and ordered him to sit at the table. Gran called up the stairway, "Lass, there's someone here to see you."

Hannah descended the stairs and stood silently at the base of the stairway. Philip stood there too. He couldn't believe how beautiful she looked, her hair wild about her face. Surprised to see him in her living room, her hands flew up to her mouth to stifle a scream. She hadn't seen him since the hospital ward in France. He had been sent to rehab the next day. If he hadn't heard her singing the lullaby, they could have been in the same place at the same time, without ever seeing each other. Their lives had crossed, and then, they had been separated again. She awkwardly stood at the bottom of her stairway, suspended in time. Then he opened his arms, and the next moment, she was in them.

Later that day, Philip returned to Giorgio's and Elisabetta's house. Giorgio crushed Philip in his arms, so happy to have the young man back in his home.

"We'a worried about you, Filippo." Elisabetta was in tears. This young man had filled an emptiness in her heart that had been left by the loss of her baby so many years ago.

As he sat down to a meal with them, he realized that they had also filled a hole that had been left in his own heart after having to leave his parents. But now, he was no longer a boy. And, as such, although he felt a responsibility to take care of these two special people, who had taken him into their home when he was in need, it was also time for him to find a place of his own. After all, he wanted to ask Hannah to marry him and he would need a home to take her to. So he explained all this to Giorgio and Elisabetta. Giorgio said, "Capice, Filippo. But know that you always have home'a here, whenever you need'a one."

"Grazie, Giorgio. I will not be far away and I will visit you often."

Elisabetta said, "Bene!"

On Thursday, May 29th, a reception was held at the Opera House for all the local young men who had returned from war and for those who had survived the Civil War, as well. The orchestra from the Tidewater Inn entertained them all. Flags, buntings, and electric lights were hung from the rafters above. Flowers decorated both the stage and floor. Seated at the tables were veterans from Sayville, West Sayville, Bayport, Oakdale, and Bohemia, all enjoying a Thanksgiving Dinner of Roast Turkey with all the trimmings. No women were present at the reception, they had left the men to enjoy it as a "stag" affair.

The following morning, Sayville celebrated having survived both the influenza epidemic and the Great War, and rejoiced that the soldiers had returned home. That Decoration Day, the Sayville Band played as Grand Marshal W. N. Raynor and his assistant, A. C. Edwards, led the parade that marched down Main Street, greeted by cheering crowds.

A record number of cottages had been rented for the season, mostly by families from Brooklyn. The streets were full of people enjoying the beautiful sunny day.

Miss Louise Ockers, daughter of the Oyster King, drove an automobile that gave accommodation to Civil War veterans. This was followed by the young soldiers of the recent war, the Fire Department, the Boy Scouts and the Girl Scouts, and finally, Hannah marched with the Suffragists. She and the other women were proud that their efforts had finally been rewarded with sweet success. In November 1917, New York State had given women the right to vote, and now, the Congress was expected to pass the 19th Amendment in just five more days, guaranteeing women the right to vote across the nation.

The parade was followed by the West Sayville Fife and Drum Corps. It made its way through Sayville, stopping first at Union Cemetery and then at St. Ann's Cemetery where flowers were laid at the graves of deceased soldiers, sailors, and firemen.

All the pomp and circumstance was to be followed by a dance that night at the Opera House. Philip stopped in at Harry Hildebrandt's Barber Shop at 18 Main Street to get his mop of hair trimmed in preparation for the big night. He wanted to look his best for Hannah.

At the dance, Philip saw Andrew standing with a group of other baymen who were all veterans of past wars. He tapped Andrew on the shoulder and asked, "Sir, can I have a moment of your time?"

Andrew nodded and walked next to Philip to a quiet area beside the building. Philip said, "Sir, I hope you will find me worthy of asking for your Hannah's hand in marriage."

Andrew looked hard at this young man who had come into their lives so unexpectedly, and said, "She is not your typical woman, Philip. She will not walk a step behind you. She will never allow anyone to put their foot on her neck. She will stand up for the people and things she believes in and will fight for the right to have her thoughts heard by others. She will not be tamed and domesticated by married life. Are you willing to accept her on her terms?"

Philip smiled as he listened to Andrew describe Hannah and said, "Those are all the reasons I have come to love her so much. I wouldn't change a thing about her."

"Well then young man, you have my permission. God Bless you and give you the strength of character to protect Hannah when you can, and to stand beside her when you can't."

Hannah wore a silk and chiffon dress in emerald green that accentuated her rosy skin and red hair. Her hair was pinned up in a respectable manner and decorated with ivory combs. When she saw Philip and her father enter the Opera House, she opened her fan of peacock feathers to shield her expression. Suddenly, she felt shy among the crowd, an unusual emotion for her that she had not been expecting. But it passed as soon as Philip took her arm and whistled low, "You are the most beautiful woman in this room." Hannah blushed, but withdrew the fan and looked directly at Philip as she said, "And you look quite dashing in your dress uniform, Sir." Philip swept her in his arms and cared little for the looks of dismay on those who were gathered around them on the dance floor. He whispered in her ear, "Come with me outside for a moment, would you please?" Hannah nodded, as the band had started to play, and it was hard to hear each other above the music and the voices that surrounded them.

Outside, the moon was shining in the sky and the two walked arm in arm toward town. "I want to show you something," Philip led Hannah to the store front he had seen a couple of weeks ago. He gestured to the sign in the window that read, "Sold." "Hannah, I bought this building and am going to open a Photography Studio."

Hannah was so proud of him, "Oh, Philip, that's wonderful!"

He replied, "I'm very excited about it. It has an apartment upstairs and they've given me the key. Would you like to see it?"

Hannah hesitated for just a moment. It wasn't proper for her to enter the building alone with Philip, but she brushed her worries away. After all, it was Philip, and she chided herself, since when had she been concerned about what others thought? She nodded, "I would like that." They climbed the stairs to the apartment. The parquet floors glistened in the electric light. The plaster walls were a blank canvas of white. Her voice echoed in the empty room as she said, "It's lovely, Philip. I'm so happy for you." Philip smiled, "I hoped you would like it, Hannah." Then he reached into his pocket and knelt before her. Tears of surprise sprang to Hannah's eyes. Philip's own eyes swam in tears as he held out the diamond ring he had purchased for her, "Hannah Trumball, will you make me the happiest man on Earth and marry me?"

Hannah was so overcome with joy, she nodded her head and choked out the word, "Yes."

# CHAPTER THIRTY-FIVE

## 1920

Andrew felt ill-at-ease in the vestibule of St. Lawrence the Martyr Catholic Church on this Saturday in March. It had been his wife who had insisted that the children be brought up Catholic; he himself didn't have much use for religion. In fact, he had not stepped inside this church since his wife's funeral. Now, he admired his beautiful daughter dressed in white satin and lace, and prepared himself to walk her down the aisle and into the arms of another man. If he had the choice, he would take her hand and run as far from this church as he could. If only he could keep her as the child who accompanied him on his oyster sloop for a little longer. He missed those days and would give anything to have them back. He took a deep breath and was assaulted by the smell of burnt ashes that hung in the air following the Easter holiday. The gothic altar was grand and imposing and the stone eyes of the statues silently watched those who gathered within the walls.

In an attempt to soften the setting, pink and white bows had been tied to the dark mahogany pews. Andrew watched the men at the altar. Philip and Harry stood there along with Pastor Thomas

Duhigg. This same pastor had come to Sayville only a year before Hannah and Harry were born and, at that time, this church hadn't even been built yet. From 1895 through much of 1896, the Catholic Diocese had rented the old Methodist Church on the north side of Main Street and east of the Kensington Hotel. In September of 1896, Hannah and Harry were two of the first babies to be baptized in the church in which they now stood.

Andrew noticed that in the first pews sat Giorgio and Elisabetta, Carmine and Rosa, Pasquale and Francesca, and the rest of the Ferrara family. Andrew was glad that Philip had found family here after having arrived alone. On the opposite side of the church, John Ellis Roosevelt sat with his daughter, Gladys. Andrew had made peace with his wife's ex-employer. He had realized that the Commodore had not been the reason his wife's health had failed her. Rather, he had cared for her and had taken Hannah in as a dear companion to his own daughters. John Ellis Roosevelt had looked out for Hannah's welfare at a time when Andrew had been drowning in his own sorrow in alcohol. Andrew thought it was a good thing that he had given up the drink before prohibition had been enacted. It was good to feel like life was worth living again.

He saw Hannah grab onto Ilsa's arm as the organ music began. Ilsa had married Will Amundsen in February at the True Holland Church on Atlantic Avenue and Hannah had been her maid-of-honor. Now Ilsa was standing up for her. While Andrew waited to escort his daughter, he watched as Jean Roosevelt began the long walk down the aisle ahead of them. Ilsa patted Hannah's hand to steady her, "You'll be all right. Look at him up there. He truly loves you."

Hannah looked at Philip standing in front of the alter with Harry at his side. She said, "He's so handsome and I love him so much."

The organ pipes began as they blared and echoed in the cavernous church. Then, Ilsa followed Jean and walked toward the alter.

Andrew wove Hannah's gloved hand through the crook in his arm to take possession of his daughter for one last time. He said, "Are you ready, dear?"

Hannah nodded, "Yes, Pa."

Andrew felt the tears well up in his eyes and they blinded him for a moment. If only Maggie were here with him now. It would be so much easier to bear losing Hannah if he still had his wife. He took the first step and then another, accompanying her as she walked toward her new life.

Following the wedding, the reception was held at The Elmore Hotel.

Once on the dance floor, Andrew held his daughter in his arms as they glided across the room. She rested her head against his shoulder and he fought the tears back once more. When the song ended, he said to her, "This is the beginning of your life, Hannah. So many wonderful things lie ahead. Be brave, be strong, persevere when troubles come, and always remember that without love, there is no true joy or sorrow. To have love, is worth the pain."

John Ellis Roosevelt sat beside Gladys and Jean while he watched as Andrew and Hannah finished their dance. He shared some of the feelings that Andrew was experiencing. He, himself, felt protective of Hannah; but he also knew his place. As often happened when he was in the presence of Hannah, he thought of Pansy, who was now nearly forty years old. So much time had passed since that fateful day, one he and Hannah, alone, shared in memory. The memory brought about a terrible thirst in him. He wished more than anything, that the bar at the Elmore could be opened, but the law forbade it. He remembered with some nostalgia, the many times he and his cousin Teddy had enjoyed a glass of whiskey, or two, at Nohowec's tavern. He missed Teddy, the President had passed away in January of 1919, just before the 18th Amendment had been ratified, banning the sale of alcohol. A one-year grace period had been granted to the citizens of the nation before it was put into effect. But that year had come and gone now. He thought of the whiskey in his desk at Meadow Croft.

He rarely came to Sayville anymore. The house held too many sad memories for him, and the wall of fence still stood between his property and that of his brother's. It had become just another reminder of memories that haunted him. Meadow Croft belonged to his daughters now, it would be a summer place for them to bring their own families. It was time for him to have a change of scenery. Perhaps he would move to Florida? Quietly, he excused himself. His daughters watched worriedly as he let himself out the door of The Elmore. The Commodore found his driver waiting for him. The driver said, "Where to, Sir?"

Wistfully, he said, "Take me home."

Eight months later, Hannah voted in the presidential election on November 2, 1920. The following day she read in the newspaper that Republicans Warren G. Harding and Calvin Coolidge, were elected President and Vice President, respectively. The losers were Democrats James M. Cox and his running mate, Franklin D. Roosevelt. Hannah found that the power to vote in a presidential election had filled her with pride. She, and others, had fought hard and long for this privilege. Right or wrong, for better or worse, she now had the ability, and legal right, to cast her vote for her choice. The tears that filled her eyes blurred her vision for a moment. Philip asked, "Is something wrong, Hannah?"

She looked up at him and said, "I have written articles and given speeches for years now, but this is the first time that I feel I've been heard. I am validated, I am now a true citizen of the United States of America, and I am so proud of our country for giving women this right." A thought crossed her mind then and she added, "But I fear that even the law won't protect the right to vote for some women. Some states have instituted laws requiring voters to be literate, and there are still those who will intimidate women who approach the voting booth." She took a deep breath, "Native Americans and Chinese Immigrants still don't have the right to vote. There is still so much work to be done."

Philip nodded, "Even in my time, prejudice and fear still exist. But I promise you, all will have the right to vote and those rights will be protected and enforced. But, as they say, the wheels of change turn slowly."

He kissed the top of her head, "But you, my dear, are one of the gears that will make those wheels turn."

# CHAPTER THIRTY-SIX

### 1921

The winds kicked up on this warm May day as Hannah ran up the dock holding on to her straw hat. She watched intently, as the ferry carrying Philip returned from Fire Island. He had been helping Harry and Edmund move. Harry had been hired to manage the Cherry Grove Hotel. The hotel was the only building on Cherry Grove to have a telephone and electricity, and Edmund had landed the job of electrician and maintaining the generator.

While Philip was helping them settle in, she had taken the opportunity to visit her doctor and had received the news that she had hoped for. After two months of missed cycles, she now knew for certain that soon their family of two would become three.

She caught a glimpse of Philip on the ferry and waved to him. In letting go of her hat, she nearly lost it to the bay. She quickly reached up and caught it before it was taken away by the wind. By the time Philip disembarked from the ferry, she was bubbling over with the news. She ran into his arms and he laughed, "I missed you too, Hannah, but I've only been gone for a day."

Hannah's eyes sparkled with anticipation, "I have some news for you, Mr. Ferrara."

Philip adored his wife and was so proud that she had continued as a reporter for The Suffolk County News even after they were married. Other men scoffed at him allowing his wife to work, but he just shook his head at them and said, "My wife is an intelligent woman with a gift for putting her thoughts into words. Why would I ever keep her from something she feels so passionate about?"

The men often told him, "Well, she ought to be at home tending to you rather than following the next story."

Thinking that she must have scooped a new story, he kissed his wife and walked beside her toward the road. "So tell me, what have you uncovered now?"

Hannah leapt and twirled around, holding onto his hand the whole time. "Well, you know how we have been wondering how to furnish the second the bedroom in the apartment?"

Confused, he replied curiously, "Mmm, yy-es?"

Hannah replied, "Well, I think a crib would look just perfect in it."

Philip stopped in his tracks. "Hannah?"

Hannah nodded gleefully, "Yes, Philip, you will soon be a papa."

Philip was overjoyed and stopped himself from lifting her up in his arms, fearful that he might hurt her. Instead he just wrapped her in an embrace and kissed her passionately. "I love you, Hannah Ferrara."

"I love you, too, my husband."

Philip asked, "When? When will it happen?"

"The doctor says by Thanksgiving. We will have something special to be thankful for this year."

# CHAPTER THIRTY-SEVEN

### 1923

Philip took the photo as Ida Gillette held a shovel in her hand. She stood on the ground across the street from St. Ann's Church. Hannah scribbled on her pad of paper as the dedication ceremony began. They were thankful for the helping hands around them who kept their little boy, Frankie, busy while they worked. Gran, Andrew, Giorgio and Elisabetta, all pitched in to keep the active child safe while his parents covered this momentous event for The Suffolk County News.

Hannah's notes would be turned into an article accompanied by Philip's photographs. They made a powerful team when it came to keeping the community up-to-date on the town's developments and activities. The group that had gathered together consisted of both community and church leaders along with a generous number of onlookers.

Hannah asked, "Miss Gillette, for my article, can you please explain how you came into possession of the land, what made you donate it to the Episcopal Church's Church Charity Foundation, and finally, what are the plans for its future?"

Ida told her, "I inherited the land from my cousin, Margaret Ann Smith Brush. She was the widow of Dr. George R. Brush who had passed away in 1918. I donated the land in 1921, after hearing that the Episcopal Church's Church Charity Foundation Orphanage in Brooklyn had burned to the ground. It's taken years of planning, but now, on this first day of December, the cornerstone is about to be laid for the first Cottage. As there is already a house on the property, Gray House, which was originally built in the 1880s for the Arthur family, it can temporarily be used to house some of the children. But we are now breaking ground for the Brush Cottage. Each building will hold twenty children, one for the boys and one for the girls. We hope to erect a third building on the property, and to name it the Swett Cottage after our Episcopal Reverend, Canon Swett. Eventually, the Gray House will be used as the central building for the children to gather together, while the two cottages will be used to house the children."

Ida turned her attention toward the audience before her and announced to the group that was gathered, "This institution will not be known as an orphanage, but rather, it is intended to provide a suitable home for any needy children of the Long Island Diocese. Once the construction of the Brush Cottage is finished, it will house the girls, while the boys will reside in the Gray House until such time as the Swett Cottage can be completed."

Gran smiled with pride as she watched Frankie giggle and play with Sage. He was a plump rosy-cheeked child with enormous hazel eyes that could melt her heart in an instant and, at two years old, he had become the focus of her every breath. Although her health was not what it used to be, she was grateful to have lived long enough to see this child. He gave her hope for the future and a reason to live as long as possible to watch him grow. She tried to ignore the pain that came and went in her abdomen. When others suggested that she see a doctor, she refused. She often said, "If I go into a hospital, I won't come out alive." Gran could be every bit as stubborn as her daughter and granddaughter. After all, they had, in fact, inherited that stubborn streak from her. Cathleen O'Connell didn't live for 86 years because she lacked strength of character and will; quite the opposite was true.

Gran said to Elisabetta, "He is a handful, but such a pleasure."

Elisabetta's heart swelled, "Tesoro, such'a treasure!"

Elisabetta gathered the child up in her arms and kissed each of his cheeks. Frankie squirmed to be free and as soon as his feet touched the ground, he once again grabbed Sage and began to tug at the dog, wanting her to follow him. Sage considered Frankie her own responsibility, and so she allowed the child to tug at her. She would do her best to follow the boy and keep her own eye on him.

When the ceremony ended, Philip lifted the little boy onto his shoulders and said, "We were lucky with the weather today, but one look at the sky and you can see that snow is on the way. We'd better get home before the heavens open up."

Andrew held onto Gran's arm as she walked with her cane to their wagon. Hannah placed the crate on the ground and helped Gran climb up onto the seat. Although they weren't far from home, the distance was too much for her to walk. Giorgio and Elisabetta climbed into their own wagon and followed them. Back at Andrew's house, Hannah and Elisabetta helped Gran prepare dinner for the family. Sage sniffed at the ground and found crumbs to munch on. Like Gran, Sage was slowing down too these days. At eleven years old, her back legs had a habit of giving out on her on the stairs. Gran smiled at the dog, "Okay old girl, here's a treat for you." She dropped a piece of the roast onto the floor for the dog to enjoy.

As they sat at the table, Philip announced, "Hannah and I have some news. We rented a three-bedroom cottage on the water in Sayville. It seems our little apartment above the photo shop is getting a bit tight for us."

Andrew asked, "Will you rent out the space after you move?"

Philip nodded, "That's the plan. The extra income will help. We plan to move into the cottage after the holidays."

Hannah held her stomach, "We need space to grow." Philip's broad smile spread across his face.

Gran asked, "Do we have another little one on the way?"

Hannah nodded happily.

The weeks passed and Philip and Hannah, prepared the cottage for their move while spending the rest of the winter in the apartment. Hannah painted a mural of an oysterman in his sloop on the wall, in what would be Frankie's new bedroom. Hannah was quite a talented artist as well as a singer and Philip enjoyed taking a moment just watching his wife from the doorway before he let her know he was there.

"Hannah, it's beautiful."

Hannah blushed, "I know it's silly. After all, he can just look out the window and see the oystermen on the bay, but I wanted to bring the scene inside so that it surrounds him. He is a lucky little boy to have a life near the bay, and I want him to love it as much as I do."

"He will, how can he not, coming from such a long line of oystermen?"

Hannah laughed, "I would hope so, but he seems more fascinated by locomotives than oyster sloops. Maybe we should have bought a home next to the railroad?"

Philip gathered her in his arms, "Frankie can be whatever he wants to be. You and I are going to make sure of that. The sky's the limit!" Then he made a motion with his hand as if an aeroplane was flying through the room.

Hannah's eyes opened wide, "No aeroplanes for him. They are much too dangerous."

Philip shook his head, "Hannah, fear has never stopped either one of us from doing what we wanted. Why should it stop him?"

She set her chin in a stubborn fashion and said, "Because I said so."

Philip laughed heartily at that reply.

# CHAPTER THIRTY-EIGHT

## 1923

While they fixed-up the cottage, they continued to live in the apartment above the store. One night, Philip was awakened by someone banging on the shop door downstairs. He was surprised when he opened his eyes and saw a red glow by the front window. He checked his watch, it was four-o'clock in the morning. He rubbed his eyes as Hannah awoke next to him. "What is it?" she asked.

"I don't know. Stay here and let me check it out."

As Philip descended the stairway, Frankie started to cry in the next room. Hannah went to Frankie and lifted him up in her arms. She noticed the red glow at the window and pulled back the curtain. What she saw made her catch her breath. There was a cross burning in front of their building.

When Philip entered the shop, he could see the cross burning through the glass windows. Judging from the men standing by the door, it had to be about fifteen feet tall. Sewell Thornhill and his sons were there; Sewell Jr. was still pounding. They backed away as he opened it and a second later, he heard the fire truck rambling up the road. Philip was having a hard time comprehending what was happening. He had no experience to reference such an event. It was something out of a history book, but why was it burning in front of his store and home?

Once the fire was extinguished, the chief explained to Philip, and others who had gathered, "It's happening across the south shore of the island tonight. The Ku Klux Klan is burning crosses in every town. We just came from putting out another cross at Carl Munkelwitz's property between Railroad Avenue and Greene Avenue." Carl Munkelwitz was a blacksmith. He shoed horse and made rakes and tongs for the baymen.

Philip felt Hannah join him as she put her hand on his back. She held onto him and said, "It's all right, Philip."

He shook his head, "No, it isn't."

The Fire Captain could see that Philip was in shock, so he directed his comments toward Hannah now. "I'm sorry, they are burning wooden crosses soaked in oil and gasoline in front of properties owned by Jews, Negros, Italians, and Catholics."

As the cross stood smoldering, the smoke blew in their direction and Frankie began to cry again. "Ma'am, take your baby and husband inside. We'll clean this up."

Hannah turned to Mr. Thornhill, "Thank you for waking us and calling the fire department."

He shook his head, "I'm so sorry, Hannah. My son saw the flames. He was going into the drug store early to prepare some prescriptions when he saw it. He called me from the store and we came running over. I wish there was more we could have done."

"It's all right. Thank you so much, Mr. Thornhill."

Hannah pulled on Philip's arm, as his shock was wearing off. He followed her into the store and up the stairs to their apartment. "I'm sorry Hannah, I can't believe that happened. It's because I'm Italian, isn't it?"

Hannah said, "We are both Catholic."

She put the coffee on the stove and took a bottle out of the icebox for Frankie. She warmed the bottle in a pot of water beside the coffee pot. When it was warm, she tested it on her wrist and then placed the nipple into the crying toddler's mouth. "Shush, my little one. Everything is going to be all right." She started to sing her lullaby then and the baby drank and closed his eyes. She placed him back in his crib and then went back to the kitchen to attend to her husband.

She poured coffee into two cups and sat beside him at the table. Philip took a sip and as the warm liquid flowed through to his stomach, he started to revive from what seemed like a trance. But he was feeling responsible for putting his family in danger and that was far more upsetting than anything else. He looked across the table at his beautiful wife and said, "Who would have done this?"

She took another sip of the coffee before responding, "Have you heard of The Ku Klux Klan?"

He nodded, "I've heard that it was popular in the south, I didn't know it was something that had been here, in Sayville."

"Well, it is, and yes, as I'm sure you have realized, they are our neighbors. They are men who do not like the changes they see happening here. They may have once been new to this town, but they don't welcome others who are different from them who want to make Sayville their home as well."

Philip hesitated to ask the next question, "Who, Hannah? Do you know who they are?"

"They meet at The True Holland Church on Atlantic Avenue in West Sayville. I've never been to a meeting of course, and they keep their faces covered in public. But they have been known to march in our town parades in the past. It seems like they are having a revival of sorts."

The sun was coming up on the cold morning of Tuesday, February 13th, when Philip walked back down to his shop to ready it for opening. The cross was gone, the only indication that it had really been there was the charred ground beneath where it had stood.

Two days later, on February 15th, there was a meeting of the Ku Klux Klan in West Sayville. The attendance was smaller than normal and the guest speaker who had been scheduled to be at the meeting was a no-show. A man dressed in a white robe and hood stood at the pulpit and addressed his audience, "The Klan came into existence in time to save America from doom, the like of which the world has never seen."

Along with the rest of the men gathered in the pews, Will Amundsen cheered.

# CHAPTER THIRTY-NINE

## 1924

The baby was born in June, another little boy, and they called him Bobby. As much as his brother, Frankie, looked like Philip, Bobby favored Hannah. Both children were home births, but instead of Gran bringing this baby into the world, the doctor had been called to assist. Hannah missed having Gran by her side as she labored, but she was glad to be able to bring the baby for a visit to meet his great-grandmother.

Gran wasn't in her usual place when they arrived. Instead, Elisabetta was in the kitchen by the stove. Elisabetta explained, "She's in'a her bed'a."

The doctor had prescribed laudanum to keep Gran comfortable. The cancer that was taking over her insides was beyond the medical treatments of the time. But she was able to be propped up in bed for a moment to hold the new baby in her arms.

Gran kissed the baby's forehead, "May the luck of the Irish be with you, my lad." The baby opened his eyes wide and started to cry. So

Gran sang her lullaby; and the baby, contented to be serenaded, quieted down and closed his eyes once again.

Two days later, Gran passed away in her sleep.

At the funeral, Carmine, Rosa, Pasquale and Francesca, paid their respects. Dressed in somber black, the women sobbed as the men stood solemnly by. Outside the funeral parlor, Carmine's son, Filippo, held a baby boy in his arms. Philip approached Filippo, "And who is this? A new member of the family?"

Filippo proudly extended his arms to hand Philip the child. Filippo said, "This is my son, Angelo." Philip faltered for just a moment, then he reached out and took the baby into his own arms. He looked down into the sweet face of the infant and then kissed his soft cheek. The eyes that looked back at him were so very familiar. They were the eyes of his own grandfather. His mind reeled, he was holding his own grandfather in his arms. This child would grow to have a son of his own named Thomas, Philip's father.

In the weeks that followed, for Philip and Hannah, it seemed it was a time of letting go of those they loved. In the week following Gran's death, Sage found a quiet place in the yard under a tree, where she lay down for the last time. Not even a month later, the Roosevelts' dog, Billy, died on July 3, 1924, and was buried along the trail he had loved to inspect, sniffing happily as he had investigated the hiding places of every rodent he could find.

Right Reverend Frederick Burgess, bishop of the diocese and president of the CCF Board of Managers, dedicated the two Sayville buildings on July 5, 1924. The girls' cottage and Gray House were ready to accept children.

Sister Dorothy was charged with the task of watching over the children. By Christmas 1924, The Brush Cottage housed eight girls and the Gray House housed eight boys. The "Inmates" were all between the ages of five and twelve years old. The CCF and the Sayville community at large, funded and managed the Cottages. The community also paid the Sayville Schools $100 per child each year to educate the children.

The children of The Cottages were gathered together under a Christmas tree decorated with ribbon and paper cutouts. They sat on the bare wooden floor and watched Hannah with haunted eyes as she handed them each a bag of candy. She knew that they had experienced painful losses in their young lives and it showed on their sweet faces.

One boy sat against the wall, away from the others. Hannah knelt down beside him and held out the last bag of candy. His eyes moved from the candy to her face, but he did not take the bag. She sat down beside him then. She untied the ribbon from the bag and pulled out a piece of peppermint candy. "Do you mind if I have one?"

He silently shook his head, no.

She unwrapped the candy and then popped it into her mouth. "Mmmm, it's good. Are you sure you don't want any?"

The boy swallowed hard and looked away from her again.

She felt a pang in her chest, what if Frankie and Bobby had been left alone in this world. She would hope that someone, somewhere, would show them kindness and love. She asked him, "Can I tell you a story?"

He looked up at her and nodded. She judged he was about twelve years old, but he was small for his age. Although they were missing the flecks of green, his huge light brown eyes reminded her of her Philip's, and she felt a fresh stab of pain in her heart. She began, "I met a boy once who saved my dog. The puppy had been caught in a raccoon trap and I couldn't release her paw from its jaws. The boy was stronger than me, he was able to pull the jaws apart. If he hadn't been there, I don't want to think of what would have happened to

Sage. Well, that boy was there at a time when I needed him, but in order for him to be there, he had to lose his entire family."

The boy was interested now. She had his full attention. "This is hard to believe, I know, but I am going to tell you a secret."

The boy's eyes widened for a moment, a brief relief from his sorrow appeared while listening to her story. "Well, you see, this boy, he had come from the future. He had left his whole family in another time and had come back in time to help me. Through the years that followed, we became good friends, and now, we are married, and our children and I are his family. Sometimes that happens. We lose one family and feel sad, but then we find another family. We never forget the family that we lost, but we find a way to be happy again with our new family."

The boy reached his hand out and took the bag of candy. Hannah said, "My name is Hannah. What's your name?"

With a mouth full of peppermint, he said, "Louis." And Hannah caught her breath and repeated his name, "Louis" as a memory of Philip telling her about the old man he had encountered at the beach came back to her.

# CHAPTER FORTY

### 1925

The trolley that had once connected Sayville to Patchogue had ceased operation in 1919. As more cars were added to the roadway, it had become dangerous to cross the trolley tracks. The crushed oyster shell and dirt roads were now being paved over, covering the old tracks. Sayville was changing along with the times, and the first Bohack grocery store opened on the corner of Main Street and Greeley Avenue. The owner of the store, Henry C. Bohack, had often summered in Sayville and had recently purchased the home of Samuel W. Green. He built his store on the property at the northwest corner of Greeley Avenue, and had the house moved to a spot behind the store. For the first time, the people of Sayville knew the convenience of being able to purchase all grocery items from one location.

Philip enjoyed this modern convenience, but knew he would miss the personal feel of the individual shops. He thought about all the changes that were yet to come and remembered how he liked to skateboard past the ferries when he was younger, watching as the boats were lowered into the water in the spring and then taken out in the fall. Each year passed almost unnoticed, until, years had gone by. Sayville was changing, it was becoming more recognizable to him; but he hoped the changes wouldn't come too quickly. He liked the way things were.

However, he was concerned that some changes weren't coming soon enough. Tuberculosis was spreading like wildfire through the island and he worried for his family and friends. He had been vaccinated against the threat of tuberculosis when he was little. And although the vaccine had been developed in 1921, it wouldn't be available for widespread use for many more years to come.

Life was changing, and as every bayman knows, life on the bay can change in an instant as well, and with it, the fate of those who toil upon it. One misty morning, the smell of the bay hung so heavily in the air that it almost seemed as if the land had been swallowed by the sea. In spite of that, Andrew set out long before dawn on his schooner in search of oysters and hard clams.

Hannah looked out the window of her cottage and watched as the sky over the bay turned dark and angry, accompanied by the sound of thunder in the distance. The wind grew stronger and began to howl furiously as she shut the window against the April storm. Bobby whimpered in the crib behind her. She lifted the child into her arms and rocked him gently as she sang sweetly. The baby, distracted by her voice, quieted and stared wonderingly into her eyes. Hannah thought, *"This is the best part of motherhood."* As she carried him into the kitchen, she marveled at the fact that he was already ten months old. Soon he would be walking and following his big brother around the house.

In the kitchen, four-year-old Frankie played with his blocks on the floor. Hannah was thankful that he was such a patient child. He was easily amused by himself and was generous about allowing her to have time with his younger brother. She announced, "Time for lunch." Frankie looked up from the tower of blocks and ordered,

"Mommy, knock them over!" She nudged the blocks with her toe and the tower tumbled to the floor. Frankie clapped his hands and started to build once again. "Not now my little man, it's time for lunch. Sit at the table like a big boy." Hannah placed Bobby securely in his high chair and gave him a baby spoon and some homemade apple jelly in a bowl.

Frankie then climbed onto his own seat, on top of a telephone book, and waited while his mother made him a sandwich of peanut butter and apple jelly. As the boys ate, she hummed and danced around the kitchen to his delight. She opened the ice box and took out the ingredients for the night's dinner so that it could thaw. She returned the breakfast dishes to their cupboard and wiped down the counter. All the while, outside the storm raged on. Moving the kitchen curtains aside, she watched as the waves beat against the wooden barrier that separated her property from the bay. She hoped the water wouldn't find its way over the bulkhead and into her home. Her sailboat was tied to the dock in the creek that ran alongside her home. She prayed it would survive without damage. It had been a birthday gift from her husband and one that she had been overjoyed to receive. It was just large enough for her little family and it afforded them the opportunity to journey to Fire Island on hot summer days.

The hours passed and the storm with them. Soon the sky opened up and a rainbow appeared in place of the clouds. She let out a deep breath, thankful that the danger was now over. An hour later, she had dinner ready when Philip returned home from work. But instead of reaching for them with his usual bear hug that included them all, he kept his head down as he hung his raincoat on the hook by the door. Immediately, Hannah felt the mood in the room change. Warily she asked, "What's wrong?"

Philip didn't know how to tell her the news he had just heard. He wrung his hands while trying to find the right words. There was no way to tell her without causing her pain. "Hannah, I . . ." But he didn't have a chance to finish. Harry burst into the kitchen and said, "Hannah! He hasn't come back."

Hannah shook her head. She felt the goosebumps rise on her skin. "Who, Harry?"

"Pa. George Gunderson came to fetch me at Cherry Grove. He said Pa was out on the bay this morning, but he didn't come to the cull shack when the storm hit. Everyone's out looking for him now. We've got to go out to find him."

Hannah felt the panic rising in her chest, "I should go. I should be looking for him, too."

Frankie tugged at her skirt, "Momma? Momma, what's wrong?" She looked down into his saucer shaped hazel eyes and bit back her own tears. She shook her head, "Nothing, baby. Everything's all right." She turned then to Philip and Harry. "Go, both of you, take the sailboat."

Philip nodded and kissed her on the cheek. "We'll be right back."

She nodded, "You'd better be." Then she hugged both him and Harry before they left the house.

She turned to Frankie, "It's time for dinner, sweetheart." She held his hand and walked toward the table. After feeding both children, she put Bobby down for another nap and told Frankie to practice writing his letters at the table. Then she took her shawl from its hook and walked outside. She looked out over the bay and searched the horizon for any glimpse of her father, brother, and husband. But the bay was empty. Her father was seventy-three years old, but a bayman never retires from the water. He works until the inevitable takes him from it.

It was hours before Philip and Harry returned and the sun was sinking into the horizon. The sky lit up in red and orange as if it were bleeding into the blue sky. Harry reached her first, "Jorge Gunderson found his sloop full of oysters, but there was no sign of him. The waves must have washed him off." Harry gulped for air, "Oh, Hannah, Oliver Amundsen found his body floating over east."

Hannah wasn't surprised. She had known before they left that her father was gone. His first lesson to her when she was a girl was a warning that the weather on the bay could turn quickly. "Hannah," he would say, "don't get caught up in whatever you're doing and forget to watch the sky. You will see the change in the sky before the bay knows what's coming."

Harry was sobbing now, he held onto her arm, asking, "Did you hear me, Hannah? He's gone."

Hannah's face remained as smooth as porcelain, but her heart was broken in pieces. She raised her chin and said, "Harry, he loved the bay. If he could have chosen a way to go, this would have been it."

She turned and walked back into the house, she kissed Frankie's head and walked into the Bobby's bedroom. She lifted the sleeping baby into her arms and silently cried as she buried her face against his soft body.

# CHAPTER FORTY-ONE

## 1926

After Andrew's death, Philip hired Carmine and Pasquale to expand his father-in-law's house alongside Brown's River. He knew just how it should look. After all, it was the house Philip had grown up in. The little kitchen on the side of the house became an indoor bathroom. Gran's room became part of a larger living room, a new kitchen was put in, the roof was dormered, and a bathroom was added on the second floor along with enlarging the current three upstairs bedrooms. The construction was completed in about a year, and the family moved in, in late August of 1926.

It was early November when Hannah heard the coal wagon pull up to the house. She went out into the cool morning air to greet the driver. Peyton Vann worked for Charles N. Aldrich and had been delivering coal and wood to houses in Sayville for nearly thirty years. As children, Hannah and Harry had often been thrilled to have a ride on his wagon while he went about his deliveries.

Hannah called out, "Hello, Mr. Vann! How are you today?"

"Doin' well, Miss. Thank ya' for askin'."

Frankie held onto her skirt as Peyton placed a chute through their open basement window. Peyton addressed Frankie, "Young man, you want to help an ole man out? Come on over here and climb up on the wagon. See that lever? Now you pull it wit' me." Together the man and child pulled the lever back, and the coal slid down the chute into the basement. From there it would be carried upstairs in a coal scuttle to fire their stove. Frankie jumped in his seat on the wagon and screamed in excitement at the day's entertainment.

Peyton's skin was as dark as the coal he transported and all the locals knew his story. Born in North Carolina in 1879, Peyton had come north for work when he was only fourteen years old. At first, he had been employed by the Hawkins Brothers of Lake Grove. Later, when he was about twenty years old, he had come to Sayville to work for Mr. Aldrich, and had been his trusted and faithful employee ever since. Peyton was a humble man, but he was also a man of considerable strength. His wife, Sadie, and daughters, sixteen-year-old Marjorie and eleven-year-old Dorothy, were the center of his world. They lived in a house at 143 Henry Street across from the Aldrich Coal and Wood Company, just north of the railroad tracks. And, as far as Hannah knew, they had been the first *colored* family to live in Sayville.

But Peyton Vann was also an entertainer. He brought his fellow entertainers from Harlem to Sayville for an annual bang-up Vaudeville show in late August, and this year's show had been the largest yet. Broadway stars, like Mr. and Mrs. Dyke Thomas and Mr. and Mrs. Chadwich, performed along with Bob Slater and his "colored" entertainers. Hannah's favorite part of the night was always the cakewalk. A tradition that was carried over from the days of slavery, it was now, more or less, a game of musical chairs that ended with the participants winning prizes.

Hannah called to him, "Mr. Vann, is it true that an electrical transformer that some men were adjusting on a pole fell on your head?"

Peyton laughed, "I told them, 'Listen, white boy! You want to be a little more careful. You made me bite mah tongue.'"

"But, Mr. Vann, it's no joking matter, you could have been really hurt!"

Peyton looked up to the sky, "I has Someone watching over me for sure. Now Miss Hannah, would Frankie here like to join me for my rounds today?"

Frankie screamed, "Yes, Momma! Say, yes! Please!"

As Hannah heard Bobby calling out to her from his crib, she laughed, "Why sure. That sounds like an offer that works out for the both of us today."

Peyton's laugh echoed with a deep rippling in his chest as he said, "Mah pleasure."

Frankie adjusted himself on the wagon and pulled his cap down over his ears. "Thanks, Momma!"

"You be careful now and do as Mr. Vann tells you," she called out to him, as the wagon rumbled away.

Hannah returned to the bedroom and lifted Bobby into her arms. She had only just entered the kitchen when the telephone rang. Placing the toddler on her hip and adjusting her stance for his weight, she answered. Jean's anxious voice reached her from the other end. "Hannah, there's been a terrible accident. It's Gladys. She's dead."

Hannah could not believe what she was hearing, "What? What do you mean, Jean? What, what happened?"

Jean explained, "She was riding her horse and she took a jump," her voice broke into a cry, "Her horse landed on her, it crushed her."

Hannah paced as she held the phone in her hand, and repeated the same word over and over again, "No. No. No."

But Jean just said, "Yes, Hannah, she's gone."

The next day, it was all over the newspapers and the radio. Gladys Roosevelt Dick had died on November 2, 1926, while jumping her horse over a five-foot barrier in Brookville, New York, during a fox hunt. The horse had caught his hoof on the fence and tumbled down, landing on top of Gladys, and crushing her to death. Although married, Gladys had died childless.

# CHAPTER FORTY-TWO

1927

Hannah piloted her sailboat across the bay to Fire Island. She looked down into the depths of the water, as clear as a running brook. At thirty-one, she was firmly in her prime. Bearing two children had added a suppleness to her formerly lithe figure, but confidence and accomplishments had brought an exuberance to her features. In spite of being a wife and mother, she had been able to continue her career as a writer for the local newspaper. Some of her peers thought her continuing to work outside the home was an outrage and didn't even try to hide their opinions of her. But she had long ago learned that the only way to be happy was to be true to herself. She often thought that it was a good thing that Philip had come to her from the future, for she was pretty sure that she would be hard-pressed to find such an open-minded man in her current time.

Once on the beach, Philip and fifteen-year-old Louis, helped carry their tents and camping equipment over to the ocean side of the island. They set up their tents, one for Louis and Frankie and the other for Philip, Hannah, and the baby.

Although Louis still lived at The Cottages, he had become an extended member of their family. Louis was grateful for their generosity and enjoyed the adventures that Philip took him on. He especially liked catching snapper turtles from Brown's River. Locals called them torp, and catching them was not an easy task, as these turtles were notoriously fast-moving with razor sharp teeth and claws. But Hannah made a great turtle soup. Hannah was also a storyteller, and she would often come to the Cottages to entertain the children with her stories.

After the tents were set, they settled down around a campfire. Louis said, "One of the boys told me that Captain Kidd buried treasure here on the Fire Island. Is that true?"

Hannah nodded, "It's true. In fact, although many years ago some of it was found, they believe that more treasure is still buried here. My father told me that he had heard of a fisherman who had been hired by three men to ferry them across the bay to Fire Island. One of the men carried two pistols, another who spoke Italian, and the last who was a deaf-mute. The fisherman was worried the men would kill him, so he asked his friends to watch the men's horses which were left on the Sayville shore. He was afraid they might try to escape after shooting him. He hoped that his friends could then find him in time to save his life. The fisherman said the three men drove a stake in the ground when they landed on Fire Island. Then the next day, they walked west until they could see a church steeple from across the bay in Babylon. The men then split up and one of them returned to the stake. They then walked toward each other, one from the stake, and the other two from the place across from the steeple. They walked until they met each other in the middle of the two points. The deaf mute then dug down into the sand until they retrieved four leather bags. The fisherman rowed the men back across the bay to Sayville. The fisherman's friends were there, and they watched as the men mounted their horses. My father said that as the men sped away, they were flinging back silver coins to the fisherman. The fisherman then shared the coins with his friends and they swore each other to secrecy, still afraid for their lives."

Louis asked, "Then how did your father hear about this?"

Hannah shrugged, "Alcohol often loosens tongues."

Later in her tent, Hannah lay awake while the others slept. A sound from outside suddenly put her on alert. Not wanting to disturb the others, she quietly crawled to the tent opening and peeked outside. She saw a boat in the moonlight, about 400 yards down the beach. Three men, one of them armed with a rifle, while the other two had shovels. They were burying something in the sand. Of course, she thought about the old stories of pirates who had buried their treasures on Fire Island and wondered what these men were about. She wanted to get closer to them to get a better look, but then heard the rustling of the baby behind her. So instead, she closed the flap of the tent and went to Bobby to comfort him and ease him back to quiet slumber. When she looked outside again, the men were gone.

The next morning, she told Philip what she had seen and they all decided to take a walk in the direction of where the men had been digging. "Here it is," Philip announced. It was almost undetectable. If they hadn't known where to look for it, they wouldn't have seen the signs of the disturbed sand.

Louis took a shovel he had brought with them and started to dig. It wasn't long before he hit something hard. He carefully unearthed the wooden crate and sat back on his heels. It took all of both Philip and Louis's strength to lift the crate out of the hole and onto the surface. With the edge of the shovel, Philip broke the seal and opened the lid. Inside, lay dozens of bottles of rum packed in hay.

The sound of men approaching caused them all to look up at the same time. Two men walked toward them coming from the bay side of the island. Each man carried a shovel and were evidently on their way to dig up the crate that Philip and Louis had just unearthed.

With one baby in her arms and Frankie clinging to her leg, a moment of fear passed between the group until Hannah recognized the men. They were William Smythe and Clarence White, two of her father's baymen friends.

Both men were getting on in years now and William was breathing heavily from the exertion of walking over the dunes. Catching his breath, he said, "Hannah? What are you doing here?"

Hannah hesitated to answer, she could surmise now what was going on, but decided to ask the men some questions anyway. "What are *you* doing here, Mr. Smythe?"

Remembering the little girl who had so often accompanied them as they shucked oysters in the shack, he answered as both men lessened the distance between themselves and Hannah, "That crate belongs to us."

Hannah shook her head in disapproval, "Why would you do this?"

Mr. White hung his head as he spoke, "Hannah, the oyster industry isn't what it once was. There's no room for independent baymen anymore. They pay us good money to come here and dig up a crate and bring it across the bay. We then hand it off to men who bring the crate to the speakeasies."

Hannah tried to wrap her head around this revelation. These men were decent men. They were law-abiding family men, not criminals. She stammered, "I-I still don't understand. Why take the chance? It's dangerous." She pointed to the ocean, "The men you are dealing with are armed and lawless. They are without scruples. They belong in prison."

Mr. White continued, "I know all that you've been told by the Temperance Society and the Anti-Saloon League, but the truth is that there are more speakeasies and roadhouses now than there were saloons before Prohibition was put in place. They are in almost every hotel, restaurant, fishing and hunting lodge on Long Island."

She was worried for them and so she asked another question, "But what about the alcohol itself? Is it safe? What chances are people taking by drinking it?"

Mr. Smythe replied, "I can't speak to the safety of it. Truth is, it would be safer for everyone if they changed the law. When alcohol was legal, there were regulations in place. There were inspectors to make sure the alcohol was made under sanitary conditions and imported through proper channels. The way it is now, no one knows what they are drinking. But people are going to drink. No law is going to stop them."

Hannah asked, "Aren't you afraid of being caught? You could be arrested."

Mr. White nodded, "Sure, we know. The Coast Guard is patrolling these waters and they are looking for the rum runners. But we are just two old men digging for buried treasure." He smiled a toothless grin.

"How does it work? Please tell me."

The men looked at each other before answering. Mr. White leaned on his shovel for support, "There are agents in all the villages on both the south shore and on the north shore of Long Island. They guarantee delivery. It's very organized with men from the vessels at sea and all. The money passes through only a few hands. Very hush, hush. We only know where to pick up the crate and where to drop it off. That's all. The money's already in the crate when we dig it up. We never see or talk to anyone else. We just get a telegram that's in code telling us it's time to take another trip to Fire Island."

Mr. White reached into the crate and took out an envelope full of cash. He took out several bills and offered them to Hannah. Hannah backed away, "No thank you. You keep it."

The men both nodded and Mr. White said, "Much obliged." Each man grabbed a side of the crate and carried it back to the bay side of the island.

Two days later, Philip watched Hannah as she scribbled on a piece of paper. "What are you up to, Hannah?"

"I've got to tell this story."

Philip worried for her safety, "You'll get those men in trouble if you do."

"No, I won't. I won't say who they were."

"Someone will find out. At the very least, they'll lose the opportunity to make money. There are dangerous people out there."

Hannah lifted her chin as she remembered her father telling her that she should be careful. He had always worried, and for good reason, that her propensity for being outspoken would get her in trouble. But she needed to tell the truth. "It's what I have to do." She was a reporter and she needed to report what was happening. And so, without another word, she returned to writing the article.

The article appeared in the Suffolk County News on the following Thursday. She wrote in favor of the unpopular view that the 18<sup>th</sup> Amendment needed to be revoked. Instead of making their communities safer, it had invited criminals and dangerous practices. It had enticed good citizens to break the law and had, in fact, not prevented the practice of drinking. The encounter and subsequent research, had convinced her that it had only succeeded in making the business unregulated and hazardous for all involved. She had discovered that government officials and the police force, itself, were involved in the underworld of mob activities and that enforcement of prohibition was impossible because of alliances between those involved in boot-legging and those who were charged with enforcing the law.

But for all her bravado, once the article was published, the reaction to it set her on a tailspin. A week later, Philip came home to find Hannah sitting at the kitchen table with her face in her hands. Tears and sobs spilled between her fingers. Alarmed, Philip pulled up a chair beside her and placed his hand comfortingly on her back. He gently asked, "What is it, Hannah? What has happened?"

Hannah looked up at him with her tear stained face, "Ilsa told me Will won't allow Ollie to play with Frankie. She said that Will has told her to cut her ties with me. That I am seen as a 'pot-stirrer' and he has forbidden her from seeing me and has forbidden their children from playing with ours. Oh, Philip, it is horrible enough that this animosity is directed toward me. I've dealt with it before. But to have it directed at our children is something I just can't bear."

Philip took a deep breath, "I was fearful of what the reaction would be to your article, but I've had some time to think about it. I am so proud of you, Hannah. You only need to stand by your convictions and time will show that you were right. This is something that I know. Others will find out eventually and see how smart and percep-tive you really were. Someday, you will be remembered for your bravery and will be revered by future generations. That is worth the rebuffs of people like Will Amundsen. He is not half the person you are."

For a while, Hannah was publicly ostracized by the respected members of the community; but secretly, many applauded her for speaking out. And one of those was The Grand Dame of Sayville, Ida Gillette. Since the article had hit the newspaper, Hannah often walked through town with her eyes cast down, avoiding the stares and sneers of those around her. So, she was surprised when she heard Ida's voice addressing her.

"Hannah darling, lift your chin, straighten your back. You are a force to be reckoned with. Don't let anyone cast shade on your sunlight." And just like that, Hannah felt a weight lift off her shoulders. Ida said, "There you go," and gave Hannah a nod of approval before walking away.

# CHAPTER FORTY-THREE

### 1928

The planes looped, circled, and spun as they plunged toward the Earth, only to recover and soar once again to the clouds. Frankie's eyes widened as he watched the flying circus above him. It was the grand opening of Islip Airport and much excitement had been building for weeks as word spread that Charles Lindbergh might attend. Lindbergh was Frankie's idol. He clutched his paper airplane in his hand, it was a replica of The Spirit of St. Louis, the single-engine Ryan monoplane that had carried Lindbergh from Long Island to Paris a year earlier. Frankie had been overwhelmed when he had seen the paper planes being sold at Thornhill's and had begged his parents to buy him one. It was a bit tattered now, but it was among his most treasured possessions.

Perched on his father's shoulders, he saw several people ascend the platform in front of him and heard the announcer say, "We are honored to be joined today by none other than the darling of aeronautics, Miss Amelia Earhart." Frankie's heart pounded. At seven years old, he had become a huge fan of these remarkable pilots. The announcer informed the crowd, "In June, Miss Earhart became the first woman to fly across the Atlantic Ocean in her Fokker F7 named Friendship. She completed the flight in 20 hours and 40 minutes."

Next, the man introduced a pretty teenager, "And here we have 'The Flying Flapper of Freeport', Miss Elinor Smith. At only sixteen years of age, she received her pilot's license from the Federal Aviation Administration, and it was signed by none other than Orville Wright! Since then, she has become known for her daring stunts, and much is expected and anticipated for the future of her flying career. Better watch out, Amelia!" The crowd roared.

A man walked up to the microphone and Frankie asked his parents, "Is that him? Is that Mr. Lindbergh?"

Philip said, "I don't believe so, son."

The announcer continued with his introductions, "Standing here is Clarence Chamberlin. Last year, he and Charles A. Levine, flew from Roosevelt Field to Mansfeld, Germany, completing a record 3,911 miles in 43 hours, and beating Lindbergh's 3,600-mile flight to Paris."

Clarence Chamberlin bowed his head and replied in deference to Lindbergh, "Indeed, but as you all know, Lindbergh's flight was solo, whereas, mine was not."

The announcer looked out at the crowd, waiting in anticipation, "Finally, Mr. Lindbergh has sent his regrets that he was not able to make it to this celebration today." The crowd sighed in disappointment. "Now, now, hold on folks. There is still much more to enjoy today. So please, raise your eyes to the sky once more and be amazed at the bravery and skill gathered here today for your enjoyment. And now," he announced, "'The Voice from The Sky'!"

From far above the crowd, music reached their ears as it was broadcast from a tri-motored Fokker. The crowd of over 10,000 people let out a cheer. Never before had any of them heard music broadcasted from the sky.

As they drove home later, Philip told Frankie, "I hope you weren't too disappointed that Charles Lindbergh wasn't able to make it."

Mature beyond his years, Frankie responded, "Well, I would have liked to see him. But it was a great show! I'm gonna be a pilot like them some day. I'm gonna fly across the Atlantic Ocean and I'm gonna beat all of their records."

Philip chuckled, "Well, Hannah, it looks like our son is going to need some flying lessons."

Hannah frowned and remembered a time when Frankie was fascinated by trains and she had sworn that her son would never be a pilot. "Perhaps it is just a phase. There's plenty of time for that, he's far too young at the moment."

"No I'm not, Momma! Elinor Smith started taking lessons when she was only ten years old."

Hannah turned to look at her son in the back seat of their automobile, "And you are seven."

"Yeah, mom, but she's a girl."

Hannah scoffed, "And why does that make a difference?"

"Well, you know, mom." But he didn't say anything further. Looking at his mother he knew he had better leave that one alone.

"I do know, my son." Then she smiled at him, and he let out a sigh of relief.

# CHAPTER FORTY-FOUR

1929

Between Jean's world travels and both women starting families, life had gotten busy for both Hannah and Jean Roosevelt. They hadn't seen much of each other over the past several years. Together now, the two women watched over their children playing in the Meadow Croft pool. Jean held her baby boy, Philip, in her arms. The child squirmed as he tried to reach his older sister, three-year-old Phillipa. Phillipa screamed as Hannah's boys, eight-year-old Frankie and five-year-old Bobby, splashed her while they raced around the pool. Hannah also held a baby in her arms, her youngest child, Nancy. The little girl she had hoped for, was turning out to be the easiest of her children. Hannah rested her cheek against the soft downy head of her sleeping daughter.

Jean had married her second cousin, Philip James Roosevelt, in May of 1925. Their husbands sat in lounge chairs near the pool discussing business. Hannah could hear Jean's husband trying to persuade Philip to invest in the stock market. But as usual, Philip refused.

Philip warned, "I don't trust the market, nor banks for that matter, and you shouldn't either."

A guffaw erupted from Philip James' throat, "I don't understand you. You are an intelligent and forward thinking man. The real money to be made is on Wall Street, not on Main Street."

At thirty-five years old, Philip was used to people trying to convince him to trust banks and invest in stocks. But Philip knew something that no one else did, there was going to be a crash and it was going to happen this October. There was no way for him to warn others without giving away his secret. So he tried, as well as he could, to convince them that he believed it to be too risky and hoped that they would take his advice.

As his business grew, he had chosen to have a cast iron safe installed in the basement of his photography shop. The safe was hidden behind a false wall to insure that it would be protected from thieves. Over the years, he had developed a reputation as a prudent man who paid cash for whatever he bought and invested in nothing but his own business and property.

Philip James continued, "Don't you see that your money could be tripled in just a few minutes?"

Philip responded, "And it can be lost in a day."

Jean's husband shook his head, "Never. That could never happen."

Philip took a deep breath and said, "Don't say I didn't warn you."

Jean called over to them, "Philip!" She chuckled and then, as the heads of both men turned toward her, said to Hannah, "It is convenient that we both married men named Philip, we only need to call one and they both come." Then to their husbands she said, "Enough talk of money. Come join us in the pool. The children want their fathers. Hannah, do you remember the time my Philip and our cousin, Kermit, rode their bicycles all the way here from Oyster Bay just because he wanted to see me."

Hannah said, "I don't think so. I remember hearing about the visit by horse, but not by bicycle."

Jean responded, "Well, it was September of 1904 and Kermit, the second son of the president, was fifteen at the time. He and Philip, who was then twelve, rode their bicycles all the way from Oyster Bay to Meadow Croft."

Philip James boasted, "We made the journey of 42 miles in less than five hours. We were a bit worse for the wear and Aunt Nannie threw us into the bath to make us presentable for the dinner table. But we did have a blast, fishing, and then automobiling."

Jean added, "And making eyes at me?"

Philip James responded, "Of course, my dear. I have always only had eyes for you."

Hannah and Philip exchanged a look of amusement at the love that was so evident between Jean and Philip James. And yet, Hannah did not envy them their relationship, because it was complicated by wealth and fame. After all, her own relationship was as deep and wide as any, but she and Philip did not have to gain the approval of family members.

Hannah now admired her husband. He still kept himself in shape, and the sight of his tanned firm chest made her heart beat faster. He was her home, her safe place. She trusted him with every fiber of her being and loved him even more than that. Theirs was a good marriage. Of course, they had had their moments, but all in all, it had been better than any other marriage she knew of. As Philip James mentioned, her husband was a forward thinking man. But only she and Harry knew why. Hannah had not shared that information with anyone else, not even with Jean.

Philip asked, "Where is your father, Jean?"

"He doesn't come out from the city much anymore. He's actually thinking of moving down to Florida. He is done with the cold and snow each winter. Meadow Croft hasn't been the same for him since Gladys died. Well, for that matter, it really hasn't been the same for him since Mother passed away. But he put up with it for us; until the accident. And now with Pansy gone, he doesn't need to be here to look out for her well-being."

Hannah knew that Jean's oldest sister, Pansy, had died of an illness in February, while still living in an institution in Whitestone, Queens. This had left Jean as the only surviving child of John Ellis Roosevelt and Nannie Vance.

Hannah asked, "I suppose the running of the house is up to you now."

Jean shrugged her shoulders gently, as her baby had finally fallen asleep as well, "I hired a new man, a Mr. Loughlin, as caretaker a few years ago."

Philip's ears perked up and without thinking said, "Barney Loughlin?"

Jean looked confused, "Well, no, his name is Michael Joseph Loughlin, but his youngest son is named Barney; the child is four years old. Do you know him?"

Philip faltered, "I-I must know a different Barney Loughlin. The Barney I knew was an older man."

Jean replied, "Perhaps a relative?"

Philip answered, "Yes, perhaps." But he thought of the man who owned a vineyard behind Meadow Croft in 2012 and knew that this little boy, was one and the same.

Jean continued, "Anyway, he seems very competent. He used to work as a Motorman on the trolley in the city. He took his family to Ireland for a while around the time of the Great War and then returned a few years ago. In fact, young Barney was born in Sayville, shortly after Joseph took the position as caretaker here. We've had a little cottage built for them on the property so that they can live here year-round. No more worrying about the place when we're in the city or elsewhere."

Hannah responded, "I'm sure that is a relief."

The men played with the older children as Hannah and Jean took their babies back to the house and laid them down for naps. Jean had been redecorating Meadow Croft and putting her own stamp on it. There were mementos from her trips around the world, including the months she had toured the Far East after the death of Gladys. In addition, there was now a dial telephone on her desk, a large radio that complemented the furniture in her parlor, and electric fans to help keep the rooms cool. The kitchen was equipped with a variety of up-to-date electric appliances including a toaster and mixer. Hannah admired everything and made a mental note of what she would need in her own home.

With the babies asleep and the older children occupied with their fathers, Hannah and Jean decided to play a game of cards. As they played, Jean asked, "How is your brother, Hannah? Did he ever marry?"

Hannah felt her own back arch in defense. She was so used to defending him against those who judged him harshly. "No, he purchased a barge home on Fire Island last year and manages the Cherry Grove Hotel. He spends most of his time there."

Jean responded, "I'm sorry; a barge home? What does that mean?"

"After they closed down Camp Upton in Yaphank, they floated buildings from the camp across the water on barges to Cherry Grove. It was quite a sight to see, houses floating on the bay!"

Jean smiled, "Fascinating, I imagine."

Hannah nodded and let the conversation drop. Harry had always been different. He had never said what she knew to be true, but Harry was not interested in women the way most men were. Harry told others that Edmund and he were just roommates, but as his twin, Hannah knew instinctively that there was more to it than that.

After that pleasant day spent together, it was months before Hannah heard from Jean again.

On October 29, 1929, the stock market on Wall Street crashed, leaving many, both wealthy and working class men, penniless. Jean called Hannah on the phone, "Hannah, I just wanted to say, your Philip was right. The crash has destroyed the lives of so many, I wish my Philip had listened to him. But we will be all right. However, do you remember Walt?"

Hannah hadn't heard his name in years, but it still stirred emotion in her to hear it, "Yes, of course."

"Well, darling, he and his family have lost everything and his father has taken his own life. Jumped out of the window of a twenty-story building."

Hannah replied, "I'm so sorry to hear that Jean. Some Sayville men lost everything as well. Now they are working in the city, doing manual labor, helping to build the new Triborough Bridge and a tunnel being built between New York and Long Island. Others want to stay close to home, and they are putting in drainage pipes from Main Street down to the Bay, on both Foster Avenue and Green Avenue. They're also putting in sidewalks and curbs. The men are working for 10 cents an hour. They are employed by the government, the WPA. It's supposed to stand for Works Progress Administration, but everyone's been calling it, We Potter Around."

Jean whispered, "A friend of my father's lost his fortune. He rented a hotel room and turned on the gas. He died of asphyxiation. There are bread lines wrapping around blocks in the city. There's no decent work to be had. How are you and Philip doing?"

"We're fine, thank you. Philip was prepared for something like this and we are doing what we can to help others. We have been organizing clothing and food donations for those who lost their jobs. I suppose, in a way, it has become a great equalizer. So many are now in *the same boat*, as they say. Together, we will all get through this."

Jean replied, "Yes, dear. But prudence, as in the case of your husband's business ventures, has proven to be an education for us all."

# CHAPTER FORTY-FIVE

1930 – 1931

Giorgio and Elisabetta passed away within a few months of each other and Philip felt as if he had lost his parents once again. On his deathbed, Giorgio handed Philip a letter and told him, "You have been a son to us and we couldn't have loved you more if you had been born to us. I have written down my wishes in this letter. I am leaving our home and whatever we have left, to you."

Philip responded, "Giorgio, you don't have to do that."

Giorgio lifted his hand to quiet Philip, "All I ask is that you do the same for others. Other children who find themselves alone. There is no greater joy than to share what you have with those who have even less."

Philip took the letter and his thoughts immediately went to Louis. He nodded through his tears and promised Giorgio he would do as he requested.

That June, Louis graduated from high school and his eighteenth birthday was only a month away. Louis had been dreading this birthday for years. At eighteen, he would have to leave the Cottages and fend for himself. He was grateful for all they had done for him, for giving him a safe place to grow, an education, and even, a "family". But for all that they had done for him, he still felt unprepared to face the world alone and wondered what he would do next.

Louis opened the door to Philip's shop. Just inside the door was a glass case that displayed the cameras and film that were for sale. Beyond that was a photographer's studio where Philip took pictures of Sayville residents and visitors in front of backgrounds painted on screens. All the way in the rear of the building, was the darkroom. A metallic smell lingered in the air from the chemicals used in developing film.

A colored couple was posing in front of a backdrop of the beach, while Philip, perched behind his camera, directed them into position. The man, who was dressed sharply in a tailored suit, was shorter than the generously plump woman standing by his side. Philip knew who they were, they were infamous in Sayville. To some, Father Divine was a savior, to others, he was a pestilence.

Addressing the woman, Philip suggested, "Mother Divine, perhaps you could tilt your head toward Father Divine. Yes, that's it. Perhaps, just a little bit more."

The woman's shoulder lowered as her head tilted and evened out the difference in height between the couple.

Louis waited patiently, not wanting to disrupt the photo session. He admired how Philip was able to bring out the best images of his clients. Sayville was a resort town, and as the bungalows had filled with city visitors each year, the slots for Philip's photography sessions had filled as well. But the Great Depression that now gripped the country, had put a large dent in people's bank accounts. Luxuries, like photo sessions, were put off in favor of putting food on the table and clothes on the backs of growing children.

Noticing Louis, Philip asked, "Louis, could you bring that chair over for Mother Divine to sit on?"

"Sure, sir." Louis placed the wooden chair where Philip directed and Mother Divine sat heavily into it, her white dress fanning around her. Father Divine stood beside her now and smiled broadly into the camera. Clearly, this was a position that he preferred.

When the photography session ended, Father Divine reached his hand out to Louis. "I don't believe we have had the pleasure of meeting, young man."

Louis took the man's outstretched hand and said, "I don't think we have, Sir. But I have heard much about you."

Father Divine chuckled, "I hope all good!"

Louis' face paled, not all had been good, but he said, "Yes, Sir. Of course."

Father Divine asked, "Where do you live, son?"

"At The Cottages, Sir."

Father Divine observed, "You're getting a bit old for that place I imagine."

"Yes, Sir, I'll be graduating from high school this month and turning eighteen in July. So it won't be home for much longer. That's true."

"Well now, you come by and see me sometime for dinner then. 42 Macon Street. Any day of the week is fine. We'll fill your belly up with a good home-cooked meal whenever you need one."

Thinking this was very generous, Louis' face glowed, "That is very kind of you, Sir."

"Not at all, it is my work as *God* to help guide my people."

Father Divine then turned to Philip and said, "How much for today?"

Philip responded, "That will be $25 for the session."

Father Divine took out a crisp $50 bill and laid it on the glass display case as he said, "Keep the change."

As soon as the couple left, Philip warned Louis, "Be wary of Father Divine, Louis. He believes himself to be Jesus Christ. He says that he came to the world the first time as a white man and now has returned as a black man. He doesn't say he serves God; he says he *is* God."

Louis nodded, but thought he would still take Father Divine up on his offer for dinner. After all, a meal was a meal.

Philip looked concerned for a moment and then he turned to put away his equipment. As he did so, a thought came into his head, "Louis, when school ends, would you like to come to work for me?"

Nodding vigorously, Louis responded, "That would be great! Yeah. Wow! That would be a big help, Sir."

"Okay, help me clean up here and I will give you your first lesson in developing film."

The following Sunday, Louis walked up Macon Street to check out the address that Father Divine had given him. The large house was not hard to find. Cars lined the street while others were parked on the lawn. The two-storied, many-gabled house had wide open windows shaded by striped awnings. Everywhere, people milled about. Mostly colored, but also white folk.

Nervously, he stood outside and watched the excited crowd. A middle-aged colored woman saw him standing there and asked if he needed help. Louis explained, "I met Father Divine a few days ago and he invited me to stop by for dinner. He said any time was good, but it looks like he's busy today. I'll come back another time."

"Now, now, don't be silly. Come on in, dinner's about to be served and there's always room for one more."

She turned and started walking toward the house. When he didn't move, she looked back toward him and said, "I don't have all day. Come along, now."

The room was huge; a table was set for about fifty people. The woman showed him an empty seat near the foot of the table and said, "Welcome to Heaven." Father and Mother Divine were both seated at the head of the table, Father Divine nodded when he caught sight of Louis. Then he stood and asked those gathered to pray with him. "My children, let us be thankful for our bounty and each other's company. You come to my table today to fill your bodies, but with prayer, I will also fill your souls. There is no reason for death. My followers, you will be saved from such an ending as long as you believe in me and are without sin. I will heal you in your time of need."

The table erupted, "Praise Father Divine! Praise the Lord!"

When Father Divine took his seat again, women walked into the dining room carrying trays of food that they then placed on the table. Louis' eyes grew large as trays and bowls of macaroni, rice, potatoes, peas, baked beans, corn, mashed turnips, baked tomatoes, turkey, ham, cornbread, biscuits, cake, pie, peaches and salad were set before him. Never had he seen so much food in his life.

After dinner, Father Divine called for him to come and take a seat beside him. Louis was conscious of the palpable jealousy that this aroused from some in the room. However, feeling honored to be chosen, he sat beside Father Divine.

"Did you enjoy your meal, Louis?"

"Yes, Sir, I did. Everything was delicious."

"Are you sure you don't want any more?"

"Oh no, Sir. I couldn't eat another thing."

Father Divine seemed pleased with this answer, "I tell you what," he said, "I will have the ladies pack some of it up for you to take with you."

"Oh, really, Sir, I would appreciate that."

"Yes, you can share it with your friends at The Cottages."

Louis nodded vigorously, "That is very generous of you, Sir."

Father Divine shook his head, "Not at all. So tell me, Louis, where will you go when you leave The Cottages?"

"Mr. Ferrara has offered me a job at the photography studio. But I will need to find a room to rent in the area."

Father Divine looked deep into Louis' eyes. Louis could feel his heart beat faster. This was a man who held a power over others. He was charismatic and his smile made you want to please him. "Son, when the time comes, you have a room at my house if you'd like."

"Really? I-I don't know how to thank you, Sir."

"Don't worry, we will make the necessary arrangements. You will see. You will have a home with us."

On the day after his eighteenth birthday, Louis packed his small suitcase with his personal belongings. As he parted, he told his young friends, "I'll still be here; I'm not going far. Sayville is still my home."

He walked to 42 Macon Street and was greeted by Mother Divine who showed him to his new room. It was simple, but adequate. It was the first time in his life that he had a room to himself. His possessions were so few, that they only filled two of the four drawers in the dresser assigned to him. In the closet, he hung his only suit and his winter coat. All of these items had been donated to the Cottages by the community.

In the days that followed, he learned that after the daily meals, each just as large as the first he had experienced, a jubilant congregation spent most of the night in adulation, praising Father Divine as Jesus Christ and thanking him for the bounty offered to them and asking for peace and forgiveness. The voices carried on through all hours of the night and sleep was nearly impossible.

Each day, he dressed for work in the morning and appeared at the photography studio with increasingly weary eyes in spite of his full belly. Knowing how Philip felt about Father Divine, Louis refrained from telling him he was now living at Heaven. Instead, he just told Philip that he had rented a room nearby. Each week, Louis turned his entire paycheck over to Father Divine in return for his room and board. He worked all summer, but had nothing to show for it at summer's end. He soon realized that under these terms, he would never be able to move out of Father Divine's house. Concerned about this situation, he approached Mother Divine one day and expressed his desire to keep some of his pay for savings. She told him, "You don't need anything beyond what we give you at Heaven. To think about yourself is a selfish thought. And selfishness is a sin."

As the weeks went by, Philip tried to give the boy the opportunity to come to him with whatever it was that was bothering him, but Louis became less and less talkative.

Toward the end of summer, Philip asked Louis, "Mrs. Ferrara is making a roast tonight. Would you like to join us for dinner?"

Louis hesitated for a moment too long. "What is it, Louis? Something has been bothering you. Are you not happy working here?"

Louis looked conflicted and almost afraid to answer. "Come now, you can tell me. We're old friends, aren't we? Whatever it is you have to tell me, it's all right." Louis reminded Philip of himself at that age, set adrift in a world he didn't quite understand. He remembered feeling like the secrets he held were too much of a burden to share with others.

Louis took a deep breath, "Sir. I've been living at Father Divine's house; the house they call Heaven. He offered me a place to stay and, well, I didn't have anywhere else to go. There's so much food. But . . ."

Philip's concerned deepened even further at the mention of Father Divine. "But what?" Philip asked.

"But, in return I have to hand over my paycheck each week and I have to praise him as Jesus Christ like his other followers do. If I don't, I can't stay there, and I don't have anywhere else to go."

"Louis, why didn't you tell me this earlier? You know I would have helped you. Haven't I always been there for you?"

"Yes, you have. You've been very generous to me over the years. But I thought I could do this on my own, and with you and Hannah having three children, I didn't want to bother you and the Mrs."

If it wasn't for Louis, Philip would never have known Hannah. He wouldn't have the family he now treasured so much. He felt guilt. Guilty at not following up more closely on what was happening in Louis' life. Guilt at having introduced him to Father Divine. And guilt at perhaps looking the other way, so as not to have another obligation added to the list he already had with the store and a growing family during this damned Depression.

"Louis, the tenants just moved out of the apartment above the store. They moved to Ohio to be with family. It's vacant and it's already furnished. It has everything you need. You can stay here, if you'd like. If you need me to, I will go with you to Divine's house and we will gather your things and bring them here."

Louis wiped the back of his hand across his wet face, embarrassed at the tears. After all, wasn't he a man now at eighteen? Men didn't cry.

He looked down at his feet and said, "That won't be necessary, I can go myself. But I would like to take you up on the offer. Both actually, for dinner and for the apartment. I am forever in your debt. Anything I can ever do for you, don't hesitate to ask, Mr. Ferrara. You have been too good to me."

Not wanting to embarrass Louis further, Philip agreed to let him go for his things, but he said, "First, come to the house for dinner. Then after dinner, you can go to Divine's and pack up your belongings." Lifting a set of keys off of a board behind the cash register, Philip handed them to Louis and said, "Here's the keys to the store and the apartment. The apartment is yours as long as you need it."

Over dinner, Philip and Louis explained the situation to Hannah. She shook her head, "Something has to be done about Father Divine. There was a young woman who stayed at Heaven in April, she was an undercover reporter for The Suffolk County News. She's not from around here, so her face wasn't familiar to anyone at Heaven. She told of the grand dinners and non-stop parties that went on at Heaven. The neighbors have lost all the value of their homes, no one wants to live near that place because they carry on all night long. Not to mention that those who follow him are told to leave their families and become his disciples. Men and women both, have abandoned their families. Those who owned properties, handed over their deeds to him. Those who have paychecks hand them over as well. But no matter what the authorities charge him with, he always gets away with it. He's taking advantage of people, but the authorities say it is not a crime to think you are Jesus Christ, nor for others to believe it."

When Louis left them, he headed straight for Heaven. Father Divine stopped him at the door, "You missed dinner tonight, Louis."

"I was invited to dinner at Mr. Ferrara's house. He also offered me the apartment above the store to stay in. So I want to thank you for helping me out when I needed it. But I'm going to go get my things now, and I'll be moving out tonight."

Father Divine stared at Louis, his eyes penetrating, no longer friendly. "We have no personal possessions in this house. Whatever we come here with, becomes the property of all who reside here."

Louis understood, he was being told that he was not allowed to gather his own meager belongings. "But Sir, it's all I have. Not just my clothes, there's some personal things that have. They're of no value to you, but mean everything to me."

"What things?" Father Divine asked.

"There's a box, it has a lock of my mother's hair in it and a picture of my family along with a few other things I've collected over the years."

Father Divine took a deep breath before asking, "Where is this box?"

"It's in the top drawer of the dresser in my room."

Father Divine turned to Sister Jane, a woman who had lived in the house with him for years. "Go up to Louis' room and find a box in his dresser. Bring it to me."

When Sister Jane returned with the box, Father Divine took it from her and opened it. As Louis said, there was nothing of value in it that he could see. He shoved it at Louis and spoke loudly so that all in the house could hear him. "I cannot protect you any longer. You have sinned against me, and you will suffer for it. I cast you out. Go now, and don't ever come back."

Over the next year, the residents heard more and more tales of what was going on in the house on Macon Street. Where once the storekeepers where happy to take his cash for their goods, they drew the line at the harm that Father Divine was doing to families. The Court House on Railroad Avenue was bombarded with suits against the man as children were left homeless, and as their fathers continued to turn the deeds to their homes over to Father Divine. In addition, accusations were thrown at Divine by husbands whose wives had left them to follow Divine in order to appease his sexual appetite.

After another night of carousing on Sunday, November 15th, on the early morning hours of the following day, the residents of Sayville had had enough. On November 20, 1931, the Court House was filled with several hundred spectators lining the street outside. Justice Charles H. Duryea presided over the court and, after a four-hour trial, found 28 of the 32 followers of Father Divine, guilty as charged, of disturbing of the peace.

The People had been represented by Joseph S. Arata, Jr. Witnesses reported that "Heaven" had been disorderly on the night in question. Divine's defense attorneys from Manhattan, Arthur A. Madison and Eileen J. Lovelace, had brought five witnesses who resided in the house at 42 Macon, who testified that there hadn't been any noise on that night. But Mr. Arata's witnesses for the prosecution far outnumbered the meager defense. All testified that they heard screaming and hollering all Sunday night and into the morning hours of Monday, November 16th. 46 persons had pled guilty and were charged a fine of $5 each, but only nine of the 46 could pay their fine.

Before dismissing the court, Mr. Arata asked Justice Duryea, "What about these unpaid fines? They total $185 due the court." Father Divine stepped forward at that moment and producing a crisp $500 bill, he laid it on the bench to the astonishment of the court.

A few days later, at 8 p.m. on Monday, November 23rd, a large crowd of 700 residents held a massive meeting at the Sayville Court House. The entire town, afraid that their businesses would be ruined by the continued presence of Father Divine and his followers, called for Divine to leave Sayville. With the entire community now against him, Father Divine moved his congregation to Harlem in January, leaving a few of his followers to continue to occupy the home on Macon Street.

# CHAPTER FORTY-SIX

1931

F rankie ran home as fast as he could. He had exciting news to share with his mother. When Hannah saw his face all flushed, she asked him, "What in the world has gotten into you, son?"

Out of breath, he blurted out, "I got a job! Mr. Thornhill said he's in a bind and needs someone to deliver medicine for him. I was in there, just to get one of those horehound candies, you know? And he says to me, 'Frankie, do you want a job?' And I says, 'Sure do!' Well, then he explains to me that the boy who usually delivers his medicines for him broke his ankle and can't work right now. So, you see, he needs someone in the meantime. What do you think, Mom? He told me I had to ask you first."

Hannah gave Frankie a glass of water. The sun was blazing and the boy had run all the way home from Thornhill's and now stood before her, sweat plastering his hair to his head. "Sit down and drink this."

"Okay, Ma, but please say yes."

Frankie was only ten years old, but being her firstborn, he had grown up quickly and had become her right hand at home. He was smart and did well in school, he was athletic and enjoyed playing softball with his friends. He was the child she thought she didn't have to worry about. Bobby, on the other hand, didn't like to leave her side. She could hear Nancy crying, awakened from her nap by all the excitement.

"Well," she replied, "I guess we can give it a try. It's a big responsibility though. Are you sure you're up to it?"

"Of course, Ma!"

"All right, then."

Frankie jumped off his seat almost toppling over the half-filled glass of water. "I gotta go tell him! He may need me right now."

"Okay, but I want you home for supper."

"I will be, Mom. And, thanks." He gave her a quick peck on her cheek before running out the door. Frankie grabbed his bicycle and headed back toward town. When he reached Thornhill's, his new employer was amused and gratified to see Frankie's eagerness to perform his first task. Mr. Thornhill took a paper bag off of a shelf and handed it to him. "Here's your first job, Frankie. Take this package to Miss Gillette. The address is on the bag." Frankie placed the paper bag in his bicycle's basket and peddled off to deliver the medicine.

Ida Gillette was now 80 years old. Although she had never had children of her own, she considered all of the children of Sayville to be hers. When Frankie came to her door, she recognized him as Hannah's son. "How is your mother, Dear?"

"Oh, she's fine, Miss Gillette. Thank you for asking."

Ida smiled, "Such a nice boy. Your mother has taught you well."

Frankie beamed back at her, pleased that she thought his mother had done a good job in raising him. Ida lifted her right hand and said, "Hold on a moment, dear. Let me get something for you."

Ida shuffled away from the front door of her home and came back a moment later. She handed Frankie a shiny quarter and the boy stuffed it in his pants' pocket for safekeeping.

Ida opened the bag to check that it contained the right medicine. She read the label, Vinol. She chucked, "Yes, the cure for everything that ails a woman." Then she looked back at Frankie, "Now what are you going to buy with my quarter?"

"I'm saving it, Ma'am."

"And what are you saving it for?"

"For flying lessons, Ma'am."

"Flying lessons! Ah, you are your mother's son. Well, then, young man, here's another quarter." When she handed it to him, he shook his head.

"That's too much, Ma'am."

"Nonsense. If my quarter feeds your aspirations, then it is a quarter well spent. What is your name young man?"

"Frankie."

"I will tell Mr. Thornhill that his new delivery boy is a great addition to his staff. Unfortunately, that other boy he had before you often left his manners on the sidewalk." She made a distasteful grimace. "Now, I feel better already. Come by and have a visit when you have time. I may have some work for you here. I'm getting old and could use an enterprising young man, such as yourself, to help with the garden. I'll pay you well, mind you."

Frankie's eyes widened in the anticipation of making more money, "Well, thank you again, Ma'am. I will come back when I can."

"Good. In the meantime, I will write up a list of tasks for you to do."

Frankie rode back to Thornhill's and felt like he was on top of the world. He now had two jobs and a plan to get those flying lessons he wanted so badly.

Sewell Thornhill was so impressed with Frankie's work over the next few weeks, that he was happy to give him the job, permanently, after his previous delivery boy decided not to return to his employ. His customers applauded Frankie's efficiency and Sewell appreciated the work ethic that Frankie exhibited. But the Depression had affected every business in Sayville, including Thornhill's. Although he was used to working seven days a week, from early in the morning until late at night, recently, he had cut back on his own hours. Instead, he now took half-a-day off, every week, to take a drive on the Long Island roads. Sewell enjoyed finding places for quiet walks in the woods. Although he hated to admit it, at sixty-four years old, it was time to slow down; just a little bit.

By late October, the trees were full of color. Tomorrow was Halloween and Sewell was anticipating the children who would be visiting his store for a treat. Sayville was growing, it was changing. As traveling by car and train became easier, more people were moving out to the island. Men who lost their jobs in the city, were being put to work building roads and adding track to the railroad on Long Island. Whereas Sayville had once been the summer playground of millionaires, it was developing into a little town of middle-class hardworking families. After many of those millionaires had lost their fortunes in the crash, the hotels and summer resorts had been only half as full as they had been a couple of years before. The people who lived in Sayville year-round and who depended on the influx of those millionaires for their seasonal jobs, were struggling. Just when some hotels had invested in central heating so that they could be open year-round, people stopped coming. Restaurants and shops were starting to close up. Times were changing.

After an invigorating walk, Sewell returned to his car which he had parked at the side of the road, and sat down at the wheel. He thought he would close his eyes for a moment, but awoke to the sound of rain on the roof, and found that the sun was already low in the sky. He pressed his thumb and forefinger against his eyes, readjusting to the dark. With only minor trepidation, he put the car in gear and headed south toward Sayville. The hard-packed dirt road was slippery with oil, rain, and wet leaves. As he struggled to see the road ahead of him, he realized that perhaps it was time for a new prescription for his glasses. When he misjudged a ninety degree turn in the road that had suddenly appeared before him, he was startled to hear the sounds of crunching metal and shattered glass just before all went blank.

He felt his broken body being lifted into strong arms as a young man moved him. He heard the man say, "Mister, I'm going to take you to Mather Memorial Hospital in Port Jefferson. You've been hurt bad." The young man had quickly assessed the injuries and knew this was serious, the older man's chest had crushed the steering wheel to bits and his head had been driven through the glass windshield.

"No, please. Call someone to come and get my car and take me home to Sayville. My name is Sewell Thornhill. You can call my store; the phone number is 589-0001."

So instead of taking the injured man to the hospital, the young man drove to his own house, which was nearby, and called to have someone pick up the damaged car. He then called Thornhill's Drug Store to let them know what had happened and that he was driving Mr. Thornhill to Sayville. Sewell felt himself going in and out of consciousness as his body was painfully jostled along the dirt road to Sayville. Upon arrival at Thornhill's, the decision was made to bring him directly to Dr. MacDonell's office. One look at the injuries, and

Dr. MacDonell called for an ambulance to transport him to South-side Hospital in Bay Shore.

As the doctors were assessing his injuries, he lay on the operating table. Sewell Thornhill had only one thought in his head, and asked, "Please, where is that man who has been so good to me?" He reached out for Dr. MacDonell's hand and said, "Find out his name and his address. I must thank him for all he has done."

He never got the chance to thank that young man, four days later, Sewell Thornhill died of his injuries on November 4th, 1931.

At the funeral, Frankie stood beside his parents and watched as members of the Sayville Masons carried the coffin from The Sayville Congregational Church to the hearse that waited outside. The crowd of townsfolk was considerable. After thirty-five years as the town's pharmacist, Sewell Thornhill had gained the love and respect of them all. He was laid to rest in St. Ann's Cemetery, and Frankie watched as Mrs. Thornhill and their sons, Sewell Jr. and Robert, wept for their loss. Standing beside them was William Thompson, the man who Mr. Thornhill had wanted to thank for helping him after his car had crashed into an oak tree on a lonely dark dirt road. Frankie admired Sewell Thornhill and had grown confident in himself due to his employer's encouragement. As he watched the coffin being lowered into the grave, he knew that he would remember Sewell Thornhill for the rest of his life.

# CHAPTER FORTY-SEVEN

## 1933

The Great Depression was reaching its tendrils out to the suburbs and beyond. Farms were abandoned, storefronts bordered up, families were destroyed when fathers were unable to get more work. As a result, the Sayville school teachers took a 10% cut in salary, but thankfully, no one lost their jobs. Superintendent Travis did what he could to keep the children's programs in place.

Some jobs came to Sayville when the Long Island Lighting Company office opened on Main Street to support the increased electricity use as more people left the city and moved father east on the Island. Simple entertainment became the glue that kept people together. Residents enjoyed silent films at the Sayville Theatre which were accompanied by The Oysterman Bank's, William Ryther, on the piano.

In spite of what was happening in the world, life and death went on for individuals. Philip and Hannah had welcomed another daughter into their family in early 1932 and they named her Filomena, but they called her Fanny. And now, one of the women who had inspired Hannah the most, had passed away.

It had been years since Hannah had taken the Brooklyn Ferry to Manhattan and her jaw dropped at the sight of the newly built Empire State Building piercing the sky. Hannah spoke with awe, "It's the tallest building in the world." Philip smiled at her amazement, "The Empire State Building will remain one of the grandest sights in New York City for years to come. But the World Trade Center will one day be the tallest."

"Did you visit this World Trade Center?"

"No. Unfortunately, when I was a boy, the twin towers of the World Trade Center fell to the ground after two airplanes crashed into them."

"Oh, my! That's awful!"

"Yes, it was an act of war. But, in 2012 they were rebuilding. I didn't get to see it finished though." Philip's heart sank for a moment, thinking that he would never see it rebuilt. But then Hannah leaned her head on his shoulder and his arm automatically brought her even closer to him. The smell of her hair, the way her body fit next to his, reminded him that he had gained so much more than he had lost. Again, he looked up at the skyline before him that was forever changed by this building that had only just been finished in 1931.

"Later, can we go up to the top of the Empire State Building?" Hannah asked.

"I'm sure we can."

They hired a car to take them uptown. On the way, they passed long breadlines where people stood waiting on sidewalks to receive food. Families in Sayville were going through difficult times, but the struggles were so much more apparent in the city. Hannah thought of how thankful she was that Philip had known to prepare for the crash and, although business was slow in Philip's store, they had enough to tide them over and keep them comfortable. So many others didn't. She reached her hand across the seat of the car to grab onto Philip's hand. He looked at her with concern for a moment, but then she smiled at him. Relieved, he smiled in return and patted her hand.

At Saint Thomas Episcopal Church on 53rd Street and 5th Avenue, Hannah watched as Alva's coffin was carried by the all-female pall-bearers into the church. They sat next to Jean Roosevelt and then looked around the church. Hannah recognized many familiar faces in the pews around her, suffragists she had admired along with members of famous families such as the Vanderbilts and the Roosevelts, including the former Governor of New York and newly-elected President of the United States, Franklin D. Roosevelt, and his wife, Eleanor. After the service, a small contingent made their way to the Bronx to bury Alva Smith Vanderbilt Belmont beside her husband, Oliver Belmont, in the Belmont Mausoleum at Woodlawn Cemetery. But Hannah and Philip did not join them for Alva's final journey. Instead, they took a car to 33rd Street and walked through the massive doors of The Empire State Building.

Philip was surprised to see that the inside of the building looked much the way he remembered it to be. Gilded walls, giant elevators, and shiny floors. At the top of the building, they stepped out onto the glass enclosed landing. Then they strolled around the perimeter of the building and admired the view from all angles. They could see New Jersey from one side and Long Island from the other. Philip recognized the distinctive Chrysler Building with its arched and spired top. But the 77-storied Chrysler Building was no match for the 102-floor Empire State Building.

Hannah remarked, "I never imagined I would see something like this."

Philip turned to her, "Hannah, I have the strangest feeling. It's like we are standing on the precipice of our lives. We can see behind us, and we can see ahead of us, all at the same time."

"What lies ahead, Philip? Tell me."

Philip frowned, "There is a war coming, Hannah. A war unlike any we have encountered so far. The man we saw today at Alva's funeral, President Roosevelt, will lead us through most of it. Bombs, powerful enough to wipe out an entire city in one moment, will finally end that war. The United States will become the leading world power and an economic boom will follow as more people spread out from the cities."

They watched as a dirigible airship passed over Manhattan, and Philip said wonderingly, "Commercial airplanes will fill the sky and take people around the world within hours. Medicines and vaccines will be discovered that will treat and cure diseases that have plagued mankind for centuries." He pointed up at the moon that could now be seen in the late afternoon sky, "And men will take a rocket to the moon and will walk on its surface."

Hannah shook her head, "So much ahead of us."

He held her closer again and kissed her full lips, "We will see it together. The good and the bad. The happy and the sad."

She smiled at him, "Yes. Whatever it is, as long as we are together, we will be fine."

Philip traced her face with his finger and said, "I love you." Her smile grew wider, "And I love you."

# CHAPTER FORTY-EIGHT

### 1934

Five-year-old Nancy played on the floor with Hannah's tin of buttons. The child matched buttons of the same color or same size and shape. Who had started the tin? It was a mystery to Hannah. She knew that her mother and grandmother had added buttons to it, but the tin itself, and some of the buttons in it, were part of her family for long before her grandmother was born. Sometimes when she searched for a button to match one that had been lost, she wondered about the people who had worn the buttons long ago. Their stories had been lost along the way, but the buttons had continued to be handed down through the generations.

Nancy could play with the buttons for hours, and Hannah was grateful for it while she packed the boys' bags for their overnight Scout trip to Cherry Grove. Thirteen-year-old Frankie and ten-year-old Bobby were to meet their Scoutmaster, Reverend Joseph H. Bond, and the rest of Troop 16, at the River Avenue ferry, leaving at 6:15 p.m. She had just finished packing the bags when she heard the baby crying. She found her youngest child trying to climb over the crib railings. Hannah lifted Fanny into her arms and carried her to the table to change her diaper. She said, "If you are big enough to climb out of the crib, little miss, then you are big enough to learn to use the toilet." Fanny just looked up at her mother with wide happy eyes and said, "baba?" Hannah responded, "In a moment young lady, give me a chance to finish changing you first."

Bobby came running into the bedroom, "We have to hurry Mom, we're going to be late for the ferry."

Hannah finished the diaper change and lifted Fanny into her arms again as Bobby raced back into the kitchen to check the bag full of supplies and snacks for the night. "Mom, can't we bring some chocolate?"

"It will melt honey. I packed plenty of snacks for you to take. Now don't start taking everything out of that bag that I just packed."

She took the bottle of warmed milk from the pot on the stove and handed it to Fanny. The toddler happily stuffed it into her mouth with satisfaction. Just then, Philip entered the room and said, "Where are my boys? Hop to it, we're gonna be late."

Bobby whined, "That's what I keep telling Mom!" Hannah placed Fanny in her highchair and repacked all the snacks that Bobby had just taken out of the bag. Frankie came into the room then and said, "Ready, Dad."

Philip and the boys lifted bags and then Philip kissed the heads of both Nancy and Fanny before kissing Hannah. "We'll be back in the morning. That is, if we all survive the night."

Hannah slapped Philip's arm, "Don't even joke about such a thing! Be careful boys. I love you." She hugged each of them and watched them leave the house together before turning around to see the mess left in the kitchen. She sighed heavily as she started to put things away and clean the table and counters. As her family grew, she found she had less time to write for the local newspaper. She missed her old life, but she wouldn't trade a minute of being a mother to her gaggle of little ducklings for anything in the world. It made her think of Philip's mother for the first time in a different light.

As a mother herself now, it was hard to let her boys go for a night. She couldn't imagine how difficult it must have been for Grace to have let go of her son forever. She could feel the physical pain in her stomach as she contemplated the choice Grace had had to make. According to the letter Grace had left in Philip's backpack, their great-grandson and great-great-granddaughter had already been in Grace's life. Grace had to sacrifice her years with her son in order for them to exist. She looked at her little girls now and wondered, which child would give her this grandson and great-granddaughter. A moment of panic struck her then when she wondered why it was that Philip only knew about this one grandson and great-granddaughter. Why hadn't her other children produced offspring? She sat down in a kitchen chair and watched as Nancy made towers out of the buttons and Fanny dipped her fingers into the chocolate pudding that now smeared her chubby cheeks. Tears filled her eyes.

Meanwhile, on the ferry to Fire Island, the Captain let each of the scouts take a turn at the wheel. Philip never imagined himself as a father, but here he was spending this bonding time with his sons and knowing how quickly this time would pass. Charles Richter sat beside Philip on the ferry, "It's good to see the boys having some fun. We've had a devil of a time with things since the crash. I'm thankful that St. Ann's sponsored Nelson, or we wouldn't be here."

Philip replied, "It's true, things have been tough, but they've been tough for everyone. Times like this bring out the best and worst in people."

Charles laughed, "Isn't that the truth!"

"I hear that there's talk of TERA, you know, The Temporary Emergency Relief Administration, creating some jobs in the area."

Charles nodded, "Yeah, I heard that too. They want to build a new adult infirmary at the Suffolk Tuberculosis Sanatorium in Holtsville and I've caught wind of a project that would build a road and bridge at Smith's Point. I'm ready for whatever projects come available. A guy's got to put food on the table."

Charles had worked at the Telefunken years ago, and had done some local handyman work since then, but not many people had work for him these days. Everyone was holding onto their dimes. More and more houses and stores were going into foreclosure. The economy was struggling, and the breadlines were getting longer.

Once on land, they followed the boardwalks past Duffy's Hotel until the boys found their cabin and prepared their bunks for the night. Then joining their fathers; they worked to start a campfire under the instructions of the men and settled in for a dinner of hot dogs and beans and a night of ghost stories and pirate lore.

The next day was filled with activities. They learned how to make various nautical knots, collected driftwood to be painted and tied together to make American flags, and made slingshots from branches, rubber bands, and masking tape.

When they arrived back in Sayville at 5:45 in the evening, Hannah and the girls were waiting for them at the dock.

Near the summer's end, the boys were eager to squeeze in a few more carefree days. They baited their hooks with shrimp and dropped their fishing lines from the little bridge between Sayville and Bayport across the road from Meadow Croft and into the brackish water of Brown's River and waited for the tug they hoped would follow. Chewing on their bubble gum, they challenged each other to blow the biggest bubble until they had gum smeared all over their faces.

Nelson rode by on his bicycle and called out to them, "Hey guys, we've got a softball game tonight against the Shoreham kids. You com'in?"

Bobby answered, "Sure! Wouldn't want to miss the chance to beat those fancy boys." The boys snickered at Bobby's reference to the sons of the families who still summered at the Shoreham. Although they were living through the Depression, there were some wealthy families who had been able to retain their fortunes, depending on where they had invested. The rivalry between the local boys who swam at the public beach and the wealthy kids who swam at the private beach had been going on for years. The local boys would swim west to sneak past the boundary of the private beach's waters. And this year, after a summer of swimming and boating competitions, a challenge had been hurled at the local boys to face the Shoreham boys in a ball game. Tonight would be the game that settled everything.

Nelson asked, "Catch anything?"

Bobby answered, "Naw! Not yet, anyways."

"Well, I've got to get home, my ma said if I do my chores, I could go to the game. See you guys there. Don't forget, 5 o'clock!"

Bobby, replied, "Don't worry, we'll be there."

After an afternoon of fishing, the boys tied their bamboo poles and buckets full of snappers to their bicycles and then waved to Captain Nick Munsel who was serving customers on his floating clam bar just south of the bridge. Nick called out, "Got anything for me?" Frankie answered, "No, Sir, Mom said we were to bring any fish we caught home to her."

"All right, son. If you ever want to sell your catch, you know I'm here."

At the game, Bobby fit his hand into his three-fingered catcher's mitt and crouched behind home plate. Frankie stood on the pitcher's mound, Nelson at second base, Ollie at first base, Barney Loughlin was ready at third base, Barney's brother, John, in right field, Nelson's brother, Arthur, in left field, and Carl's son, Teddy Hendricks, was playing center field.

Bobby flicked his fingers to signal a curve ball as Frankie watched, but Frankie shook his head. Bobby now made his signal for a fast ball, Frankie nodded. It was the top of the ninth inning with two outs and they were tied six to six. As the home team, the Sayville kids would have one more chance if the city kids were able to bring in another run. Frankie looked to his right and his left, checking the boys who stood on third and first before throwing his pitch. The ball connected with the bat and a line-drive sped past Nelson on second base. The ball hit the ground and Teddy picked it up and threw it to first. Ollie missed the catch and by the time he picked up the ball and threw it to Bobby, one runner had made it home and one was safe at second and another had made it to first. Frankie took a deep breath and tried to calm his nerves. He faced the next player and waited for Bobby's signal. A curve ball again, this time Frankie nodded. He threw the ball and the batter swung wildly and missed. Strike one. Frankie looked again to his left and right, there were now runners on first and second. He wound up the next pitch and threw a fast ball, the batter swung again but just missed the ball. Strike two. Frankie dug his sneakers into the dusty worn dirt around the pitcher's mound. He licked his lips and could taste the salty sweat that dripped down his face. He swiped his hand across his forehead and threw another curve ball. Acting as umpire, Louis yelled out, strike three, as again the batter missed the ball. The batter threw the bat to the ground and walked to the dugout. The teams switched on the field, the Sayville kids now needed one run for a tie or, better yet, two runs for a win.

Barney Loughlin was up first, and as his bat made the connection to the first pitch, the boys in the dugout roared. The ball found a pocket in the outfield and he was able to make it safely to first in time. Ollie was up next, he was a lefty and had an unusual stance that the others teased him about, but the kid was a slugger. The pitcher had sandy hair and a perfect nose and an obvious attitude of superiority. Ollie smashed the ball into the outfield, but it was caught by a kid in a red shirt. Louis called, "Out!" Frankie was up next, he was a great pitcher, but his batting left something to be desired. He spit into the palms of his hands and gripped the bat. He let the first two pitches go, waiting for the right one. Now with one strike and one ball, he faced the pitcher again. The ball came right in his sweet spot, he hit the ball and it grounded to the infield. The second basemen picked it up and tagged Barney out but Frankie was safe at first. With two outs, Bobby stood at home plate and took a deep breath. He made the sign of the cross and stared the pitcher down. Bobby pulled his bat back and the pitch came, Bobby smashed the ball. As he ran toward first, he could see the ball sail over the head of the centerfielder. Frankie ran ahead of him around the bases and made it home before the outfielder was able to get the ball back to the second baseman, too late to catch Bobby who had made it all the way to third base. The score was tied. Teddy took the bat now and let the pitcher throw three balls. One more, and he would walk. Then the pitcher threw a fast ball and Louis yelled, "Strike!" Teddy was not going to let his nerves get to him and he wasn't going to let these fancy boys beat them. One more run, and they had it. He stepped back from home plate and collected his nerves. Once again he stepped forward and the ball left the pitcher's hand. His bat connected with the ball and a line drive headed straight for the pitcher. As Teddy ran toward first plate, Bobby ran toward home. The pitcher started to lift his mitt to catch the ball that was hurling toward him, but he was too slow and the ball hit him square in his nose. Blood spurted out and poured down his shirt as the ball rolled on the ground and Bobby crossed home plate. Louis called out, "Safe!" The boys in the dugout jumped up and ran out to the field smacking Bobby and Teddy on their backs. "Yeeha! Woot! Woot!" The boys yelled and danced around the field. The pitcher, a boy named Clement, swiped at his nose as it started to swell and threw his mitt down onto the ground in anger.

# CHAPTER FORTY-NINE

## 1935 – 1936

Ida Gillette loved her gardens and Frankie had proven to be a quick learner when it came to helping to care for them. Her ill health had kept her from her normally active life, so it lifted her spirits to be able to look out her window and see the colorful blooms on her property. She watched Frankie, hard at work, pulling weeds that tried to strangle the flowers. Just then, she heard the knock on the front door and called out, "Come in, Karl, it's open."

Karl Pausewang took off his hat and nodded a greeting to the old woman and Ida asked him to take a seat. A man in his forties, he was tall and blonde with sturdy German roots. Karl's Aunt Rosa and his father, William, had been friends of Ida's for a long time, but both had recently passed away. Ida's father, Captain Charles Gillette, had once said that Rosa and William's parents, Leopold and Clara Pausewang, were the most handsome couple he had ever seen. After Clara's death in 1924, the land she and her husband had owned on Moscow Avenue was divided among her children and grandchildren. Early on, Karl had earned quite a reputation in Sayville as an expert mechanic and pilot. He owned Pausewang Brothers' Machine Shop, a successful business that had secured contracts with Sperry Gyroscope and Grumman Aircraft Company, as well as, over the years, foreign governments. But most recently, he had constructed the first airport in Sayville.

Not one to beat around the bush, Ida was direct in her approach to the subject. "Karl, thank you for coming today at my request. I have a young man in my employ that I would like you to take 'under your wing', so to speak. He has been helping me with my garden for the past four years and he has shown himself to be very industrious. He has told me often that he's determined to learn to fly. I thought it might be helpful if you took him on as an apprentice at your shop to teach him the mechanics behind airplanes. I also would very much appreciate it if you would give him flying lessons. He's been saving for years to be able to afford the lessons, but if there is any shortfall between what you charge and what he has saved, I will make up the difference. There's no need to let the boy know that. But mind you, I want him to be safe, and the more he knows about the mechanics, the safer he will be in the air."

Karl smiled, "I would be happy to do so, Miss Gillette. How old is this young man?"

"He's fourteen and he's gardening for me at the moment. I would like for you to meet him today so I can be assured that the connection has been made." She called out the window, "Frankie, come in will you? I have someone I'd like you to meet." Frankie brushed the dirt from his hands onto his overalls and entered through the back door not knowing what to expect. Ida beckoned him to come closer and Karl extended his hand to him. The two shook hands. Frankie again wiped his own hand against his overalls, "Sorry, Sir. My hands are dirty."

Karl smiled again and said, "Never apologize for the hard work you do. Look at my own hands young man." And Karl showed him hands that had been stained by oil and roughened with calluses from years of hard work.

Ida interrupted, "Frankie, Karl here owns the airport just north of town. He has agreed to take you on as an apprentice mechanic and, if you do well learning the mechanics behind flying, to then teach you how to fly."

Frankie's eyes opened wide in disbelief. "T-Thank you. I-I, well, I don't know what to say. I've saved up some; how much does it cost?"

Karl replied, "Never mind about the cost for now, we will work that out."

Ida, pleased with herself said, "Of course, you have to ask your parents for permission first. But I think this will work out just fine."

Karl asked, "Who are your parents, son?"

"Philip and Hannah Ferrara."

"Ah, you mean, Hannah Trumball?"

"Yes, Sir."

"Well, I'll be. Hannah's boy. I think this will be just fine. Little Hannah Trumball. Well, not so little anymore I suppose. My younger brother, Clarence, was sweet on her when they were kids. Poor Clarence, he passed away a few years ago. But this would have made him very happy. Tell me, when can you start?"

"I've just got to ask my parents, but I'm ready to start whenever you need me."

Ida suggested, "Well, why don't you run on home then and ask them. If you get their approval, then you know where to find Karl at the shop."

"Well, thank you-all again. I-I will get back to you, Sir, as soon as I can."

Karl replied, "I look forward to it."

Frankie started to leave, but then he came back to the kitchen once again and extended his hand to Karl. Once again they shook hands and then Frankie left. Karl said to Ida, "A nice young man. Good manners."

She agreed, "That was the first thing I noticed about him, myself."

A year later, on a hot August day, Karl Pausewang watched Frankie as he landed his first solo flight. The boy was one of his finest students, taking to the air like a natural. He felt a sense of pride in having been able to bring flight into Frankie's life.

Frankie exited the airplane to the applause of the workers on the ground. They each patted his back and shook his hand as he walked past them. "Great job, son!" he heard one call. Flying had been all he had hoped for. He felt at home in the air, soaring through the skies. It was a sense of freedom; a sense of going beyond the bounds of nature. He clasped his hand to Karl's, "Thank *you*, Sir, for making this possible."

"No need to thank me, son. It's been my pleasure. I think you are ready to do some mail delivery for me. What do you think?"

"Sure, that would be great!"

"You can start tomorrow, then. Be here at dawn."

Frankie nodded as he pulled off his gloves, "At dawn!" he said excitedly. On his bicycle, he rode home, trying to ride fast enough to experience the euphoria that he felt when flying. He saw his mother waiting for him anxiously as he rode into the driveway.

At the sight of him arriving home safely, she felt like she could breathe again. Not wanting him to see the worry that his flying caused her, she put on a smile and asked, "How did it go?"

"Great, mom! Mr. Pausewang asked if I would start delivering mail for him tomorrow. I've got to be there by dawn."

With conflicting emotions, she responded, "Very well."

As they entered the house, Frankie explained, "Mom, I love it! I mean, I feel like I'm supposed to be flying. I know, that sounds crazy, but it's true. From the first time I went up, I felt just . . . comfortable with it. And now, to fly alone, to be up in the sky and look down on everything, I can't describe the feeling. But it's everything to me, Mom. Thanks for letting me take the lessons. If it weren't for Miss Gillette and you, this wouldn't be possible."

Hannah took a deep breath, "Frankie, I'm afraid I have some sad news to tell you. Miss Gillette has passed away today, dear."

Frankie stood still as this news sunk in, "What happened?"

"Nothing happened, Frankie, she was nearly 85 years old. It was just her time."

Frankie turned away from his mother, not wanting her to see the tears in his eyes. Hannah touched his shoulder. With a tone of defeat, he said, "Everyone dies." He was thinking about Mr. Thornhill, Grandpa Andrew, Giorgio, and all the others he had lost in his short life.

Hannah said, "Yes, everyone dies. But that's why we need to live while we can. Look at all Ida was able to do in her years; all those she was able to help. That all counts toward a life worth living."

He swiped at the teardrop on his cheek with the back of his hand, "I guess you're right, Ma, but it still hurts to lose people you love."

Hannah smiled at her tender-hearted son, "It does. So we have to make sure we use our lives to make them proud." She wanted to give him a hug, but didn't want to embarrass him. She just kept her hand on his back, feeling him breathe beneath her palm.

Just then, Bobby burst into the house and Frankie said, "Excuse me mom." Frankie retreated to his bedroom, as Bobby, unaware of the heavy mood in the room, excitedly described sailing with the Wet Pants Sailing Club on their annual August club-wide picnic and sail to Fire Island. "Mom, it was so funny! Jimmy had to take all these little kids over on his boat and they nearly drowned! The kids were all crying when they got to Fire Island. The parents wouldn't let the kids go back in Jimmy's boat. But they wanted me to take them! Jimmy was really mad at me, but I don't care. It was great! He always thinks he's such a hot shot! He tries to beat everyone and doesn't care if he causes other boats to pitch kids in the water. All he cares about is winning and it wasn't even a race."

Hannah pulled Bobby into her arms and gave him the hug she wished she could have given to Frankie. At twelve, Bobby still allowed such displays of emotion by her. Seven-year-old Nancy stomped into the kitchen then. The girl was soaking wet but she was smiling. Nancy tugged at her mother's apron, "Did Bobby tell you? Jimmy nearly drownded us!"

Hannah asked Nancy, "Did you have a good time at the picnic?"

"Yeah, but I'm glad Bobby was there because he's a good sailor. I'm not ever going in Jimmy's boat again." She stomped her foot on the floor to emphasize her determination. "I think he should win the pants."

Hannah asked, "What pants?"

Nancy giggled and said dramatically, "Short may they be; long may they wave."

Bobby explained, "There's these old pants that I think belonged to one of the first members of Wet Pants, and each year, someone wins custody of the pants. It's a real honor and a tradition."

Just then, four-year-old Fanny came running into the kitchen, "You're ho-o-o-me!" Fanny was glad to see Nancy back from her sail-over. She felt left out when her siblings all went out for the day and she was left home with no one to play with. "Nancy, come see what I did! I made a tent in our bedroom with a sheet and put our dolls to bed."

Nancy and Fanny ran off to their bedroom. The August afternoon was stifling even with the windows open. Hannah turned up the fan to a higher speed and gave Bobby a snack even though it was so close to dinner time. It seemed to her that the boy was always eating. No amount of food ever seemed to be enough to satisfy him for long. She could hear the girls laughing in their bedroom and she felt a sense of relief. All of her ducklings were home and safe for the moment. It seemed that once she became a mother, worry lines started to pop up on her face. But she treasured each line because they represented her love for her lively children.

# CHAPTER FIFTY

1937

The children spread B-V Mosquito Chaser on each other before they followed twelve-year-old Barney Loughlin through the wooden paths on the grounds of Meadow Croft. The girls, eight-year-old Nancy and eleven-year-old Philippa Roosevelt, helped the younger children, five-year-old Fanny and six-year-old John Ellis Roosevelt Jr., as they each collected colorful leaves in paper bags. Nine-year-old Philip Roosevelt, caught up to Barney and said, "Let's head toward the cemetery."

The boys led the way toward the cemeteries and the railroad tracks. Paths intersected the property of Meadow Croft with some leading toward St. Ann's Cemetery and Union Cemetery.

The old moss-covered gravestones of Union Cemetery stood in rows as the children walked among them. The children were not yet used to the shorter autumn days and the sun was already sinking low in the sky. As they walked, Barney repeated the stories his father had told him about the more famous residents of the cemetery, including heroes from the Civil War.

As the shadows lengthened, little Fanny said, "I hear a bell. Where's that coming from?" Philippa shook her head as she responded, "I don't hear the bell from St. Ann's. Actually, I don't hear any bell."

Six-year-old John Ellis said, "I think I hear a bell."

Barney looked at the youngest members of their group and said, mysteriously, "Well, they say that, a long time ago, when people were buried here, they buried them with a bell inside the coffin."

Nancy asked, "Why would they do that?"

Barney answered, "So that if they had made a mistake and buried someone alive, the buried person could ring the bell and someone would hear them and dig them up before they suffocated to death."

Philippa, close to tears said, "Stop Barney, you're just trying to scare us."

He shook his head, and said defensively, "I'm not the one who heard a bell."

Philippa shot a warning look at Barney, "We'd better head back before it gets dark."

Just then, Fanny stopped in her tracks and tilted her head. She pointed toward a gravestone and said, "There! It's coming from there!" And she ran toward the sound as the others watched in horror. Nancy called out, "Fanny, don't!"

But Fanny kept running until she reached a grave five rows from the rest of them. By the time the others reached her, she was crying. "What's wrong, Fanny?" Nancy asked.

Fanny said, "Her name is Phoebe. She said that no one comes to see her anymore. She heard us talking and rang the bell so that we would come to visit her."

Philippa shook her head, "Fanny, it was just your imagination."

But the little girl said, "No, it wasn't. She said she wants a friend and thinks that you should stay with her."

Philippa grabbed Fanny by both arms, "Fanny Ferrara, are you making this up?"

"No. I'm not. She's standing right there. She said she's waiting for *you* to join her. That's what she said!" Again, Fanny pointed, to the gravestone. Philippa read out loud, "Phoebe Hawkins. She died in 1857 at seven years old." Philippa accused Fanny, "Fanny, you read this name and just made up that she was here talking to you."

Nancy's eyes and grown to the size of saucers after hearing what Fanny had said. She tugged at Philippa's arm, and shook her head, "But Philippa, Fanny can't read yet."

Barney said, "Let's get out of here."

Nancy grabbed Fanny's hand and pulled the younger child along as they all took off running, following Barney out of the cemetery and back to Meadow Croft through the maze of wooded paths. When they reached the house, the moon had risen to light the dark sky. Philippa said, "Don't anyone tell the adults what happened today. They'll never believe us anyway."

# CHAPTER FIFTY-ONE

## 1938

The children rode their bicycles to school on Wednesday morning, in spite of the light drizzle in the air. That morning, Hannah had listened to the weather report on the radio and heard the announcer say, "The hurricane that was headed toward Florida earlier this week has made a turn and is now headed safely out to sea. Expect the rain and overcast skies that we have been experiencing to continue today and into tomorrow." Nancy and Fanny parked their bicycles outside of Old '88 as Frankie and Bobby continued past St. John's German Church to the high school. The boys leaned their own bicycles against the fence and waved to their sisters, signaling that all was well before entering the building.

But as the morning passed, the rain increased and the winds picked up, a storm was brewing outside. Around two o'clock, Bobby watched as the trees behind the building started to bend in the wind. Class was interrupted an hour later as the winds continued to increase. His teacher, Miss Cobb, was called into the hallway by the principal. She came back a moment later and said, "Children, the weather is becoming a concern. There is a tropical storm off the shore. For those of you who take the school buses and live in Oakdale, Bohemia, Lake Ronkonkoma, Lakeland, Lake Grove, and Holbrook, you will remain at school for the duration of the storm. Those who live closer, you are to go home immediately and stay there for the rest of the day."

A buzz erupted from the students in the classroom as those who lived nearby got ready to leave and the others wondered how long they would have to stay. Bobby met up with Frankie outside as they grabbed their bicycles and headed toward Old '88 to find the girls. They passed by Mr. Case, the crossing guard, at his post in front of St. John's. He was telling the Brady brothers to go to their grandparents' house on Main Street. He said, "Don't try to get back to Bayport. You'll never make it." Then turning to Frankie and Bobby, he said, "You too, go straight home boys, this is going to be a doozy!"

Frankie and Bobby reached the girls quickly and Frankie instructed, "Bobby, you stay in the rear, I'll lead. Girls you stay in the middle. Okay?"

In theory, it seemed like a good plan to Bobby, but as they headed toward home, it became evident that Fanny, being so small, could not keep up with Frankie and Nancy. As hard as she peddled, she struggled to keep the bicycle from being blown away from under her. Bobby stayed with her as the distance between them and Frankie and Nancy widened. The sound of the splitting wood only reached him an instant before the tree fell in front of them, just missing them by a few inches. He could feel the vibration in the air around him as the ground shook beneath him. Fanny started to cry and Bobby quickly checked her for injury, "Are you hurt?" She whimpered, "No."

He called above the wind, "Well, we're blocked off here, let's go back and turn up the side street."

When they finally reached town, they saw their brother, sister, Louis, and their father standing in front of Philip's photo shop and quickly joined them. Frankie, afraid he was going to be in trouble for leaving his brother and sister behind, yelled at Bobby, "Where did you go? You were supposed to be right behind us!"

Bobby defended himself, "A tree fell and Fanny couldn't peddle fast enough to keep up with you anyway."

"Never mind," Philip interrupted above the roar of the wind, "Put your bicycles in the store and I'll drive you home. Louis, do you want to come with us? No one is going to come out in this storm to shop."

Louis declined, "Thanks, Philip, but I'll be all right here in the apartment. I'll keep an eye on things and make sure no one comes in after the storm with any ill intentions in mind."

"Thanks, Louis."

"No problem, boss."

But instead of heading directly to the house, Philip drove down to the shore. The water had been pulled out to sea, boats that had been floating just hours before, were now stranded on the exposed sandy bottom of the bay. People had gathered to stare at the phenomenon of the bay emptying over Fire Island and into the Atlantic Ocean. Philip knew what this meant, it meant a tidal wave was coming. When they arrived home, Hannah met them at the door in a panic. The girls ran to meet her and Fanny dramatically burst out, "I was nearly crushed by a tree, Momma!" The children were soaked through, but at least now they were safely home. Hannah told them to take their shoes off and go to their rooms to change immediately, "You'll catch your death in those wet things!"

As the storm increased, the family gathered in the living room. The sound, like wind howling and whistling through a tunnel, surrounded the house. The clouds darkened the skies and brought the approaching night closer. The announcer on the radio spoke in disbelief, "Not since 1815 has a tropical hurricane of this strength hit the northeast." His voice faltered, "Our only blessing is that most of the summer resorts have closed. If this had been a month ago, the loss of life would have been astronomical. For those of you still on the shores of Long Island and New England, may God be with you."

When a transformer blew, the loud explosion caused Nancy and Fanny to scream. Fanny ran into Hannah's arms and Nancy snuggled closer to Philip. Philip spoke into Nancy's ear, "I love you to the moon and back." She whispered back in a tiny frightened voice, "I love you more." The electricity failed as the waters from the bay filled the streets, and in the dark, Frankie loaded a roll onto the player piano and started to pump the pedals. Frankie and Bobby's voices accompanied the music, Hannah joined in singing, *"My bonnie lies over the ocean; my bonnie lies over the sea. My bonnie lies over the ocean; Oh bring back my bonnie to me."* Nancy left Philip's side and slid onto the piano bench next to Frankie, while Fanny rested on the couch in her mother's arms. Fanny tried to sing along, but not knowing all the words, her tiny voice lagged behind the others and made a sort of echoing effect.

Philip looked outside to gauge the large trees that were within reach of the house. The walls shook beneath the torrential rain and gale force winds. For just a moment, he wondered if, perhaps, there was a full moon tonight. He remembered Super Storm Sandy and wondered if it were possible to return home on a night like this. After all, it was September 21st, the autumnal equinox, a time when both the sun and the moon combined to effect the greatest pull on the Earth. If he headed toward Meadow Croft . . . but then he took his eyes away from the storm outside and focused back on his wife and children. He smiled at himself; who was he kidding? He wouldn't leave them for anything or anyone, not even to return to his old life. This was his home now and they were his family. His mother had been right to let him go. For so long he had been angry with her for choosing Jenny over him. But no longer. Now, he knew the love a parent had for their children. Now, he understood how difficult it must have been for her to let him go. And now he felt a love for Jenny that was even greater than the one he had before. One day, probably after he was long gone from this world, she would be his legacy, his great-granddaughter. Her father would be his grandson. That seemed the oddest of all, but it was true. He felt particularly blessed at this moment. He had known them in the future and had also been able to meet his own great-great-grandfather in the past. But most importantly, he had the opportunity to build a foundation for those future generations with his own children in the present. What an amazing gift he had been granted in this singular life.

The boys brought down their sleeping bags, the girls brought down blankets and pillows and settled on the floor of the living room while Philip and Hannah each took a couch. They spent the fitful night together, listening to the howling winds and driving rain and being thankful for the shelter of their home. Hannah tossed and turned all night, not able to sleep while the wind howled around the house. She whispered, not to wake the children, "Philip, I'm worried about Harry and Edmund. If it's like this here, what must it be like on Cherry Grove?"

Philip responded, "There's nothing we can do now. Tomorrow, I will take the boat over to check on them."

Early the next morning, they were awakened by a pounding on the door. Philip answered and Harry rushed in. Hannah ran to him and patted his arms and face, checking to see if he had come to any harm, "Are you all right?" she asked worriedly.

Harry exclaimed, "Holy Toledo! Cherry Grove is a mess! Eighty percent of the cottages have been swept off of their foundations and most of those are now floating in the bay!"

Philip went into the kitchen to put coffee up on the coal stove and checked the electricity, but it was still out. Hannah, Harry, and the children came in to sit around the big wooden table.

"Tell us what happened, Uncle Harry!" Nancy excitedly asked.

"I was lucky, I was working at the hotel when it hit and I decided to stay there for the night. We watched from the windows as the storm surged around us and cut us off from the rest of the island. We could see the cottages fall apart and get carried away by the waves. The sand dunes were flattened. The boardwalk broke to pieces and disappeared into the bay. And the whole time, Frenchy was asleep upstairs in his room!"

"Who's Frenchy?" Bobby asked.

"He's the assistant bartender at The Cherry Grove Hotel. He slept right through the hurricane!"

Hannah asked, "How did you get back here?"

"The ferry evacuated us this morning. It was tough making our way to the ferry because the boardwalks that are left are at angles that make it difficult to walk on."

Hannah was so grateful that Harry was safe now, but she had more questions for him, "Is your house in one piece?"

He shook his head, "It's gone, like most of the others. You have to see it; Cherry Grove is a wasteland right now."

"Was anyone hurt? What about Edmund?"

"Edmund was with me at the hotel. We came over on the ferry together this morning, but he went back to his parents' house. I don't know about everyone else, yet. There were some people who looked pretty banged up on the ferry ride back here. Do you mind if I stay here for a little while?"

Philip looked at his brother-in-law, "Of course you'll stay here. You can have Bobby's bed and he can bunk with the girls until you figure out what you want to do next."

Philip grabbed his camera and went out into the yard to see the damage to the property, a tree had come down and crushed their fence, but thankfully, had missed the house. Frankie joined him and the two waded through the flooded streets and surveyed the neighborhood's damage and took photos of the storm's aftermath. Trees, stripped of their leaves, leaned on houses and telephone poles. Their neighbors were milling around, stunned by the damage and wondering how they were going to get power restored. As Philip and Frankie attempted to walk toward the bay, the damage increased tenfold. The water rose to their waists and engulfed the streets and flooded the homes. Even with the barrier island as protection, the south shore had been brutalized by the storm tide. Boats along the harbor were tossed and pulled from their moorings. One lay on its side up against a house after having been left there by the damaging waves. Frankie let out a whistle, "Boy, I've never seen anything like this."

Philip shook his head, "There was no warning. No one had time to prepare or evacuate. It just hit like a ton of bricks." He looked across the bay to Fire Island and knew that it was even worse there. "Uncle Harry is lucky he wasn't hurt." Then looking around himself he said, "We all are. Let's check out the town and see how the store held up."

In town, they saw men sawing trees that had fallen on telephone lines while electric lines sparked in the streets around them. The bell tower of the Methodist Church had been reduced to splinters and sheared off of the building. There were watermarks on the church where the tide had risen but had now receded. Philip found that the water had also seeped into his shop under the front door. But, thankfully, other than some equipment being destroyed, most of the shop had been left intact.

The following day, Philip stepped off a ferry at Cherry Grove with his camera. Accompanying him was Timber Koman, an Islip Town police officer and the brother of both Jack Koman, who had been with him at Camp Upton, and Ilsa's friend, Anna Koman. Together they walked along what was left of the boardwalk and photographed the damage left behind by the storm. Hearing about the damage was one thing, seeing it with their own eyes was another. Timber said, "It's amazing that anyone survived this."

Philip agreed, "I haven't seen devastation like this since the war."

The newspapers used some of Philip's photos to capture the destruction that the hurricane of '38 had left behind. Prior to this hurricane, the only inlet along Fire Island was the Moriches Inlet which had been created during a northeast storm in 1931. But the hurricane of '38 had caused a wall of high water, ranging from thirty to forty feet high, to wash over areas of the south shore. The storm wave carved several more inlets in the bay, and after the storm, there were now ten inlets. Some they planned to repair eventually, but the Shinnecock Inlet would be kept. Westhampton and Fire Island had been hit the hardest. Twenty-nine souls had been lost. The loss was heartbreaking. Philip found Hannah crying in the kitchen as she read the newspaper. He put his hand on her shoulder and asked, "What's wrong?"

She shook her head, finding it difficult to speak. Philip picked up the newspaper and read,

*"Stanley J. Teller, the chief of the two-man Westhampton Beach police force, was on the beach with his fellow officer, Timothy Robinson, trying to evacuate a group of people from an oceanfront house when the high surge of water came upon them. There were about seventeen people gathered in that house, and among them there were three small children named McCooey. I was carrying two of them, twin boys, about six years old from the house to my car which was parked on Dune Road. I had a twin slung over each shoulder. The big wave came over the dunes behind me and picked me up and lifted me into the cross arms of a telephone pole. The telephone pole was thirty feet high, so the wave must have been thirty feet high or higher. The two twins disappeared. While I was hanging to the top of the telephone pole, Tim Robinson's rubber boots came floating by me. I recognized them as Tim's because he had been wearing black boots with white soles. So*

*there were Tim's boots but there was no sign of Tim. Don't ask me*
*what happened next or how it happened, but the next thing I knew I*
*was out on Quantuck Bay, floating on the roof of the house I had just*
*left—the telephone pole had crashed into it—and all of the people who*
*had been in the house were with me now, including Tim and the*
*twins. We floated on the bay on that house for the next five hours. We*
*finally landed in the middle of the village at Quogue, behind the*
*Breezed Lawn House, around nine o'clock that night. I went back to*
*Westhampton and got to work, and I didn't get a chance to change my*
*clothes, the same clothes I was wearing when the big wave hit me,*
*until three days later."*

Another report came from Fire Island from a woman named Mrs.
Overton,

*"About three thirty in the afternoon my friend and I were forced to flee*
*my brother's cottage because massive waves were washing over it. As*
*we fled, a wave now estimated at thirty feet high came roaring after us,*
*carrying the remnants of the wooden crosswalks we were on with it,*
*plunging us into water and washing us to the closed cottage behind us.*
*Mr. and Mrs. H were there with their little boy, calling to us to help*
*them break in the door. Their own cottage opposite had already broken*
*up and was floating away in pieces. No sooner had we gotten inside,*
*through broken glass, then this cottage began to break up around us.*
*Windows blew in and water rose to our waists. We climbed a ladder*
*through a trap door to the pitch-black attic. There was no exit to the*
*roof, and even if we could have gotten out and tried clinging to the*
*chimney, we would have been swept off the roof by the wind and the*
*water washing over it. We huddled at the opening of the attic, frozen*
*and wet, and watched the water below rise to our hanging feet. The*
*floor of the attic only consisted of crossbeams, so we could not stand on*
*it to get higher above the water. We knew the tide would continue to*
*rise for two more hours, and not one of us four adults expected that we*
*would get out of that trap alive. It is strange what resignation you feel*
*at a time like that. The little boy was a wonderful sport, frightened, of*

*course, but worrying more about his Teddy bear and the kittens he had
left behind. His mother sang to him, and confided to me that when the
final crash came, she would hold his head under the water so that he
might drown quickly before being injured by the force of the waves and
wreckage. We could hardly believe our eyes when the water began to
recede a few hours later. We climbed down the ladder and discovered
that the cottage had been carried three quarters of a mile across the
beach, from the ocean dunes to the shore of the bay, where it had lodged
beside a fallen telephone pole, half in and half out of the water. We
picked up a box of crackers, a package of apricots, a can of soup, and a
carton of cigarettes we found in the kitchen and went outside. There
was a newly-cut inlet from the ocean to the bay. We spent another
night in the grocer's cottage and finally saw people on the ferry dock
the next morning. The men came running toward us, simply astonished that we were alive and unharmed."*

Hannah looked up at Philip and said, "I keep thinking how close
Harry was to this happening to him." Philip took her in his arms and
let her cry.

A week after the storm hit, Hannah heard that the body of her
father's friend, Frank Wilkens Greene, a bayman who had worked
for years with her father, was found two miles north west of Cherry
Grove. His was the only death in Sayville, but in Westhampton, the
death toll had climbed to over fifty. With Fire Island nearly swept
away, Sayville was now left defenseless against the fury of the next
storm and the ocean waves. The storm had moved on to New
England, but not before ravaging Long Island with 120 mph
sustained winds and gusts up to 185 mph with an approximate pres-
sure of 941 mb and an estimated average storm surge of 15'. It had hit
the south shore of Long Island, on September 21st, 1938, without
warning, as a Category 3 hurricane. Following this hurricane, for the
first time in Sayville's history, science teachers were hired so that they
would never again be taken unaware by such a storm.

# CHAPTER FIFTY-TWO

## 1939

Nancy watched from the window of the train as the landscape flew by. The farms and pastures with cows and horses slowly changed as the Queens County border grew nearer. Housing developments appeared between old farmhouses until the two-story brick attached-homes took over. She started to see trees with funny looking leaves and pink flowers, "Daddy, what kind of trees are those?" Philip leaned over his daughter to get a better look, "Those are mimosa trees. They were my mother's favorite." Nancy blinked, her father never spoke about his parents. "Did they have mimosa trees in Pennsylvania?" Philip hesitated a moment and then said, "Um, sure. Of course." Nancy pressed her nose against the window, this was a very exciting day for her, it was her first ride on the train and they were on their way to the 1939 World's Fair!

She thought about her father as a young boy, she couldn't imagine being left alone without her parents and trying to find a way to survive. The window of the train was partly opened and the breeze moved the soft hair at the top of her head. Her thighs stuck to the leather seats in the hot train car. She readjusted her dress to cover as much of her skin as possible beneath her.

Once at the fair, her father paid the admission price of 75 cents for each adult and 25 cents for each child and then told Frankie and Bobby, "Just meet us back here at five o'clock," and the boys went off on their own. She noticed a little girl rush past the admissions booth to join a family ahead of them. The man in the booth shook his head, but didn't call the family back.

The excitement just about burst out of her as she craned her neck to see all the wondrous sights. Buildings of blue and orange surrounded her, and statues and water fountains abounded. At the center of it all was The Perisphere and The Trylon. Towering above the crowds and the buildings, these steel monoliths were breathtaking. One as round as the Earth and the other rising to pierce the sky. Nancy had never seen anything like them before. She held onto her father's hand as Fanny held onto their mother. It was always this way when the four of them were together and she felt pride in being the one her father chose to take with him.

Of all the wondrous things they saw that morning, her favorite was Electro the Moto-Man. A seven-foot-tall robot that talked and could differentiate colors. He even smoked a cigarette as they all watched in amazement. Nancy liked the idea of robots, she thought that one day she might become someone who built them. She tugged on her father's shirt, "Daddy, who made the robot?" "I suppose engineers did, honey." She tried the word, "en-gin-eers. Like the engine in a car?" Philip nodded with a smile, "Sure. Like an engine in a car." "Daddy, I think I'll be an engineer when I grow up." Philip responded, "I think you would make a great engineer. You'll need to go to college, so you better study hard now and get good grades." She was determined, "I will."

In the RCA pavilion, they watched President Franklin D. Roosevelt give a speech on something called a television. She saw her mother laugh at the sight of it and heard her mother say to their father, "So that is the box you told me about when I first met you!" Her father pulled her mother close to his side and kissed the side of her face. "It is." This puzzled Nancy, how could her father have known about television so many years ago?

Just before lunch, they gathered at the Westinghouse Time Capsule Exhibit. Her father told her "This time capsule will not be opened until the year 6939, five thousand years from now." Philip read aloud, "This tube contains writings by Albert Einstein and Thomas Mann, copies of Life Magazine, a Mickey Mouse watch, a Gillette safety razor, a Kewpie doll, a dollar in change, a pack of Camel cigarettes, and millions of pages of text on microfilm." He laughed at that, "Microfilm? 5,000 years from now? They better bury a microfilm machine in there too!"

At lunchtime, Hannah and Fanny saved their seats at a picnic table as Nancy accompanied her father to purchase their food. People crowded around by the food stands and, as Philip let go of her hand, she fell back from the crowd of bodies pressed against each other. From the corner of her eye she saw movement. Looking toward what had caught her attention, she saw the same little girl she had seen that morning who ran past the booth to catch up with her family. Only the little girl was alone now. She came out of a shop and unwrapped a piece of candy she took from her pocket and then placed it in her mouth. She then went into another store and came out with another piece of candy. The girl pulled out a handful of assorted candy that she had already accumulated in her pocket and examined her treasure.

Curious, Nancy approached the little girl. "That's a lot of candy. How much does it cost?"

On closer inspection, Nancy saw that the little girl's face and clothes were dirty. And her hands were black with dirt caked around her fingernails. The little girl said, "It doesn't cost nothin'. It's free."

Nancy said in surprise, "Free?"

"Yeah, you can go into each of the shops and they will give you a free piece of candy. Look what I got!" She reached into both pockets and took out two handfuls of candy. Then said, "I've been going into the shops all mornin'. I've got plenty now. Do you want one?"

Nancy shook her head, "You'll get a belly ache if you eat all that candy."

The little girl shrugged her shoulders, "It's food."

Nancy looked around her, "Where are your parents?"

"I dunno. My ma said that pa went out to get cigarettes and never came back. Then ma left after that and she didn't come back neither. I heard about the fair and wanted to see it. Everyone talks about it, you know."

"Who do you live with?"

"No one."

"What's your name?"

"Marie."

"That's a pretty name. How old are you, Marie?"

"Um, I think I'm eight." She hesitated, "Anyway, seven or eight, or nine, I think. Not sure though."

"You don't know your birthday?"

"Nope. I know it's in the winter though. I remember my brother giving me a cookie for my birthday and there was snow on the ground."

The little girl started to walk away and Nancy followed. "Then that wasn't your family I saw you with when you ran past the entrance booth?"

"Oh, you saw me?"

"Yes. And you are all alone?"

Marie found a shady corner and sat down on the ground taking the time to count the candy she had in her pockets. Nancy sat down next to her, "Do you go to school? I can see that you can count."

Marie squeezed her eyes and made a funny face, "No. My brother taught me. I'm really quick at grabbing apples and things off of the vegetable stands in the city. They never catch me. I'm too little for them to see over the tables of fruits and stuff. I even get fish sometimes. Ma used to like it when I came home with fish. Anyways, Ma said it wasn't always like this. Pa lost everything in some crash and then we had nothin'." Marie looked down at her dress. Embarrassed, she said, "It's really a potato sack. But heck, it's better than nothin'." Marie sighed.

Nancy thought about all of this and wasn't sure of what she should do but thought her father would know. "Would you come with me? My father is buying lunch and I'm sure there will be enough for you to have some too." Marie looked at her warily, "Grownups make believe they don't see me. You see, they-they don't want to see me."

"Not my parents, they will help you."

Marie doubtfully cocked her head to the side, "Okay." The girls stood up and Marie stuffed the candy back into her pockets. As they moved out of the shadows, Nancy heard her father call to her with panic in his voice, "Nancy! Where have you been? You scared the living daylights out of us!"

Philip's heart was racing, he had been terrified when he turned around and Nancy was nowhere to be found. He had returned to the picnic table with the trays of food and had hoped to find her there. The panic really set in then as he and Hannah looked around at the endless crowds.

Philip grabbed Nancy's hand and started to pull her away. "Daddy, wait!" For a moment, she wondered if what Marie had said was really true. It seemed that even her father hadn't seen the little girl that was standing next to her. "Daddy, this is Marie. Can she have lunch with us?"

Philip looked confused, "What?"

"Daddy, this is my friend, Marie. She's hungry, can she eat lunch with us?"

Philip finally noticed the girl beside Nancy. He saw her thin arms and legs and the dirt on her face. He had seen many children like her in the city whenever he had the occasion to go there over the last ten years. These children would steal your wallet from your pocket if you weren't careful. He knew it wasn't their fault, but there were so many of them. He couldn't be expected to save the world. Could he? But he looked again at Nancy's upturned face with that expression on it that told him how much she thought of him. Then looking at Marie, he saw a girl who had lost faith in ever finding someone who might help her. He thought of what Giorgio had said to him on his deathbed, took a deep breath, and then bent down to Marie's height and said, "Sure, Marie. Come with us. Have some lunch, there's plenty."

When they reached the table, Hannah crushed Nancy in a hug. Finally letting her go, she looked her daughter up and down to make sure she wasn't harmed. Nancy protested, "Mom! I'm okay!"

Hannah stood back and said, "Where did you go? Why did you leave your father? Don't you know how worried we were?"

"I was talking to Marie."

Hannah finally noticed the girl beside her daughter. Marie whispered in Nancy's ear, "See, I told you, they don't see me."

Philip got Hannah's attention over the girls' heads and said, "Marie is going to join us for lunch."

Over lunch, Nancy explained what Marie had already told her about her family while Marie ate, ravenously. The child stuffed handfuls of the sandwich in her mouth as if she were afraid someone would take it away from her if she didn't finish it quickly.

Nancy suddenly had an idea, "Mom, can Marie come home with us?"

Hannah held her breath and looked toward Philip for help. Philip said, "Nancy, she has a family. We can't just take a child home with us. Perhaps we should take her to the police station and they can help her there."

"No!" Marie yelled with wide eyes, "No! The cops will put me in jail for stealing."

"No, honey," Hannah said, "They'll help you."

Marie shook her head, "That's not what happened to my brother. They took him away. I saw them. I ran away and I haven't seen Nick since."

Philip said, "Well, why don't you spend the day with us for now. Okay?"

Marie shrugged, "Yeah. Okay, that's good."

After seeing a few more exhibits introducing electric typewriters, florescent light fixtures, and nylon stockings, they visited the Pavilions of Foreign Nations. Philip noticed that Germany was not represented. Nancy heard Philip tell Hannah, "The war is coming soon." Again, this left her with an uneasy feeling. Why were some of the things that her father knew making her feel like there was something he hadn't told her. She was his "special girl". He called her that when Fanny couldn't hear. What wasn't he telling her? She wasn't a baby anymore and things just weren't adding up now that she could think for herself.

Philip saw the look on her face and realized that soon, he would have to tell her the truth of where he had come from. But for now, he just said, "Let's go over to the carnival rides."

The three girls were thrilled by the rides. But when Philip saw the parachute ride he said without thinking, "They will move that to Coney Island after the fair." Nancy finally said, "How do you know that, Daddy?"

Philip said, "Because I heard that's what they're planning to do."

"Daddy?"

"Yes?"

"How do you know so much?"

Philip joked, "Because I'm from the future."

Nancy giggled and said, "Well, that makes sense."

Philip's eyebrows raised high on his forehead, "It does?"

Nancy answered, "Sure." And then she giggled.

They walked past the side shows to "Frank Buck's Jungleland." The girls admired the variety of birds, reptiles, wild animals and performing elephants. According to the girls, the highlight was Jiggs, the trained orangutan, who amazed them with his human qualities. When they came to the camel rides, Marie, shied away in fear of the towering animals. As Fanny and Nancy climbed on top with the help of a trainer, Marie slipped her hand into Philip's and hid her face in his side. He said, "Marie, you don't have to ride if you don't want to."

Marie shook her head and rustled his shirt. The muffled sound came from her lips "I don't want to."

"Okay." Philip put his arm on her shoulder and she pressed her little body against him. He felt her vulnerability then and knew she needed his protection. All the voices in his head that told him he was crazy, were drowned out by this little girl's need for protection. He thought back to his first moments in 1912 and how alone he would have been without Hannah.

Hannah looked at Philip and knew that this child had already melted his heart. She nodded to him over Marie's head and Philip nodded back.

At five o'clock they met the boys at the entrance and introduced Marie to them. Philip said, "We are going to have a guest staying with us for a little while." Nancy and Fanny who had both become attached to Marie during the afternoon said, with excitement, "Really?" Philip nodded, "At least until we can figure out what to do next." Marie felt a sense of relief. Life had been such a struggle for her and she had given up hope that anyone would ever help her.

Diners were new, and most people from outside the northeast had never seen one, so it wasn't surprising that a diner was on exhibit at the fair. But Sayville had its own diner. The Modern Diner was originally opened on the north side of Main Street in 1930, but in 1935 it was moved across to the south side of the road. When the family returned home, they piled into the diner for a late night meal. The owners, George Devlopoulos and Tom Pitsanoites, greeted Philip and Hannah. Noticing Marie, and seeing the condition she was in, George said, "And who is this?" Philip answered, "She's my late cousin's daughter. Marie, is going to be staying with us for a while. We just got home from picking her up in the city."

Mr. Devlopoulos said, "Ah, well, welcome Marie." Marie looked around her. Everything was unfamiliar to her here, so far away from the city. She felt her heartbeat race and tears threatened her eyes. Nancy put her arm around Marie's shoulder, and said, "It's okay. You have a family now." Philip, overhearing his daughter, knew that Marie was not just going to be here for a visit. She was going to become part of their family. He knew that this would have been impossible in 2012, but in 1939, no one noticed a little girl left to fend for herself on the street, and no one would mind if he took her in and cared for her. He was glad that it was Nancy who had found her. Marie could have ended up in the hands of someone who meant her harm.

# CHAPTER FIFTY-THREE

1940 – 1941

Hannah met the milkman from Tioga Dairy, on the front stoop and paid him for a week's worth of milk. "Thank you Charlie, today is moving day for us." Hannah pointed toward Philip's truck, already loaded with boxes. "We'll be moving to the new house on the bay, and a relative of Philip's will be moving in here. We'll leave a couple of these bottles for them to tide them over till next week. You have our new address, Charlie?"

"Sure do, Hannah. Good luck with the move and I hope you have many years of good health in your new home."

"Thank you, Charlie."

Charlie carted away the empties and continued up the block. As it had been a particularly cold winter, he was glad that spring had finally arrived. A moment later, Hannah's children waved to him as they rode past on their bicycles on their way to school. Everything seemed peaceful here, but there was a war escalating in Europe. As he waved to the children, the two older brothers, and then, three little girls, it crossed his mind that if America became involved in the war, these boys could soon be soldiers. The bottles he carried clinked against each other as he placed them on another doorstep and he inhaled deeply to smell the budding flowers along the walkway. He tried to put the foreboding thoughts out of his mind, but even the hope of spring could not do so.

Hannah carried another box into the kitchen and filled it with glasses, wrapping each one in newspaper to keep them safe for the move. Philip asked, "Almost done?" Hannah nodded, "It will be sad to leave this place. I was born here. But I am excited to move to the new house on the bay."

Philip kissed her and picked up another box to bring out to his truck and said, "I grew up here as well. We are both leaving our childhood home."

He felt a mixture of emotions, sad to be leaving this home by Brown's River, but excited to move into their new home by the bay. Hannah had loved living by the bay in their little cottage. And moving to Andrew's house, had made sense at the time. But when the cottage went up for sale after the hurricane, Philip bought the property. Pasquale and Carmine demolished the little cottage and built, in its place, a larger house for Philip and Hannah's family. He laughed to himself as he thought about how things had somehow worked out the way he knew they were supposed to. After all, this new house was the house that Jenny would one day grow up in. While, Carmine's son, Filippo, and his wife, Caroline, were about to move into Andrew's house with their teenage son, Angelo. Philip knew that one day, Angelo would marry an Italian-born girl named Virginia, and they would have a son named Tom, who would, in turn, marry Grace, and raise Philip and his brothers in this house alongside Brown's River. Houses in Sayville, stayed in families for generations. This was just the way things were done here.

When the move was completed, Philip carried his wife over the threshold to the applause of their children. The family was filled with excitement while they walked together through the rooms of their new home. Nancy and Fanny had decided to continue to share a bedroom, while Frankie, Bobby, and Marie had each been given rooms of their own. The house was much larger than the one on Brown's River. Hannah's dream kitchen looked out over the bay and their bedroom had a terrace where she and Philip could sit, alone, and enjoy a cup of coffee together.

A week later, Hannah looked out her kitchen window at the bay and thought about John Ellis Roosevelt. He had died on March 8th, 1939 in Florida at the age of eighty-seven. Incredibly, he had lived twenty-seven years without the love of his life, Nannie. The last thing he had said to Hannah before leaving for Florida was, "All the money in the world can't buy happiness. Tend to your family. Cultivate the soil that will allow them to grow strong. They will make you smile and cry, but they will also make the whole damn thing worthwhile." He had wiped away the tears that spilled down her cheeks. She had also lost so many, and she somehow knew that she would never see him again.

Now, in a few days, it would be her twentieth wedding anniversary. She wondered how the years had flown by so quickly. She turned her attention back to the dishes in the kitchen sink and finished tidying up.

The following Saturday, Philip led her to a seat at the kitchen table. "Sit here, Hannah. I have something for you."

He went outside for a moment and brought back a wrapped box and placed it on the table in front of her, "Happy Anniversary, Hannah."

"Whatever have you brought me?" She untied the ribbon and opened the box to find a soft furry golden puppy looking up at her. Immediately, she lifted his little body out of the box and held him close to her heart. Caressing the puppy, she said, "Oh, Philip, I love him, thank you!"

She missed Sage, it had been too long since she had had a puppy to cuddle with. The puppy licked her hands and looked up at her with trusting brown eyes. Immediately, she knew his name. She tried it out, saying it out loud, "Your name is Trusty. Oh, Philip, he's perfect! Thank you!"

When the girls saw him, they took him outside to show him the back-yard. Fanny held him as she introduced him to the chickens and was completely surprised as the puppy leapt from her arms to the ground. Trusty ran around and wreaked havoc among the chickens who squawked and clucked and jumped out of his way. Marie and Nancy ran after them, trying to pick them up, but the chickens were faster than they were. All the commotion caused Hannah and Philip to come outside to see what was going on. They laughed with delight at the sight of the girls giggling and the dog barking as the chickens ran in circles. Hannah leaned back into Philip and felt his arms encircle her. Safety. Love. Family. This was all she had ever wanted.

That night, he took her out to The Foster House for dinner. He looked at his beautiful bride's face, lit by the candle on the table, and felt at peace with the world. "Hannah, there's something I've been wanting to tell you."

Hannah looked at him with concern. He smiled, "It's nothing bad. It's actually rather good." He took a breath as his eyes glazed over, "For so many years, the hardest thing for me has been that there was no one who shared my memories. I would think of something and want to talk to my parents or my brothers or, even, my friends. But they weren't here. Those were the loneliest moments for me. But you and I have been married now for twenty years and I have known you for twenty-eight years. And in that time, you have given me the gift of shared memories. When I think of something funny or sad, I know that it is something I can talk to you about."

Hannah sat back in her chair and looked up at the man seated across from her. "Thank you, Philip. Thank you for standing next to me no matter what I have said or done. Thank you for supporting me when others turned their backs. You are my rock, and with you, I can face anything. I love you."

Just then a large group entered the restaurant. The staff seated them across from Hannah and Philip. There was a glamorous woman dressed in a mink coat and jewels, surrounded by an entourage of gentlemen and ladies, city folk. One of the waiters came to clear the plates from Hannah and Philip's table. Philip asked, "Who is that?"

The waiter leaned in close to whisper, "Greta Garbo. Ever since the hurricane, she prefers to stay in Sayville rather than taking the ferry across to Cherry Grove. I'm told she's just arrived and has rented a house near the bay for the season."

Hannah smiled, "Get ready for an interesting summer season!"

As it turned out, Hannah was right. Greta Garbo was not the only person of fame to flock to Sayville that summer. A surge in visitors, the likes of which had not been seen since the crash, took place. Names like Xavier Cugat, Paulette Goddard, Pola Negri, Arlene Frances, and Earl Blackwell appeared on hotel ledgers and reserved seating lists at restaurants.

When the winter once again drew near, it was a relief to have their tiny village return to some normalcy. As Thanksgiving approached, Nancy and Fanny told Marie, "Come with us, we have something to show you. The boys used to take us, but now we can go on our own." Each armed with a shovel, they walked over to the banks of Brown's River. "There are arrowheads here, left by the Indians who used to live here." Just pick a place and start digging. Yell if you find anything."

The girls each picked a spot and spent the afternoon digging. At first they found plenty of rocks and shells, but it wasn't long before Marie held up a rock with a sharp edge, "Is this one?" The girls examined her find, the crude sharpened rock was indeed an arrowhead. "You found one! That will bring you luck!"

Marie hugged her new sisters and said demurely, "I already have good luck."

The winter of 1940-41 was spent ice skating on the creeks and ponds of Sayville. All the children gathered together and enjoyed snowball fights and sledding. But as the March winds once again caressed the shores of the Island, the children became ill. Strep Throat was the culprit. Fevers soared and parents fretted.

Hannah had her hands full as all three girls took to their beds. She tended them and soothed them with cold compresses and aspirin. But as Nancy and Marie returned to health, Fanny seemed to get worse.

When the doctor told Hannah, "I'm sorry to say, but Fanny has Rheumatic Fever." She stepped back from him with her hand over her heart. The words were terrifying. He explained, "Rheumatic Fever is the body's response to the Strep. Here is a prescription for Sulfa, it will help her battle the infection."

But the Sulfa was destructive in and of itself, as Fanny proved to be allergic to the remedy. It caused her eyes to swell and itch and her throat to close on her. But without it, she would most likely die. For three months she was bedridden and in pain whenever anyone would touch her. Hannah gently bathed her daughter's heated body and fought back the tears that threatened to frighten Fanny further.

One night, Philip was brought to tears while watching his baby suffer. Hannah wrapped her arms around her husband and said, "There's nothing we can do but pray that this ends soon."

Philip said, "Hannah, Penicillin could have cured this, but it's not available to her. Antibiotics have been discovered, but I can't get them for her." He didn't regret giving the Penicillin to Addie, and he knew that taking antibiotics had helped to keep pneumonia from setting in while his own body had fought the influenza. He also knew he probably wouldn't have survived the gun shot he suffered during the Great War without the last of the antibiotics. But that didn't stop him from feeling helpless now. His body shook, "And I had antibiotics, Ben sent them back with me. But they're gone. There are none left."

Hannah said, "None of this is your fault, Philip." But that did nothing to relieve his guilt.

She taught Fanny her school lessons and nursed her back through the nightmare. Finally, in June, the fevers broke and the painful rashes faded away. Slowly, Fanny learned to walk again after her muscles had atrophied.

Hannah thanked God for saving her child and thought that having survived this, nothing, ever again, could equal the fear or challenge that this illness had demanded of her.

In November, Hannah got word that Jean's husband had been found dead. It was determined that he had drowned when he fell off of a dingy after suffering a heart attack. Hannah and Philip rushed to Jean's home in Oyster Bay, but the roads between Sayville and Oyster Bay were few in 1941. Philip wished he was driving in a car and on roads that were available in 2012, but as it was, the roads were narrow and winding and the journey was agonizingly slow for Hannah.

The lawn of Jean Roosevelt's home was crowded with cars. As they entered the house, people milled about. Influential people. People with money and fame. For a moment, Hannah hesitated. After all, no matter how close she was to Jean, she was still the daughter of a bayman and a maid. But then Jean saw her from across the room. Hannah instinctively opened her arms and Jean ran into them.

After another moment, Jean took Hannah's hand and said, "Follow me." They walked to the outside garden and took a seat on a bench.

Jean patted Hannah's hand that still lay in her own, "Thank you for coming, Hannah. I couldn't face this without you."

All reservations left Hannah's mind as her concern for her friend mounted. "Jean, you've been through so much. I'm so very sorry."

Jean swiped at her own tears with her lace handkerchief and said, "Hannah, I wanted to tell you something. I know that it hasn't always been easy for you. Seeing my sister and me and all that we were given because of who we were born to. Perhaps it wasn't fair to hold you so close to us when so much divided us as well. But from that day when Pansy was taken away, and you were there for us, you became part of our family. All those talks in our bedrooms about all our dreams and hopes for our futures, they meant a lot to me. But I always worried for you. That it would make you unhappy to not have what we had."

Hannah protested, "No, Jean. I was happy to be with you all. I didn't need more than that."

Jean nodded and swallowed in her sadness before continuing, "What I wanted to tell you is, I love you, dearly, my friend."

Hannah embraced Jean and any residue of envy she had harbored in her heart disappeared. Jean sat back and then stood. "I have to go back inside, will you come with me?"

"Of course."

Then, the two old friends walked back to the house, and together, they faced the crowd of important, influential, wealthy, mourners inside.

# CHAPTER FIFTY-FOUR

## 1942 – 1943

 month later, Hannah, Philip, and their children gathered around the radio as they heard John Ellis's cousin, President Franklin Delano Roosevelt, say these words,

*"Mr. Vice President, Mr. Speaker, Members of the Senate, and of the House of Representatives. Yesterday, December 7th, 1941—a date which will live in infamy—the United States of America was suddenly and deliberately attacked by naval and air forces of the Empire of Japan.*

*The United States was at peace with that nation and, at the solicitation of Japan, was still in conversation with its government and its emperor looking toward the maintenance of peace in the Pacific.*

*Indeed, one hour after Japanese air squadrons had commenced bombing in the American island of Oahu, the Japanese ambassador to the United States and his colleague delivered to our Secretary of State a formal reply to a recent American message. And while this reply stated that it seemed useless to continue the existing diplomatic negotiations, it contained no threat or hint of war or of armed attack.*

*It will be recorded that the distance of Hawaii from Japan makes it obvious that the attack was deliberately planned many days or even weeks ago. During the intervening time, the Japanese government has deliberately sought to deceive the United States by false statements and expressions of hope for continued peace.*

*The attack yesterday on the Hawaiian Islands has caused severe damage to American naval and military forces. I regret to tell you that very many American lives have been lost. In addition, American ships have been reported torpedoed on the high seas between San Francisco and Honolulu.*

*Yesterday, the Japanese government also launched an attack against Malaya.*

*Last night, Japanese forces attacked Hong Kong.*

*Last night, Japanese forces attacked Guam.*

*Last night, Japanese forces attacked the Philippine Islands.*

*Last night, the Japanese attacked Wake Island.*

*And this morning, the Japanese attacked Midway Island.*

*Japan has, therefore, undertaken a surprise offensive extending throughout the Pacific area. The facts of yesterday and today speak for themselves. The people of the United States have already formed their opinions and well understand the implications to the very life and safety of our nation.*

*As Commander in Chief of the Army and Navy, I have directed that all measures be taken for our defense. But always will our whole nation remember the character of the onslaught against us.*

*No matter how long it may take us to overcome this premeditated invasion, the American people in their righteous might will win through to absolute victory.*

*I believe that I interpret the will of the Congress and of the people when I assert that we will not only defend ourselves to the uttermost, but will make it very certain that this form of treachery shall never again endanger us.*

*Hostilities exist. There is no blinking at the fact that our people, our territory, and our interests are in grave danger.*

*With confidence in our armed forces, with the unbounding determination of our people, we will gain the inevitable triumph—so help us God.*

*I ask that the Congress declare that since the unprovoked and dastardly attack by Japan on Sunday, December 7th, 1941, a state of war has existed between the United States and the Japanese empire."*

In the weeks that followed this radio address, the government requested that one son from each family, volunteer to join the service. So Frankie immediately joined the Air Corps as a pilot.

Fear ran through the cities and countrysides of America; but so did courage. Each and every American found a way to contribute, even the children. Along with other women in Sayville, Hannah organized the children to collect scrap metal, rubber, paper, rags, fats and greases. And Philip became a member of the local rationing board that volunteered under The Office of Price Administration (OPA) which was in charge of the ration books that were distributed for each citizen, including babies.

In February, Bobby turned eighteen. "I want to serve too, Mom. I was thinking maybe I'd join the Navy."

Hannah chewed on her lower lip, the idea of both of her boys fighting a war overseas was too much for her. She turned toward him and said, "Bobby, instead of the Navy, would you consider joining the Coast Guard? I can't bear to think of both you and Frankie in harm's way.

Please." She ran her hand over his thick soft red hair and knew she couldn't lose him.

Bobby was about to protest, but seeing the fear in his mother's eyes and not wanting to cause her more anxiety, he agreed. "Okay, Mom. I'll do that for you."

Bobby was stationed near Amagansett on the south shore of Long Island. His assignment was to walk the beaches to ensure that Long Island was safe from any enemy attack. There were three men who each took eight-hour turns patrolling the beach. On the morning of June 12, 1942, Bobby was awoken early by his buddy, John Cullen. "Wake up, Bob, I've got something to tell you."

Bobby immediately became alert, "What is it, John?" Bobby looked at his watch, it was only 0600 hours, his alarm wasn't due to go off for another fifteen minutes and John shouldn't be standing in front of him. He should be walking the beaches and waiting for Bobby to relieve him. "What's going on?"

John signaled for Bobby to speak quietly, then explained, "Something happened on the beach last night."

Bobby cocked his head to the side, narrowed his eyes, and looked at John with suspicion, "What could possibly go on, on a Long Island beach, John?" Bobby had become more and more frustrated that he had let his mother convince him to join the Coast Guard instead of the Navy. He felt like he was wasting his time walking a beach with sunbathers, instead of being a sailor on a ship in the Pacific Ocean. But he noticed that John was very serious and so he waited for an explanation.

"I was walking down the beach and ahead of me I see these guys burying something in the sand."

Bobby joked, "Pirate treasure?"

"Come on, Bob. I'm telling you, they were Germans. They were wearing uniforms, but they changed into civilian clothes and buried their uniforms in the dunes."

Bobby, still not quite believing John, said, "What?"

"It was more than just their uniforms; they were burying explosives."

Knowing that John would have been patrolling unarmed, he asked, "What did you do?"

"Well, this guy, the ring-leader I guess, pulls out a wad of cash and hands it to me and says, 'Hey, you didn't see anything, right? Take this and have a good time. Forget what you've seen here.' So I says, 'I didn't see a thing.'" John then took his hand out of his pocket and showed Bobby a fist full of bills and said, "There's $260 here."

Bobby shook his head, "You can't keep that, John!"

Hurt that Bobby even thought for a moment that he would keep the money and the secret, he said, "I know, I'm going over to tell the Lieutenant, I just wanted to make sure you knew before you started your shift."

Bobby asked, "How many guys were there and where are they now?"

"There were four of them and, last I saw them, they were headed toward the train station."

Bobby questioned him further, "Without the explosives?"

"I think so, they buried the explosives and what looked like detonators. Maybe they're going to come back and get them later? Or maybe there are more Germans landing as we speak? Then again, maybe they had some on them that I didn't see."

"Okay, let the Lieutenant know I've been briefed." Bobby dressed quickly and headed toward the beach.

A short while later, John led an armed contingent of officers and soldiers to the spot he had seen the men bury their stash. When the contents were unearthed, a message was sent to New York City to be on the lookout, as it was believed the men had boarded the 6:57 a.m. train, filled with commuters, heading for Manhattan.

Three days later, an anonymous call was made to the New York office of the FBI. In perfect English, the caller said, "A Nazi submarine just landed and I have important information. I'll be in Washington within the week to deliver it personally to J. Edgar Hoover." On June 19th, the same man called the FBI Headquarters in Washington D.C. saying, "I'm the man who called your New York office, I'm in Room 351 at the Mayflower Hotel." He asked to speak with Hoover but, instead, FBI agents met him at the hotel.

The man's name was George John Dasch, he had previously been a long-time waiter in New York City who had even served in the U. S. Army. He explained that there had been another group of Germans who had landed on the coast of Florida, each group consisted of four men. All of the men were either U. S. Residents or U. S. Citizens who had been born in Germany. They had returned to Germany to be trained as spies outside of Berlin. In exchange, they had been promised handsome salaries, and exemption from military service, and choice jobs after Germany won the war. They had come ashore in their uniforms so that if they were captured, they would be held as prisoners of war rather than as spies. The mission had been dubbed, Operation Pastorius, named after the founder of the first German settlement in America, Germantown, which had eventually, become part of Philadelphia. No more convincing was needed once Dasch showed them the $84,000 in cash that was given to him to bribe anyone who stood in their way.

The other men were quickly apprehended. FBI Director, J. Edgar Hoover, announced their capture, but never mentioned that Dasch had sought them out and had willingly given them the information.

As a result of Dasch's actions, the FBI was able to prevent planned attacks against critical targets such as Penn Station, The Hell Gate Bridge, and New York's water supply.

For the next two days, dumbfounded FBI agents interrogated Dasch in his hotel room with a stenographer taking down his story. He told them everything, from the sabotage training outside Berlin, to the targets identified by both teams, and contacts' addresses in America. He also handed over all the cash the German government had provided to bankroll the planned sabotage, over $82,000. Within 14 days, all eight saboteurs were in jail, a string of arrests were made from New York to Chicago.

Along with the rest of America, Hannah and Philip read about the court proceedings that followed. The trial ended on August 1st and two days later, all were found guilty and sentenced to death, including Dasch and another of the group, Ernst Burger, who had been aware that Dasch was going to reveal the plot to the FBI. But upon learning that both Dasch and Burger had decided not to go on with the plan, President Roosevelt, commuted their sentences; Burger to life in prison and Dasch to thirty years. Wasting no time, the others were executed by electric chair on August 8th

In March of 1943, Hannah anxiously pushed her cart through the Bohack Grocery Store and felt the relief wash over her as the crowd parted to reveal that there were still some cans of milk remaining on the shelf. There was a sign above the shelf limiting purchases to two cans per shopper. Many of the shelves were empty or nearly empty, and it had just been announced that canned milk and canned fish would shortly be added to the list of items to be rationed. She placed them in her cart with one hand on them to protect them. Although it wasn't general knowledge yet, Philip had told her that it was only a matter of time till meats, fats, cheeses, and butter would be added to the list. She scoured the shelves to find these items. But even though they hadn't been announced yet, people guessed at what goods would soon be in short supply and hoarded them. She put what she could find in the shopping cart, and after waiting on a long line, handed the cashier the cash and the stamps from her ration book for the items already on the list, including sugar and coffee.

The next morning, she cooked breakfast for her family with the last of the bacon, along with eggs from her chickens. She thanked God for the chickens, they would help get her family through this war. Nancy said, "Mom, our teacher said she is collecting waste fat for the soldiers. Can I take the fat from the bacon in to school next week?"

Eleven-year-old Fanny asked, "Why do the soldiers need waste fat?"

Nancy replied, "It's used to produce the explosives."

Hannah gave her permission, "After breakfast, the three of you can go door to door and collect scrap metal, rubber, paper, rags, fats and greases. And yes, Nancy, you can certainly bring the bacon grease to school on Monday."

Marie asked, "What is the paper used for?" Philip responded, "It's used to package items that need to be sent overseas."

"Oh, that makes sense," Marie replied.

The girls spent their Saturday collecting items to donate. Marie stopped in front of a sign plastered on the side of a building asking people to invest in War Bonds. "I wish I had money to buy some bonds. It would help the service men now and, someday, I could cash them in for myself, right?"

Nancy said, "Yes, the way it works is you buy the bond at half the value. The money goes to help the soldiers, and then, after perhaps ten years, you can cash it in and get the full amount. They sell them in the movie theater lobby. We should go this afternoon and pool our money together to buy some bonds."

Marie, thinking about how much she would like to help, agreed, "We should do that."

They brought home their cache in a wheel barrel with Fanny rolling an old flat car tire behind them. By the time they got home, Fanny's hands were black from the old rubber. Hannah took one look at them and said, "Don't touch a thing until you clean those hands."

"Mom," Nancy said, "Is it all right if we go to the movies later?"

"What's playing?" Hannah asked.

Fanny announced excitedly, "Frankenstein Meets the Wolf Man with Lon Chaney, Jr. and Bela Lugosi!"

Hannah laughed, "All right, but I don't want to hear that you girls can't sleep tonight after seeing that movie."

Fanny jumped up from her seat, "Thank you, Ma!"

The movie theater was packed with their friends from school. Popcorn, candy, and soda pop filled their hands and mouths as they watched the movie in terror. After it was over, they gathered in the lobby and waited in line to buy a war bond. Nancy felt so proud as she handed over the five dollars to purchase the ten-dollar bond. Fanny had given a dollar, while Marie and Nancy had contributed two dollars each, all from weeks of saved allowances. Nancy said, "In ten years, when we cash in the bond, Marie and I will get $4 each and Fanny will get $2."

As they walked out of the movie theater, Fanny heard her friend, Clara Miller, calling her name. Turning toward her voice, Fanny saw that Clara was with her older brother, Ralph, and his friends.

Fanny greeted her, "Hi!"

Clara complained, "The boys are driving me crazy!"

Nancy offered, "Then come with us. We're going over to Beers for some ice cream."

Clara sighed with pleasure, "Yes!" She turned back toward the boys, there was one more girl standing in the group. Molly Hendricks was Carl's fifteen-year-old daughter, "Molly, do you want to come with us to Beers for ice cream?"

Molly brightened at the prospect, "Sounds wonderful!"

The girls found seats at the soda fountain and ordered their ice cream. However, it wasn't long before the boys found them there. Clara Miller's fourteen-year-old brother, Ralph, said, "Hey, does anyone have a dime for the jukebox?" Joseph Campbell handed him a dime, and said, "That's money earned on my paper route. Ralph, you need to get a job." The boys horsed around, pushing, shoving, and making a scene in front of the girls. The music started and Ilsa's son, fourteen-year-old Donald Amundsen, grabbed his cousin, Molly, "Come on and dance." He motioned toward the dance floor. She brushed him away, "Naw, I'm not gonna dance with my cousin."

Donald shrugged and reached his hand out to Nancy, instead, "How about it Nance?"

Nancy blushed, "I'm eating my ice cream."

Marie said, "I'll dance with you."

She joined him on the floor and they did the jitterbug. The music was inviting and the girls started to bop in their seats. Joseph reached his hand out to Nancy, and seeing the others dance, this time she agreed. Finally, Ralph pulled Molly onto the dance floor. Fanny and Clara clapped and watched the others dance.

After dancing, they all finished off their melting ice cream. Joseph Campbell said, "My brother, Michael, is enlisting next month."

Nancy said, "My brother Frankie is overseas, he's in the Air Corps stationed in England."

Molly nodded, "My brother, Teddy, is in the Navy."

Donald Amundsen said, "My brother, Ollie's in the army somewhere in Africa. Damn I wish I was old enough to go myself."

Nancy said, sarcastically, "Well, let's hope the war doesn't last another four years just so you can go get yourself blown up."

Joseph laughed and pounded Donald on his back, "Yeah, you might trip over those big feet of yours and land on a mine or something."

Molly turned her back on the boys, "That's not funny! You all think this is a game, it's not. People are dying and I'm worried about my brother and the rest of the soldiers."

Just then, the older boys, Michael Campbell, Nelson Richter, and Barney Loughlin walked into Beers. Michael grabbed Joseph by the scruff of his neck, "What'cha doin' little bro?"

Donald said, "I heard you enlisted, Mike?"

"Yep, going in next month after I turn eighteen."

Barney said, "I won't be far behind you. My brother John is already in."

Nelson said, "I just signed up too. Maybe Mike and I can go over together?"

Fanny looked up at Michael and her heart skipped a beat. He had thick dark hair and gentle brown eyes. She said, "We collected a ton of scrap metal and paper today. I even found a car tire!"

He patted her on the head, "Good going, Fanny! I'm sure it will help." She smiled to herself, thrilled that the older boy actually knew her name.

# CHAPTER FIFTY-FIVE

### 1944

It was a Monday and the day before Halloween, Mrs. Krsnack addressed the chosen airplane spotters in the classroom. "I've chosen each of you because I know you will take this job seriously and responsibly."

The boys and girls listened carefully to the instructions. Then Nancy raised her hand, "Are we supposed to watch for submarines too?"

"Yes, Nancy. Of course, airplanes are more visible, but if you see anything in the bay that looks suspicious, please notify me immediately. If an enemy sighting is verified, you are to ring the school bell to warn the town."

A few days later, Nancy, Molly Hendricks, Donald Amundsen, Joseph Campbell, and Ralph Miller stood on top of Old '88 and watched the late summer skies and the bay.

Joseph said, "Did you see any of the shows at the Playhouse this summer? I heard that Erwin Piscator moved his acting class from New York to Sayville."

Ralph added, "Yeah, his students were looking for summer stage jobs but couldn't find any because of the war. So he told them to come out to Sayville and work at odd jobs until they earned $100 each. Then he and his wife, Maria Ley, came out here to restore the Playhouse at the end of Candee Avenue."

Nancy replied, "It was the bees' knees! That Playhouse had been boarded up since the war began. My parents let me take some acting lessons there. Did you know that Maria Ley was a famous ballerina in her time? She gave classes in movement on the beach. Some of the parents were pretty upset that the Assistant Director, Chouteau Dyer, ran around the whole time in her shorts and bare feet, coaching us students while we were wearing bathing suits. The grown-ups were outraged! Really! But I loved every minute of it!"

Ralph asked her, "Did you have a major role?"

"Oh, I only had bit parts. But it was really fun."

Ralph said, "I heard that the famous casting agent, Maynard Morris, was in the audience last week and that he signed up a cast member after seeing the performance."

Nancy swooned, "Yes! That was Bud Brando. His real name is Marlon, but everyone who knows him, calls him Bud. And you should watch out for him. He's going to be big! I can tell. He's got a gift for acting and he's just so dreamy!"

Donald listened to his friends and wished he would be allowed to see one of these plays they spoke about. But entertainment, such as this, was forbidden in his church. Still, the idle chatter helped the time go by, and he was glad that, on his watch, the skies and waters remained empty of enemy aircraft and submarines.

It was getting dark by the time Donald Amundson reached his house. His heart rate sped up when he realized he had just walked into the tail of an argument between his parents. It bothered him that his father treated his mother so badly. Although he never raised a hand to her, he talked to her in a way that obviously made her feel worthless. He had seen it for years, his mother slowly becoming a shell of who she once was. Whatever fight she had in her, had left her long ago. His father took one look at him, said nothing, and then stormed out of the house.

Trying to wipe away the tears quickly so that her son wouldn't see them, Ilsa said, "Donald, go clean up. I saved some dinner for you, let me heat it up." Ilsa was so very unhappy, but she loved her children and saw no way to leave her marriage. She also missed her friendship with Hannah. But Will refused to allow her to speak with Hannah. Friendless, this left Ilsa feeling so terribly alone and trapped in a life she had been forced to enter by her parents.

"Sure, Mom. Are you okay?"

She took in a deep breath and smiled, "Of course, I am. Don't worry about a thing."

Ten minutes later, he returned to the kitchen to find his mother looking out the back window. He thought he heard some voices in the yard and so he crept up behind her to take a look. There were a group of boys in the dark yard. They seemed to be attaching a rope to the back of a car parked alongside the house. It was hard to be sure of who they were, but some of them looked familiar to him. He said, "What's going on?" But his mother shushed him.

As they watched, one of the boys started the motor and a car that quickly pulled away, pulling the entire shelter of the outhouse with it. Inside the outhouse, Will Amundson had been busy doing his business. He now stood up with his pants down around his ankles and the lower half of his body completely exposed. Will raised his hands in anger at the mischievous boys. They were obviously pulling some pranks on the night before Halloween. Will let go of a string of curses as the boys took off, dragging the outhouse behind the car down Main Street.

Donald said, "Holy Crap!" and quickly covered his mouth. His mother did not like curse words and he had never said one in front of her. But she didn't reprimand him. She just turned away from the window with a broad self-satisfied smile on her face and said, "Sit down, son, your dinner's ready."

# CHAPTER FIFTY-SIX

1945

J apan formally surrendered on September 2, 1945 on board the USS Missouri. The day the war ended was called V-J Day, Victory over Japan Day. And there was a lot to be thankful for on Thanksgiving Day.

Hannah greased the pie dish, sprinkled some flour over it and lined the plate with the flattened dough. The kitchen' smelled of apples, cinnamon, and vanilla as the girls peeled, cored and sliced the apples. The turkey was defrosting and ready to be put in the oven on the following morning. This year, Hannah felt she had more to be thankful for than usual. Scattered throughout Sayville, were homes with gold stars hanging in the windows signifying that a soldier who had lived there had sacrificed their life in the war. But as she listened to the men's voices coming from her living room, she felt herself exhale for what seemed like the first time in years. Her sons were both home. Frankie had come back from the war in Europe, safe and sound.

She stepped outside and called for Trusty. The dark skies and the crisp cool air reminded her that winter was almost here. A shiver ran through her and she instantly heard her mother's voice in her head say, "Someone just walked over your grave." The expansive sky was filled with stars. She spoke into the darkness as tears filled her eyes, "Momma, Papa, I miss you. Thank you for keeping my boys safe and bringing them home to me." Silence followed her spoken words until she heard the sound of the dog's paws scraping against the ground as he ran toward her. Trusty licked her hand happily, tasting the pie dough. "Come inside, you wanderer." Trusty followed her into the house and he settled down in a warm spot by the oven.

At the far side of the kitchen table, Fanny wiped her face with the back of her hand and then licked her lips. She could taste the sugar that had been sprinkled on the apple slices she had already eaten. "Mmmm, so good!" She had missed sugar during the long years of the war.

Hannah laughed at her daughter, "Bring those apples over here before you eat them all."

Nancy took the bowl from her sister and said, "Really, Fanny, there won't be enough left for the pie!" She carried the bowl over to Hannah who poured the contents onto the dough in the pie dish.

Marie was using a rolling pin to flatten another ball of dough, and then, using the cover of a pot for a guide, she cut off the edges to form a perfect circle. Fanny picked up the dough from the discarded edges and played with it. Marie brought the flattened dough over to Hannah and laid it over the apples. Nancy pressed the end of a fork around the edges to adhere the top crust to the rest of the pie. Finally, Hannah poked the top of the pie with a fork to make some breathing holes. Stepping back from the last of the three pies they had made, one blueberry, one pumpkin, and the last one, apple, Hannah said, "Good job, girls. Now let's pop them in the oven. Set the timer, Nancy."

A half-hour later, Frankie and Bobby entered the kitchen, enticed by the aroma of the baking pies. Frankie put his arm around his mother's shoulders and said, "It's good to be home. I've been missing your cooking! It's been a long time since we've had your pie, Ma."

Philip entered the kitchen and seeing the flour on Hannah's nose, couldn't resist brushing it away and giving her a kiss. Hannah said, "It is such a pleasure to cook in this kitchen with every modern convenience I can think of, especially, the gas stove."

The next day, Harry, Edmond, and Louis joined them for Thanksgiving dinner. Louis had remained a bachelor, living above the shop all of these years. He was content to have his freedom and independence. It wasn't that he didn't wish to find someone to spend his life with, but in all his years, he just hadn't found the right one.

After eating his fill, Philip pushed back from the big table and patted his belly while listening to the pleasant chatter of those gathered together. He had had many Thanksgiving dinners, and as he thought back over the years, he couldn't help but feel the years were slipping away too quickly. It was in that moment that he decided it was time to tell his children the truth about his life.

"Hannah, I think we should tell our children how we really met."

Although Harry had already told Edmund the truth, the rest were still in the dark. Hannah nodded in agreement, "I think this is a good time. Let me start."

Hannah said, "Louis, do you remember when I first met you and I told you I knew of a boy who had lost his whole family? Well, that boy was Philip."

Frankie interrupted, "We know that, Mom, his family died in fire in Philadelphia."

Hannah shook her head, "No dear, his parents didn't die. In fact, they haven't been born yet."

Bobby laughed, "What kind of nonsense is that?" But Louis was watching both Hannah and Philip closely.

Philip continued, "I wasn't born in 1894, I was born in 1994. In the spring of 2012, I met Louis at a park where the Shoreham is now. He was very old at the time, in fact, he was 100 years old. I was taking a photo of the sunset and we had a short conversation. He pointed to me and told me that he knew me. He told me to go to Meadow Croft on the night of the harvest blood moon, during the sand storm. I didn't know what he was talking about at the time, but late that October, it became clear to me what he meant. On the night in question, I went to Meadow Croft. I heard your mother calling out for help and a dog crying in pain. I found them in the woods just as a terrible storm was erupting in full force. I didn't know it then, I didn't know it until later that night, but I had somehow traveled back one hundred years in time from 2012 to 1912. If your mother hadn't helped me adjust to my new reality, I don't know what would have happened to me."

Fanny broke the silence, "You're joking with us."

Hannah shook her head, "No, we aren't. His parents knew he was going on this journey through time. Without him knowing, they packed all the things they thought he would need in a bag that he had brought with him."

Nancy said, "Pa, you weren't kidding when you told me you were from the future."

Hannah looked questioningly at Philip. "Yes, at the World's Fair. That was why I knew about the future. But you didn't believe me when I told you."

Nancy replied, "I thought you were kidding."

Philip looked at the disbelieving faces in front of him. "I'll be right back." Philip found the old backpack in his bedroom closet. He brought it downstairs and showed his children. As they examined each piece of evidence, they tried to make some sense of this crazy story. Finally, Hannah said, "one of our daughters is going to have a son and a granddaughter who your father will know in his time. His parents let him come back in time because the events had already happened. And if they didn't let him go, then their great-grandson and great-great-granddaughter wouldn't have existed."

Nancy said, "I don't understand all of this, but I believe you. What are we supposed to do now?"

Philip said, "Just live your lives. History cannot be changed and it's best not to tell anyone else what I have told you. What will be, will be. I don't know anything else about your lives other than what we've just told you."

Louis said, "I'm going to live to be 100?"

Philip smiled, "Yes, you are. That is the only thing I am sure of."

# CHAPTER FIFTY-SEVEN

### 1946

Before Marie even opened her eyes, she could see the sun shining into her bedroom. She wished it was summer already so that she didn't have to get up for school. "Oh well," she thought, "only a month and half left, then I'll be free for the summer." She was rubbing the sleep from her eyes and stretching in her bed when she heard a sound come from Nancy on the other side of the room. Marie sat up and looked at her sister. Nancy's body was curled up with her knees crumpled up to her chest. A moment later, Nancy made the sound again. Realizing it was a moan, Marie stood up and approached Nancy's bed. Nancy's eyes were closed shut and the moan again escaped her lips. Marie gently shook her sister and said, "Wake up sleepyhead, you're having a dream and we need to get to school."

Nancy swiped at her sister, "Go away. I'm not feeling well."

Marie asked, "Are you on your period?"

Nancy moaned again and said, "No. Tell Mom, my stomach hurts."

"Okay."

Marie put her robe and slippers on and descended the stairs. In the kitchen, she found her parents and her brothers having breakfast. Both of the boys were now working for Karl Pausewang, Frankie as a pilot and Bobby in the machine shop. "Mom," Marie said, "Nancy isn't feeling well. She has a stomachache."

Hannah frowned, "Okay, dear. Thank you. Have some breakfast and get ready for school or you're going to be late."

Philip wiped his mouth with a napkin and put his dish in the sink. "Maybe she has senioritis."

Marie asked, "What's that?"

Philip explains, "It affects people in their senior year of high school in late spring when they don't want to go to class anymore." Then, with his hand on his lunch box, he hesitated and thought that maybe he should go check on Nancy. But he brushed the thought away, he had a full schedule at work and needed to get going. He kissed Hannah, "I'll be late tonight, I've got some scheduled photo shoots this afternoon. Between weddings, confirmations, communions, and graduation, it's almost impossible to fit everyone in at this time of year."

"Okay, dear. We'll be fine. Don't worry." Hannah responded.

The boys picked up their lunches, too, and kissed their mother before joining Philip in the car for a ride to work.

Hannah heated up some water and filled the rubber hot water bottle with it. She then filled a glass with ginger ale and took an aspirin out of the bottle in her kitchen cupboard. Fanny and Marie dropped their cereal bowls in the sink with the other dirty breakfast dishes and followed Hannah upstairs.

As they entered the room, they both heard Nancy moan. Hannah sat beside her daughter and placed the palm of her hand on Nancy's forehead. No fever, in fact, she felt cool. "Sweetheart, what's wrong? Marie said you had a tummy ache."

Nancy nodded, "It started again last night and it's getting worse now."

Nancy had been experiencing stomach issues for a few days. But Hannah said, "It doesn't appear that you have a fever, dear. But these stomachaches are troubling. I don't know what is causing them. However, no fever is always a good sign."

Then Hannah turned to Fanny and Marie, "Get going young ladies." The girls grabbed their clothes, took showers, and got dressed.

Just before leaving for school, Marie came to the bedroom door, "Is Nancy all right?"

"She'll be fine. It's probably something she ate that didn't agree with her. Now scoot you two, get to school."

Returning her attention to Nancy, Hannah said, "Put the hot water bottle on your belly, it will make you feel better. No need for the aspirin at the moment, but I'll leave it by your bedside. And here's a glass of ginger ale, the bubbles will also help to settle your stomach. There now, that will help. I'll call the doctor and see what he has to say."

Twenty minutes later, the doctor advised Hannah to keep an eye on Nancy and that if her fever began to spike, to give him another call. Hannah returned to Nancy's bedside and saw that Nancy was now sleeping. Satisfied that everything that could be done for her daughter was being done, she returned downstairs to clean up the breakfast dishes.

During the day, Hannah periodically checked on Nancy, filling up the hot water bottle again and checking for fever. But by the time Fanny and Marie came home from school, Nancy was shivering and a cold sweat had formed on her skin. Hannah placed an extra blanket on her daughter and called the doctor's office again, but he was out on a call. The nurse assured her that she would notify him as soon as he returned.

Hannah prepared dinner while waiting to hear from the doctor. The boys came home for dinner, but Philip was still at work. Hannah told Frankie and Bobby, "Nancy still isn't feeling well and I'm waiting to hear from the doctor again." Hannah was worried, but she didn't want to alarm the others if it all turned out to be nothing. "She doesn't have a fever, but she's still having stomach pains. I want you all to stay away from her room until we know better. Marie, you will sleep in Fanny's room tonight."

An hour later, the doctor appeared at the door. "I thought I'd stop by and see how Nancy is doing."

"Yes, please, come upstairs." The doctor followed Hannah into Nancy's bedroom. He opened his bag and took out his stethoscope and a thermometer. "How are you feeling, Nancy?"

"My stomach hurts."

"Where does it hurt?"

She pointed to the lower right side of her abdomen. "It started here, but it's all over my stomach now."

The doctor frowned. "Well, let's see here." He placed the thermometer into her mouth and watched the minutes pass by on his watch. When he took the thermometer out of her mouth, he checked the temperature and saw that it read 94.3 degrees Fahrenheit. He placed the stethoscope in his ears and said, "Take a deep breath now." He listened to her accelerated breathing and then pressed softly against her abdomen. Nancy cried out in a moan, "Oh! No! Ow!" She started to cry.

Hannah watched anxiously as the seriousness of the situation started to hit her. The doctor said, "Now, don't you worry, Nancy. We're going to take care of you."

He directed Hannah to follow him out of the room. Once out of earshot, he explained to Hannah, "I think it's her appendix. I'm going to call for the ambulance. She doesn't have a fever because the opposite is happening, her temperature is dangerously low. She's going into shock."

Hannah sent Frankie to get Philip and to tell him to meet them at the hospital. The ambulance arrived quickly and she rode in the doctor's car as they followed behind.

Seeing her daughter, her face pale and beaded with sweat, being carried into the hospital on a gurney, reminded her of the days she had spent in the field hospital during the First World War. Nancy, was in serious danger, and that was quite apparent to Hannah now. She prayed they had brought her to the hospital in time.

While Nancy was whisked into the operating room, Hannah waited for Philip to arrive. He and Frankie arrived together, Philip's eyes wild. "What happened? I thought it was just a little stomachache."

Hannah tearfully explained, "They think it's her appendix."

Philip asked, "What will they do? Can they operate?"

"She's in the operating room now. We have to just wait and see."

That night when the doctor finally met with them, he explained, "It was her appendix. We took it out, but the problem is, it had already ruptured. From the looks of things, I would say it ruptured several days ago. I'm afraid the bacteria have already infected her heart and lungs. We started her on penicillin, but now all we can do is wait."

Philip looked confused, "But the stomach ache that she had days ago went away and she didn't complain about it again until this morning."

"Sometimes after the rupture, there is a relief for a little while. But then the infection spreads and the pain gets increasingly hard to ignore. I'm sorry."

Hannah tried to wrap her head around what the doctor was saying.

Philip asked, "Can we see her?"

"Give the nurses a little time to settle her into a room and then they will come down to get you."

Another precious hour passed before they were able to see their daughter again. She looked as white as a ghost and was under heavy medication that kept her unconscious. Medicine dripped through tubes and into her body. Hannah looked at Philip's haggard face and Frankie's worried expression, "Philip, take Frankie home. I'll stay here with her tonight. Let the others know what is happening and come back in the morning."

Philip didn't want to leave Nancy, but he knew there was nothing he could do here. "All right." He bent over Nancy's damp forehead and kissed her. He gasped as a cry escaped her lips. Thinking about how much he missed his own mother at this moment, he whispered in her ear, "I love you, sweetheart, to the moon and back. Get better for Daddy, okay?" But Nancy was unable to respond. Tears filled his eyes as he kissed his wife and left the room with his eldest son.

The night was long for Hannah. The nurses popped their heads in and checked on Nancy without saying much to her. In the morning, the doctor came again. He checked the charts and then called Hannah to follow him outside the room.

"Mrs. Ferrara, we've done all we could, but it appears that your daughter's vital organs are shutting down. The infection is wide-spread; the penicillin is doing what it can, but her heart has sustained a lot of damage. I fear we might have been too late. It's in God's hands now."

Hannah stepped back from him as if she had received a blow. She hadn't expected him to say this. She had been praying all night and was sure that her prayers would be answered this morning; that the nightmare would end with her daughter opening her eyes. Hannah felt an emptiness in her stomach. It was more than hunger due to missed meals, it was an emptiness such as she had never felt before.

Philip arrived a short while later and she told him what the doctor had said. He argued, "But they operated and they have her on antibiotics."

"Yes, but the doctor said it might already have been too late. He thinks the infection had already spread too far."

Philip entered his daughter's hospital room and pulled a chair up beside her. He took Nancy's hand in his and felt her cool clammy skin. "Baby," his voice broke, "it's Daddy. I'm here." Again he said, "I love you to the moon and back." He longed to hear the response she had given to him so often over the years, but it didn't come.

Another night had fallen. Philip and Hannah watched as Nancy's breaths became more shallow and the number of seconds between breaths grew. It was early the next morning when Nancy took her last breath with her parents by her side.

At first, Hannah refused to even get out of bed. She wanted to be left alone in her sorrow. The grief overwhelmed her and filled her with an anger she had never known before. Nancy was laid to rest in Union Cemetery, just two rows from Phoebe Hawkins, the child that Fanny had seen in the cemetery all those years ago.

It was a week before Hannah even noticed that Philip only spoke to her when he couldn't avoid it. She didn't blame him for hating her. She hated herself. She should have known Nancy needed help; she should have insisted that Nancy be brought to the hospital.

Now, as her other children and husband returned to their lives of school and work, she stood staring at Nancy's bed in the empty house. She lifted the pillow and held it against her nose, trying to catch a whiff of her daughter's scent. She collapsed onto the bed and sobbed into the pillow. She spoke to the walls, "I'm sorry, baby. I'm so sorry." The tears soaked the pillow but no matter how much she cried, there was no relief from the pain and the guilt that she felt.

There was a knock on the front door. It became more insistent the longer she ignored it. Hannah wiped the tears from her eyes and ran her fingers through her hair before descending the stairs and opening the door. Ilsa stood there. Hannah hadn't seen Ilsa in years. Ilsa opened her arms for her old friend. And without hesitation, Hannah walked into them. Hannah cried as Ilsa comforted her. Ilsa said, "I'm so sorry to hear about Nancy, Hannah. Why didn't you tell me?"

Hannah looked at Ilsa's face, older and lined, but still the face of her childhood best friend. "I wasn't sure you cared."

Ilsa held onto Hannah's arms and said, "I've always cared. Will has been pigheaded and he's kept us apart. But when I heard about Nancy, I told him he couldn't keep me from you anymore."

Hannah stepped aside and said, "Please, come in."

The two friends sat on Hannah's sofa as they told each other about the years that had passed. When Hannah told Ilsa that Philip was ignoring her now when she needed him most, Ilsa said, "Hannah, he's just working through his own grief. Give him some time."

"Ilsa, honestly, I've thought about taking my own life. I can't see the years ahead without her. I don't know how to do this."

Ilsa's own eyes filled with tears at the despair she saw in Hannah's. "Darling, you need to go on for your children. How would they go on without both you and Nancy? You may need some more time, but you need to accept it and find a way to go on. Causing more pain will not alleviate the pain that has already been thrust on your family. Live, Hannah. Live for Nancy. Live for Philip. Live for your other children. Live for the future. Please, Hannah. Live for me. I need you as well."

Hannah hung her head and let Ilsa embrace her, "I've missed you, Ilsa."

Ilsa replied, "I've missed you too." But Hannah still lived through the following weeks in the dark.

It was late June when Jean Roosevelt called Hannah and invited her to tea. Hannah refused, "I'm sorry, Jean, I just can't."

Jean was not having it, "Nonsense, Hannah, I've lost my parents, both of my sisters, and my husband. I know, that's not the same as losing a child; still, we need to talk. Come to Meadow Croft. I'll send a car over to pick you up."

Hannah finally agreed. She put sunglasses on over her red eyes, and tied a wide-brimmed straw hat on her head to hide her face before entering the car that Jean had sent for her.

Jean took one look at Hannah and wrapped her in her arms. Jean's children, Philippa now twenty, Philip who was almost eighteen, and John Ellis who was nearly fifteen, sat in the dining room laughing and chatting amiably while having lunch. They quieted down when they saw Hannah, and Philippa said, "Mrs. Ferrara, I'm so sorry to hear about Nancy."

Hannah managed to say, "Thank you."

Jean took Hannah's arm and directed her toward her parlor where tea and sandwiches awaited them.

After Hannah explained that the loss of Nancy had taken a terrible toll on her marriage, Jean said, "Then talk to him."

Hannah shook her head, "I can't. I can't hear him say the words that he blames me. I blame myself, I can't handle hearing those words come out of his mouth."

Jean shook her head, "Nothing will be resolved if you don't talk to him. I would give anything to be able to talk to my Philip again. Don't waste this precious time while you still have the opportunity. Too many things are left unsaid when we lose someone we love."

Hannah nodded, "I know. But Jean, I still can't believe that she's gone. I walk into her room and expect to find her there. The girls walk into the house and I expect her to follow after them."

Jean hugged her friend, "Dear, the grief process is not a linear one. They say we go through phases of grief, but the truth is, it is cyclical. We are in disbelief, then we are sad, then we are angry, then we accept, and then we are in disbelief once again. Believe me, I know this."

Hannah took comfort in her friend's embrace and was thankful to have someone to talk to who understood what she was going through. "Jean, I'm sorry you have had so much loss in your life. I'm sorry I haven't been a better friend to you, but I didn't fully understand what you were going through."

Jean released Hannah and said, "None of us truly can know what another is feeling. But loss has a way of reminding us of what we still have. I love you, my dear friend. Now when you go home, talk to that husband of yours and be thankful you have more time with him. He's a good man."

That night Hannah asked Philip to take a walk with her. As they looked out over the bay toward Fire Island, they could see the tiny lights twinkling from the homes across the water. Life had returned to Cherry Grove after the hurricane that wreaked havoc a decade before. The lights looked so welcoming, shining in the darkness. Hannah's voice broke as she started to speak, "I'm sorry, Philip. It's my fault that Nancy is gone and I don't blame you for hating me."

Philip blinked with shock, "Hannah, I don't hate you."

Hannah shook her head, "Of course you do, and rightly so. I should have realized she needed to see the doctor earlier. They would have operated earlier before the rupture. They would have started her on the penicillin earlier and she would have lived." Her voice trailed off in a cry.

Philip took a deep breath, "Hannah, it's not your fault, it's mine. I should have checked on her that morning. I should have known. And I ran out of the antibiotics that Jenny's father had sent back with me. I don't know, maybe if I had held on to them instead of using them for myself, but then again, they may not have been safe to give after all these years. I could have kicked myself when Fanny got sick and had to suffer taking Sulfa. But now, with Nancy . . ." He turned away from Hannah as the tears spilled down his face.

Hannah shook her head, "Philip, if you hadn't taken those pills when you did, you wouldn't have lived. We wouldn't have had any of our children and we wouldn't have had the years with Nancy that we did have. And as far as you knowing, it was I who should have known."

Philip gathered Hannah up into his arms as she cried. "I'm so sorry, Hannah." Philip felt broken. He had blamed himself and assumed that Hannah had blamed him as well. He now realized that in doing so, he had left her to suffer alone with her own guilt.

Hannah pushed him away ever so slightly and sniffed, "Nancy, wouldn't want us to blame ourselves or each other. She was like one of those bright lights off in the distance there; she was a spark of hope. We shouldn't let her death dim her light. She is watching us, she knows our pain, and she doesn't want us to wallow in it any longer."

Philip nodded and, for the final time, spoke to the lights across the bay, "Love you to the moon and back."

And Hannah replied, "Love you more."

# CHAPTER FIFTY-EIGHT

## 1949

As time passed, the family learned to cope with the loss of Nancy. Although there were always reminders of the empty seat at their table, their lives had to be lived. The town was growing and changing in this post-war era. Some old traditions were replaced by new ones and, in 1949, Sayville decided to hold its first Easter Parade on Main Street.

Fanny, Marie, and Clara put the last touches on their Easter bonnets that were adorned with ribbons, bows, and flowers. Looking into the mirror in Fanny's bedroom, they complimented each other on their creations. Marie said, "I love the daisies and forget-me-nots in yours, Clara, they complement your blonde hair."

Exaggerating her speech, Clara said, "Why, thank you." Then she tilted the hat a little to the left to dip lower on her forehead. With her hair hanging down and almost covering her left eye, she turned toward, Fanny, "What do you think? Does this make me look more . . . mysterious?"

Fanny giggled, "Definitely! A bit like Veronica Lake, I'd say. Let's see now, who does Marie look like?"

Clara suggested, "Vivian Leigh in Gone with the Wind."

Marie smiled and said wistfully, "If only!"

Fanny picked at the flowers in her hat and moved them about. They hadn't turned out exactly as she had imagined they would. There were little pink tea roses and baby's breath tangled together in blue polka dot ribbons. But no matter how much she fussed, she couldn't get it quite right. She stuck one more bobby pin into her hair and stepped back to survey herself for the final time. Clara saw her frown, "Fanny, it looks lovely. Really, you are stunning. Why, by golly, you look just like Maureen O'Hara with those auburn curls and hazel eyes! You are stunning, Fanny. Don't be so hard on yourself."

A true combination of both of her parents, Fanny had inherited her father's eyes, green specks and all, while her hair was a compromise between Hannah's fiery red curls and Philip's chestnut brown. Fanny put her hands up in the air in defeat, "I give up! Let's go, I don't want to be late."

The girls picked up their purses and rushed out of the empty house. Everyone else in the family was already at the parade. They walked briskly, holding onto their hats while goosebumps appeared on their arms. But in spite of the cool temperatures, they were not going to cover up their new dresses on this special day. Once on Main Street, they got in line with the other women and girls just as the music started. They walked together, arm-in-arm, as the boys whistled from the sidelines. When passing the judges' booth, they gave each other a wink and then, as planned, put a touch more wiggle into their walk.

With the parade over, the judges retired to Cy Beebe's office on Main Street to tally up the votes. The girls joined their families by Sparrow Park to listen to the music being broadcast from atop the American

Legion Truck. It had been set up as a platform, with a microphone to make the announcements.

Although there would be prizes for an assortment of competitions, Fanny was only really concerned about winning one of the contests. She and other senior girls at the high school had written an essay on what Springtime meant for them and Fanny wanted to win first prize.

One by one, the winners were announced and prizes were awarded. Prizes for the competition included corsages from Reid's Flower Shop, chocolates from Frances' Sweet Shop and Beers Confectionery, nylon hose from Otto Kubelle's ladies' dress shop called La Mode, a bottle of wine from Donovan's Liquor Store, two theater tickets from the Sayville Playhouse, notepaper from the stationery store, Cherry Milk from Budenos Broadway Dairy, dinner for two at George's Modern Diner, gift services from Jost Dry Cleaners, dinner for two at Albert's, a recording of Bing Crosby's "Easter Parade", 10 gallons of gas from Village Service Station, Coty 49er gift set from Thornhill's, airplane rides from Karl Pausewang, dinner for two at the Foster House, and two minstrel show tickets from the local VFW and American Legion posts.

When they were ready to announce the winner of the writing contest, Fanny closed her eyes and squeezed Marie and Clara's hands tightly. When the judge announced her name, she let go of a breath she hadn't realized she was holding. Marie pushed her forward, "Go ahead, you won!"

Fanny walked up to the platform and accepted the pretty package of stationery as the crowd clapped and whistled. Looking over the crowd, she noticed a man standing by the sidewalk. Something about him was familiar, but it took her a moment to realize why. He was older now and the experience of war had changed him. It was Michael Campbell. The last time she had seen him, she had only been a kid. But she wasn't a child anymore and he was looking her way. She fluttered her eyelashes and blushed at his enraptured gaze.

Fanny took the gift of writing paper and fountain pen as her reward and faced the crowd. The boys they had gone to school with for years, Donald Amundsen and Ralph Miller cheered for Fanny along with Donald's older brother, Ollie. But she couldn't pull her eyes away from Michael Campbell, who along with his brother, Joseph, was talking to her brothers and Nelson Richter. Oh, how she wished she could hear what they were talking about.

When she rejoined Clara and Marie, she was bursting to tell them that her heart was jumping out of her chest. But before she had the chance, her brothers, Nelson, Joseph, and Michael approached them.

Bobby said, "Do you remember my friend, Michael?"

Fanny reached out her gloved hand to shake his and, even though the cotton, she could feel the warmth of his hand. "Of course, I do."

Michael said, "Congratulations."

Bobby pointed to the writing paper and offered, "She takes after our mother, she's the new writer in the family."

Nelson stood next to Clara and said, "You look very pretty." Clara coyly replied, "Why, thank you."

Molly Hendricks and her brother, Teddy, approached them then and she said, "You all look lovely."

Marie responded, "Thank you, Molly. So do you." Molly hadn't marched in the parade because that would have shown a measure of vanity that was not allowed in the Dutch church. But she did have on her Sunday dress and looked pretty.

As the crowd thinned, Donald Amundsen and Ralph Miller joined them. Ralph said, "What do you say? Should we meet at Fran's for some hot chocolate? It sure is a cold day for Easter."

The group agreed and headed toward the Sweet Shop. They stopped their chatter for a moment when they saw the town police officer standing in front of the shop. Timber Koman, was keeping a watchful eye on the crowds as they milled about. Clara whispered to Fanny, "Do you know that each night, after all the shops in town close down, Timber goes over to the pet store on Railroad Avenue and puts a leash on the ocelot that they keep there? He walks the ocelot through town while making sure all the stores are locked up tight and safe for the night."

The girls erupted in giggles as Fanny exclaimed, "Only in Sayville!"

Clara and Fanny took seats at one four-seater table and were quickly joined by Nelson and Michael. Marie and Molly sat at another table and were joined by Ralph and Joseph. Bobby, Frankie, Donald and Ollie Amundsen, Teddy Hendricks, and Arthur Richter had to settle for seats at the counter.

Clara spoke first, "I feel so bad for Donald." Fanny nodded, "I know, he and Nancy had been getting so close before she got ill. I don't think he's ever gotten over the loss."

Michael asked, "How are you doing, Fanny?" Fanny admitted, "I miss her every day."

Michael inched a little closer to Fanny, "I saw a lot in the war. Lost friends who were like brothers to me. I guess I know a little of what you are feeling." Fanny said, "I'm glad you came home safely." Michael beamed, "Me too."

# CHAPTER FIFTY-NINE

## 1953

Fanny looked down from the window on the people gathered below. The lawns of Meadow Croft were blankets of green, and in the flower garden stood a gazebo, decorated with roses, ribbons, and bows. The rustling behind her caused her to turn away from the window.

Hannah beamed at her beautiful daughter. The red glint in Fanny's auburn hair was enhanced by the sunlight, and her beautiful green-speckled hazel eyes, exactly the same as Philip's, made Hannah catch her breath. Hannah reached up to adjust the veil on Fanny's head, "You look beautiful, sweetheart."

Fanny blushed and lowered her eyes. "Oh, Momma, I feel so lucky to have all this. To be marrying the man I have loved for so long. To have this beautiful venue for our wedding. To have all my loved ones here to share this day with me." But the thought was followed by a piercing pain. Fanny threw her arms around her mother. "But, of course, Nancy's not here. I'm sorry, Momma. Really, I'm so sorry."

Hannah shook her head, "Now, now, Nancy wouldn't want us crying sad tears on your wedding day. She is with us, you know. I always feel her around me. Almost like she never left. Besides," Hannah pointed out the window of Jean's childhood bedroom, "she's just beyond the woods in the cemetery."

"Momma, can I tell you something."

"Of course, dear."

"Many years ago, when I was just a small child, Barney took us and the Roosevelt children on a walk through the woods to the cemetery. While the others were talking, I heard a bell ringing. It was coming from one of the graves." She said wistfully, "I'll never forget. I saw a little girl standing by the grave. She was dressed in a white gown. She looked right at me and said, 'My name is Phoebe. I've been ever so lonely. Can Nancy stay and play with me?' I turned to tell the others, but they said there wasn't anyone there. When I looked back at where she had been, she was gone. I know it's silly, but sometimes, I'm glad that Nancy can be with her now. So that neither of them has to be alone."

Hannah blinked back the tears in her eyes. "You have always been a very special child, Fanny. Of all my children, you have been the most sensitive to others. You are going to make a wonderful wife and, someday, a mother." She smiled through her glassy eyes, "In fact, I know you are going to be a wonderful mother. Come sit down, I have something to tell you."

The two sat on Jean's divan and Hannah started to explain. "Remember what your father and I told you about how we met?"

Fanny replied, "I remember what you told us, but it still seems so impossible."

Hannah smiled, "Did you not just tell me that you spoke to a ghost in the cemetery when you were younger?"

Fanny nodded, "Yes, I guess so. It's just so hard to grasp that he came to you from the future."

Hannah patted her daughter's arm, "My dear, with Nancy gone, we now know that it is you who will one day have a son named Ben, and he will have a daughter named Jenny. Jenny will be one of your father's closest friends. But she will also be his great-granddaughter. His mother knew all this would happen. As a mother myself, I know just how hard it is to let your child go, knowing you will never see them again in this life. And yet, she let him go. She had to, because if she didn't, then Ben and Jenny wouldn't exist. Your son and your granddaughter. Perhaps, she also did it for you."

Fanny had to ask the next question, "Who are Papa's parents? Do we know them?"

Hannah took Fanny's hand, "They haven't yet been born, but his father will be your son's best friend. His name will be Thomas, and he will be the son of Angelo Ferrara and his wife, Virginia. Thomas will marry a woman named Grace and they will have three boys, the last of whom, will be your father."

Fanny's head was swimming. "Why did you keep some of this from me until now?"

Hannah said, "I don't want to change what must happen. But you are about to marry Michael, and he is the man we knew you would one day marry, because he is Jenny's grandfather. Your father knows that Jenny and Ben's last name will be Campbell. All has happened as it should until now, so there is no longer the worry that your knowing will alter the events which must still occur. Their discussion ended quickly as the bridesmaids fluttered into the room in their taffeta gowns, Marie, Clara, and Molly Hendricks.

An hour later, Philip tucked Fanny's gloved hand into the crook of his arm. He looked down at his beautiful daughter and felt his heart constrict at the thought of giving her away. She had grown up much too quickly for his liking. He realized for the first time how Andrew must have felt when he walked Hannah down the aisle and into his arms. Now, it was his job to let go of his own little girl. And that brought him to the thought that was never far from his mind . . . Nancy. The daughter he would never have the chance to hand over to another man. He fought back the tears. Fanny looked up at him and said, "You've given up so much for me. I just want to say, thank you."

He looked at her quizzically, and she said, "Your family, your mother, father, brothers and friends."

Philip nodded, "I miss them, but look what I have received in return. I can only hope the life you build with Michael is as full and complete as mine has been. Things happen the way they are meant to happen." He swallowed the sadness that threatened to overwhelm him and tried to comfort her, "It's not our place to question why. It's only for us to make the most of what we are given."

# CHAPTER SIXTY

## 1969

Philip walked through town contemplating the changes he had seen. It was the same street he had walked down in 1912. He remembered the feel of the oyster shells crunching beneath his feet on the dirt road. And he could almost smell and hear the horses.

But it was also the same street of 2012. As it had been in his childhood, many of the buildings were the same and the road was now smoothly paved. It would be perfect for his old skateboard if only he was seventeen again, instead of seventy-five.

An airplane soared across the sky toward MacArthur Airport. He remembered bringing Frankie to see the grand opening so many years ago. Everyone had been astonished by the accomplishments of the pilots then. Now, men had walked on the moon.

Elaborate Christmas lights were strung across the road from telephone poles. The old Sayville Men's Store Clock, which had stood on the corner for years, and would continue to stand there for years to come, was decked out in ribbons and holly. The window of Thorn-hill's Drug Store was also decorated for the holiday.

The first snowflakes of the year were falling. Philip could hear Bing Crosby croon Irving Berlin's *White Christmas* as music was pumped through loudspeakers. People were busy Christmas shopping. He smiled at the memory of Irving Berlin's Yip Yaphank show at Camp Upton during the war. He shook his head as he marveled at the life he had been given to live. Like a paper, being folded upon itself, the two ends of his life were beginning to touch.

The country was now involved in another war and American soldiers were losing their lives halfway around the world in Vietnam. As a boy, he had been fascinated with the history of war. But now he knew that each medal or ribbon he had collected, had belonged to someone who had sacrificed for this country. He had a much more solemn view of war now than he did then.

He saw Timber Koman standing in front of the barber shop. Although he had been retired for some time, Timber still watched over the town he loved and knew so well. Timber called out, "Merry Christmas, Philip."

"Merry Christmas, Timber. Hope the family is well."

"They are fine, thank you. And yours?"

Philip nodded, "All are well." But in his heart, the question always brought the loss of Nancy to the front of his mind.

Philip tipped his hat to Timber, "Give your family my regards."

Timber replied, "Will do, and please send mine to yours."

Philip continued his walk and smiled to himself at the memory of how fearful he once was of Officer Joel catching him riding his skate-board. So long ago, and yet, still so far in the future. Both he and

Timber were good men who, separately, spent years keeping the town safe.

Sayville was busy on this December Saturday with people conducting business, purchasing gifts, and enjoying a meal or treat. He walked up and down each side of the road, passing the familiar storefronts of Heinlein's Hardware Store, Beers Confectionery, Charlotte Shops, Ehrenberg's Pharmacy, Frances Sweet Shoppe, Fritsche's Bakery, George's TV & Appliance, Greaves Stationery & Gifts, Lad & Lassie, Yards & Yards, Sayville Pizza, Stadtmuller's Jewelry, Stein's Apparel & Shoe Store, the Village Gift Shop, and Wahn's Bakery.

In front of Oystermen's Bank, Philip saw Angelo Ferrara with a young boy. "How are you, Angelo?"

Angelo's eyes widened, "Philip, it's been a while. I'm well, how are you?"

Philip answered, "I'm okay. I'm sorry I haven't been very good at keeping in touch. I was sorry to hear about the passing of your grandfather, Carmine."

Angelo nodded, "The heart attack was unexpected; it took us all by surprise."

Philip remembered the young girl whose hand had been destroyed while working at the lace mill, and asked, "And how is Addie, Pasquale's daughter?"

Angelo shook his head, "She's well. She has three grandchildren now. She's still living in Patchogue."

Philip nodded, "I'm glad to hear that." By his calculation, Addie should be about seventy-two now. He was glad she had had the chance to live a full life and wondered if he had changed anything or if she would have recovered on her own anyway. Then again, he supposed he was meant to have been there when she needed him. As his mother had once said, it all had already happened. But then, why hadn't he been able to save Nancy? His heart sunk at the thought of his daughter.

Seeing the sadness darken Philip's face, Angelo apologized, "I'm sorry that I'm full of bad news." Then he let out a sly laugh, "But on the brighter side, I just got signed up for next year's Christmas Club at the bank and got this cookbook as a gift. I didn't know what to buy Virginia for Christmas, now I think I'll wrap it up and put it under the tree for her."

Philip laughed, glad for Angelo's humor, "You may want to find something at Stadmuller's to wrap up along with it."

The little boy tugged at Angelo's hand, "Daddy, can't we go to Fran's Sweet Shop for a malted milkshake? You promised."

Angelo said, "In a moment, Tom. Tom, this is our cousin, Philip. Say hello."

The six-year-old boy reached out his hand to Philip, and said, "Hello."

Philip bent down on his knee and took the boy's hand in his, "Hello, Tom. It's nice to meet you."

Just then, Fanny called out from across the street, "Dad!" She crossed the street and joined them with her son, Ben, at her side. The boys were happy to see each other and little Tom's attention was diverted from Philip. Tom begged his father, "Can Ben come too? Can Ben come with us to Fran's?"

Angelo asked Fanny, "Would that be all right?"

"Sure, Angelo. Just drop him off at the house when you're done. I'm heading home now." Then she turned to her father, "Are you ready to go, Dad?"

Philip had a hard time tearing his eyes off of the boys, "Sure, honey." He watched as Angelo held the hand of each boy and headed toward Frances. He spoke to Fanny, "That boy is my father."

Fanny looked after her son, Ben, and his friend, Tom. "I know, and they are good friends."

Philip nodded, "Yes, they are."

Fanny touched his arm, "Come on, dad. Let's go home."

Philip allowed Fanny to lead him away.

At 4:00 o'clock the next morning, Philip was awakened by the sound of fire alarms blaring. He had spent some years in the town's volunteer Fire Department, but that was a job for men younger than he now. He nudged Hannah awake, "Something is happening, I'm going to see if I can help."

Ten minutes later, he was driving in his new Volkswagen Beetle toward Greene Avenue. He could see the flames licking the sky from blocks away. He pulled over and left the car at the side of the road and followed the crowd of people who were walking toward the scene. Old '88 was burning down.

He saw the Sayville Fire Chief, Howard Reeve, talking with the ex-chief, Barney Loughlin. They were in the center of a mass of firemen and equipment from not only Sayville Fire Department, but from Bayport, West Sayville, Bohemia, and Blue Point. But for all their collective effort, it was pretty clear that the old school building was lost.

When he returned home, Hannah was standing on a stool, hanging Christmas cards on a ribbon strung across the living room. With her back to Philip, she held one up and said, "We got a card from Jean. She says all is well in Oyster Bay. Funny how Christmas cards seem to be the only time we hear from each other these days."

When Philip didn't answer, she turned around to look at him. "What is it? What has happened?"

"Old '88 is gone. It burned to the ground. But they were able to save all the personnel and financial records. Everything else was lost."

"What happened? How did it start?"

"Howard Reeve said they think it was an electrical fire that started in the photo copy room."

Hannah shook her head, "So many buildings from my childhood are gone now. I thought that when St. Lawrence Church burned down in April of 1967, that was the worst. But this . . . Old '88, that building *is* Sayville."

Seeing how cold Philip looked, Hannah stepped down from the stool and went into the kitchen to put up the tea kettle.

Philip followed her and sat down at the kitchen table, he explained, "Way back in 1925, the South Bay House was destroyed by fire. Ten years later, The Elmore was closed and eventually demolished. The Foster House was consumed by fire in 1973. The Kensington Hotel was razed to the ground to make room for the Bohack parking lot in 1954 when the grocery store was moved to its new location. The Cedarshore Hotel and The Sayville Playhouse, where Marlon Brando got his start, were both destroyed by fire in 1959. The Opera House burned down in 1961. The Sayville Golf Course and two airports were demolished over the years to make way for housing developments and elementary schools. They're all gone now, and they are going to be forgotten by the coming generations. It's such a shame."

Hannah sat down and reached her hand across the table. She took his hand in hers, "But *you* got to see them all. And if you hadn't come back to help me and Sage so many years ago, you wouldn't have known them. But you did, and we have had a good life here. But maybe it is time for us to move away before we see any more destroyed. Let them live in our memories."

Philip agreed, "I saw Angelo and my father today. I don't know how to react when I see them. I think it is best if I'm not so close to them. I don't want to risk endangering the future."

Hannah patted his hand, "It's time. Fanny and her family can move in here and we will find a new home. We should find something that is smaller and easier to care for, anyway. This house is much too big for just the two of us."

# CHAPTER SIXTY-ONE

### 1985

Tom and Ben were glad that they had married women who were also the best of friends. Before Ben and Alice were married, Tom and Grace met each other at a party at Alice's house. So it was Ben who invited Tom and Grace to join him, now, on a visit to his grandparents' house in Noyak, near Sag Harbor.

Grace admired the pretty little ranch-style home as they walked around to the backyard. A screened-in porch was affixed to the back and the yard led directly to a tiny beach on Little Peconic Bay. Grace wore cut-off denim shorts and a yellow tank top that showed off her baby-oil tan. Tom wore an Allman Brothers t-shirt and blue-jeans.

Alice called back to the couple walking behind them, "You have to hear this story, Grace!"

Ben waited for Tom and Grace to catch up and then said, "There's some crazy story about how they met. There was a storm and my grandmother had a dog who got her leg caught in a raccoon trap. Out of nowhere, my grandfather shows up to the rescue. And they've pretty much been together ever since."

Grace giggled, "Aw, that's so sweet!"

Ben pushed open the back porch door and walking across the wooden floor called out, "Gramps, we're here!"

Philip appeared, ready to embrace his grandson, but stepped back as if hit by a blow when he saw who was with him.

"Gramps, these are my friends, Tom and Grace Ferrara. I keep telling Tom that he's got the same last name as you." And then with a laugh Ben said, "Maybe we're related?"

Philip had done his best to keep away from his parents, afraid that seeing them and spending time with them, would somehow imperil them all. He wasn't sure how all this crossing of time worked, and was very careful not to do anything that might endanger the existence of his family. Hannah came up behind Philip, unaware of what had startled him.

Again, Ben made introductions, "Gran, this is my friend, Tom, and his wife, Grace." That was enough for Hannah to realize what was happening. Her heart raced. Philip was looking at his parents, years before he was born.

Tom held out his hand to Philip and after a moment's hesitation, Philip took his father's hand in his. The touch caused him to close his eyes for the briefest of moments. When he opened them again, Grace was saying, "It's so nice to meet you both."

Hannah recovered first and ushered them into the dining room, where a delicious dinner already awaited them. She swiftly added two place settings and additional chairs.

Philip decided that maybe it was time to tell a little of the truth, "Tom, the truth is, you and I are distantly related."

Both Tom and Ben said at the same time, "Really?" Then Ben asked, "Why haven't you told me this before?"

Philip shrugged his shoulders, "I haven't seen that part of my family in a long time. I lost my parents when I was young. Then shortly after I came to Sayville, I met my distant cousins who lived in Patchogue. They were Tom's great-grandparents. But we were never particularly close." Philip took a deep breath; he was going to need to have a conversation with Fanny. In a few years, she was going to have to tell Tom and Ben the whole truth.

As everyone took their seats, Hannah served the tortellini with meatballs and sausages and Philip cut off any further discussion by announcing, "Buon appetito!"

After eating their fill, Philip sat back in his chair and patted his well-fed belly. "My wife is as good a cook as any. Whenever I taste her sauce, I remember my own mother's cooking." He couldn't help the tears that swam in his eyes as he looked at Grace and thought of his childhood.

Grace and Alice stood up to help Hannah clear the table. Grace started washing the dishes in the sink, while Alice dried them, and Hannah put them away. Hannah kept looking at Grace with interest, following her movements, and finding the commonalities that existed between mother and son. She could see that Grace had the same hazel eyes as Philip and the same nose. But when she looked at Tom, she saw the shape of Philip's face, the same thick chestnut brown hair that Philip had had in his youth.

Philip asked Tom, "How long have you and Ben known each other?"

Tom smiled, "Since elementary school. His mom, I mean, your daughter, is like a second mom to me."

This caused him to remember the days and nights when Gordy would spend time at his house. One day, Grace would be like a mother to Gordy. He hoped that Gordy and Jenny had ended up together. Gordy had always been crazy for her.

Ben interrupted, "Gramps, I think you know Tom's neighbor. I remember you talking about a Charles Richter? He used to work at the Telefunken. You told me about that story, and how a secret message was sent through Sayville, along with a couple of other wireless stations, and it was coded. Something about the Lusitania?"

Philip replied, "Yes, I knew Charles. He had a son named Nelson who was friendly with our sons, Frankie and Bobby."

Ben continued, "Well, Nelson and his wife, Clara, live across the street from Tom's family. We're both friends of their son, William. In fact, the wedding we're going to tomorrow is William's, he's marrying his girlfriend, Esther."

Philip drew in a deep breath. William and Esther were Gordy's parents, who sadly, would die in a car accident. Clara was Gordy's grandmother. He wondered why he hadn't put that together before.

When the ladies finished tidying up the kitchen, Ben said, "We're going to take a walk over to the preserve. I want to show them the chickadees."

Hannah, overhearing the plans, pulled a bag out of the cupboard and said, "Here, take sunflower seeds with you."

Grace said, "Oh, that's not necessary, I really couldn't eat another thing."

Ben laughed, "It's not for us, it's for the birds. You'll see."

The group walked down the road and turned left at the first corner. The sign read, Elizabeth A. Morton National Wildlife Refuge. Past the entrance, shady paths led through the trees. Ben told the others, "Hold out your hands, palm up." He poured the seeds into each palm and said, "Okay, now all you have to do is wait."

Grace was startled when a bird landed on her hand and just perched itself there while it looked from her face to the seeds. Finding that it was safe, the bird gathered two seeds in its mouth before flying up to settle on a branch. A moment later, more birds appeared and took turns swooping down and snatching seeds from their hands. Ben explained, "These are chickadees. We've been coming here since I was little to feed them."

The couples then walked along the wooden path to the beach and giant sand dunes. Ben and Tom ran to the top, while Grace and Alice took their time. When they reached the top of the sand dunes, they gazed out at the bay. Grace said, "It's so beautiful!"

Ben nodded as he sat down and said, "I love coming here, especially when no one else is around."

Tom responded, "It's hard to find places this quiet these days."

Grace said, "Your grandparents are really sweet."

Alice agreed, "They welcomed me into the family right away and they've been like my own grandparents ever since."

Ben stood, "We'd better get back. Gran probably has dessert and coffee on the table waiting for us. I don't want to disappoint her. Tomorrow is their 65$^{th}$ wedding anniversary. I hate to miss it, but as Tom and I are both ushers for William and Esther's wedding, it can't be helped. Thanks for coming with us today."

Alice added, "And we can't stay too late, we've got to be at the rehearsal tonight."

While the young couples were at the nature preserve, Philip took a walk out to the yard. He looked over the Little Peconic Bay and thought of the years they had lived in Sayville, it was Fanny's house now, the one that looked out over the Great South Bay. His head was spinning; it was such an odd experience. Seeing his parents again after all these years. They were so young. Knowing who they were, but they not knowing him. It was a lot to take in.

Meanwhile, Hannah retreated to her bedroom. She carefully lowered her ancient body into her chair at her old writing desk. She remembered the many articles that she had written on it over the years. Hannah gently ran her fingers over the wooden surface and was saddened to see the veins and liver spots that marred her once beautiful hands. With a deep breath and a prayer, she lifted her pen and wrote a letter. She placed the letter in an envelope and hid it in her jewelry box. She was afraid of meddling with history and what repercussions would come of that interference. What if giving Grace this letter only made things worse? She left the letter in her jewelry box and waited for the young people to return, still undecided.

After returning to the house and enjoying coffee and pastries, the couples were ready to leave when Hannah asked Grace, "Did I show you our bedroom? It has a lovely view of the bay."

"Oh, no, you didn't. I'd love to see it."

Grace followed Hannah into the bedroom which was painted in a blue that matched the water in the bay. Grace said, "Beautiful, it must be nice to wake up to that view every morning."

"It is. But wait one moment, I have something for you." Hannah walked over to her dresser and opened her jewelry box. Taking out an envelope, she turned to Grace and said. "Has Ben told you how Philip and I met?"

"Yes, he did. He said that he saved your dog who had been caught in a trap."

Hannah nodded, "Well, there's more to that story. This may sound to you like I am a crazy old lady, but I have a favor to ask of you." Hannah handed Grace the envelope. On the outside the name *Hannah* was written.

Hannah explained, "Grace, you and Tom will have three sons. The youngest will leave you to go on a journey when he is eighteen years old. You will let him go, because he must go in order for others in your family to live. But before he goes, you will fill a backpack with all the items you think he will need for his journey. Please, save this letter and add it to those things."

Grace did not think Hannah was crazy. She believed in mystical things. She had always loved to read Tarot cards and enjoyed novels about past lives. She wanted to ask more questions, but Hannah's demeanor stopped her. Grace nodded, she knew that she would do what Ben's grandmother was asking of her. She placed the envelope in her purse. "I will keep it safe and I will give it to him."

Hannah sighed with relief. "In time, my daughter, Fanny, will tell you more. But for now, from one mother to another, thank you."

That night, Hannah dreamed. In her dreams, she saw herself and Philip beside the fireplace at Meadow Croft. She saw Philip draw an assortment of items from his old backpack. Then she saw him hand her an old yellowed envelope with her name printed on the surface. Her fingers worked to open it and unfold the delicate paper that was inside. She read the words out loud,

*"Hannah, you will have a daughter one day. Shortly after the Second World War, she will tell you she has a belly ache. Take it seriously and get her to a hospital, immediately. It is not an ordinary ailment; she has a ruptured appendix. They will need to operate and they will give her a medicine that can cure her, it's called Penicillin. If you do this, it may save her life."*

In her dream, Hannah asked Philip, "A Second World War? What does this mean?"

Philip told her, "There will be a war they call The Great War, it will happen soon. Later, it will be called the First World War. World War 2 will happen in the 1940s.

The dream shifted then, and Hannah dreamed of Nancy. She saw her marry Donald Amundson and become a mother of twin daughters. She saw Nancy's full life as it should have been. When Hannah awoke in the morning, she had tears in her eyes and Philip asked her, "Are you all right, Hannah?"

She shook the cobwebs from her head, "It was just a dream. A beautiful dream."

That afternoon, Frankie and his wife, Christine, arrived from Florida with his family. Bobby and his wife, Judy, and family, took the ferry from Connecticut. Marie and her husband, Joseph Campbell, and their family, arrived from New Jersey. Louis, still a bachelor, picked up Harry and Edmund from the Fire Island Ferry and drove them to Noyak. Finally, Fanny and her husband, Michael Campbell, arrived from Sayville. With the family spread out and living in different states, it was rare for them all to be together. So it was particularly exciting to have the house filled with family and love. Hannah was just pulling the lasagna out of the oven when the last guests arrived.

Donald Amundsen and his mother, Ilsa, arrived. Hannah, surprised by their visit exclaimed, "Ilsa! It's so good to see you!" Hannah hugged her old friend whom she hadn't seen in years.

"Hannah dear, I am so happy for you and Philip. Congratulations on sixty-five years together!" Hannah looked over Ilsa, she appeared healthy and happy, "Ilsa, I'd heard that Will passed away. I'm so sorry we haven't stayed in touch."

Ilsa looked concerned, "Hannah, are you feeling well? Will passed away years ago and I married again after his death."

Hannah blinked, "You did? Are you happy, Ilsa?"

Just then, Nancy walked in with two identical blonde young women and an elderly man. Ilsa continued, "Yes, Hannah." Then she motioned to the elderly man, "You know my husband, Warren." Ilsa felt near to tears, worried that Hannah was experiencing an episode of dementia.

Hannah stepped back and grabbed her chest in shock. She reached for the back of the kitchen chair and held onto it with a vice-like grip.

Nancy said, "Sorry I'm late, mom. I had to pick up the cake from the bakery and the twins' train from the city was delayed."

Hannah was stunned; Nancy was alive. It wasn't just a dream. She thought back to yesterday and realized that the letter must have worked. It quickly dawned on her that in another time, she hadn't given Grace that letter, but this time, she had. Philip was wrong, history could be changed, and she had changed it. She wrapped her arms around her daughter and cried for joy.

Philip and the rest of the family had stopped what they were doing and were confused to see Hannah crying while hugging her daughter. Nancy worriedly asked, "Mom, what's wrong? Are you all right?"

Hannah shook her head, "I-I had an awful dream about you. I'm so glad you are here with us today!" But she couldn't stop crying.

Philip explained, "Your mother's been weeping since she woke this morning. I keep telling her, we have a lot to be thankful for. We've been married sixty-five years and we have this beautiful family." He turned to Hannah and asked, "What more could we ask for?"

He reached his arms around his wife and kissed her. Hannah replied, "Nothing more, we have everything."

# AUTHOR'S NOTE

Although Hannah and Philip are fictional characters, they interact with people who actually lived. Any events depicted here in which fictional characters interact with the lives of real people, have been presented through my imagination. The historical events that are included in this story are portrayed as they were seen and reported at the time that they occurred.

The Ferrara family depicted in this novel was inspired by the Felice family of Patchogue which were related to my husband's ancestors.

Whether if you currently live in Sayville, grew up in Sayville, or have never been to our lovely hamlet, I invite you to take a walk down Main Street and imagine the changes that have taken place over the past century. Sayville has remained "small-town America," while still changing with the times. Come visit Meadow Croft and take a tour through its beautiful halls. Finally, take the ferry over to Fire Island and enjoy the welcoming community that has developed there.

Theresa Dodaro is the author of the previously published, Tin Box Trilogy: The Tin Box Secret (2015); The Hope Chest (2016); and Reawakening (2017). She is also the author of the previously published, The Porcelain Doll (2018).

More about author, Theresa Dodaro, can be found at www.theresadodaro.com and www.raisingdrama.com. She also can be found on Facebook and Instagram @theresadodarobooks.

To set up appearances at events, you can contact Theresa at thetinboxtrilogy@gmail.com.